T0021250

Books by Leslie Meier

MISTLETOE MURDER

TIPPY TOE MURDER

TRICK OR TREAT MURDER

BACK TO SCHOOL MURDER

VALENTINE MURDER

CHRISTMAS COOKIE MURDER

TURKEY DAY MURDER

WEDDING DAY MURDER

BIRTHDAY PARTY MURDER

FATHER'S DAY MURDER

STAR SPANGLED MURDER

NEW YEAR'S EVE MURDER

BAKE SALE MURDER

CANDY CANE MURDER

ST. PATRICK'S DAY MURDER

MOTHER'S DAY MURDER

WICKED WITCH MURDER

GINGERBREAD COOKIE MURDER

ENGLISH TEA MURDER

CHOCOLATE COVERED MURDER

EASTER BUNNY MURDER

CHRISTMAS CAROL MURDER

FRENCH PASTRY MURDER

CANDY CORN MURDER

BRITISH MANOR MURDER

EGGNOG MURDER

TURKEY TROT MURDER

SILVER ANNIVERSARY MURDER

YULE LOG MURDER

HAUNTED HOUSE MURDER

INVITATION ONLY MURDER

CHRISTMAS CARD MURDER

Published by Kensington Publishing Corporation

HOLIDAY MURDER

LESLIE MEIER

KENSINGTON BOOKS

www.kensingtonbooks.com

Contents

MISTLETOE MURDER

*A very big thank you to
Dr. Clifford A. Wood of Bridgewater State College,
Debi Long, the world's best sister,
and the Twelve O'Clock Scholars.*

Chapter One

#4076 A set of the most frequently used kitchen knives, including two carving knives, a filleting knife, and a paring knife. All with carbon steel blades and rosewood handles. Our best quality. $57.

"**D**o you have any really sharp knives?" asked the tremulous voice. "Something that will cut through bone and gristle?"

Lucy Stone stifled a yawn, adjusted her headset, and typed the code for "knives" on the computer keyboard in front of her. Instantly the screen glowed with the eleven varieties of knives sold by Country Cousins, the giant mail-order country store.

"What kind of knives were you thinking of?" Lucy inquired politely. "Hunting knives, fishing knives, pocket knives, kitchen knives . . . ?"

"Kitchen knives, of course," snapped the voice. "Homer hasn't been out of the house for forty years."

Lucy hit the code for "kitchen knives," and the screen listed six sets of kitchen knives.

"I'm sure we have something that will do. How about a set of four carbon steel knives with rosewood handles for fifty-seven dollars?"

"What is carbon steel? Is it really sharp?" insisted the voice.

"Well, some cooks prefer it because it's easy to sharpen. However, it doesn't hold an edge as long as stainless steel. We also have the same set in stainless steel for fifty-seven dollars."

"I don't know which to get. Homer loves to cut and carve. He's really an artist at the dinner table." The voice became confidential. "I've always believed he would have been a gifted surgeon. That unfortunate incident in medical school simply unnerved him."

Lucy stifled the urge to encourage further confidences. "Then carbon steel is probably your best bet," she advised. She then mentioned a related product, a technique her sales manager insisted upon. "You could also get him a sharpening steel. He would probably enjoy using it."

"You mean one of those things you draw the blade against before carving? Seems to me Poppa had one of those. I think you're right; I'm sure Homer would enjoy doing that. It would add a touch of drama. How much are those?"

"We have one with a rosewood handle for eighteen dollars."

"I'll take the knives and the steel."

"All right," said Lucy, smiling with satisfaction. "I need some information from you, and we'll ship them right away." She finished typing in the woman's name, address, and credit card number. "Thank you for your order. Call Country Cousins again, soon." She arched her back, stretched her arms, and checked the clock. Almost ten. Three hours until her shift ended at one A.M.

Lucy didn't mind working at Country Cousins. Like many of the tourists who came to Tinker's Cove in the summer, she was fascinated by the quaint old country store on Main Street. Inside, there were crockery, kitchen utensils, penny candy, and sturdy country clothes as well as fishing, hunting, and camping equipment. The porch with its ten-foot-long deacon's bench, the sloping floors of scuffed, bare wood, and the huge potbellied stove were all authentic, they just weren't the whole story. For the truth was, most of Country Cousins' business came from catalog sales and was conducted at a mammoth steel warehouse on the outskirts of Tinker's Cove. There, state-of-the-art telephone and computer systems enabled hundreds of employees like Lucy to sell, pack, and ship millions of dollars' worth of merchandise twenty-four hours a day, three hundred and sixty-four days a year. Country Cousins was closed on Christmas Day. All merchandise was sold with an unconditional guarantee: "We're not happy unless you are."

"It's quiet tonight, isn't it, Lucy?" said Beverly Thompson, the grandmotherly woman who had the computer station next to Lucy.

"It sure is. And only ten days until Christmas."

"Are you all ready for Christmas?"

"Not by a long shot," Lucy said. "I haven't finished the fisherman's sweater I'm making for Bill, I still have to make an angel costume for Elizabeth to wear in the church pageant, and I have to bake six dozen cookies for Sue Finch's cookie exchange. And," she continued, "I still have quite a bit of shopping to do. How about you?"

"Oh, I'm pretty well finished. Of course, now that the kids are scattered from Washington to San Francisco there isn't so much to do." Beverly's voice was wistful. "I just have something sent from the catalog."

"Don't knock it," advised Lucy. "I have my mother and Bill's folks coming. Christmas is an awful lot of work. I like Halloween, myelf. All you need is a mask and a bag of candy."

"Why don't you all pack up and spend Christmas at Grandma's?" asked Beverly. "I'd love to have my brood back for the holidays." Beverly sighed as she thought of the neat stack of presents waiting in her closet, which she would open all by herself on Christmas morning.

"Oh, we started having Christmas at our house back in the granola years when we had chickens and goats and woodstoves. We couldn't leave or the animals would starve and the pipes would freeze! Now everyone expects it." Lucy shrugged, pausing to take an order for a flannel nightgown.

"I don't know how you girls do it," said Beverly, picking up the conversation. "You work half the night, and then you take care of your families all day."

"It isn't so bad. I like it a lot better than cashiering at the IGA or working at the bank. When I did that my whole check went for day care."

"But when do you sleep?" asked Beverly, yawning.

"Oh, I usually nap when Sara does. She's only four," answered Lucy, stretching and yawning herself. "It isn't sleep I miss, it's sex. How about you, Ruthie?" Lucy asked the woman on her other side. "Are you getting any lately?"

Ruthie whooped. "Are you kidding? He works all day, I work all night, and the baby wakes up at five." She lowered her voice and spoke in a confidential tone to Lucy and Beverly. "I've asked Santa for a night in a motel."

The three women laughed, and Lucy realized that the thing she liked best about working the night phones at Country Cousins was the companionship and cama-raderie of the other women. If you wanted to know what was going on in Tinker's Cove, Country Cousins was the place to be, because absolutely everyone worked there, or had worked there, or knew someone who did. It was an institution; it had been in business for years, selling sport-ing goods to a small but faithful following of customers. Then fashion seized upon the preppy look, and the de-mand for Country Cousins' sturdy one hundred percent wool and cotton clothes soared. Preppy was followed by country, and in a few short years Country Cousins had become a household word in most American homes.

Country Cousins' phenomenal growth, which had been the subject of an article in the business section of the Sun-day *New York Times,* would not have been possible with-out skilled management. Founded by a discouraged Maine farmer named Sam Miller in 1902, Country Cousins was still owned in 1972 by the Miller family. Fortunately for them, that was the year Sam Miller III graduated from Harvard Business School. He was followed, in 1974, by his brother Tom. Together the two brothers piloted an ex-pansion program that made Country Cousins one of the nation's largest mail-order retailers, although it was still second cousin to the granddaddy of them all, L.L. Bean.

That had meant growth and change for Tinker's Cove. Intrigued by the folksy catalog, vacationers began seek-ing out the Country Cousins store. Big old homes became bed-and-breakfast inns, motels were built, and McDon-ald's appeared on Route 1. Soon every available piece of commercially zoned land had been snapped up and Main Street was lined with outlet stores: Dansk, Quoddy, Corning, and even a designer outlet featuring Ralph Lauren seconds. Tinker's Cove residents enjoyed their new prosperity, but they also complained about the busloads of tourists who swarmed all over town making day-to-day activities difficult, if not impossible, during July and August. In those months, then, when the phones fell quiet at Country Cousins, the operators exchanged views on when was the best time to avoid the crowds at the post office and grocery store.

There was no doubt that life in Tinker's Cove, especially in the summer, required a certain amount of planning. Doc Ryder claimed he had noticed a definite increase in stress-related illness such as ulcers and high blood pressure among his patients. On the whole, however, most people in Tinker's Cove enjoyed their new prosperity, remembering the dark days of the oil embargo when the sardine cannery closed.

"You know," said Lucy, "I'm only a couple of hundred dollars short of making an incentive bonus this month."

"That's terrific," Ruthie said. "What will you do with the extra money?"

"Oh, I don't know," Lucy said slowly, savoring the possibilities. "I think I'll take the whole family out to dinner."

"Don't you want something for yourself?" asked Ruthie.

"Not really. Besides," Lucy said, brightening, "if we eat out, I won't have to cook and clean up!"

There was a sudden burst of activity as calls began coming in and the women were kept busy taking orders. Around eleven-thirty the calls finally slowed down, and Lucy found herself nodding off.

"Gosh, if things don't pick up a little, I'm going to fall asleep." She yawned. "I'll never last until one."

"Why don't you take a break and get a cup of coffee?" Beverly suggested.

"Oh, no. If I have coffee now, I won't be able to sleep later. Maybe I'll just walk around a bit and get some fresh air. I'll be back in five minutes."

Lucy took off her headset and made her way past the other operators in the phone room, out to the corridor. Walking slowly, stretching her arms and legs as she went, she passed the rest rooms and the break room with its coffee and snack machines. She pushed open the fire door to the outside. It had begun to snow, and the cars in the parking lot were shrouded with one or two inches of soft powder. Lucy took a deep breath of the clean, cold air and watched the flakes falling in the light of the lamps that lit the parking lot. They were large and coming down heavily; the town could get a lot of snow if it kept up all night.

Oh, no, thought Lucy. Not a snow day. A snow day meant that all three children would be home; even the nursery school Sara attended three mornings a week would be closed. She had so much to do to get ready for Christmas that she couldn't afford a snow day.

Lucy sighed and stepped back into the warm building. As the door closed it occurred to her that something wasn't quite right outside. She thought she heard a squawk like a duck quacking. But ducks don't quack at night, especially in December. Perhaps it was a laggard goose making a late migration south, or a dog barking. She opened the door for another look and realized she could hear an engine running. The cars were all mounded with snow, yet the hum of a motor broke the silence. This wasn't right, and if something wasn't right, Lucy had to get to the bottom of it.

Lucy took a wooden coat hanger from the rack near the door, wedged it between the door and the jamb, and went out to investigate. It wasn't very cold, and Lucy was comfortable enough in her jeans and wool sweater. Her high-top Reebok athletics left small prints filled with circles in the fresh snow.

As she drew closer to the row of parked cars, the noise of the humming engine grew louder. It came, she realized, from Sam Miller's BMW. The navy blue sedan with the SAM-I-AM vanity plates was covered with snow just like the other cars. The only difference was that the engine was running and a black rubber hose neatly capped one of the twin exhaust pipes and snaked around the car to the driver's window.

Lucy gasped and tried to pull open the driver's door. It was locked, but she did manage to pull the hose out of the window and then ran back into the building as fast as she could. She arrived in the phone room panting for breath and gesturing frantically with her hands.

"Call the police," she finally managed to say to the group of concerned women who were clustered around her.

In a matter of seconds Beverly had the police station on the line.

"A suicide in the parking lot," she repeated after Lucy. "Lucy Stone found Sam Miller's car running in the parking lot, with a hose pumping exhaust into the driver's window." She paused. "No, we'll stay right here and we won't touch anything."

Lucy collapsed on a chair and someone gave her a cup

of sweet tea to sip. "Best thing for a shock," they agreed solemnly.

"Imagine, he had a BMW and a Mercedes," commented one of the girls.

"And an indoor pool," added another.

"Really, the fanciest house in town." They nodded in unison, and then Ruthie ventured to add, "And the fanciest wife."

"Fancy house, fancy wife, fancy cars. It just goes to show," said Beverly, "that fancy isn't everything."

Then they fell silent, listening for the wail of the police cruiser's siren.

Chapter Two

#4791 These white stoneware mixing bowls with blue bands are perfect in any kitchen. Ovenproof and microwave safe. The set of three includes 1-, 2-, and 3-quart sizes. $29.

Home had never looked so good, thought Lucy as she braked to a stop in the driveway. The familiar shape of the old farmhouse comforted her, and the porch light that Bill had left burning: for her was welcoming. The old Regulator in the kitchen read 5:05, too late to make going to bed worthwhile.

While Lucy unbuttoned her coat, Patches, the black-and-white tabby, wove herself around Lucy's legs.

"You don't fool me," said Lucy. "All you want is an early breakfast."

The cat flicked her tail impatiently and meowed.

"Be quiet," Lucy hissed as she filled the coffeepot. "You'll wake everybody up."

For a moment Lucy considered waking Bill to tell him the news about Sam Miller, but she decided instead to let him sleep. She had been awakened so many times at night by hungry babies that she appreciated the luxury of uninterrupted sleep—and Bill had had his share of sleepless nights with the kids. Besides, he'd be waking up soon, anyway. She switched on the coffeepot and sat down on the rocking chair to watch it drip, smelling its wonderful aroma. She sat and rocked, letting the familiar old-house sounds and scents surround and soothe her.

Lucy loved her kitchen. She loved the old Glenwood woodstove that burned two and a half cords of wood every winter. She cherished the Hoosier cabinet she'd bought at a flea market and spent an entire summer refinishing. Bill had made the cupboards himself out of maple, and they had scraped and polished the wooden floor together. She'd sewn the blue-and-white-checked gingham curtains herself. This kitchen was really the heart of the house, with its wooden rack for wet mittens, its collection of bowls for the cat, and the big round oak table where the family gathered for meals, Monopoly, and checkers.

If she didn't do something soon, Lucy realized, she would fall asleep sitting up. She poured herself a cup of coffee and began mixing up some Santa's thumbprint cookies for the cookie exchange. She was just taking the first sheet out of the oven when Bill, looking rumpled and sleepy, appeared in the doorway.

"What are you doing?" he asked.

"Baking cookies to stay awake," Lucy answered.

"Oh," he said, and headed straight for the bathroom. He returned, poured himself a cup of coffee, and sat down at the table.

"You don't usually bake cookies so early in the morning."

"I know. I didn't get home until five and decided it

wasn't worth going to bed." She paused dramatically. "Oh, Bill! It was awful. Sam Miller committed suicide in the parking lot. I was the one who found him."

"Oh, my God. Was it really bad?" asked Bill, reaching for her hand.

"No, not really. All I saw was the hose going from the exhaust to the window. I couldn't get the door open, and I couldn't see much because of the snow. The police came, and they realized it *was* Sam Miller. He was dead when they got there. Of course, we all had to stay and answer questions even though none of us really saw anything at all. We were all in the phone room."

"Gee, I never would've thought that he'd kill himself. He had so much going for him. Maybe it was all too much—too much responsibility, too much stress," said Bill, drawing on his mug of hot coffee.

"I don't think so," Lucy said. "You and I have stress; someone like Sam Miller goes to Barbados. I don't believe it was suicide."

"Oh, Lucy. Just leave it alone. It's none of your business. Promise me."

"I don't know what you mean," said Lucy, lifting the cookies one by one onto a rack to cool.

"You know perfectly well what I mean. You can't just leave things alone. Well, for your information, there are people called police who investigate these things."

Bill paused to take a swallow of coffee and noticed Lucy's jaw had become set in a certain way he'd come to recognize. "Lucy, don't be like this. I'm just saying I don't think you need to get us involved."

He got up from his chair and stood behind her, slipping his arms around her waist and nuzzling her neck with his bearded chin.

"It's Christmastime. Let's just enjoy the holidays, and the kids. We don't have to get involved with Sam Miller's"—he turned her around and looked straight in her eyes—"unfortunate death." As he put his hand on her chin and tilted her face up to meet his kiss, a high-pitched voice broke the morning stillness.

"Mommy and Daddy alarm. Stop that kissing!"

Seven-year-old Elizabeth squirmed her way between them, demanding, "Elizabeth sandwich! Elizabeth sandwich!"

Bill caught her under her arms and lifted her up between them while Lucy covered her sleep-warmed pink cheeks with kisses. Elizabeth squealed and giggled in delight. Elizabeth's happy cries attracted her little sister, Sara, who wrapped herself around Lucy's legs, and her older brother, Toby, who leaned against the doorjamb with all the sophistication a ten-year-old could muster and asked, "Are we really having cookies for breakfast?"

It seemed to Lucy as if years had passed before she finally drove Sara to nursery school and returned to the empty house, hoping to catch a few hours of sleep. She had the foresight to turn on the answering machine, but it seemed as if she had barely dropped off when she was awakened by a loud banging and rattling at the back door.

Wrapping her log cabin quilt around her, Lucy staggered down the back stairs and across the kitchen to the door. Through the lace curtain she could see a massive blue shape: Officer Culpepper. Opening the door, she realized there was someone else with Culpepper, a slim, serious man wearing a Harris tweed sport coat under an unbuttoned London Fog raincoat.

"Sorry to wake you up, Lucy. A few questions have

come up that we need you to answer. This is State Police Detective Horowitz. May we come in?"

Lucy stepped back, allowing the men to enter, and followed them into the kitchen. Officer Culpepper sat right down at the kitchen table as if he belonged there. Indeed, he had often sat at Lucy's table planning Cub Scout and PTA activities. Detective Horowitz was more self-contained. He took off his coat and folded it carefully, then laid it across the back of one of the chairs. He placed his briefcase on the table just so, opened it, and took out a manila folder. Then he closed it and placed it on the floor next to the chair with his coat. Finally he sat down, drawing his chair up to the table and sitting stiffly with his hands on the folder. Lucy herself had collapsed on the corner chair, leaning her elbows on the table and trying to hold up her head.

"Gee, Lucy, you look beat. Let me make some coffee for you."

"What time is it?" she asked.

"About eleven. Do you have to pick up the kids or something?"

"Not till twelve. I slept longer than I thought."

"Not surprising. You had quite a night." Culpepper slipped three mugs of water into the microwave and pushed the start button.

"The instant coffee's in the cabinet over the sink. Excuse me for a minute."

Looking in the bathroom mirror, Lucy decided she'd rarely looked worse. Quickly she washed her face, brushed her teeth, and ran a comb through her hair. She smoothed a dab of moisturizer under her eyes, straightened her sweat suit, gave herself a quick spritz of Charlie, and returned to the kitchen.

A cup of hot coffee was waiting for her, and she sipped

it carefully. Detective Horowitz, she noticed, had opened his folder and was clearly ready to begin.

"Now, Mrs. Stone, about last night. What made you decide to go outside? Wasn't that unusual?"

"Not really. The calls had slowed down, I was feeling sluggish, and I didn't want to drink coffee so close to quitting time. I thought a breath of fresh air might perk me up."

"I see. You weren't drawn outside by any unusual noise or occurrence?"

"Oh, no. In fact, the phone room has no windows. When you're in there you have no idea what's going on outside. Sometimes we'll be completely surprised if a storm has blown up during our shift."

"So it was just a normal night for you. There was nothing out of the ordinary until you discovered the car."

"That's right. When I looked out I knew something was wrong, but I couldn't quite put my finger on it. Then I realized it was the car motor running."

"Was that unusual?"

"Oh, yes."

"You didn't think it might be someone arriving for the next shift or picking up one of the girls?"

"It was too early for that. Besides, when you get out of work at one A.M. nobody picks you up. If you've got car trouble, you just get a ride with one of the other girls."

"I see," said the detective, pursing his lips and making a tiny notation on his yellow legal pad. He had a slight lisp, Lucy noticed, and his upper lip was elongated, rather like a rabbit's. Lucy looked at him closely, thinking what a very serious man he must be. He was such a contrast to Officer Culpepper, who had rolled up his sleeves and was cheerfully washing the breakfast dishes she had left soaking in the sink. Perhaps it was his job that made him serious. A man couldn't investigate sudden death all the time without being affected by it.

Looking around her homey kitchen, Lucy thought how living in Tinker's Cove had insulated her, until now, from the random violence and cruelty that was twentieth-century life. Of course, in the fifteen years she and Bill had lived in Tinker's Cove, things had changed, sometimes drastically. When they'd first moved into the old farmhouse, they had heated entirely with wood, and Lucy, like many others, did all her cooking on the old Glenwood. In those days she often took down the long-handled popcorn popper from its hook on the wall and shook homegrown kernels over the wood fire until they popped. It took a little time, but she never felt rushed in those days. Nowadays she was more likely to put a package of preflavored popcorn in the microwave and zap it. Somehow the long, leisurely afternoons with children and friends had vanished; now Lucy was measuring her life in seconds.

"You didn't see any footprints in the snow, or any sign of disturbance?" insisted the detective.

Lucy shook her head. "No. The snow was clean and unbroken. There were only my footprints."

"According to your account last night, the car was locked. Is that right?"

"Absolutely. Once I saw the hose I tried to open the car door. I couldn't, so I just pulled the hose out of the window and went in to call for help. I don't know what else I could have done."

"Oh, you did the right thing, Lucy," Culpepper interrupted. "It was too late to save him."

"Did you know the deceased personally?" asked the detective.

"Well, everybody in Tinker's Cove knew Sam Miller. I wasn't a close friend, I was never invited to his house or anything. But I certainly knew him to say hello to in the street. Most people did. If you work for Country Cousins, he personally hands you your profit-sharing check, and Country Cousins is the biggest employer around."

"That's right," agreed Culpepper. "Everybody knew him."

"And envied him," Lucy added. "That's what I can't understand. Why did he kill himself?"

The detective and Culpepper exchanged a meaningful glance; finally Culpepper broke the silence.

"There's no harm in telling you, I suppose. It'll be in the paper tomorrow, anyway. Sam Miller didn't kill himself. He had quite a bump on his head. He was unconscious when somebody stuffed him in the car and rigged up the hose. Sam Miller was murdered."

Chapter Three

#5532 An intricately patterned vest knitted in 100%
Shetland wool. Designs include Christmas trees,
reindeer, and ice skates. Dry clean or hand wash.
Natural color with green and red. Women's sizes:
S(6–8), M(10–12), L(14–16), XL(18–20). $58.

Lucy leaned back in Sue Finch's antique rocking chair and took a sip of mulled cider. She inhaled the spicy scent of the potpourri Sue had left simmering in a little copper pot on the woodstove and let out a long breath. After the last few hectic days it was wonderful to relax among friends in Sue's beautifully decorated house.

Christmas was Sue's favorite time of year, and she loved using all the decorations she collected at flea markets and antique shops throughout the year. She had no fewer than three Christmas trees: one in the living room, bedecked with baby's breath and ribbons, which were carefully coordinated to go with the Victorian color scheme; one in the family room, decorated with ornaments her daughter, Sidra, had made; and one in the kitchen, trimmed with cookie cutters and gingerbread men. A collection of teddy bears was gathered in a hutch, lamp tables held a large and valuable collection of St. Nicks, and a twelve-inch feather tree with tiny German glass ornaments stood on the coffee table. Crocheted and starched snowflakes hung in the windowpanes, and a single candle burned in each window.

Looking around at the rosy-cheeked faces and eyes sparkling in the candlelight, Lucy realized she'd known most of these women for her entire adult life. A few were natives of Tinker's Cove, but most were transplants or "wash ashores" like herself and Bill, idealistic young college graduates who had avoided the rat race and looked for an alternative lifestyle "back on the land." With their *Mother Earth News* to guide them, they'd chopped wood, planted gardens, and recycled everything.

Through the years she'd attended Lamaze and La Leche League classes with these women. In those days they wore hand-wrought silver earrings in their pierced ears, and they drove ancient pickup trucks or huge Chevy Impalas filled with apple-cheeked and overalled children. Conversations had centered around how to get a baby to sleep through the night or how to keep the cabbage moths away from the kohlrabi.

Now they drove Jeep Cherokees or Dodge Caravans, and the dangling earrings had been replaced with discreet gold buttons or cultured pearls. Their faces were still scrubbed clean morning and night, but Oil of Olay was carefully smoothed under the eyes and just a hint of makeup applied. The long, flowing hair of the seventies had been cut, tinted, and permed. Now they didn't look very different from their mothers.

Their lives, however, were different from their mothers'. They all had jobs, some full-time, but most part-time like Lucy. They helped in their husbands' businesses or answered the phone at Country Cousins, and some weren't above waiting on tables during the summer. "How else can you make a hundred dollars in a few hours?" they'd ask each other as they sunned themselves on the beach. They were the mainstay of the Scouts and the PTA; they were the class mothers. The cookie exchange was an established part of their Christmas season.

Sue Finch had been the hostess for five or six years. It gave her an opportunity to show off her decorations, and it gave her friends a chance to socialize during the busy holiday season. Sue held the number of participants to an even dozen, and each woman brought six dozen of her best Christmas cookies. All the cookies were arranged on a long pine trestle table, and the high point of the evening was a leisurely procession around the table, each woman taking six of each cookie. All went home with the same number of cookies they had brought, but each had a dozen different varieties.

And what varieties! It was a point of honor to bring cookies rich in butter, chocolate, and nuts, cookies that required a bit of fussing. Of course, the cookies were to be taken home and saved for Christmas, so Sue always provided a dessert, too. This year it was an elaborate bûche de Noël, a sponge cake filled with chocolate-flavored whipped cream and decorated with meringue mushrooms and drizzles of chocolate and caramelized sugar.

"I just don't know how you do it, Sue," commented Lucy. "Everything is so lovely."

"Oh, well, I'm not working like you are." Sue shrugged. "Lucy, you look exhausted. Are you doing too much?"

"I don't think so. But I haven't been getting much

sleep. The police kept us so late the night Sam Miller died."

"That's right," said Pam Stillings, whose husband, Ted, was editor of *The Pennysaver.* "You actually found Sam, didn't you, Lucy?"

"I did and I wish I hadn't. I may have discovered the body, but I didn't even see him. Everyone asks me about it, but I really don't know anything."

"Were you scared?" asked Pam.

"No, not really. Just kind of sick and let down the way you feel when the adrenaline stops flowing. Of course, I thought it was suicide. I didn't realize he'd been murdered."

"Why would anyone think a man like Sam Miller would kill himself?" demanded Rachel Goodman. "He had everything, including Marcia."

"If you ask me," Franny Small informed the group, "I think Marcia is the prime suspect."

"The wife usually is," agreed Lucy. "But I can't imagine her being mechanical enough to rig up a hose. She might have gotten her hands dirty."

"She really is a stuck-up little bitch. She thinks an awful lot of herself," commented Rachel, running the side of her fork around her dessert plate and licking it clean with her little pink tongue. "When I invited her to join the Friends of the Tinker's Cove Library, she just turned me down flat. Made me feel as if I were social climbing or something. I was just trying to be friendly," Rachel defended herself.

"They may live here in town, but the Millers have never really been part of the town," Sue said. "I mean, there's a certain distance. You wouldn't just drop by for a cup of coffee and a chat."

Lucy chuckled. "Imagine dropping in on Marcia Miller!"

"Oh, Sid got to know her pretty well," announced Sue. "He's spent quite a lot of time in her bedroom."

"Oh, really?" inquired Lucy. "How did that happen? Why aren't you upset?"

"It wasn't like that," Sue admitted. "He installed a closet system for her."

"Tell us more, Sue," said Lucy. "What did he say when he got home?"

"He said she had a lot of clothes, and"—Sue stretched the words out, dearly saving the best for last—"they have separate bedrooms."

"Really?" Lucy was incredulous. "Lydia, you're always the first to know about these things. Weren't the Millers happy?"

Lydia smiled. "It's not my fault. Kindergartners tell their teacher everything. They just can't keep secrets. But little Sam seems happy enough. He's a quiet little fellow. Not abnormal. I thought, well, maybe he's just a well-brought-up boy with good manners."

"That's not much help," complained Lucy. "What about your mom, Franny? She always knows everything that's going on."

"You can say that again," agreed Pam indignantly. "I saw her at the IGA and she told me that Jennifer had gotten her first period, and that was before Jennifer even got home from school."

Franny moaned. "It's not as bad as it sounds. She's awfully good friends with the school nurse."

"I dread to think what you've heard about my kids," Lucy worried.

"I don't listen to her," admitted Franny. "I've got my own life to live."

"Don't we all. Too much life, in fact. I'm never going to be ready for Christmas. But I still can't help wondering why someone would kill Sam Miller," Lucy said pensively.

Chapter Four

#1939 Classic neckties made by McMurray woolen mills, weavers of handsome plaid and solid-color woolens for over 100 years. Made in Canada. Dry clean only. Three lengths: boys, regular, and tall. Be sure to specify size and pattern on order form. $12.

The next morning Lucy made breakfast, kissed Bill good-bye, packed lunches for Elizabeth and Toby, kissed them on their cheeks, and waved them off on the school bus. Then she made the beds, washed the dishes, and swept the kitchen floor. Chores completed, she sat down at the big oak table with a cup of coffee and a pencil and paper to take stock of her Christmas situation.

Only seven days until Christmas. One week. Yesterday she'd finished the sleeves of the sweater she was making for Bill. Now all she had to do was sew the parts together and knit the neckband. The tools she'd ordered from Brookstone had come, and she'd used her Country Cousins discount to buy some other clothes for him. Bill was taken care of. She put a check next to his name.

Next on the list was Bill's father, Bill senior. She had used her Country Cousins discount again and bought him a fly-tying set, which was sure to be a big hit. She put a check next to his name.

Below him on the list was "two moms," hers and Bill's, with a row of question marks next to them. Lucy fought down a rising sense of panic, scratched her head thoughtfully with her pencil, and added another question mark to the row.

This afternoon she would finish Elizabeth's angel costume, really just a sack with armholes made from an old sheet. With her long blond hair, a little tinsel, and wings provided by the church, Elizabeth would look lovely. She put a check next to "angel costume."

Looking over her list of toys for the children, Lucy decided there was no way around it. She had to work tonight, and that only left tomorrow, Saturday, for a final trip to the Tons of Toys store in Portland. She wrote "Sat" next to "toy store" and went on to the next item, "meals." Just then the phone rang. It was Sue Finch.

"Sue, I was just going to call you! I had such a nice time last night, and it's great having all those cookies in the pantry."

"Thanks for coming and bringing those Santa's thumbprints. Everybody loves them. Listen, Lucy, are you going to Sam Miller's funeral?"

"I want to," said Lucy. "I'm sure it's going to be the social event of the year in Tinker's Cove. But I have to do some major Christmas shopping in Portland."

"So come to the funeral with me and we'll zip into Portland afterward. You'll hate yourself if you miss it," coaxed Sue.

"Okay, great," said Lucy. She hung up the receiver and called for Sara to come and put her jacket on.

"Come on, honeybun. We've got to get some groceries."

Lucy enjoyed her little outings with Sara. She had just turned four, and she still loved going to the grocery store, the bank, or the story hour at the library with her mother. Before she knew it, Lucy realized she'd have another touchy preteen like Toby to cope with.

Sara and Lucy took their time strolling through the aisles at the IGA. They debated the relative merits of Cheerios and Lucky Charms and found a great deal on fabric softener, and Lucy decided that a package of cupcakes wouldn't hurt just this once. When it was time to check out, Lucy saw her friend, Miss Tilley, standing in the checkout line behind Barb Cahoon, who was the mother of three basketball-playing sons and had the grocery order to prove it.

"Miss Tilley, is that heavy cream in your basket? You shouldn't be buying that."

"Nonsense, I've had oatmeal with cream for breakfast every morning since I was a little girl. Hasn't hurt me a bit. Of course, I'm only seventy-three years old."

"You don't look a day over eighty," teased Lucy.

"Don't get smart with me, young lady," retorted the old woman. "Now tell me . . . about this Sam Miller business. Who do you think killed him?"

"I haven't got the foggiest idea," answered Lucy, tucking a stray clump of hair behind Sara's ear.

"I seem to remember that you love to read mysteries. I used to save the good ones for you at the library." Miss Tilley had been the town librarian until the board of trustees finally gathered the courage to retire her forcibly on her eightieth birthday.

"I don't have time for mysteries these days. In books or in real life." Lucy shrugged. "Everybody's saying Marcia killed him."

Miss Tilley raised an eyebrow. "Why do folks think that?"

"I guess because it's the usual thing. Husbands and wives usually kill each other."

"I wouldn't know," observed Miss Tilley. "I've never been married. I would imagine he was killed by someone who had something to gain by killing him."

"Well, Marcia might have gained a lot. First, she got out of an unhappy marriage. Did you know they had separate bedrooms?" Lucy nodded for emphasis. "And, he probably left her a lot of money. Money, and the freedom to spend it. Sounds like a pretty good motive to me."

"Not necessarily. She received a settlement when she married, but that's all she got. Sam's money is all tied up in the business."

"That's interesting," said Lucy, remembering that Sam Miller's mother and Miss Tilley were close friends. "Who really runs the business? Is it a family board of directors?"

Miss Tilley laughed. "Old Sam hated family squabbles, and he had plenty of them with his wife's family, as I remember. He left the whole kit and caboodle to the two boys, Sam and Tom."

"That means Sam's brother, Tom, might have quite a lot to gain."

"That nasty Viennese doctor probably had a name for it," said the old woman.

"Sibling rivalry," agreed Lucy. "Sam always did over-shadow Tom."

"Now Tom will be able to run Country Cousins any way he sees fit," said Miss Tilley, unloading her basket of groceries onto the conveyor belt. "I wonder if there will be any changes."

"I wonder," said Lucy, shaking off the anxious feeling she got when she thought about going back to work. Chances were, she thought as she watched the girl ring up Miss Tilley's order, that Sam Miller's death had something to do with Country Cousins. After all, that's where his body was found. Maybe it was where his murderer would be found, too.

For the rest of the day Lucy tried not to think about Country Cousins. She was scheduled to work at five, and as the afternoon wore on, she began to feel tense and uneasy.

When the old Regulator in the kitchen read 4:45, she climbed into her little Subaru, feeling exactly the way she had the day she went to the dentist to have her wisdom teeth pulled. As she drove the familiar route, she couldn't help thinking about Sam again. He might have been killed because he saw something he shouldn't have. Nobody in Tinker's Cove talked about it much, but like many coastal communities, the little town had had its share of smugglers and mooncussers.

The Pennysaver occasionally reported drug busts made by the Coast Guard, so Lucy knew Tinker's Cove wasn't immune to illegal traffic, but she didn't think she knew anyone who was involved. Country Cousins itself imported goods from all over the world, and Lucy, with her flair for the dramatic, had occasionally wondered if something a little more potent might be coming in along with the Peruvian knitwear and Mexican rugs.

As she parked in her usual spot, she wished it wouldn't get dark quite so early. Anyone could be lurking out there, in the dark beyond the bright lights. They certainly hadn't done much for Sam Miller, and she felt like a sitting duck as she crossed the brightly lit area to the safety of the warehouse.

Walking down the hall, Lucy noticed a group of women clustered around the bulletin board in the break room.

"What's up?" she asked Beverly.

"It's just a memo saying the police are investigating Sam's death and asking everyone to cooperate."

"Oh, no," wailed Lucy. "I don't think I can go through that again."

"I'm sure it's just a formality," Bev reassured her. "I haven't seen any sign of police."

"It feels so creepy coming back here," Lucy confessed. "I didn't want to come."

"The sooner you get back to work the better. Come on, hang up your coat," said Bev in a no-nonsense, motherly tone of voice.

Lucy obeyed, and followed Bev to her desk, where she found a bouquet of supermarket flowers waiting for her.

"Oh, you guys are so nice," she exclaimed.

"We knew it would be hard to come back," said Ruthie. "It's been hard for everyone. We're all scared."

"Lightning doesn't strike in the same place twice," Bev said, settling down at her computer station.

"It does if there's a maniac loose out there," grumbled Ruthie. "What did the police ask you, Lucy?"

"Just what I saw, which wasn't much." Lucy put on her headphone and logged onto the computer. "What did they ask you?"

"They haven't bothered with me," Ruthie complained. "But I heard they were in and out of the office all day. They spent a lot of time with Tom Miller and George Higham."

"I suppose they would," said Lucy, taking a call. She was soon busy taking orders, some from as far away as Alaska and California, and talking to the customers made her forget her anxiety. The lines were busy and she didn't even get to take a breather until ten-thirty. She was just coming out of the rest room and heading for the machines in the break room when she met George Higham, the customer service manager, in the hallway.

"Hi, George," she said, and then, plucking up her courage, she asked, "Have the police made any progress?"

"Not as far as I know. Of course, as the memo requested we're asking everyone to cooperate," replied the little bearded man. He was wearing his usual navy blazer, button-down shirt, gray flannels, and tasseled loafers. Lucy noticed that all his clothes were from the catalog.

"I can't help feeling nervous," admitted Lucy. "You don't think Sam's death had anything to do with the company, do you?"

"Of course not," he snapped, bridling at the suggestion. "Now, isn't it time you got back to work?"

"Well, I'm actually on my dinner break right now. I worked right through my coffee break. I'm supposed to get a half hour for dinner, and a fifteen-minute coffee break."

"You don't need to lecture me about the state labor laws, Lucy," said Higham, his face flushing. Then he caught himself, probably remembering one seminar on employee motivation, and stretched his mouth into something resembling a smile. "I see you're quite close to earning an incentive bonus, Lucy. Keep up the good work."

Lucy watched him as he walked down the corridor to the executive offices; then she went into the break room. She bought a package of cheese crackers and a diet soda from the machines and sat down at the table opposite Bev.

"Sam Miller's only been dead for two days, and already things are going to pot around here."

"What do you mean?" asked Bev.

"With Sam gone, guys like George Higham are going to have more power," Lucy said, ripping open the cellophane package.

"Sam was a nice man to work for," Bev agreed, "He had a smile for everybody, and then he left you alone to do your job."

"Those days are over, Bev. George Higham will be looking over our shoulders and poking into everything. He won't be able to pass up a chance to flex his managerial muscles."

"You're probably right, Lucy. But there's nothing you can do about it. Take a word from a survivor and watch your step. Higham's real friendly with Tom Miller. He's the one to watch these days."

Chapter Five

#2100 Orthopedically correct back cushion for comfort on long drives. Car manufacturers insist on designing automobile seats that are sheer torture for people with weak or injured backs. These sheepskin-covered forms of flexible, durable polyfoam are guaranteed to solve the problem. $57.

As she climbed awkwardly into Sue's big Jeep the next morning, Lucy lamented her friend's knack for looking perfect. Her gray tweed coat and black beret were just right for a Tinker's Cove funeral, where too much black would be considered excessive.

"I thought I'd just put this scarf over my shoulder when we go to Portland," said Sue, pulling a piece of red paisley out of her enormous shoulder bag. "I don't want to look as if I've been to a funeral."

That was just the sort of thing Sue would do, thought Lucy, who was making do with a castoff coat of her mother's. There was no point in being jealous; no matter how hard she tried she would never have Sue's sense of style. Lucy would much rather spend an afternoon reading the latest P. D. James than studying the latest *Vogue*. She loved shopping with Sue, though, because no one had a surer nose for a bargain.

Arriving at the white clapboard church with its tall steeple, they paused for a second and looked up at the weather vane. It was a gilded rooster, and Lucy loved the way it sparkled against the clear blue sky.

Neither woman was surprised at the large turnout. They managed to squeeze their way through the crowd to the balcony, where they found two vacant seats behind the clock. They would have to crane their necks to see, but at least they had seats.

Looking around, they saw that everyone in Tinker's Cove seemed to be there—from the selectmen right on down the social ladder to Sol Smith, the man who owned Sol's Septic Service.

At precisely ten o'clock, a hush fell over the congregation as the Miller family entered. First came Marcia Miller, leaning heavily on the arm of the funeral director. She was swathed in a black veil reminiscent of the one Jackie Kennedy wore at JFK's funeral. Next to her, holding her hand, walked five-year-old Sam IV, looking like a small solemn owl in his tiny blazer and short gray pants. The undertaker indicated the front pew and Marcia entered it, alone except for young Sam. Sue and Lucy exchanged a glance, and Lucy found herself working very hard not to giggle.

Following Marcia was Tom Miller, Sam's younger

brother, escorting his mother, Emily. Emily Miller, usually a hale and hearty type, looked very old and frail today. Tom helped her sit down and get settled.

Tom had always been considered something of a mama's boy. He still lived in the big Miller house out on the point with his mother. Lucy had always thought of him as a pale imitation of his brother. He and Sam looked a lot alike, but where Sam had a fine head of glossy black hair, Tom's was light brown and thinning.

Sam had always been a bit of a show-off. He drove the BMW with its SAM-I-AM plates, he had the glamorous wife and the architect-designed house with Palladian windows and an indoor pool. Tom, on the other hand, was often seen at local theater productions with his mother and was known to collect stamps. Lucy had long suspected that he was gay. After all, no one's sex life was nonexistent, and since Tom didn't have a public one, she assumed he must have a hidden one, though she'd never voiced her suspicions. Homosexuality was not an approved lifestyle in Tinker's Cove.

The next three or four pews behind Tom and Emily Miller were filled with an assortment of more distant Miller relatives and senior executives of Country Cousins. Lucy noticed with satisfaction that George Higham was not included in this group, although she was sure he would have liked to be.

The organist struck a few familiar chords, and the congregation all rose to sing "Rock of Ages." Then they sat and read together the Twenty-third Psalm. A period of silent prayer accompanied by several mournful tones from the organ ensued. Then, formalities completed, Dave Davidson, the minister, rose to deliver the eulogy. Lucy thought he looked awkward and uncomfortable standing before them in the black robe he wore for services. His hands clenched nervously as he grasped the lectern and gazed out at the congregation. He glanced once at Marcia Miller in the front pew and began.

"Sam Miller was a man everyone knew and no one knew. He was not a simple man; his life was a paradox. Sam himself was an enigma."

It seemed to Lucy that a rustling, perhaps even a wave of resistance, emanated from the Miller clan, but Marcia sat perfectly still, while Sam IV fidgeted beside her.

"To many of you, Sam was the man who had it all. He owned the biggest store in town, had the biggest house and the biggest bank account. Sam could afford things most of us can't, and many of us envied him.

"You might be surprised to learn that Sam envied you.

"To many of you, Sam was your boss, your employer. He was a good man and a fair man; he was a good man to work for. It's hard to work for a man and be his friend, too.

"You might be surprised to learn that Sam wanted to be your friend.

"Sam Miller knew that the success of his business and the prosperity it brought had changed Tinker's Cove. Sam Miller felt badly about that. Sam Miller wanted to be your neighbor.

"Sam Miller was a wealthy man, a powerful man, and a successful businessman. Yet he grew up here in Tinker's Cove and the values of Tinker's Cove were his values, too. He believed in family. He believed in hard work. Let us remember him as he would have liked to be remembered: as a neighbor, a friend, a man who was one of us." Here Davidson paused, looked around the church at the congregation, and picked up the large Bible that lay on the lectern before him.

As he stood there, holding the Bible in his upraised arm, Lucy thought of the prophets of old, of unforgiving Cotton Mather and fanatical John Brown.

"The Bible tells us that we must love our neighbor, and teaches us that it is a sin to kill.

"Sam Miller was murdered. His death was carefully planned—engineered—by one of his fellow beings. We do not know, yet, who his murderer is." Here Davidson paused and scanned the congregation, as if he expected the guilty one to leap to his feet and confess.

"I do not think Sam Miller was killed by one of you. Sam Miller was a man of our town; indeed, he embodied all that is best in our town. This evil person"—and here the minister paused before hissing—"this sinner, must have come from outside our town.

"Every night the evening news tells us of the violence that pervades the cities of our country, of international syndicates dealing in drugs and death, and of political terrorism.

"This is the lesson of Sam Miller's death. We must fight the evil that is overtaking so much of the world, and we must keep our town as a good place to let our love for each other shine as a beacon of light in an ever-darkening world. Amen."

Davidson turned away from the pulpit and almost collapsed onto the ornate, gothic armchair that stood behind the pulpit. He stayed there, leaning on his elbow and covering his face with his hand, while they all sang the final hymn.

When it was over, Marcia sailed serenely out of the

church, her veils billowing around her face. No one, of course, could see her expression. Lucy did happen to catch a glimpse of Tom Miller's face as he watched Marcia climb into a large black limousine, and she thought he looked perfectly disgusted.

"What did you think of that?" she asked Sue as they drove down the highway to Portland.

"Well, I was surprised to learn that Sam Miller wanted to be my friend. I would have invited him over for potluck if only I'd known."

Lucy laughed. "Me too. And what was Marcia trying to do? Did you believe that veil?"

"I don't know," said Sue, shaking her head. "She had to do something. The rumors are terrible."

"I don't see how she could have done it. She always wears such high heels. I couldn't walk in shoes like that, much less kill someone."

"One thing you can be sure of," Sue advised her friend. "If she did kill him, she wore exactly the right outfit." They both laughed. "She could have hired someone to do it."

"Maybe," admitted Lucy. "But I saw them dancing at the profit-sharing dinner, and they looked so nice together. I just can't believe it. I've heard that some people think it was Tom Miller."

"Tom?" Sue's voice rose in disbelief.

"Yeah, an extreme case of sibling rivalry. You only have one kid, Sue. If you did, you'd know how murderous things can get. And Sam really did overshadow Tom. Tom might have been seething inside for years."

"Well, I've never noticed him seething. He seems like such a nice boy." Sue laughed mischievously. "And he takes such good care of his mother."

"You're probably right," conceded Lucy. "Dave Davidson could be on the right track. It must be some maniac from outside town. A prison escapee or something. But I thought those guys always play with their victims first. I don't think a homicidal maniac would choose carbon monoxide."

"You think it was a professional?"

"No, I think it was somebody who was afraid of blood. Somebody who wasn't terribly handy with guns and knives." Lucy paused for a minute, then blurted out, "Somebody like me!" She laughed. "That's what I'd choose, if I were going to murder somebody. No mess, no bother."

The rest of the day passed in a frenzy of spending that Lucy feared might wear the numbers right off her Visa card. At the very least, she hoped the closing date for next month's bill had passed.

After they finished shopping at Tons of Toys and loaded the oversized boxes into the car, Sue insisted on a quick trip to her favorite shop, the Carriage Trade. Lucy went along just to look while Sue tried on dresses, and she noticed a basket of scarves marked fifty percent off.

"Do you think my mother and Bill's mother would like those?" she asked Sue as she pulled two, one blue, one red, from the pile.

"Why not? Those are silk. A scarf like that can really make an outfit."

"Okay, you've sold me. Now, let's get out of here."

"Not so quick, Lucy. Bill asked me to be Santa's little helper. He wants you to pick out an outfit for him to give you for Christmas. How about this Oriental poppy dress?"

"Look at the price! I can't get that!"

"Just try it on," coaxed Sue.

In the dressing room, Lucy grumbled to herself as she struggled out of the too tight black skirt she'd cleverly disguised with an oversize gray sweater. The silky red dress slipped on as if it had been made for her. Lucy shook out her hair and looked at herself in the mirror. Even to her critical eyes the dress was perfect. It slimmed her hips, emphasized her bust, and made her skin glow.

"How are you doing?" asked Sue, shoving the curtain aside. "Oh, Lucy. I can't let you out of this store without that dress."

"I give up," agreed Lucy as she handed the dress over.

As they drove back along the highway to Tinker's Cove, the last rays of weak winter sun disappeared and the sky turned dark. Remembering that they'd skipped lunch, Lucy and Sue made a quick detour through a Burger King drive-thru and ordered burgers, fries, and soda.

"I shouldn't be doing this," Lucy said with a moan. "I'll get a zit."

"You've got to live dangerously once in a while," observed Sue, wiping a trace of ketchup off her perfect little chin. "You know, Lucy, I've been thinking. If Sam Miller got killed at Country Cousins, it's probably because somebody there is a murderer. I hope you're careful."

"I don't think I've got anything to worry about," said Lucy. "Why would anybody want to kill me? But I do think Sam got killed because he saw somebody doing something they didn't want him to see. That makes the most sense to me."

"Well, I don't want to scare you. But you *are* the one who found his body. The murderer might be afraid you know more than you do. If I were you, I wouldn't go poking around any dark corners."

"Don't worry about me. I don't have any opportunities to go snooping around, even if I wanted to."

"You can't fool me, Lucy. I know you too well," said Sue, turning the radio dial to a classic rock station. As they drove along together listening to old John Lennon tunes, Lucy thought how glad she was that she had a friend like Sue. The trip home went quickly as they munched their fries, talked, and sang along with the radio. Soon they had turned off the highway onto Route 1 and had passed through Tinker's Cove center and turned onto Old Red Top Road. Lucy's driveway was just ahead.

As Sue pulled into the driveway, the headlights picked out a huddled clump of black-and-white fur.

"Oh, Lucy! Isn't that your cat?"

"It sure looks like it. Probably hit by a car. Stupid. cat. I never could teach her to stay out of the road." Lucy began unloading her bags and packages. "I don't know how I'll tell Elizabeth. She loved that cat." She waved to Sue and trudged over to the little furry body. It was definitely Patches.

Lucy took a deep breath and marched toward the house, clutching her Christmas presents and bearing bad news.

Chapter Six

Lucy stashed her packages in the ell off the back door and let herself into the house. She followed the sound of voices into the living room, where she found Bill perched on a stepladder in a tangle of Christmas lights and greenery.

"You're putting the tree up," accused Lucy. "Weren't you going to wait for me?"

"Of course. We were only getting it ready," Bill reassured her as he climbed down. He looked at her closely. "Did shopping tire you out?" he asked sarcastically. "I've got a big pot of clam chowder sitting on the stove, I've spent quality time with my children—a lot of quality time, I might add—and I'm ready for a beer. Do you want something?"

"A glass of wine?"

Bill went off to the kitchen, and Lucy hugged Sara,

who was tugging on her coat and squealing, "What did you get us?"

"Yeah, what about us!" demanded Toby.

"Seven days till Christmas and you're asking for treats?" Lucy raised her eyebrows in disapproval.

"Don't you know that Santa might be watching?" inquired Bill, returning with the drinks.

"Oh, nobody believes that stuff," Toby grumbled.

"Nobody believes in Santa?" Bill was incredulous. "Do you believe in Santa, Elizabeth?"

"Yes, I do." She nodded her head gravely.

"What about you, Sara?"

"I believe in Santa, Daddy."

"Well, I'm glad to hear it. It seems to me that you're in the minority here, my boy." Bill looked sharply at his ten-year-old son. "Perhaps, you'd better rethink your position."

Lucy laughed and drew three candy canes from her pocket. "You can chew on these while you mull things over."

The three children happily grabbed the candy canes and went off to watch the *Garfield Christmas Special,* which was playing on the VCR.

Bill and Lucy retreated to the kitchen, where Bill stirred his chowder and Lucy slumped at the table, sipping her wine.

"Patches is out by the road. She must have gotten hit."

"Shit, what a crummy Christmas present."

"I don't know how I'm going to tell the kids."

"Don't look at me," said Bill. "That's your department. I'll handle the graveyard patrol."

"Maybe we can find a little Christmas kitten. They'd like that," said Lucy, sitting up straighter.

Later that evening, after the family had eaten their chowder supper and trimmed the tree, Lucy supervised the Saturday night baths while Bill went out to bury the cat. It was a clear, starry night and not too cold. He picked a spot near the compost heap and began digging. The ground wasn't frozen yet, and his shovel went into the loamy soil easily. As he worked he couldn't help thinking that if an occasional dead cat was the worst thing he and Lucy had to face, they were pretty lucky.

But when he picked up the dead animal to place it in the small grave, he noticed a bit of cord around its neck. He turned on his flashlight in order to get a better look, and he saw that the cat had definitely been strangled with the cord. He dropped the cat into the grave and began shoveling the earth back as quickly as he could. As he replaced the shovel in the toolshed, he tried to think who would do a thing like that. He wondered if Toby had had a fight with someone at school. He couldn't imagine an adult strangling a cat. Not an emotionally healthy one, anyway. Entering the house, he shook off the sense of unease he'd felt outside. From what he could hear, Lucy had her hands full in the bathroom.

She had put both girls in the tub together and was trying to convince Sara that washing her hair every now and then was really necessary.

"What do you mean we can't stay up and watch the *Peanuts Christmas Special?"* interrupted Elizabeth.

"It's too late. Daddy will tape it and you can watch it tomorrow."

"I want to see it tonight."

"Me too."

"Well, you need your sleep tonight. Tomorrow you're in the Christmas pageant." Lucy's knees were beginning to get sore, and her leg muscles ached from leaning across the tub. "Let's get finished here."

Toby appeared in the doorway, causing Elizabeth to scream and grab for the shower curtain.

"Relax, Elizabeth. I don't think he's interested in your little pink shrimp body. What's up, Toby?"

"Mom, I can't find Patches. Have you seen her?"

"Actually, I have." Lucy paused, and all three children stared at her, the two girls pink from the hot bath and Toby in his striped pajamas. "Patches got run over," she said slowly, watching their faces carefully for a reaction. "I don't think she even knew what happened. She was a happy cat, right up to the moment she died," Lucy reassured them as she wrapped Sara in a towel and began to dry her. Noticing the tears welling up in Elizabeth's eyes, she said softly, "I'm sure she's in cat heaven right now."

"Patches was the best cat we ever had," Toby asserted. "She used to sleep with me."

"And she'd ride in the doll carriage," added Elizabeth. "Sometimes she'd let me dress her up."

"But then she'd scratch and run away," remembered Sara, ever the realist. "See my scratches." She pointed to two red lines on her forearm.

"She didn't scratch because she was bad," Elizabeth said, defending her pet.

"It's just the way cats are," added Toby. "I didn't mind the scratches. I loved Patches."

"Well, we all loved her and we'll miss her," said Lucy, folding the towels and hanging them up. "Maybe Santa will bring a new kitten."

After she had finally gotten the children tucked in bed and read them the Patches memorial bedtime story, James Herriot's *The Christmas Day Kitten,* Lucy was exhausted. It had been a long day and she was glad to sink into a hot bath herself and let her tense muscles relax. It was an effort to make herself climb out of the tub and get dried off. Then she pulled about ten yards of flannel nightgown over her head, smoothed Oil of Olay under her eyes, and brushed her teeth. On her way to bed she detoured through the living room, where Bill was stretched out on his recliner, flipping through channels with the remote control. She stood next to him and smoothed his hair affectionately.

"I'm going to bed early tonight."

Bill nodded. "Toby having any trouble at school?" he asked.

"Not that I know of. Why?"

"Patches wasn't hit by a car. There was a string around her neck. Somebody strangled her."

Lucy was stricken. "Who'd do a thing like that?"

"Most probably a boy of a certain age."

"You don't mean Toby? He's really upset."

"No, not Toby." He stroked her hand. "Maybe some kid with a grudge against him. Has he said anything?"

"Nope. He seems to get along with everybody." Lucy's voice was defensive.

Bill shrugged. "Don't worry. Go to bed. I'll be up soon."

"That was a nice thing you did today. Thank you." Lucy sat on his lap.

Bill grunted. "What do you mean?"

"You know. Having Sue make me buy an outfit."

"What did you get? Something sexy?"

"No, something beautiful. And expensive. Sue said money was no object."

"I didn't tell her that." Vertical lines appeared on Bill's forehead.

"I can take it back," Lucy said quickly.

"No. I'm just teasing. I like to see you in new things. Are you going to model it for me?"

"You'll see it on Christmas," said Lucy, yawning. "It'll be a surprise."

Bill smiled. "Okay. Go to bed, sleepyhead. I just want to see the end of this hockey game. I'll be up soon."

Once she was tucked under the down comforter in the antique sleigh bed, Lucy realized she wasn't as tired as she'd thought. She reached for the latest Martha Grimes novel she'd pounced on at the library. Soon she was absorbed in the adventures of Detective Inspector Richard Jury and his faithful sidekick, Detective Sergeant Wiggins. What exactly, she wondered, was a Fisherman's Friend?

In the book they came in packets. Perhaps they were cigarettes or a candy of some kind. Maybe a cough drop. She imagined the sharp smell of tobacco and the clean, astringent scent of camphor. When she was at summer camp years ago, she had been terribly homesick. For some reason she couldn't remember, the camp nurse had given her cotton balls soaked in camphor. Remembering the smell made her feel small and sad. Camphor and gray wool army blankets. She'd hated the rough blanket, so unlike the soft blue one on her bed at home. One night she'd kicked off the sheet and become entangled in the coarse gray wool. Somehow she hadn't been able to free herself from the gray wool cocoon and she'd screamed and screamed until the counselor had finally come. The counselor was huge and fat and unfriendly and made her feel small and helpless. The counselor had laughed at her and Lucy had perversely held on to the wool blanket. In her dream she had waited to be free of it; now she held on to it for protection. Now she smelled the sooty, chemical smell of an automobile's exhaust. It was a comforting, familiar smell and she wanted to yield to it, to the great throbbing sensation of the automobile motor, but she knew she mustn't. She must fight to stay awake. She felt warm fur on her face as if the cat had curled up to sleep there. The cat began purring softly and then louder and louder until it sounded like one of Bill's power saws. Lucy's heart began beating faster and faster; it was pounding within her chest and she couldn't breathe. Her lungs were bursting and she finally fought her way free of the suffocating covers. Gasping and gulping for air, she realized she was sitting up in bed. Her nightgown was soaked with sweat and she was shaking with fright. She put her hand to her forehead to push her hair back and realized that her hair was soaking wet. It must have been a nightmare; there was nothing to be afraid of. Bill was lying there beside her, sound asleep. She took a deep breath and tried consciously to relax her arms and legs the way she had learned in Lamaze class. She really ought to get up and go to the bathroom if she wanted to be comfortable, but she was afraid to leave the safety of Bill's side. The thought of walking alone through the dark, silent house terrified her. Instead she turned on her side and curled against him, spoon fashion, to try to go back to sleep.

Chapter Seven

#997S Traditional Christmas wreaths made by skilled craftswomen from genuine Maine balsam. Each wreath is decorated with a weatherproof red bow. $16.

"Mommy, isn't that wreath big?"

Lucy smiled down at Sara, who was dressed in her prettiest Polly Flinders dress and was sitting beside her in the crowded church pew.

"Yes, it's very big," agreed Lucy as she admired the enormous green wreath that hung behind the pulpit. Lovingly assembled by the flower committee, the wreath was the only decoration in the plain Protestant meetinghouse. Sunlight streamed through the tall windows and reflected off the white walls. This church had no stained glass or carved-wood paneling; there was no kneeling, no sense of hushed anticipation. Members of the congregation greeted each other and chatted while children ran up and down the aisles. This was the Sunday of the Christmas pageant, and the church was overflowing with families. A chord from the organ brought everyone to order, and the congregation rose to sing an old carol, "Venite Adoremus."

Lucy loved the pageant. It was the same every year, and she enjoyed watching the children progress through the ranks. The very youngest were angels, naturally angelic with their plump rosy cheeks and soft baby hair, but they soon graduated to become sheep and other animals. After a year or two the animals went on to become shepherds. The very oldest had the important parts: Mary, Joseph, the Three Wise Men, Herod the King, and the angel Gabriel. This year Elizabeth was a lead angel and Toby was a shepherd. Little Sara was still too young, so she was watching with her parents and dreaming of next year, when it would be her turn.

Lucy had grown up in New York City, where her family had attended a large and wealthy Episcopalian church. As a child she had taken part in the Christmas pageant there, dressed in elaborate costumes donated by a rich parishioner. That pageant had been a very elaborate affair, complete with hired actors and singers for the main parts. It had been wonderful in its way; the darkened church had smelled of evergreens and the candlelit, glittering processions had been dramatic and mysterious. Yet Lucy much preferred the sunlit, homemade pageant in Tinker's Cove.

Hearing the familiar strains of "Angels We Have Heard on High," Lucy craned her neck to see Elizabeth. She nudged Bill and they beamed with pride as their daughter, glowing with self-consciousness, paraded down the aisle. This year she even had a line. Lucy perched anxiously on the edge of the pew until Elizabeth announced, "Behold, I bring you tidings of great joy!" and she could safely relax.

Leaning against the straight back of the pew, Lucy thought how different the atmosphere in the church seemed today from yesterday. Yesterday's mourners had been replaced with families intent on celebrating Christmas. It was wonderful to see so many young families in the church, thought Lucy. When she had first started attending, Toby had been a baby and she had come to services with him cradled against her chest in a Snugli.

The congregation then had consisted mainly of old people; some Sundays the youngest member was sixty-seven years old! The women in particular had made Lucy feel welcome. They had fussed over baby Toby, delivered casseroles to her house. when she caught pneumonia, and given her slips and cuttings from their gardens. Lucy was truly fond of some of the old members like Miss Tilley. She smiled to see her gaunt figure and straight back across the aisle.

When Miss Tilley had been the librarian at the Broadbrooks Free Library, she had been legendary for her strict overdue book policy and her tart tongue. She was not likable, but she had a penetrating intelligence that earned her the town's respect. It was rumored that she had been friends with Longfellow's daughter, Alice, and Lucy always meant to ask her if it was true.

Next to Miss Tilley sat Faith Willets. Faith was a simple, good-hearted woman who dressed in plain old polyester from Sears—and had the most beautiful garden Lucy had ever seen. Faith was the president of the Organic Gardening Club, and wrote the "Garden Checklist" that appeared in *The Pennysaver* each week. The acre surrounding her Cape Cod house was planted like an English cottage garden with fruit trees, perennial flowers, herbs, and even vegetables. Faith was the primary donor to the Memorial Day plant sale, and Lucy was a faithful customer.

In fact, Lucy had first discovered the Tinker's Cove church through the annual plant and used-book sales. One year Bill had discovered a treasure trove of erotica in the paperback section and had returned hopefully every year since. When she felt lonely and depressed after Toby's birth, Lucy began attending services. She'd given up trying to be an Episcopalian in her teens when she'd decided she just couldn't believe in God. She'd missed the hymns and sermons, however, and had been delighted to discover the friendly, informal community church. Shortly after she'd become a member, old Dr. Greenhut died and the congregation called a new, young minister, Dave Davidson.

Dave and his wife, Carol, were not a traditional ministerial couple. Carol avoided the Women's Club meetings like the plague and rarely attended Sunday services. Instead she poured her energy into her career as a sculptor and turned the old barn behind the rectory into a studio. The congregation didn't seem to mind; in fact, the Davidsons brought a new energy and vitality to the old church. Sunday school classes were organized and filled rapidly as many young families realized something was missing from their lives that church could provide.

The service was ending. Everyone rose to sing the "Hallelujah" chorus from Handel's *Messiah*. *No* one could resist joining in, and the church was filled with the sound of joyous if somewhat off-key voices raised in celebration.

Lucy left Bill in the line of parishioners waiting to greet the minister and, taking Sara with her, went to find Toby and Elizabeth. Truth be told, she always felt awkward around large male authority figures like Dave and could never think of anything to say to him.

Back home and changed out of their Sunday best into jeans, Lucy and Bill made lunch and planned the rest of the day. Since the weather was so beautiful, they decided to take turns staying with the kids and going out for a run. Once the dishes were washed, Lucy put on her sweatpants and running shoes and headed out alone along the network of dirt roads that crisscrossed the woods. They were originally made by early settlers who cut timber for firewood, but nowadays they also led to hunting and fishing camps. They were ideal for a peaceful jog when the weather was warm; once the ground was covered with snow they were perfect for cross-country skiing. Today Lucy stood for a while on the back porch, taking a few deep breaths and deciding which route to take. Because she hadn't been running much lately, she decided on an easy four-mile loop without hills that went around Erskine's Pond. She did her stretches and set out, enjoying the bright sunshine and mild weather. The last few winters had followed a pattern of mild weather until Christmas; then once the holidays were over, bitter cold and heavy snowstorms set in. It seemed as if this year was going to be no exception.

Once she got past the mile mark—an old Chevy truck that someone had left to rust in the woods—Lucy found her stride. The first mile was always the hardest, but she'd learned that if she didn't give up, the rest was easy. She felt as if she could run forever along these soft roads, smelling the sharp, piney scent of the trees and catching glimpses of the pond sparkling through the trees. Problems and anxieties receded, leaving nothing but the pounding of her heart, the rhythmic in and out of her breath, and the regular thud of her feet on the path. All too soon she saw the tall, narrow chimney of their house, and rounding the bend, she saw Bill and the kids in the yard. Bill and Toby were tossing a football back and forth, and the girls were mixing up pine cone and stone soup. Lucy cooled down by walking around the house and then went in for a drink of water and a shower. As she closed the door she saw Bill wave as he started off on his run.

Since Bill was a more enthusiastic runner than she was, Lucy didn't expect him back for a while. After her shower she settled down to stitch together the pieces of the sweater she had knitted for him. The girls were happy in their room playing with their Barbie dolls and Toby curled up in a corner of the couch with his book report book. It was only when she noticed the light getting dim and reached to switch on the lamp that she realized how late it was. According to the old Regulator, it was almost four, which meant that Bill had been gone for nearly three hours.

Lucy tried to fight her rising sense of panic. Something must be wrong; he could have—indeed he had— run the Boston marathon in that time. She didn't think he would have attempted anything so ambitious today. He knew she had to leave at five to pick up her mother at the airport.

Something must have happened to him, she thought. But what? He was a big strong man in his prime. Of course, Sam Miller had been in his prime, too, and someone had managed to kill him. She knew she was being ridiculous. No one wanted to kill Bill. But when she switched on the porch light and stood looking out the door, she couldn't help remembering Patches' lifeless body lying in the driveway. It was getting too dark to wait any longer, she decided. She would have to take out the Subaru and look for him. She piled the kids into the car and slowly and carefully drove along the rutted, twisted dirt road. Running along these roads was one thing; it was quite another to drive them at night, even in a four-wheel drive. The woods were gloomy, filled with dark, shadowy shapes, and the branches brushed and snapped against the car.

Lucy gripped the steering wheel in clenched hands, her neck and shoulders rigid with anxiety as she searched for him. When she finally saw his familiar figure in the road, the tension drained from her body, leaving her with a terrific headache and aching muscles.

Bill was moving slowly, however, and as he came closer, Lucy could see he was limping.

"What happened?" she asked as he climbed into the car.

"I must have pulled a muscle or something. God, my knee hurts."

"Do you need a doctor?"

"No, I'll put some ice on it when I get home. How late is it? Don't you have to get to the airport?"

Lucy checked her watch. "It's almost five. I'll drop you at the house and get the kids something to eat on the way. McDonald's okay, kids?"

As Lucy sat on the molded plastic seat in the airport, she knew she had made a mistake. Having grown up on a steady diet of tofu and brown rice, the kids adored McDonald's. Their excitement, fueled by excessive amounts of sugar, caffeine, and saturated fats, was almost unbearable. Her mother's plane was due at seven o'clock, and Lucy very much hoped it would be on time. She could see her reflection in the expanse of plate glass that overlooked the runway. She was a very small figure, surrounded by a moving blur of brightly clad children.

"Please sit down and wait nicely for Grandma," she begged through clenched teeth.

"Ooh, here comes another one!" shouted Toby. The girls screamed and jumped from their seats, running to press their hands and noses against the window.

"Is it Grandma? Is it Grandma?" they demanded.

Lucy checked her watch. Five minutes past seven. "Maybe," she said. "I hope so." Actually, she rationalized, this isn't so bad. At least she wouldn't have to face her mother alone. Ever since her father had died six months ago, Lucy had dreaded being alone with her mother. When she last saw her mother, the pain of her loss was so palpable that Lucy could barely stand to be with her. One look at her grief-ravaged face and Lucy had wanted to flee back to the safety of Bill's arms, back to the cocoon of her house. "There is no safety, no security," her mother's reproachful eyes always seemed to say. "I thought there was, but I was wrong."

Lucy crossed her arms across her chest, pressed her

lips together, and looked up to see the automatic doors opening. Her mother picked her way carefully along the rubber matting, holding herself together only by the tightly wound threads of restraint and good breeding. She might well have been the survivor of some dreadful battle or holocaust, a witness to unspeakable horror, scarcely sure herself whether she was alive or dead.

Chapter Eight

#8990 This canvas-and-leather bag is accepted by airlines as carry-on luggage and can be neatly stowed under the seat. Seasoned travelers advise that one's necessities should not be entrusted to the airlines, as they can be lost or delayed. Sturdy webbing shoulder strap included. 16" x 12" x 10". $89.

"Hi, Mom," said Lucy, rising from her seat and brushing her cheek against her mother's.

"Hello, Lucy," her mother responded tonelessly.

The children gathered around her, waiting expectantly to be fussed over, but their grandmother didn't seem to notice them.

"How was the flight?" Lucy asked, searching her purse for change to give the kids so they could buy gumballs from the machine.

"It was fine," her mother answered automatically.

"Well, do you have a baggage check or anything? How do we get your bags?"

"A baggage check?" Her mother seemed never to have heard of such a thing.

"Didn't you hand over your luggage at the ticket counter?" Lucy demanded.

"I guess I must have. I don't have it now."

"No, you don't," agreed Lucy, fighting the urge to take her by her shoulders and shake her. "You must have checked your bags, and they gave you a ticket. Do you remember what you did with it?"

"No, I don't," admitted her mother. "I don't remember that at all."

"Well," said Lucy, speaking softly and patiently as she might to one of the children, "how about looking in your pockets and your purse. I don't think that man will let you take a suitcase without your ticket stub." She indicated an extremely large uniformed baggage attendant.

The older woman obediently went through her pockets and found nothing, so Lucy led her over to the row of seats so she could sit down and search her purse.

"It isn't here," her mother announced.

"What is that pink paper?" asked Lucy, spying a corner peeking out of an inner zipped compartment.

"I don't know," she replied, and pulled out a stub printed with large black numbers. She sat and looked at the paper, turning it over and over.

When she made no effort to move, Lucy said, "That looks like it. Let's give it a try, okay?"

"All right," her mother agreed, following her over to the baggage carousel.

"What does the bag look like?" asked Lucy. "How many are there?"

"Just one."

"Do you see it?" asked Lucy.

"No, I don't recognize any of these."

Lucy bent over and began comparing the strips attached to the bags with the stub in her hand. She soon found a bag with matching numbers and asked, "Is this it?"

"It could be." She was open to the possibility.

Lucy picked up the bag. "Now, where did the kids go?"

"The kids?"

"You know. My children. Your grandchildren," snapped Lucy, her patience exhausted. "They were here a minute ago."

"They were?"

"Here they are," said Lucy as the three kids ran up. She was almost hysterical with tension and relief, and her head was pounding. "We've got the kids and we've got your bag, I guess we're all set."

"Did you bring us presents?" Toby asked boldly.

"No. I haven't shopped yet." All three children's faces fell with disappointment, but their grandmother ignored their crestfallen expressions and turned to Lucy. "I didn't want to carry the presents on the plane. I thought you and I could go shopping together this week."

"I'm sure we can," Lucy answered in a cheerful voice, but inwardly she was furious with her mother. One week until Christmas and her mother had just assumed she would have time to take her shopping. Somehow they would have to fit it in, but Lucy already felt deluged with Christmas preparations.

"I'll carry the suitcase, Mom. You take Sara's hand. I don't want her running around in the parking lot. Elizabeth, Toby, stay with me and watch out for cars, okay?"

Lucy had the sudden feeling that now instead of having three children, she had four. She was going to have to take care of her mother as well as her children. The realization absolutely overwhelmed her.

As she led her little cortege out of the terminal, Lucy noticed a taxi pulling up. She was surprised to see Marcia Miller and little Sam IV climbing out of the backseat. As she loaded her mother's suitcase into the Subaru and waited for the kids to pile in, she watched the cab driver unload suitcase after suitcase. Lucy couldn't help but notice that these were not the canvas bags sold in the Country Cousins catalog; these bore the distinctive gold logo of Louis Vuitton. A long trip to someplace warm, thought Lucy as she put the key in the ignition. Not a bad idea at all. She wondered if she could stow away on their flight.

Arriving home, Lucy installed her mother on a corner of the couch, switched on the TV for her, and sent Bill in to keep her company.

"How's the knee?" she asked as he hobbled past her.

"The ice helped, but it still hurts. If it's not better tomorrow, I'll go and see the doctor."

Lucy sighed and went upstairs to get the kids ready for bed. Toby and Elizabeth could change into pajamas themselves, but Sara needed help. It was way past her bedtime, and she burst into tears when Lucy told her it was too late for a story. Bending down to kiss her good night, Lucy noticed that her forehead was awfully warm. A quick check with the thermometer revealed a temperature of a hundred and one. As Lucy counted out the cherry-flavored tablets, she wondered idly what else could go wrong this week.

That night she ran her bath as hot as she could stand and in a fit of self-indulgence poured in the last of her treasured Vitabath. As she leaned back in the delicious suds, she sighed and felt tears prick her eyes.

This was going to be an awful Christmas. It had been terrible to lose her father just a few months earlier. He had died suddenly of a heart attack. He had left for work as usual one morning, and by dinnertime he was lying in the intensive care unit of the hospital.

Lucy had rushed to her mother's side and supported her through the hurried hallway conversations with doctors, who held out no hope, through long visits during which her father gave no sign he knew them, and she helped her make the difficult decision to forgo heroic measures and let nature take its course. Then there were the funeral and cemetery to arrange, accommodations to find for out-of-town relatives, and food to prepare for all of them.

After two weeks in the city Lucy was exhausted. She needed to go home. She helped her mother find an accountant to help put her affairs in order and then she left, feeling tremendously guilty but knowing that her place was in Maine. She called once or twice a week and made the occasional brief visit, but even though her mother had seemed awfully depressed over the phone, it had still been a shock to find her so passive and out of touch at the airport.

She had to face the fact that the mother who had been a friend and confidante was gone. Lucy promised herself that she was not going to worry about taking her shopping. If the weather was too bad, or if there was no time, she could just tie a twenty-dollar bill to a candy cane for each of the kids. Feeling somewhat relieved, Lucy was again flooded with depression when she remembered that Bill's parents would be arriving on Friday. Christmas seemed like a huge snowball increasing in size as it rolled downhill. She was a small figure in its path, toiling up a mountain of baking, shopping, and wrapping.

She was reluctantly pulling herself out of the water when Bill appeared in the bathroom.

"Now, there's a sight for any man," he said, grinning and handing her a towel.

"Oh," she groaned, "I'm getting so fat."

"No, you're not," he said, drying her back. "You're just right. There's something the matter with your mom, though. She keeps talking about things that happened years ago. She's mad at Aunt Beverly for borrowing a pair of stockings sometime during World War Two. Beverly just took them without permission and got a run in them."

"Doesn't surprise me. Just the sort of thing Aunt Beverly would do." Lucy nodded.

"Aunt Beverly? She's a sweet old thing who weighs about ninety pounds!" exclaimed Bill.

Lucy laughed. "You didn't know her in her prime. I think she borrowed a boyfriend along with the stockings. I know what you mean about her state of mind. It's not good. Maybe after she's been here for a few days she'll get better. I hope so. I don't know what I'm going to do if she doesn't."

Chapter Nine

#3221 Hand-knitted ski hat worked in 100% llama wool by Peruvian natives. These unique hats are attractive and warm. In shades of brown, taupe, and natural. One size fits all. $39.

At a few minutes before five the next afternoon, Lucy pulled into the employees' parking lot at Country Cousins. She sat for a few minutes, waiting for a song on the radio to finish, and smiled wryly to herself. For the next few hours all she had to do was answer the customers' calls and press a few buttons on her computer keyboard.

"You need a pair of waterproof boots? We have just the thing. What size do you need? Where shall I ship it? What is your credit card number?" The next day the boots would be on their way. If the boots went out of stock, Lucy would know immediately, thanks to the computerized inventory system that Sam Miller had pioneered. The computer would suggest an alternative style and indicate when the next shipment of boots would arrive.

Out-of-stocks were unusual at Country Cousins because Sam Miller had also developed a computer program that tracked the ebb and flow of customer preferences in the past and projected future sales. Lucy had come to develop a real respect for the computer, which always greeted her personally when she logged on. The screen would blink a friendly "Good evening, Lucy!" after she logged on with her password, Patches.

"You look beat," Beverly said sympathetically. "Christmas getting to you?"

"Sort of," agreed Lucy, taking a call for a decorative maple sap bucket. Calls came in pretty steadily for about an hour, and the time flew by as she placed orders for a chopping block, a fishing rod, a camp stove, and lots of deerskin slippers. There was a lull around six, dinner hour, and the evening was slow.

"Except for a few last-minute orders for slippers, it seems as if everybody's got their shopping done," Beverly observed.

"I've sold quite a few slippers, too." Lucy laughed. "You'll never guess who I saw at the airport," she said, pausing for emphasis. "Marcia Miller and little Sam and a big pile of suitcases. It looked as if she were planning to be away for a while."

"I guess the police don't think she's a suspect, then."

"Do they really say that?" came Ruthie's voice from the computer station on Lucy's other side. "Don't leave town, ma'am," she said, mimicking Jack Webb on *Dragnet.* "I don't think they can. Unless they indict you, I think you can go wherever you want."

"It kind of makes her look guilty, leaving like that so soon after the murder," Beverly commented.

"How could a woman kill a man after she'd had his child?" asked Karen Hall, pausing on one of her frequent trips to the restroom. She rubbed her huge tummy absent-mindedly. "It just doesn't make sense to me."

"I know," agreed Lucy. "But they say that the spouse is always the first suspect. She didn't have to do it herself. She might have had a boyfriend, or even hired somebody. She certainly could have afforded to."

"But why? Why would she kill him?" questioned Ruthie. "He seemed nice enough. And she had everything she could want. That nice little Mercedes, that big house, all those clothes."

"Money's not everything," said Beverly, shaking her head.

"They had separate bedrooms. For all we know, she could have hated him." Lucy broke off the conversation, nodding her head toward the end of the row of work-stations, where George Higham had suddenly appeared.

Karen scuttled off and the rest of the women bent their heads over their desks in an effort to look busy. Lucy hoped he would pass by, or that someone would call with an order, but the indicator on her phone refused to light up. She hunched over her desk and began making a tally of the items she had sold that night.

"Lucy, how are things going?" As George stopped behind her he blocked the overhead light and a shadow fell over her tally sheet.

"Just fine, George. I've been selling a lot of slippers."

"Keep up the good work," he said, letting his fingers linger as he patted her on the shoulder. Then he moved along down the row.

Lucy stood right up and marched off to the restroom.

She resented George touching her, and even though she washed her face with cold water, her cheeks remained flushed with anger.

Back at her station she muttered to Bev, "I think somebody ought to check up on George's whereabouts last Wednesday night."

"Just because he's obnoxious doesn't make him a murderer," Bev cautioned her.

"Everyone knows how ambitious he is. And Sam Miller never gave him the time of day. Maybe he figures his chances are a lot better with Tom Miller," Lucy said darkly.

"Speak of the devil," whispered Bev. Lucy looked up and saw George and Tom Miller standing together by the door to the phone room. Tom cleared his throat rather loudly, and George rapped on a file cabinet to get the women's attention.

"I just want to let you know that we're having a problem here," said Tom in his high-pitched voice. He paused and the women shifted on their seats, waiting nervously.

"We have a mouse in the house." He smiled apologetically. "A few field mice have apparently moved into the building." A few of the women giggled.

"This is a serious problem for us," he continued. "They could damage the computer. We've discussed the options, and I've decided the most humane course of action is to trap them."

He held up a small wire-mesh box.

"This is a Havahart trap. We don't want to hurt them, we just want to catch them and release them out in the woods where they belong. I just wanted you to know how we're dealing with this. Any questions?" He waited, glancing around the room.

"We want to make one thing very clear," added George. "It is company policy to allow eating only in the break room. If any of you are discovered with food in your desks, I can assure you that you will be dealt with severely." He turned and ushered the senior executive out of the room.

"Better clean out your desk, Karen." Lucy giggled, watching as Karen pulled out wads of crumpled candy wrappers.

"It's just that I get so hungry," Karen confessed. "I'm hungry all the time."

"I know. Being pregnant is the one time you can eat without feeling guilty," Lucy reassured her. She continued thoughtfully, "I guess we can eliminate Tom Miller as a suspect."

"I didn't know he was," observed Bev.

"I heard he was," Ruthie agreed, giggling. "Who knows what evil lurks behind that mild-mannered exterior?"

"I don't think a man who uses a Havahart trap to catch mice is going to murder his brother," said Lucy. "Dave Davidson is probably right. Sam Miller must have been involved in something outside Tinker's Cove, something illegal like drugs."

"Smuggling cocaine in the Peruvian ski hats?" asked Ruthie.

"Oh, I don't know," Lucy admitted. "It's hard to believe Sam would be involved in anything like that."

"That's it!" exclaimed Karen. "They wanted him to smuggle in dope and when he refused they killed him."

"I think you better answer your phone," observed Bev.

"Oops! Country Cousins. May I help you?" Karen babbled automatically. When she finished taking the customer's order, Lucy heard her muttering.

"What's the matter?"

"I'm out of order forms."

"I'll get 'em for you," offered Lucy. "They're kind of heavy."

"Thanks," said Karen. "I'll cover on your computer."

Lucy went over to the corner of the big phone room where the boxes of computer order forms were kept, but she discovered that the usual supply of boxes was gone. She would have to go to the storeroom.

She hesitated. The storeroom was down a long, dimly lit hallway. The furnace room was along there, and the maintenance department. But no one would be there now; the offices would be dark and empty.

Before Sam Miller's death she'd never given her safety a thought at Country Cousins. But now she was reluctant to leave the brightly lit phone room and the safety of the group of chattering women.

Straightening her shoulders, she pushed open the door and marched down the hallway, away from the phone room. She turned right where the hallway branched into the executive suite and the maintenance offices. The door to the storeroom was unlocked, and she pushed it open, reaching for the switch.

She was relieved to see several pallets of paper neatly stacked near the door and hurried in to pull a box from the top. Juggling the heavy cardboard box, she turned to leave when she saw George's figure in the doorway.

"What are you doing in here, Lucy? You're not supposed to leave the phone room."

"I just came to get order forms," explained Lucy. "There were none in the corner where they usually are."

"You should have notified your supervisor," George admonished her.

"I didn't want to waste the time, George. Now, can I get by? I want to get back to work."

"Let me carry that, Lucy. It must be heavy."

As George took the box of paper, his fingers brushed against her breasts. "You know in many ways you're a model employee. And you're very pretty, too." George's voice had become hoarse.

"Thank you." Lucy smiled at him sweetly. "You know, George, my husband is six feet tall, and he pounds nails all day long. If I told him that you touched me, he'd beat you to a pulp. He would." She nodded. "Shall we go back to the phone room?"

"I guess you can manage this box after all," said George, thrusting it at her. His face was very red, and there were beads of perspiration on his brow. Lucy hurried off. But inwardly she shuddered, unable to forget the sickening feeling of George Higham's clammy hands on her sweater.

Back at the safety of her desk, Lucy was suddenly exhausted. She answered the phone mechanically and couldn't help keeping an eye on the clock. The calls dribbled in, and the clock seemed stuck at twelve-thirty. Finally, at one, it was time to go home.

As they were putting on their hats and coats, Ruthie looked over her shoulder uneasily. "I'll tell you one thing," she said. "I hope they catch whoever killed Sam Miller real soon. It feels creepy around here."

"Ladies, don't forget your paychecks." George stood by the door with a handful of envelopes. Country Cousins had always followed the old Maine custom of paying on Monday. That way, the paternalistic mill owners had reasoned, the workers wouldn't drink away their earnings over the weekend.

Lucy snatched her check from George, refusing to

look at him. Before she left the building, she made sure that her car keys were ready in her hand. She went straight to her car, scanning the parking lot to make sure no attacker was lurking. She unlocked her car door quickly, made sure no one was hiding in the backseat, and climbed in, locking the door immediately. It was only after she was safely in her car that she noticed the other women clustered together by the door. She started the car and circled around the lot to the group, rolling down her window.

"What's the matter?" she asked.

"I've been laid off," announced Bev, her voice flat with shock.

"Me too," Karen said with a moan.

Lucy ripped open her envelope immediately, but only her check was inside. She still had a job, but she wasn't sure she wanted it.

Chapter Ten

#4152 These heavy-duty coffee mugs are favorites with merchant seamen and railway crews. They are extremely sturdy and keep coffee hot for a long time. $8.

"It's a crime, I'm telling you, a crime." Officer Culpepper's voice boomed over the din in Jake's Donut Shop. Jake's was everybody's favorite coffee shop, and today, four days before Christmas, it was packed. Lucy didn't go to Jake's very often; somehow her days didn't include time to dawdle over coffee, and even if she had the time, she didn't want to be tempted by the doughnuts.

But at noon Bill had come home early and announced that his knee was bothering him and he was going to take the afternoon off. Sara was feeling much better, so Lucy decided to seize the opportunity and take her mother shopping. They had gone through most of the stores in town, and everywhere they went her mother had the same comment.

"I just don't see anything here that I want to buy," she

would say, shaking her head and clutching her purse with two hands.

Lucy couldn't decide if she really found all the shops uninspiring or if she just couldn't bring herself to part with any money. Lucy knew her mother had been well provided for, but she suspected that the loss of her father's weekly paycheck had made her nervous about spending anything at all. Passing Jake's, Lucy had seen an empty table and suggested they stop for coffee. She needed a break, and her mother could certainly use the calories.

"I've heard those Bavarian cream doughnuts are delicious. Wouldn't you like to try one?" she urged her mother.

"Oh, I never snack."

"You've been losing weight. You should have a snack now and then," said Lucy, forcing herself to make eye contact with her mother. She hated to see her dull eyes, sagging cheeks, and lank hair.

"Oh, I eat very well. I eat three meals every day."

"Well, it's obviously not enough. You must have lost twenty pounds since Daddy died."

"It isn't because I don't eat enough," she insisted. "I do."

"That can't be true. You're using up more calories than you're taking in. If you want to stop losing, you're going to have to eat more. Have a doughnut."

"Just coffee, please," her mother told the waitress.

"Me too," said Lucy, resigned to losing another round. Looking around the shop, she saw her friend Lydia Volpe, the kindergarten teacher, just coming through the door.

"Hi!" She waved, and Lydia headed over, cheeks cherry-red from the cold.

"What a day! Those kids have got too much Christmas spirit!"

"I can imagine. Lydia, this is my mother, Helen Hayes."

"I'm not the actress," Lucy's mother announced.

"No, I can see that. I mean, you don't look at all like her," said Lydia. "It must be confusing sometimes to have the same name as a famous person."

"Usually I use my husband's name, Mrs. Bernard Hayes, if I'm reserving a hotel room or ordering something over the phone. I started doing that because once when I went to Washington, D.C.—it was during the war and I was visiting my sister who was stationed there. Well, I reserved a room at the Hilton because it was the only hotel that had any vacancies. I just gave my name, Helen Hayes, but when I got there they took me up to an enormous suite. It was just beautiful and was filled with fresh flowers. They thought I was the actress."

As she listened to this story for the hundredth time, Lucy thought how bright and animated her mother had become. It was as if her real life had been some time in the past, and the present was just a pale imitation, which she didn't find very interesting.

"What did you do?" asked Lydia. "Did you stay in the suite?"

"Of course not. I couldn't have afforded it. But it was lovely, and they let me take one of the flower arrangements to my new single room, courtesy of the management. They wanted to thank me for being so cooperative."

She nodded virtuously, certain in the knowledge that she was not one to make a scene, and sipped her coffee.

"What's Culpepper so het up about, Lydia?" asked Lucy. "He's been ranting and raving since we came in."

"Probably the warrant for the special town meeting. Haven't you seen it?"

"No, I've been a little out of touch lately," said Lucy, glancing at her mother.

"Everybody at school was talking about it. It calls for a one-year moratorium on all building, and sets aside most of the undeveloped land in town as conservation land. Sam Miller had been working on it before he died. It's kind of his legacy to the town."

"No wonder Culpepper's upset," commented Lucy. "First the layoffs and now this. There won't be any jobs left in town."

"I heard about that. Are you okay?"

"So far." Lucy shrugged, watching as Barney Culpepper grabbed a young man wearing a ragg sweater by the shoulders and shook him.

"Who's that?" asked Lucy.

"Jonathan Franke, the new APTC director," answered Lydia. "Association for the Preservation of Tinker's Cove," she added for Helen's benefit.

Conversation in the coffee shop had stopped. Everyone watched to see if there would be a fight, but Culpepper merely dropped his hands and mumbled something to Franke, who left.

"It's just not fair," the officer said to his companions. "People in this town care more about ospreys and owls than they do about people. I've worked here my whole life, but I can't afford to buy a house. In fact, my rent's going up next month and I don't know how I'm going to pay *that.*"

His companions nodded and murmured assent.

"Now they want to stop building houses for a year. What's that going to do to you, Mark?"

"I'll have to go someplace else, I guess. Especially since Patti got laid off last night. I sure as hell ain't gonna make it here."

"I'm thinking of switching to remodeling," admitted Frank Martignetti, a master builder known for his expensive custom homes.

"Good luck," said Culpepper. "You'll have a devil of a time getting anything approved by that planning commission. Nope, this town is a good place to live if you're an owl or a salmon, but it really stinks if you're a workingman." He set his police cap squarely on his head, shifted his holster, and stalked out the door.

"Gosh, I hope nobody's double-parked out there," Lucy quipped.

"He has a point, Lucy. It's very hard for young people to get a start here," said Lydia. "Most of my students' parents are really struggling."

Lucy nodded. "The average house costs about a hundred and fifty thousand dollars."

"Right," said Lydia. "Say he makes twenty-five thousand, and she makes twelve, that's thirty-seven thousand a year. Most people don't even make that; a lot of our kids get subsidized lunches. But, say a family is doing pretty well, they're both working, they still can't afford twelve hundred a month for a mortgage payment—and that's if they've managed to get together thirty thousand for a down payment."

"We're lucky we bought when we did."

"We are, too. But you know there was talk of affordable housing for town employees like cops and teachers. Not that I like being considered a town employee lumped in with the road crew and the water department." Lydia's dark eyes flashed. "I'm a professional with a master's degree. But it would have helped some of the younger teachers. If this plan is passed by town meeting, I don't know what will happen to that."

"I didn't realize Sam Miller was behind all this. Maybe that's what Dave Davidson was talking about in his sermon. It didn't make sense to me," Lucy confessed.

"Maybe. Maybe it was just something Marcia put him up to saying. Socking it to the family that Sam didn't want to be like them, he just wanted to be one of the folks. She hated the Millers. You know what else I heard?" Lydia's eyes grew large and she dropped her voice. "I heard she had an affair with Culpepper."

"No." Lucy giggled. "With Culpepper? The woman who brought Donna Karan dresses to Tinker's Cove?"

"And sculptured nails!" Lydia laughed.

"And black eyeliner!"

"Don't forget black stockings." The two women burst out laughing.

Noticing that her mother had withdrawn from the conversation and was just sitting at the table fingering her napkin, Lucy reached over and caressed her hand.

"What do you say we make a quick trip to Portland? There's a big toy store there."

"I don't want to buy them toys." Helen shook her head. "They have too many toys already."

Lucy tapped her fingers on the table. "We've been to every store in town, and you didn't find anything. What do you have in mind?"

"I don't know. I'll know it when I see it," she said, frowning.

Lucy rolled her eyes and looked at Lydia, who asked, "Have you been to Sandcastles?"

"What's that?"

"A little shop behind the fire station. It's cute. She does T-shirts and sweat suits. She'll monogram them or put designs on whatever you want."

"There wouldn't be time now to have something monogrammed," Helen argued.

"Oh, sure there is. She can probably do it while you wait."

"Let's check it out, Mom. Thanks, Lydia. See you later."

Just as Lydia had promised, Sandcastles was located on pilings behind the fire station. As they walked along the boardwalk the cold wind from the bay whipped their clothes and faces. Lucy took her mother's arm and guided her along protectively, afraid the wind would be too much for her. Once inside the little shop filled with brightly colored clothes, they began to warm up.

Energized by Jake's coffee, Lucy convinced her mother to buy each of the girls a sweat suit printed with dancing hippos. While they waited the proprietor applied rhinestones in strategic places, a detail Lucy knew would thrill Sara and Elizabeth. For Toby they found a warm sweatshirt with a surf design.

"Lucy," complained her mother, "I didn't really plan to spend this much."

"The kids will love them. How much did you have in mind? I'll make up the rest."

"You don't need to do that. I'll manage." She sighed.

"Good."

"I'm not made of money, you know."

"And you're not the actress, either," said Lucy, piloting her mother back along the boardwalk to the car.

"Christmas only comes once a year. Let's try to enjoy it, okay?"

"I'm trying," answered the older woman.

"I know you are," Lucy said, and as the wind whipped round them in a savage burst, she felt tears sting her eyes.

Chapter Eleven

#1009 This rugged compass is an essential survival tool that no hiker should be without. Sturdy plastic case with a leather strap. $11.

Waking up the next morning, Lucy experienced an almost paralyzing sense of dread. She knew with certainty that something awful was going to happen today but couldn't remember what. She checked the calendar, but no dentist appointments were penciled in and she hadn't forgotten anyone's birthday, but she knew that there was something unpleasant in the offing. When the phone rang promptly at eight, it all came clear.

"Lucy, this is Marge Culpepper."

"Hi, Marge."

"Listen, Lucy. I can't help you with the Cub Scouts this afternoon. I've got to take my mother to the doctor."

"Cub Scouts?"

"Don't tell me you've forgotten? You and I promised to fill in for Kathy—she's leaving today to spend Christmas with her family in Pennsylvania."

"I did forget. I haven't got anything planned."

"Well, you've got until two-thirty to think of something. I wish I could help you, but Mom's feeling pretty poorly. You know, it's a nice day and not too cold. Why not take them for a hike?"

"That's a good idea. They can work off some of their excess energy."

"Sure. And I'll send my husband over with some hot cocoa. It's the least I can do. He'll be at Indian Rock at, say, three-fifteen. Okay?"

"Sounds great. Thanks, Marge."

Lucy hung up the phone and started washing the breakfast dishes. At least now she knew why she was depressed. Cub Scouts always depressed her.

Of course, Toby loved being a Cub Scout. He loved wearing his blue-and-gold uniform to the after-school meetings every Wednesday. He was doggedly working his way through the wolf book, bringing it to her to sign after he finished each task and proudly supervising the addition to his uniform of each bead and patch that he earned. Toby was the ideal scout, and Lucy felt guilty that she couldn't be the ideal den mother.

She did help out from time to time, and when she did she always took two aspirins before the meeting. No matter how much time she spent planning activities and projects, it never took the boys more than five or ten minutes to lose interest. Then came the choruses of "We're bored" and "What's next?" As far as Lucy could tell, all the boys really wanted to do was wrestle with each other and pick on Stubby Phipps, who, they all agreed, was a nerd. Oh, well, she sighed, maybe today would be different.

Leaving her mother in charge of Sara and Elizabeth,

Lucy was waiting in the elementary school cafeteria at two-thirty for den five to assemble.

"Where are we going today?" asked the boys.

"We're going to hike up to Indian Rock," she announced enthusiastically.

"A hike. . . ."

"I'm too tired."

"We'll never make it, it's too far." They groaned in protest.

"You sound more like Girl Scouts than Cub Scouts," Lucy teased.

"But what about a snack?" demanded Stubby. "Aren't we going to have a snack?"

"No snack!" Den five was dismayed.

"I've heard a rumor that an old Indian, the last of the Sockatumee tribe, may have left a peace offering at Indian Rock."

"What? What tribe?"

"Haven't you heard of the Sockatumees?" Lucy asked incredulously. "Don't you know their secret word?"

"What secret word?" Toby was suspicious.

"I'll teach it to you. Repeat after me. Oh."

"Oh."

"Oh-wa." Lucy waited.

"Oh-wa," repeated the boys reluctantly.

"Oh-wa-ta," said Lucy, drawing out each syllable.

"Oh-wa-ta," the boys intoned.

"Oh-wa-ta-foo," Lucy smiled.

"Oh-wa-ta-foo," repeated the boys.   .

"Oh-wa-ta-foo-lie." Lucy restrained the urge to giggle and kept her voice low, stretching each syllable out as long as she could.

The boys repeated after her, "Oh-wa-ta-foo-lie," really beginning to get in the spirit of magic Indian words.

"Oh-wa-ta-foo-lie-yam," droned Lucy, and the boys shouted back: "Oh-wa-ta-foo-lie-yam!"

Lucy beamed at them. "Now, say it faster."

"Oh, what a fool I am!" they screamed.

"Gotcha!" said Lucy.

"You tricked us," Toby reproached her.

"I didn't spend five summers at Camp Wah-wah-tay-see for nothing," Lucy confided, leading boys out the door and across the baseball field, where the trail to Indian Rock began. "Now, let's see who'll be the first to reach Indian Rock."

"Last one there is a rotten egg," shouted Eddie Culpepper, and the boys ran ahead along the trail, except for Stubby. Stubby was a little overweight, and he was content to walk along beside her.

"Mrs. Stone, did you really spend five summers at camp?"

"I did."

"My mom wants me to go to camp this summer." Stubby didn't sound very happy about the idea.

"Don't you want to go?"

"Nah."

"Why not?"

"I don't like sports much," Stubby confessed. "I like to read. The Three Investigators are my favorites."

"Toby likes them, too. There'll probably be time to read at camp. I used to read Nancy Drew books. Lots of the girls had them, and we'd borrow the ones we hadn't read."

"Yeah? I still don't think I'll like it."

"You might be surprised." Lucy smiled. "We'd better catch up with the others." She had been keeping track of the boys' progress by listening to their voices, but she hadn't heard them for a while.

When they rounded the last bend in the trail she was relieved to see the seven other members of den five perched on the huge boulder.

"Stubby Phipps, Stubby Phipps," Rickie Goldman chanted. "It ought to be Chubby Hips, Chubby Hips."

"That's enough, Rickie," reproved Lucy. "Who knows the story of Indian Rock?" She was wondering where Officer Culpepper and the hot chocolate were.

"It was left here by a glacier," Stubby said. "Mr. Hutchins told us about it."

"That's truc," agreed Lucy, who knew better than to dispute anything a teacher said. "But I was thinking of the Indian legend. Does anybody know that?"

The boys were quiet, so she began.

"The story goes that a long time ago there was an Indian chief named Maushop. Maushop was a great chief, and his people loved and respected him. His tribe was very rich and they had lots of corn in their storehouses, and deerskins and wampum. But even though he was very rich, Maushop's greatest treasure was his little son, Queeg. Maushop taught him to fish and hunt and track, and Queeg grew up to be the best hunter in the whole tribe.

"But then a sickness came and many people died. It was a hard time for the tribe, and there was a great deal of suffering. The people came to Maushop and said that since he was the chief he should do something.

"So Maushop climbed up the hill where we're standing and called to the Great Spirit.

The Great Spirit answered, but he demanded that Maushop give him something that was dear to him.

"So Maushop went home, wondering what he could offer to the Great Spirit. He looked at his favorite bow and arrows, the moccasins his wife had sewn for him, even his best knife. While he was doing this Queeg entered the lodge, and Maushop knew what was dearest to him. So he told Queeg to go to the top of the hill.

"Queeg climbed the hill, just like you did today. Maushop followed behind him, and when Queeg got to the top he called out to the Great Spirit. 'Great Spirit, here is my offering, my dearest son.' Then a great eagle came out of the sky and swooped down, grabbing Queeg in his enormous talons and carrying him off.

"Maushop stood there, all alone, crying for his son. The Great Spirit spoke to him. 'Because of your great sacrifice the people will live and prosper. To remind them of your great sacrifice, I will put a mark here so they will remember Queeg and how you loved him very much, but you loved your people even more.' Then the eagle came flapping out of the sky, holding this rock in his talons. He dropped it here, and it's been here ever since."

The boys were quiet, looking thoughtfully at the rock and glancing at the sky.

"I don't believe it," Eddie announced.

"Me neither," agreed Rickie.

"But it was a good story, Mrs. Stone," Stubby reassured her.

A sudden squawk made them all jump, and Lucy looked up. Officer Culpepper was pulling into the parking lot in his police cruiser. He climbed out of the black-and-white car and walked over to the group, carrying a large Thermos and a bag of doughnuts.

"You boys ready for some hot cocoa?"

Rickie had already opened the bag and the boys were pushing and shoving, grabbing for the doughnuts.

"Hey," he thundered. "That isn't how scouts behave. Get in line. Take turns. There's enough for everybody."

"That's amazing," commented Lucy as the boys obeyed. "I'd give anything for a voice like yours."

"Well, Bill probably wouldn't like it very much."

"No. I don't think he would." Lucy laughed. "It would make being a den leader a lot easier, though."

"I s'pose," agreed Culpepper, taking an enormous bite of doughnut.

"Any new developments in the Sam Miller case?" asked Lucy. "Have they found out who did it yet?"

"Not that I know," Culpepper said. "Of course, I'm just a town cop. They don't tell us much. We're just supposed to direct traffic and find lost bicycles and leave the investigating to the state police." He shrugged. "Last year the town wouldn't even give us a cost-of-living increase. Nobody thinks much of us."

"These scouts certainly think you're something special," said Lucy, indicating the boys, who were admiring the officer's uniform and cruiser.

"Is that a real gun?" asked one of the boys.

"It sure is. It's a police-issue nine-millimeter Smith and Wesson," he answered, drawing the revolver from its holster. Lucy eyed the gun distrustfully. "Don't worry, Lucy. I made sure the safety's on."

Culpepper held the gun out in the flat of his hand for the boys to admire, then twirled it around his finger a few times before replacing it at his side.

"What else have I got in my belt? This here's my walkie-talkie. We use this when we're working in a team—say, for the Fourth of July parade or a search. A situation like that." He held up the instrument for the boys to see and then stowed it in his belt.

"I tell you, this belt gets heavy. At the end of the day I'm sure glad to take it off. Now these," he said, "these are handcuffs. Who'll volunteer?"

All the boys stuck out their hands, but Culpepper picked his son, Eddie, and clapped the cuffs on him. "Now, see if you can get loose," he challenged. The boys gave Eddie all sorts of advice, but no matter how he twisted and turned the cuffs held fast.

"Okay, I'll unlock him. I've got the key right here." A sudden burst of sound from the radio in the cruiser caught Culpepper's attention as he unlocked the cuffs. "I have to answer that. Want to see how the radio works?"

The boys all followed him over to the black-and-white vehicle. Lucy remained leaning against Indian Rock, overwhelmed by a sudden sense of recognition. She'd heard that sound before. But when? Not in the course of daily life; she'd heard it in connection with something major. How else could she explain the uneasy feeling that threatened to overwhelm her? She followed the boys over to the cruiser and tried to remember if she'd seen a police cruiser at her father's funeral. Death. She knew the sound meant death.

This is ridiculous, she thought to herself, and then she remembered. She'd been standing in the doorway at Country Cousins watching the snow fall. She'd stepped inside and closed the door. Then, she'd heard a sound. Because of the sound she'd gone out and found Sam Miller. And it wasn't a dog barking, she now realized with horror. It had been the crackle of a police radio. She was sure. That meant a police cruiser had been in the

Country Cousins lot when Sam Miller was dying. Had it been Culpepper's?

As Lucy watched him pushing buttons and talking into the mike, smiling and nodding at the scouts, bits of information fell into place. It was rumored that Culpepper had had an affair with Marcia Miller. Even if that wasn't true, Miller's role in the planning commission might have been enough of a motive. Just yesterday at the coffee shop she'd seen him nearly sock Jonathan Franke over the commission's proposal. He had certainly looked as if he'd wanted to kill Franke.

"That's enough, boys," said Culpepper, looking up at Lucy. He looked away furtively, and she realized he knew that something was wrong.

"Boys!" she called. "It's getting late. It's time to go back." They had run off down the trail without her. She half turned toward Culpepper, stretching her lips across her dry teeth in something she hoped looked like a smile.

"Thanks so much for bringing the cocoa," she said. "I'd better catch up with the boys."

"Not so fast," said Culpepper, causing her to stop in her tracks. She stood nervously while he hauled himself out of the cruiser, calculating her chances. She was perhaps twenty feet from the cruiser. If she ran immediately, she would have a good head start. She was used to running, and a glance at Culpepper's belly where the buttons on his uniform strained to hold the gaping fabric together indicated that he wasn't. If she ran hell for leather down the path this instant, she could catch up to the boys and be safe. But she felt frozen in place; her feet felt like lead and her breath was coming too fast. She watched as he came closer and closer, fascinated by the red veins on his nose, the hairs that sprouted between his eyebrows, and his little blue eyes. Piggy eyes. Had Sam Miller felt like this before he died?

"Lucy, breathe into this bag." Culpepper shoved the doughnut bag against her face and picked up her hands, cupping them so she could hold it herself. "You're hyperventilating. Here, sit in the cruiser for a minute until you feel better. Just take it easy. You'll be fine," he reassured her.

"I don't know what's the matter with me," Lucy admitted as he climbed in beside her. "For a minute there I thought you killed Sam Miller."

Culpepper looked up sharply, and again panic swept over Lucy. Why couldn't she keep her suspicions to herself, at least until she was safe at home?

"I know you didn't," Lucy reassured him. "But everyone's saying you had an affair with Marcia Miller."

"What?" Culpepper was incredulous. "Me and Marcia Miller? That stuck-up bitch?"

Lucy shrugged. "You know the kinds of things people say. I thought it was possible."

"You did?" Culpepper sucked in his gut and straightened his shoulders. "Do you think Marge knows?" Then he corrected himself. "I mean, do you think anybody said anything to Marge?"

"No, they wouldn't." Lucy shook her head. People gossiped according to the rules in Tinker's Cove. They talked about each other, but they never made direct accusations.

"And then I saw you and Jonathan Franke in the coffee shop. You looked as if you wanted to strangle him."

"Those conservationists make me sick," Culpepper confessed. "Not a one of 'em knows what it's like to work for a living."

"But Barney . . ." Lucy weighed her words carefully. "I'm almost positive I heard a police radio the night I found Sam Miller. In fact, I know I did."

Culpepper dropped his head on the steering wheel. "I was afraid you'd remember. I tell you, I was sweating like a pig that day Horowitz had me come along to interview you. Boy, was I glad when you didn't remember. I guess it'll all come out now," he said, raising his head and looking at Lucy.

"What will come out? What were you doing in the parking lot?"

"I was a fool," said Culpepper. "I can't believe I was so stupid."

"You're really in trouble, aren't you?"

"You know it. If this gets out, I'll lose my job." Culpepper shook his head. "It's not much of a job, but it's all I've got."

"It can't be that bad," Lucy reassured him. "What did you do?"

"I don't know what I was thinking of," Culpepper admitted. "You know that magazine? *Modern Mercenary?* Well, I've had a subscription for years. Real man stuff, y'know. Lots of action. I love it. In the back they have a classified section. Dirty deeds done dirt cheap, y'know what I mean?"

"I think I saw something on TV about it."

"Yeah, I think *60 Minutes* did a story on it. Well, I put an ad in. Partly it was just for kicks, just make-believe. But partly I thought something might come from it. The pay for this job is lousy, and we could use some extra money. So I put an ad in."

His eyes glowed with pride as he remembered the words. "'Resourceful, enterprising man of action available for assignments in Maine, Massachusetts, and New Hampshire.' I didn't want to be away from home overnight, you know." He cocked an eyebrow and nodded at Lucy.

"Barney, why don't you drive while we talk? When the boys' parents come to pick them up, they'll wonder if I'm not there."

"Okay." He started the car and headed down the road.

"I only got one response to the ad, but it was a doozy. Someone wanted me to kill Sam Miller. Offered me ten thousand dollars. I said I wouldn't do it, wasn't really my line, and they hung right up."

"Who do you think it was? Was it a man or a woman?"

"It was a man, but I don't have any idea who. I didn't recognize the voice and there wasn't time to trace the call. Then I didn't know what to do. If I warned Sam, I'd have to explain about the ad, and I was embarrassed, I might even have lost my job—moonlighting's against the regulations. So I just tried to keep an eye on him. Checked in on him every so often. That night I happened to see him on the road, heading toward the warehouse. Then I got a call to go to the Anchor Bar and give Bill Maloney a ride home. When I got back to the parking lot, Sam was already dead. I didn't have any reason to be in the parking lot, so I left."

"You'd really get in trouble if this got out?"

Culpepper nodded. "Probably get suspended without pay for a month, something like that. I can't afford that." He shook his head and then smiled. "Don't look so worried, Lucy. I'll think of something." He indicated the anxious row of mothers peering into the cruiser and laughed. "I guess I'm not the only one with some explainin' to do."

"I didn't feel well," said Lucy to the small group of curious women. "Officer Culpepper gave me a ride down from Indian Rock."

"These children have been unsupervised for at least fifteen minutes," said Mrs. Phipps, the wattles under her chin shaking with indignation.

"I'm sorry. It couldn't be avoided." Lucy shrugged. Seeing their skeptical expressions, she didn't think she'd convinced them.

"Don't forget," she added brightly, "there's no meeting next week because of school vacation. C'mon, Toby, let's go home."

Chapter Twelve

#6775 This genuine wool blanket woven by Mac-Murray Weavers of Canada is an authentic reproduction of the blankets the Hudson Bay Company traded for furs. The lines on the side of the blanket indicate how many skins it was worth. White with red, yellow, and green stripes. Specify twin, $95; double, $135; or queen, $175.

"I'm seriously thinking of committing suicide."

"Don't you think you're overreacting just a tiny bit?" Sue's crisp, rational voice came over the phone wire.

"Probably," admitted Lucy. "But you should've seen the way they looked at me. I thought Stubby Phipps's mother was going to lose her bridge. She just kept standing there with her mouth hanging open, looking at Culpepper and looking at me and trying to make one plus one equal something illicit."

"Well, I wouldn't worry about her. If Stubby manages to graduate from high school, he'll be the first in that family."

"But she's influential. People listen to what she says, and she always has a lot to say. I bet the phone wires are just buzzing, and meanwhile my reputation is going down the tubes."

"What if Bill finds out?"

"Sue! There's nothing for Bill to find out! I'm not attracted to Barney at all."

"A lot of women are."

"I have trouble believing that."

"Why? These things happen, you know."

"Culpepper's belly hangs over his pants."

"Just because you don't find him attractive doesn't mean that other women don't."

"Well, I do know Barney. He's a family man, he likes kids, he's kind of an overgrown kid himself. And even if hc wasn't devoted to Marge, where would he carry on an affair?"

"There's lots of camps out in the woods. A roaring fire, a Hudson Bay blanket, a man with a gun . . . it could be kind of exciting."

"Whatever turns you on," said Lucy, neatly turning the tablcs on her friend. "Seriously, it's an awful feeling when you know people are talking about you. I feel so exposed. I can understand how Marcia Miller must have felt. No wonder she left."

"That, or a guilty concience?"

"Who knows?" said Lucy, growing impatient. "Look, I've got to go."

She hung up the phone and turned to see her mother entering the kitchen. She was glad to see she was still in her robe and slippers. So far during her visit she had appeared fully dressed each morning. When Lucy went in to tidy Toby's room she found both twin beds neatly made and her mother's suitcase zipped shut and placed at the foot of the bed.

"Did you have a good night?" asked Lucy.

"I did," answered her mother, pouring a cup of coffee. "I've slept better here than I have in a long time. I think it's sleeping in the same room with Toby. I hear his breathing, and it's so peaceful that I fall right to sleep. I haven't done that in a long time."

"You must miss Dad a lot."

"Especially at night. I don't like being alone. If I hear a little noise, I get frightened. I'm nervous all the time."

Lucy nodded. "I know what you mean."

"I wonder if you do. I don't think anybody knows what it's like until it happens to them. Losing a father isn't like losing a husband."

"Maybe," said Lucy, not quite willing to admit that losing her father was insignificant compared with her mother's loss. "What would you like for breakfast?"

"Just an English muffin."

"How about an egg or two? Or some hot cereal?" asked Lucy, eyeing her mother's flat cheeks and stick wrists.

"No, just a muffin. That's what I always have."

"Marmalade?" Lucy asked hopefully.

"That would be nice." The older woman took a sip of coffee. "Lucy, last night I was thinking that I really ought to send some Christmas cards. I wasn't going to, but now I've changed my mind."

Lucy almost dropped the knife she was poking into the marmalade jar. "I think you should. I'm sure you can find some conservative ones."

"I thought I'd look in that gift shop in town and see what they have."

Lucy's heart sank. She wanted to encourage her mother to keep in touch with her friends, but with Sara still sick and a long list of things to do, she felt frantic at the prospect of another trip to town.

"Mom, I'd love to help, but I just can't drive you today."

"I could drive myself. I have a license."

This was news to Lucy. "You do? Dad always drove."

"He did, but I never let my license expire. I've been out a few times and I've done quite well."

"In the city?" Lucy was incredulous.

"Only around the neighborhood, but I'm sure I could manage these roads. There isn't much traffic."

"Okay," Lucy agreed. She certainly wasn't going to discourage her. In fact, new possibilities were opening before her. "Would you mind picking up a few things for me?"

Lucy watched as her mother drove the Subaru very cautiously down the long driveway. As she turned out onto the road a large egg truck swerved to avoid her, narrowly missing a collision, but she continued on her way. Lucy wasn't sure if her mother had noticed or not. She sighed. There was nothing she could do now except send up a quick prayer and keep her fingers crossed. She poured herself a second cup of coffee and sat down with the morning paper. She wanted to find a kitten for the kids to replace poor Patches, so she turned to the classifieds.

The first ad she saw read "Kute, Kuddly, Kristmas Kittens." Lucy chuckled and dialed the number, but the woman who answered told her that the kittens were all gone. She hung up and turned back to the paper to check the next ad. "Free to a good home," it read. "Pretty Calico Kittens."

"I'm calling about the kittens," began Lucy when the woman answered.

"We do have some kittens," the voice admitted cautiously. "But we want to make sure they'll be well taken care of."

"We've had lots of cats. We're very experienced cat owners, and I can promise we'll take good care of the kitten," Lucy promised.

"How many cats do you have?" inquired the voice.

"None at the moment," Lucy confessed. "Our last cat was killed. . . ." The moment she said it she realized her mistake. She should have said "died of old age," but she continued, hoping to convince the kitten owner that she was not a kitten abuser. "Our children have been very upset. They miss old Patches very much, and I was hoping to give them a new kitten for Christmas."

"You have children?" The voice was shocked. "I'm sorry, but our kittens are not used to children. Good-bye."

Lucy tapped her fingers on the table and looked at the next ad. She scratched her head thoughtfully and thought about Culpepper's ad in *Modern Mercenary* magazine. Someone had read those ads looking for a hit man to kill Sam Miller just as she had gone through the ads looking for a kitten. When she didn't get a satisfactory response, she just went on to the next ad. And whoever had called Culpepper had probably just gone on to the next ad when he'd refused the job.

Lucy dialed the next number. She heard the phone ring six times and was about to hang up when she heard the receiver being picked up. She could hear a baby crying in the background.

"Hello?"

"Hi," piped a child's voice.

"Can I speak to your mommy?"

"Okay." There was a long silence. Lucy thought of the times she'd found the receiver lying on the counter, the caller forgotten, as some distraction interrupted Sara or Elizabeth as they searched for her.

"Hello?" said a grown-up voice.

"I'm calling about the kittens," Lucy said.

"How many do you want?"

"Just one."

"How about two? Two are definitely more fun than one."

"Two would cause fights," said Lucy, suddenly overcome with Christmas spirit. "Do you have three?"

"Sure, come on over."

"I must be crazy," Lucy said, stricken with second thoughts.

"It's Christmas. Live a little! Crystal, put that kitten down!"

Lucy wrote down the directions and told the woman she would come the next day, Christmas Eve. What am I getting myself into? she thought as she replaced the receiver. Three cats. It wasn't all that ridiculous, she tried to convince herself. The house was big, and the kids would be thrilled to have one cat each. Maybe three cats would be content to stay safely at home. Anything was possible.

She shuddered involuntarily, thinking of poor Patches and Sam Miller, too.

"I know I shouldn't do this," she said aloud, dialing the police station. When she got Culpepper on the line, she just plunged in.

"Barney, I think I know how we can find Sam Miller's killer."

She explained how the idea had come to her while she had been looking for a kitten in the classifieds. Culpepper was skeptical.

"Lucy, this is crazy. Just let the state police handle it."

"What do you mean? Yesterday you were worried about your job. I'm just trying to help."

"I shouldn't have been crying on your shoulder. This is my problem," insisted Culpepper.

"Do you still have the magazine? I'd love to see the ad."

"You would?" Culpepper was flattered.

"You didn't throw it away, did you?"

"Oh, no, I've still got it," he admitted.

"Well, let's see who else advertised. Maybe one of them was the killer. I can't wait to get started. When can we get together?" she demanded.

"Now, hold on, Lucy. I still think I should handle this by myself."

"Barney, people just hear your voice and they know you're a cop. You need me for this. Besides, I want to make up for suspecting you."

"Lucy—"

"No, Barney, don't 'Lucy' me. Just get over here as soon as you can. I've got all the Pinewood Derby cars. You can pick Eddie's up, and you can show me the ad.

Okay? I can't leave the house because Sara's got the flu and my mother took the car."

"And you think you're gonna help me? Some hotshot detective you are," accused Culpepper.

"Yeah. The original gumshoe, that's me. And when I say gum, I mean Double Bubble." Lucy laughed and bent over to peel a large pink wad from the bottom of her Reebok high-tops.

Chapter Thirteen

#9137 Fishing the old-fashioned way can be frustrating. This newfangled sonar scanner actually finds and tracks schools of fish so you can put your hook where the fish are. Can be operated with 10 "D" batteries or connected directly to a power source, Solid-state, UL approved. $345.

If Barney Culpepper were a dog, thought Lucy as she opened the kitchen door for him, he would be a St. Bernard. Doorways were always too small for him and ceilings too low; he had to bend his head as he came through the doorway into the kitchen. As he stood there unzipping his jacket, his cheeks seemed to droop into jowls. Slowly he took off his regulation blue jacket and tossed it on the corner chair, ran his hands through his shaggy brown hair, and squared his burly shoulders before sitting down at the kitchen table.

When Lucy had first met Barney, back in the granola years, she'd thought of him as a typical redneck. He was a recent Vietnam vet, and she'd been a bit leery of him, expecting him to explode into violence whenever he encountered members of the college-educated peace brigade who were moving into Tinker's Cove. But when the battery in the Malibu she'd been driving died one day, he'd gone out of his way to get her car going again. She'd been struck by his quiet, assured helpfulness.

Then she began meeting him on some of the same volunteer committees she was serving on, especially the Cub Scouts and the School Improvement Council. She had come to respect his willingness to work, and his practical approach. He was the sort of man you could count on; sometimes she wished she'd had a big brother like Barney.

She eyed the well-thumbed copy of *Modern Mercenary* that he placed on the table in front of him and gave him the little box containing the Pinewood Derby car kit.

"Eddie won last year, didn't he?" she asked. "He made a fast little car."

"It broke, though, on the last heat. This year he wants to put on a rubber bumper. That kid's always thinking," Barney said proudly.

"You know, I've never seen one of these magazines before," she said, sliding a cup of coffee in front of him and picking up the magazine.

"Now, Lucy. I'm not sure you should get involved in this."

"What do you mean, 'get involved'? I found Sam Miller's body. I worked for him. I live in this town. I *am* involved, and I'm not just going to shut my eyes and pretend I'm not. I can't let people get killed practically in my backyard. I have a family to raise."

"That's what I mean. Your kids need you. This could be dangerous."

"Don't you think it's dangerous living in a place where people get murdered in their own cars? I won't stand for it," said Lucy, shaking her head. "Besides, Christmas is two days off and I'm going to be cooped up with my mother and Bill's folks, and I'll go crazy if I don't have something else to think about. Where are the ads?"

"In the back," Barney said, capitulating.

Lucy leafed through the magazine quickly, noting the ads for weapons and camouflage suits and the action-packed adventure stories complete with lurid illustrations. There was even a comic strip, *Mercenary Max.* The classified ads were just after the comic.

"You know, this kind of reminds me of *Boy's Life,*" Lucy commented absently.

"Naw. *Boy's Life* is for kids. This is for men."

"Oh." Lucy smiled to herself. "Here we are, 'Courageous Captain at your service.' He sounds more like a stud for hire than a hit man."

"He probably is. I got a few calls for that kind of service myself," admitted Barney, blushing.

"You did?" Lucy's voice rose.

"I turned 'em down, of course."

"Hmmm," Lucy said thoughtfully. So much for Sue's theories. "None of these ads have phone numbers. They're all boxes."

"That's right. If you're a professional killer, you're hardly going to put your phone number in an ad. If you kill somebody, you don't want to leave a trail of phone calls, especially long distance. No, you get a post office box using a false name, or you can have the magazine give you a box number. Then they hold the mail and send it on to you. That's what I had them do."

"So we just have to write to these ads?"

"Yeah, just drop 'em a line, tell 'em to call at a certain time."

"I thought phone calls were out," said Lucy.

"They'll use a pay phone."

"Oh." Lucy rummaged in the Hoosier for paper and envelopes. "Somehow I thought this would be more exciting."

"Let's just hope it doesn't get too exciting. Lucy, you'd better have a good story ready when they call."

"How's this? I want somebody to kill my husband because he's mean to me."

"Mean to you?"

"Say he beats me. Brutally. I saw that on *60 Minutes.*"

"Okay. It's a little lame, but hell, I guess it's happened before. How much are you going to offer for doing the job?"

"Twenty-five thousand?"

"Sounds good."

"Do you think they'll go for it?"

"Well, if they do, we've got a possible suspect. But I don't think most of these ads are genuine. Real hit men probably don't advertise. Most of 'em are probably just guys looking for a little excitement like I was. Or selling sex like Courageous Captain there. But it's worth trying, I guess. After all, somebody did call me." He scratched his chin. "You never know, we might get lucky."

"What do we do then?" Lucy asked.

"Then we take it one step at a time. We can try to set up a meeting. Very carefully. Don't do anything without me." Culpepper's voice was earnest. "I want to keep an eye on things."

"Okay," Lucy agreed. "This guy looks serious. 'Man for Hire. Professional and efficient.' Gives me the willies. What should I write?"

"How about, 'If interested in twenty-five thousand dollars, call . . .' and put down your phone number and the time you want him to call," advised Barney.

Lucy thought for a minute. "I don't want him to call when the kids are home, so it has to be during school hours."

"Now you're thinking like a pro," Barney teased.

"Don't laugh. My kids could scare off the meanest, toughest criminal. And I certainly don't want hit men calling during Christmas when Bill's folks are here. What would they think?"

Barney shook his head. "It'll take a couple of weeks if the mail's forwarded."

Lucy checked her calendar. "How about nine-thirty A.M. on Wednesday, January fifth?"

"Sounds good." Culpepper ran his finger down the column of ads. "Put down 'Man for Hire' at nine-thirty, 'Pest Control'—I don't think he's serious at ten, and 'Bad Guy' at ten-thirty. Is that enough for one day?"

"We can fit one more in at eleven, but then I have to pick up Sara at nursery school."

" 'Ex-marine' sounds promising, put him down for eleven. Then on Thursday you can have 'Combat Veteran' for nine-thirty and 'Cool Professional' for ten. That's it." He put down the magazine.

"You know," said Lucy, licking an envelope, "this is an awful lot like paying bills."

"A lot of life is like that." Barney smiled ruefully. "I wanted to be a cop because I thought it would be real exciting. High-speed car chases, shoot-outs, the works. Like on TV. You know what I spend most of my time doing? Paperwork! Paperwork and traffic duty. I sure didn't expect that." He shook his head and took a big gulp of coffee.

"You drink too much coffee. It's not good for you."

"Gotta take a risk sometimes, Lucy. Have that extra cup of coffee, drive without a seat belt, have one beer too many. You know what I mean?"

"I do. I always hated Nancy's slogan, 'Just say no.' So prim and proper. I'd rather say yes."

"Lucy, I hope you're not going out on a limb for me." Culpepper was looking straight at her, and the direct eye contact was making her uncomfortable. She shifted on her seat and glanced away.

"Now, don't get all mushy on me, Culpepper. I have an ulterior motive."

"Uh-oh." Now it was Barney's turn to shift uncomfortably on his seat.

"Yup. Pack twenty-seven needs a new cubmaster next year."

"They do?" Culpepper gulped.

"They sure do. I figure you're the perfect man for the job."

"Lucy," said Culpepper, rising and reaching for his jacket, "if I'm not in jail, I'll be glad to do it."

Lucy watched as he drove away, then went upstairs to see how Sara was doing. Her fever was down and she was demanding food, so Lucy set her up on the couch, where she could watch TV and nibble on some toast.

Then she put a casserole together for supper and prepared for the afternoon onslaught when Toby and Elizabeth came home from school.

Much to her relief, her mother and the Subaru returned intact. Lucy showed her where the salad fixings were in the refrigerator; then she left for work.

At Country Cousins, she punched the time clock and hung her coat up slowly; ever since the layoffs she hadn't enjoyed going to work. She missed Bev and Karen and the others; the phone room seemed empty without them.

"You know, I used to like working here," Ruthie said as they went to their computers. "The pay wasn't very good, but there used to be a nice atmosphere."

"I know what you mean. Now, I'm always expecting to get laid off, and I don't think I'd mind if I was," admitted Lucy.

"Oh, they won't lay you off. You're a good producer. They always go for the ones who are going to retire or have a baby—the ones who actually use the benefits." Ruthie sounded bitter but resigned.

"Is that why Karen and Bev were laid off? That's terrible."

"Look for yourself, Lucy. You can see who survived the cuts. I haven't noticed any drop in sales, have you? I think they just wanted to get rid of the deadwood."

"Sales always drop off after Christmas," Lucy reminded her.

"But they never had layoffs before. Not when Sam was in charge," Ruthie argued. "Lower payroll means higher profits. This'll be a feather in somebody's cap."

"Do you think George was behind this?"

"Doesn't really matter whose idea it was, does it? The

whole board of directors had to approve it. They don't care about people like us." Ruthie clicked on her computer and started pounding away angrily at the keyboard.

Lucy was kept busy all night trying to keep up with the calls. She frequently had several callers waiting, something that had never happened to her before. The customers weren't very pleased at having to wait to place their orders, and by the time she could take her break, her tact was exhausted.

She sat alone in the break room, sipping her diet soda and reading last week's *Pennysaver.* George Higham stopped in the doorway and looked at her, but she shot him such an evil glance that he beat a hasty retreat.

She was sure George had masterminded the layoffs. Ever since Sam Miller's death, George had been the one to watch. His star was certainly ascending, and Lucy thought she knew why. Of all the people at Country Cousins, he seemed to have gained the most from Sam's death. She took a long pull on the can of soda and took a deep breath. She'd love to be able to prove that George had killed Sam.

Chapter Fourteen

#9001 Fire starters. These pieces of genuine Geor-gia fatwood make starting a fire easy and quick. Five pounds in a decorative gift box. $25.

"It's Christmas Eve! Tomorrow is Christmas!" shouted Toby as he ran into the kitchen.

Lucy finished pouring herself a cup of coffee and smiled at Bill, who was sitting at the table, reading the *Herald*.

"You know what they say about Christmas Eve, don't you? It's supposed to be the longest day of the year," Bill said in a teasing voice.

"No, it isn't," answered Toby. "December twenty-first, the day of the winter solstice, is the shortest day. Now the days are short and the nights are long."

"Oh," said Bill. "I must have had it wrong. To me, Christmas Eve always seems longer."

Lucy sighed. "I wish it was the longest day. I need a long day to fit in everything I have to do."

"I want to work on the Dempsey house this morning

and make up some of the time I lost earlier this week. I'll try to knock off a little early so I'll be here when my folks arrive."

"Okay. I have to go grocery shopping and do some last-minute errands."

"What about us? What'll we do?" Toby demanded.

"You're going to stay home with Grandma," asserted Lucy. "Maybe she'll show you how to make popcorn chains."

"I have a better idea," said Helen, entering the kitchen and heading straight for the coffeepot. "We'll eat the popcorn and make paper chains."

"Okay," agreed Toby. "That sounds like fun."

Lucy felt light-hearted as she slammed the hatchback shut on twelve brown bags of groceries. She'd put in a busy morning doing a lightning job of housecleaning by dusting the tabletops, fluffing the couch pillows, and bundling all extraneous objects into a large trash bag, which she'd stuffed in the back of her closet. When she'd left the house, her mother had been vacuuming the rugs and the girls had been chattering away with her, asking what Christmas was like when she was a little girl. Now Lucy had just one errand left, and that was to pick up the kittens.

She carefully followed the directions she'd been given and soon found herself on a road she didn't know in a part of town she'd never seen before. Scattered along the road, like toys left on the living room floor and then forgotten by a careless child, were worn-out house trailers, shacks constructed from bits and pieces of other buildings, and an assortment of battered, rusting cars and trucks. Lucy pulled up in front of a little brown house with rough-sawn siding that had probably once been a hunting camp.

She stepped cautiously onto a rotting step and knocked timidly on the door. She was surprised when it was opened by a pretty girl with dark hair. She didn't look more than seventeen, wearing a bright T-shirt and jeans and balancing a plump, nearly naked baby on her hip. Her eyes were suspicious and defensive as she looked Lucy over, but she had an air of vulnerability that Lucy found attractive.

"I've come about the kittens," explained Lucy, indicating the plastic cat carrier she was holding.

"Oh, great, come on in!" said the girl, revealing a beautiful, wide smile. She opened the door and stood aside. "I'm Lisa Young," she said, introducing herself. "Never mind the house. Honestly, with this heater it's full blast or nothing. Now, where are those kittens?"

From her spot by the door Lucy received the full blast of the heater, but she knew that in really cold weather the camp, perched as it was on cement block pilings, must be freezing. She unzipped her jacket and tried not to look as if she were inspecting the one-room house. Houses like this were common on the back roads, but she'd never been inside one before.

At first it was difficult to see much. It was dark in the house even though a bare bulb was burning in the center of the ceiling. Sheets of plastic had been taped over the windows to keep out the wind. As her eyes adjusted Lucy saw that the stud cavities had been filled with batts of fiberglass insulation; in places pieces of recycled paneling with worn and rounded edges had been nailed over the insulation. One end of the room was the kitchen, with an early-model propane stove that was also a heater. There was a table covered with an ugly plastic cloth and an assortment of chairs. A tiny plastic tree with twinkling lights stood on the table. There was no sign of running water or even an indoor bathroom. A dented and rusty refrigerator hummed noisily, bearing a picture of a Biafran child. His head was enormous, his eyes huge, and his tiny sticklike arms were crossed over his protruding ribs. Beneath the picture was written, "Before you yell about mac and cheese again, be grateful for what you got."

Lucy swallowed hard and looked at the other end of the room. There an old sheet hung from a length of cord, separating a neatly made double bed from a set of camp-style bunks. All of the beds were covered with handmade log cabin quilts, faded with washing and drying in the sun. Sitting on the top bunk was a tiny little girl, a replica of her mother, with her dark hair and full lips.

"I was playing with the kittens, Ma," she complained.

"It's time to say good-bye to them," Lisa said firmly.

"We'll still have Tiger Lily, right?"

"That's right." She scooped up the kittens and held them against her chest for Lucy to see. "This one here is Midnight because he's black, and this one is Jumbles, and here is Boots. We weren't very original, but we wanted them to have names. You'll probably want to name 'em yourself."

"I'm sure my kids will have some ideas," said Lucy, smiling a bit too broadly. "Let's put them in the carrier, okay? I feel so lucky to have found them. Our cat was killed, and my kids are pretty upset. Having their own kittens will make Christmas special," she gushed, suddenly wondering how this family was going to celebrate Christmas. "Is ten dollars apiece okay with you?"

"What?" Lisa's face was blank.

"Ten dollars. I'm afraid I can't go much higher."

"They're free. I'm just glad to get rid of them. Pet food's expensive and you can't use food stamps for it."

"Well, I won't take them unless you let me pay," said Lucy, holding out three ten-dollar bills.

"Okay. I won't say I can't use the money. Thanks."

As Lucy carried the kittens out to the car, she was overwhelmed with guilt. She'd never thought of herself and Bill as wealthy; every month they had to juggle the bills, and the Visa balance stubbornly refused to shrink. But today the sum of their material possessions embarrassed her.

As she put the kittens on the backseat she noticed a box of candy canes poking out from one of the grocery bags. Remembering the very tiny Christmas tree on the table, she dug a little deeper and pulled out a roasting chicken, aware that she had a freezer full of food at home as well as money in the bank. She rummaged through the other bags and added cranberry sauce, stuffing, potatoes, a few cans of vegetables, and a bottle of apple juice. Looking for something sweet, she shrugged and tossed in a bucket of dastardly mash ice cream. Give till it hurts, she thought.

She was tempted just to leave the bag on the porch, but instead she made herself knock. When the door opened she said, "I'm really so grateful for the kittens, won't you please take these groceries?"

Lisa pulled herself up to her full height and said unsmilingly, "Thank you, but I already have Christmas dinner planned. We're having macaroni."

Lucy smiled encouragingly. "My husband and I had

tofu and brown rice for Christmas once. We decided never again. Please take it."

Lisa shrugged and then smiled, accepting the bag of groceries. "Merry Christmas!" she said, and shut the door.

"Now, little kittens, how am I going to keep you a secret until tomorrow?" Pulling the car off the road a few feet before her driveway, Lucy put the carrier on the floor behind the driver's seat and tossed a blanket over it. Then she pulled in the driveway and started unloading the groceries. She carried one bag and a gallon jug of milk into the kitchen, pausing at the door to see if any of the kids were around. She heard a low murmur from the front of the house, so she put the groceries on the table and dashed back to the car. Covering the kittens with the blanket, she ran as quickly as she could back to the kitchen and scooted down the cellar stairs. She put the carrier next to the furnace and, apologizing to the kittens for not finding them, was back in the kitchen before the kids realized she was home.

"Help me with the groceries, Toby. Grandma and Grandpa Stone will be here any minute.

"How'd everything go?" she asked her mother.

"Come and see the tree!" demanded Sara. "We made it so pretty."

Helen shrugged. "All right, I guess."

"Well, it sounds as if you've been busy. Let me see the tree," said Lucy, allowing the girls to pull her along.

Just then they heard the crunch of tires on the gravel driveway. Bill's folks had arrived. The house was soon full of confusion and bustle as hugs and kisses were exchanged, groceries put away, and suitcases and shopping bags full of presents carried in.

At last, Bill's parents were settled and everyone was gathered around a cheerful fire in the living room. The scene looked Christmas card perfect: the lush tree twinkling in the corner, three children playing quietly on the rug, the adults relaxing on the couch and easy chairs. Lucy perched on the edge of her grandfather's cane chair, took a deep breath, and tried to still the butterflies that were churning in her stomach. Now she ought to be able to relax. After working toward it for weeks, Christmas was finally here. The house was clean, the cookies baked, the presents wrapped. Everything was under control, she realized, except for the people. She was so worried that her mother's depression would return and dampen the holiday, or that Bill's father, always unpredictable, would say exactly the wrong thing.

She had always found the elder Mr. Stone intimidating. She would never forget the first time she had met him. She had been terribly nervous and as Bill's fiancée had wanted to make a good impression. She hadn't known what to say when Mr. Stone suggested that she escort Brother, Mrs. Stone's retarded brother, to the bathroom. She could still remember the blood rushing to her face as she stammered out an excuse, and Bill had rushed to her rescue, leading Brother out of the room. That meant she was left alone with Mr. Stone, who'd muttered something and left the room, too. All by herself in the Stones' living room, she had felt totally abandoned and suspected that she had failed some important test.

She had always marveled that Bill's mother never seemed upset by her rude husband. She was a small, plump, cheerful woman who serenely managed to smooth the feathers that her husband continually ruffled. Now she was sitting on the couch with Helen, and the two women were chatting together.

Bill's father was sprawled on the recliner, puzzling over a fishing reel Toby had asked him to fix. Suddenly he looked up and demanded, "Don't you have any cookies? What's Christmas without cookies?"

"I've got cookies," Lucy snapped to attention. "Would you like some coffee or tea to go with them?"

"Sure, whatever," he answered gruffly.

"Tea would be very nice," said Mrs. Stone. "Can I help?"

"No, I can manage. Just relax," answered Lucy.

"Of course, there's only one really good Christmas cookie. You don't have 'em. They're Italian. Called pizza or something."

"Do you mean pizelle?" asked Lucy.

"Yeah. They're made on a little waffle iron thing. Had 'em once and never forgot 'em."

Lucy couldn't help smiling as she went off to the kitchen, because high up on a shelf in the pantry, in her tin of cookies from the cookie exchange, were six lovely pizelle made by Lydia Volpe. Lucy hummed as she put the water on to boil and set out cups. She added three glasses of milk for the children, and then she climbed up the stepladder and carefully brought down the cookies. She arranged them attractively on her special Christmas plate, clustering the delicate pizelle together. When the kettle shrieked she poured the tea and proudly carried the tray out of the kitchen. She couldn't wait to see the expression on Grandpa Stone's face.

Chapter Fifteen

#4840. New Englanders have long known the luxury of 100% cotton flannel sheets. Warm to the touch, flannel ensures a good night's sleep. Each set includes one fitted sheet, one flat sheet, and two cases. In blue, yellow, or ecru. Specify twin, $29; double, $39; queen, $49; or king, $59.

Christmas Eve really is the longest day of the year, thought Lucy as she glanced at the kitchen clock on her way to bed. It was two in the morning and Bill was still snapping together the dozens of interlocking pieces of the Barbie town house. Everything else was ready. The presents were arranged under the tree, the stockings were filled, and Santa had nibbled his cookies and poured his warm milk down the kitchen drain. The house was quiet; everyone was asleep, presumably dreaming of sugarplums. Lucy went down to the cellar to get the kittens.

She found them all asleep in a pile in a corner of the cardboard box she'd made their temporary home. She picked up the carton and tiptoed upstairs with it. Setting it down next to her bed, she climbed between the sheets and put all three kittens in her lap.

"Time for some exercise," she told them, and smiled as they climbed clumsily over each other and explored the mysterious hills and valleys her legs made in the covers. She picked each one up and examined it carefully, relieved to find they all appeared healthy, with no sign of fleas.

"Well, what have we got here?" asked Bill, coming into the room and beginning to strip off his clothes.

"Christmas kittens," said Lucy, admiring the long, lean curve of his back as he bent over and pulled on his pajama pants. "How are we going to manage this? We can't really put them in the kids' stockings."

"Never you worry," Bill boasted. "No job is too difficult for Super-Santa!"

"You are a super Santa. Did Barbie's house go together okay?"

"Nothing to it." Bill shrugged. "Fifteen pages of directions, innumerable tiny plastic parts, all pink; anyone with a degree in engineering could do it in five hours, easy."

Lucy laughed. "Don't expect to get any credit. You know what Toby told me? He says he doesn't really believe in Santa, but he can't believe we'd spend that much money on presents!"

"Well, I can see his point. All year long we say, 'You can't have that because it's too expensive,' then at Christmas it's all under the tree." He lifted the covers to climb into bed, and the kittens all tumbled into Lucy's lap.

She laughed and handed one to Bill. "Aren't they sweet?"

"Almost as sweet as you," said Bill, nuzzling her neck. "Boy, Dad sure loved those cookies."

"I think it's the first time I've managed to do anything that pleased him. I was worried he'd choke on those pizzelle."

"When he absolutely has to, he can say something nice. He's a lot happier, though, when he can find something to criticize." Bill shook his head. "It's too bad. When I was a kid I used to knock myself out trying to please him. I was never good enough for him. If I got a base hit, it should have been a home run. If I got a ninety-five, it should have been a hundred. That's probably why I became a hippie carpenter instead of an insurance underwriter like him."

"You'd be a terrible insurance underwriter," said Lucy, stroking his hand. "You're a good father."

"I don't want to be like him. I make mistakes, but they're not the same ones he made. If Toby strikes out, I tell him he looked good up there. I tell him even Pete Rose strikes out. I tell him he'll get a piece of it next time."

Lucy snuggled up to him. "How about a piece of it right now?"

"Nope. I'm a liberated modern man. I'm not afraid to admit that I'm too tired."

"Poor Santa. Well, kittens, it's time to go to sleep." She put them back in their box one by one and tucked the box in a corner of the room. Then she hopped back into the warm bed and curled around Bill. Nestled together, they were both asleep before they knew it.

Chapter Sixteen

#6175 These practical cushions for pets are filled with cedar shavings to repel fleas. The removable cover is machine washable and comes in green, red, or plaid. Three sizes: small, $25; medium, $39; and large, $60.

"Mommy, can I go downstairs and see if Santa came?" Toby's whisper was so earnest that Lucy had to smile as she groped for the clock.

"It's six o'clock," he assured her. The family rule was that nobody woke up Mommy and Daddy before six.

"Okay, but be quiet. Don't wake your grandparents. Elizabeth, you go, too, and help carry the stockings."

Lucy sat up and rubbed her eyes. She yawned and smiled at Bill. "I feel as though I just got to sleep."

"I'll make coffee," Bill volunteered, climbing out of bed.

"Sara, hop in here. You must be freezing without your slippers."

Soon the whole family was gathered in the sleigh bed.

Lucy and Bill sipped coffee and smiled indulgently while the children pulled small treasures from their stockings. Reaching into a stocking and finding an oddly shaped, mysterious package—to Lucy that was what Christmas was all about.

"What's this?" asked Sara, holding up a little catnip mouse.

"It's a cat toy," Toby informed her. "Santa must have made a mistake."

"Maybe Santa hasn't heard about Patches," Elizabeth said reasonably.

"Or maybe he knows something you don't," said Bill thoughtfully.

"What's that box doing in the corner?" said Lucy. "I didn't put it there."

"I'll see," Toby shouted, jumping out of bed. "It's kittens! Three of them!"

"Careful, Toby," Lucy cautioned as he picked up the carton and brought it over to her. "Look, Santa brought one for each of you. Now, who wants the little orange one?"

"Oh, I do." Sara sighed and reached for the soft furry bundle.

"Be gentle. Remember, he's just a baby," said Bill.

"Mom, I want the black one. The black one should go to a boy," Toby argued.

"Okay. That leaves the calico one for you, Elizabeth. Is that okay?"

"Oh, yes." Elizabeth sighed. "Calico cats are always girls."

"Well, that worked out well," Lucy said. "What are you going to name them?"

"I'm naming mine 'Softy,'" said Sara, "'cause he's so soft."

"I'm naming mine 'Mac' 'cause he's so tough," said Toby, holding up a very tiny fluff of black fur with two bright eyes.

"I'm going to wait until I know my kitten better before I name her," said Elizabeth. "This is the best Christmas ever."

"I'm sure Santa wants you to take good care of your kittens," Bill announced. "No rough stuff, make sure they get plenty to eat and lots of rest. Okay, gang?"

As she leaned back against the pillows, watching the children dangle Christmas ribbons for the kittens to chase, Lucy rubbed her eyes and yawned again. Bill put his arm around her shoulder and gave her a squeeze as Bill's father appeared in the doorway.

"So, you started Christmas without me? What have you got here, kittens? Well, don't do another thing until you open my present," he said, producing a large, gaily wrapped box.

"You want us to open this now?" said Bill.

"Right away."

"But Mom's not up," Bill protested.

"Doesn't matter. Open it up," he ordered.

Bill shrugged and began to open the package but stopped in amazement when he realized what it was.

"This is a video camera," he said as if there were some mistake.

"That's right. You can film the whole day. Hurry up! You're missing some cute shots of the kids and the kittens."

"Okay, okay. Just let me figure it out."

"It's ready to go. All you have to do is push that red button."

"Really?"

"Yeah. They're great. Fantastic gadgets." The older man bounced around them, barely able to restrain himself from grabbing the camera.

Lucy protested, "You really shouldn't have done this. They're so expensive."

"Nonsense. You only go around once, right? Can't take it with you," said Bill senior. "Besides, Edna wants videos of the kids she can show off to her friends."

Lucy laughed, then threw up her hands in horror as Bill turned the camera on her. "Don't, Bill! I haven't even combed my hair yet."

"Doesn't matter. It looks like Christmas. It looks just like Christmas should."

Indeed, the day was just the way Christmas should be. Eventually the two grandmothers appeared in their robes, with their faces washed and hair combed. Forewarned about the video camera, both had dabbed on some lipstick.

Lucy served coffee and juice while the grandparents opened their stockings, and then everyone moved into the family room to open presents.

After waiting such a long time for Christmas, the children hurried through their piles of gifts, ripping off the paper as fast as they could. Toby was fascinated with the giant insects Lucy had found and was also quite taken with the football his grandfather gave him, but he swore he would never wear the argyle sweater Aunt Madeline had sent him. The girls shook their heads over the red sweaters Aunt Madeline had sent them, but they adored the Barbie house, and the dolls, and the ice skates, and all the other wonderful presents they found under the tree.

The grown-ups opened their packages at a more leisurely pace, stopping to admire each new treasure. Lucy was relieved that Bill approved of the red dress she'd bought at The Carriage Trade, especially after she tried it on for him. Bill senior declared he couldn't wait to try out the fly-tying kit, and both grandmothers immediately draped their scarves over their robes. Lucy was extremely touched by a lovely pair of gold earrings from her mother.

"I wanted to give you something special. I don't know what I would have done without you," her mother said, her eyes glistening with tears.

Lucy worried that the day might be too much for Helen, reminding her of all the Christmases she had shared with her husband. She disappeared for quite a while to get dressed, and when she finally reappeared, she seemed withdrawn and quiet.

"Helen, how about a game of Ping-Pong?" invited Edna. "Elizabeth needs a partner."

To Lucy's surprise, Helen joined the game and even seemed to enjoy herself. Toby and his father and grandfather all went outside to try out Toby's new archery set, and Lucy fussed over the roast.

At four o'clock the family gathered around the long harvest table for Christmas dinner. Candles shone in crystal holders, the silver gleamed, and the centerpiece of golden glass balls and holly sparkled. The children were dressed in their best clothes, Bill and his dad wore their new plaid sport shirts, and the women were all wearing touches of red. Lucy served the roast beef and Yorkshire pudding; dinner was perfect, even the gravy. Lucy had made chocolate mousse from a recipe Sue Finch guaranteed was fool-proof, and everyone adored it.

Finally, when the dishes were all done and put away, and the children changed into their new pajamas, they sat around the TV and watched a replay of the day on the VCR.

"Honestly, this ought to be titled *The Perfect Christmas,*" said Edna.

"I know," Lucy agreed. They looked up as Bill came into the room.

"Lucy, there's a phone call for you."

When Lucy picked up the receiver she was surprised to hear a male voice on the other end.

"Mrs. Stone, this is Officer Findlay. I'm calling for Mrs. Culpepper. Her husband's been hurt and she wants you to stay with Eddie so she can go to the hospital."

"Of course," said Lucy. "Is he badly hurt?"

"I can't say. I'm not even sure he's alive. His car went off the road near Barrow's Light."

"Oh, my God," Lucy said with a gasp. "I'll be there as soon as I can."

Chapter Seventeen

#5714 Shaker stitch hat and scarf set is knitted from 100% virgin wool yarn. This classic style is comfortable and warm. One size. Red, blue, or green. $21.

As Lucy sped through the night in her little car, she repeated over and over, "Please let Barney be all right, let Barney be all right." The car was frigid; the drive was too short for it to warm up, and Lucy's stomach tightened as her hands clenched the wheel. When she pulled up in front of the little ranch house, she was shivering from cold and anxiety.

She tapped on the door and stood blinking in the light and heat that hit her when it was thrown open. Marge looked terrible. Always a large woman, she had given up the struggle to contain her weight some years ago. But now in spite of her bulk she suddenly seemed frail and vulnerable. Her face was pasty white, and the harsh overhead light revealed dark circles under her eyes.

"Don't worry, Marge," said Lucy, rushing to hug her friend. "I'll stay as long as you need."

"Thanks, Lucy." Marge stepped back but grasped her hands. "I hate to take you from your family at Christmas."

Feeling Marge's hands trembling, Lucy gave them a gentle squeeze. "Don't be silly—it can't be helped. I'm glad you called. Honest. Now, get going," she said, giving her a little shove. "And call me as soon as you have any news."

Lucy stood in the doorway for a moment, watching Officer Findlay lead Marge down the icy path to the patrol car; then she shut the door firmly against the dark and cold. She tiptoed down the hall. It wasn't difficult to figure out which room was Eddie's. Pausing outside the door that had been left slightly ajar, she peeked in. Enough light from the hall filtered in so that she could see Eddie sleeping peacefully. His face was plump and round, and asleep he looked much younger than he did in the daytime. Although he was a big, strapping boy, he wasn't really very old—only ten, like Toby. He still needed his parents, thought Lucy. Both his parents.

Returning to the living room, Lucy sat down on the plaid Herculon couch. She drew her knees up to her chest and hugged them. She was still shivering slightly, and she let out a long, quavering sigh.

The Christmas tree stood in the corner, glimmering as the tinsel wafted gently in the updraft from the baseboard heat. The lights were still on, twinkling gaily, and the opened presents were spread out beneath the pine branches. Among the presents she noticed a hat and scarf set from Country Cousins. It was one of the less expensive items in the catalog and was a very popular gift.

Lucy alone had sold hundreds of them. Seeing a little gift card tucked in the corner of the box, she took it out and unfolded it carefully. "To Marge," the card read, "because you need more than love to keep you warm." It was signed "Barney."

Lucy dropped it as if it had suddenly burst into flame in her hand and wrapped her arms around herself. Her glance fell on the worn recliner in the corner that was clearly Barney's chair. The lamp table beside it was well stocked with the hard candies he had sucked on steadily since giving up smoking, and his *TV Guide* and remote control awaited his return.

"Damn," muttered Lucy. She didn't for a moment believe that Barney's crash had been an accident. He was an expert driver; in fact, he'd taken many specialized driving courses for police officers. He loved driving the big cruiser with its antilock brakes and heavy-duty suspension, and often said that if you knew what to do, you could control any skid.

Of course, the road to Barrow's Light was full of curves, and black ice was always possible this time of year. But Barney would have known that and driven accordingly, thought Lucy.

She rose awkwardly to her feet and went out to the kitchen, remembering the many hours she'd spent babysitting as a teenager. Then, as now, the refrigerator had an undeniable appeal. Marge wouldn't mind if she had a snack. Pulling open the door, she peered in; the remains of the Christmas turkey were wrapped carefully in aluminum foil. Lucy took out the packet and placed it on the table. In the breadbox she found a loaf of homemade bread, and the covered butter dish was placed nearby. Lucy smiled approvingly. She hated refrigerated butter herself and always kept her butter out, except in the hottest days of summer.

With nothing else to do except worry about Barney, she made a project of constructing a sandwich, slicing two perfectly even pieces of bread. She put them in the toaster and watched carefully so she could take them out when they were just lightly toasted. Then she spread them with the soft butter, covering even the corners and watching the butter melt into the little air holes. Taking out a large carving knife, she cut two thin slices of breast meat and laid them on the bread. She dusted the meat with salt and pepper, then fished a head of lettuce out of the crisper and peeled off a nicely wrinkled leaf. Adding this to the sandwich, she placed the second piece of bread on top. With geometric precision she cut the sandwich from corner to corner in four triangles. Opening the refrigerator again, she pulled out a bottle of Moosehead Ale, then sat down at the table to eat her snack.

What if the cruiser had some sort of mechanical failure? It was possible, but unlikely. Barney and the other cops maintained the cruisers themselves, in a garage underneath the police station. They didn't trust the black-and-whites to just any mechanic; they knew their lives could depend on the cars and followed a strict maintenance schedule religiously.

Could the car have been sabotaged? Could someone have cut the brake line? Lucy didn't think so. The saboteur would have been taking an enormous risk, unless he was someone the cops knew well—someone who was above suspicion or perhaps someone who was interested in cars. Lucy couldn't get away from the fact that Sam Miller had been killed in a car, and Barney had almost been killed in his.

Lucy chewed her sandwich and sipped her beer thoughtfully. The last time she'd seen Barney he'd been brimming with life, complaining that his job was boring. Had he finally gotten the high-speed chase he'd wanted? She suspected that whether he knew it or not, he'd discovered something that made him dangerous to Sam Miller's murderer. And whatever it was, it had driven the murderer to attempt a second killing.

If he died, how was Marge going to manage? Now, more than ever, families needed two incomes to get by. In her heart Lucy knew that security was just an illusion. She'd never fallen into the trap her mother had of building her life completely around her husband. Down deep she knew there was only one person she could count on—herself. Paychecks, houses, husbands, children, could all be lost in an instant. There are no certainties in life except death, she thought. We are all on slippery ground indeed.

Tragedy, however, was no excuse for leaving dirty dishes. Lucy washed up the dish and knife she'd used and wiped the table. She found a piece of paper and a pencil and began making a list of people who could help Marge. Checking the clock, she realized it was only a little bit past nine, not too late to call Sue.

"Hi, Sue—it's me, Lucy. Did you have a good Christmas?"

"Did I? You'll never guess what Tom gave me—a gorgeous aviator's jacket."

"Lucky you. But I didn't call to compare Christmas presents. Something terrible's happened."

"What's the matter?" Sue's voice was immediately full of concern.

Lucy told her the news, including the few details she knew about Barney's crash.

"I just can't believe it. What a terrible thing, especially at Christmas."

"I know. It's awful here in their house. All the presents are under the tree and everything."

"Marge will need a lot of help. Her mother's been sick and she doesn't have any other relatives around here."

"She'll need someone to take care of Eddie," said Lucy.

"He's good friends with Adam Stillings. Maybe Pam will take him tomorrow."

"That's a good idea. I better get off the phone and leave the line free. Marge promised to call."

"Okay. I'll give Pam a call tonight. Adam's probably covering the accident for *The Pennysaver.*"

"Let me know if you hear anything, okay?"

Lucy replaced the receiver and tiptoed down the hall to make sure she hadn't disturbed Eddie. Seeing that he was still sleeping deeply, she went back to the kitchen. She stood leaning against the kitchen sink, savoring the last drops of beer and reading the collection of notices attached to the refrigerator with magnets.

There was a birthday party invitation printed with brightly colored dinosaurs; an identical one was on Lucy's refrigerator. Toby and Eddie and the rest of the Cub Scout den had been invited to Richie Goodman's birthday party. The school calendar and the lunch menus for December were neatly clipped in a magnetic holder, along with the rules for constructing the little Pinewood Derby cars the Cub Scouts would race in January. Lucy made a mental note to have Bill help Eddie since Barney wouldn't be able to. There was a postcard from Opryland that an Aunt Liz had sent last August and a photograph of Barney dressed as a giant bumblebee, which made Lucy grin.

She yawned and glanced at the clock. It was almost ten.

She was exhausted, she realized; she had had only a few hours of sleep last night. She checked the TV listings and decided to watch the last hour of *It's a Wonderful Life*. Stretching out on the couch with an afghan over her, she watched only a little bit of the movie before she fell asleep.

Thanks to the Moosehead, she woke up around midnight to go to the bathroom. She switched off the TV and turned off all the lights except for the hall and the outside porch light in case Marge came home. She returned to the couch, and next thing she knew sunlight was streaming through the picture window and the phone was ringing.

"Unnnh," said Lucy in the direction of the receiver.

"Lucy, it's Marge. Did I wake you?"

"That's okay. How's Barney?"

"They took us to Portland last night in the air ambulance. He was in surgery for five hours and guess they've put him back together. They say he'll recover well from his physical wounds. The problem is that he's in a coma. He could come out of it anytime, or not at all. We just have to wait."

"That's awful!" Lucy blurted.

"I know. I'm just trying to be glad he's alive. I'm not giving up hope. He's strong. They said nine out of ten wouldn't have survived the surgery."

"He'll be fine, Marge, I know he will," said Lucy, struggling to keep her voice from breaking.

"I'll probably be home this afternoon. I'm going to catch some sleep now, and then Dave Davidson is going to bring me home. He's coming up after services this morning. I hate to ask—but could you keep Eddie?"

"It's no problem. Everyone will want to help."

Indeed, Lucy could see through the kitchen window that a car was pulling up in front of the house. A short figure climbed out and began walking toward the house carrying a foil-covered dish.

"In fact, here comes Franny Small. I bet she's got a dish of Austrian ravioli for you."

"I bet she does." Marge laughed weakly. "It's good to know I can depend on people."

"You know you can always depend on Franny to bring Austrian ravioli." Lucy chuckled. "Don't worry about things here. Just take care of yourself and Barney."

Lucy opened the door for Franny, "Goodness, you're up and about early, Franny. Want some coffee?"

"No, thanks, I have to get Mother to church at eight for choir practice. I had this in the freezer and thought Marge might be able to use it. It's Austrian ravioli."

Lucy stifled a smile. "That's so sweet of you, Franny. It's still frozen, so I think I'll just put it in the freezer. Goodness knows when Marge will get back."

"I've got to run, Lucy. Mother hates to be late."

Lucy was making herself a cup of instant coffee when Eddie appeared in the kitchen, barefoot and in pajamas.

"Where's Mom?"

"Your mom and dad were called away on an emergency last night, Eddie. I spent the night here. What do you usually have for breakfast?"

"Scrambled eggs."

"I'll mix 'em up while you get dressed," Lucy said cheerfully. "And be sure to put something on your feet."

While she cooked Lucy wondered how to tell Eddie the bad news. She wanted to get some food in him before she told him, and she wanted him to have something else to think about. She quickly dialed Pam Stillings and asked if Eddie could spend the day with Adam.

Eddie soon reappeared, dressed in new Christmas clothes. Lucy set a plate in front of him and sipped her coffee while she watched him eat.

"Did you have a good Christmas, Eddie? What did Santa bring?"

"Electronic football. I really wanted that."

"Sounds like fun. Maybe you could take it over to Adam's house. I'm going to drop you off there on my way home, okay?"

"Sure. Where are Mom and Dad?"

"Eddie, your dad had an accident last night." Lucy spoke softly. "They took him to the hospital in Portland. Your mom called a little while ago. Your dad had surgery, and he did real well, but he's still unconscious. He's a big strong man, Eddie, and I think he'll be fine."

"Dad once lifted a car off a little girl."

"I remember that," said Lucy, "It was on the TV news."

"Yeah." Eddie's eyes shone with pride.

"Well, he'll probably be in the news again. Meanwhile, you're going to Adam's. Mom will be home later, and you'll probably have leftover turkey for supper. Do you like that?"

"Yeah." Eddie nodded, swallowing hard.

"Let's get a move on," said Lucy. "How about combing your hair and brushing your teeth?"

"Do I have to?"

Lucy raised an eyebrow and smiled to herself as Eddie headed down the hall. The phone was ringing again and she could see Bev Thompson coming up the walk carrying a pie basket.

Chapter Eighteen

#8260 Everything you need to begin cross-country skiing. Fiberglass skis with polyurethane foam cores are extremely durable. Fish-scale provides traction and does not require waxing. Bindings are adjustable to all snow boots. Fiberglass poles are sturdy and lightweight. Blue. $139.

"I couldn't believe it when I heard," said Bev, shaking her head. "I was going to take this pie to the Friendship Circle dinner tonight, but I've got time to make another one. It's apple."

"Thanks. I know Eddie will enjoy it." Lucy took the pie, and as Bev turned to go she spoke impulsively. "Do you have a minute? I'd love to have a cup of coffee with you."

"Sure, Lucy. I've been missing you and the other girls at work." Bev settled herself at the kitchen table, and Lucy poured two cups of coffee.

"Have you been thinking about getting another job?" Lucy asked.

"Not really. Fred left me well provided for," Bev admitted, taking a sip of coffee. "Actually, I'm thinking of traveling a little. I'd like to visit my son in D.C. Then I could go on to Florida and stay with my sister for a while—she's always after me to come. Then if I flew to San Francisco where my daughter lives and stayed with her a while, winter would be pretty well over." Bev raised an eyebrow and tapped her mug, waiting for Lucy's reaction.

"I'm speechless," said Lucy, smiling. "You've never been one for traveling."

"I know," admitted Bev. "I was perfectly happy to stay here. But now that I don't have my job anymore, there's nothing to keep me here."

Lucy nodded. "Have you seen Karen?"

"I have. She's really mad. Thinks they laid her off because of the baby. Something about the insurance."

"She said she was only working to get the insurance."

"I know," agreed Bev. "She's taking the company to court."

"Really? Good for her." Lucy chuckled. "I don't think the company should get away with it. There were never layoffs when Sam was in charge. I think George was behind it."

"I never liked him. At least now I don't have to be polite to him." She paused. "I saw him, you know. In MacReed's. I didn't say a word to him. I just glared at him." She blushed, remembering her rudeness.

"What were you doing in MacReed's?" asked Lucy. MacReed's was a bait and gun shop.

"Oh, I was seeing about selling Fred's guns and fishing tackle. I'll certainly never use them, and the money would come in handy for the trip. It was odd seeing

George there. I never thought of him as the sporting type."

"What was he doing there?"

"I don't know. He was in the gun side of the shop, though. Maybe he thinks he better get himself some protection now that he's laid off half the town."

"Mrs. Stone, can I watch TV?" Eddie's hair showed signs of recent combing, and there were dribbles of toothpaste on his shirt.

"Sure. Come here a minute." Lucy rubbed at the stains with a damp corner of a kitchen towel. "We'd better get this show on the road."

Bev, quick to take a hint, rose to her feet and began putting on her coat. "Be sure to tell Marge that I'd be happy to help. All she has to do is call."

"I'll do it. Take care, now." Lucy closed the door and started washing up the dishes. It didn't take long for her to tidy up the little house, folding the afghan on the couch, straightening Eddie's bed, and giving the bathroom and kitchen a quick wipe. She wanted it to look nice for Marge when she returned.

Then she had Eddie pack up some toys and they drove over to the Stillingses' house. Pam opened the door for them, smiling her huge smile and welcoming them in a voice that could probably be heard in Alaska.

"Hi, Eddie," she shrieked. "Adam's playing in the living room."

"What did you tell him?" she whispered loudly to Lucy as Eddie made his way down the hall.

Lucy shrugged and smiled apologetically. "I'm operating on a 'need to know' basis. I told him his dad had an accident, he's in the hospital, and that his mother's with him. I told him she'd be home this afternoon. I tried to keep things as normal for him as I could."

"Good." Pam nodded approvingly. She belonged to a generation that took their children's mental health as seriously as their temperatures. "It's best to let Marge decide how much to tell him. Just as long as he doesn't think the accident was his fault."

As she spoke, Pam gave up trying to whisper and her voice rose to its usual piercing decibel. Lucy had often thought Pam's loud voice, and her understanding of child psychology, were the remnants of her brief career as a nursery school teacher.

"The most important thing," she said, concluding her lecture, "is to maintain his usual routine. Children find that very reassuring." She moved aside so her husband could get through the door.

"Hi, Lucy. Good bye, Lucy," said Ted. The two women watched him stride down the path toward his car, his reporter's notebook sticking out of his back pocket and his camera bag slung over his shoulder.

"Ted's been so excited, having a big story," confided Pam. "There's never even been a murder in Tinker's Cove before this. Ted says the police are very suspicious about Barney's accident."

"You mean someone tried to kill him?"

"That's what they think. After all, Barney had driven that route at least once a day for fifteen years or more. There's no way he could have made a wrong turn. And the car had just had a complete overhaul, so they're certain it wasn't a mechanical failure. They think it must have been attempted murder. First Sam Miller and now Barney!"

"I was thinking the same thing," admitted Lucy. "Well, you can read all about it in *The Pennysaver.*"

"I will," Lucy promised, giving Pam a wave.

As she drove home Lucy wondered about what Pam had said. Ted generally had a pretty good idea of what was going on in Tinker's Cove. After all, he was the editor, publisher, and chief reporter for the weekly paper that featured ads, coupons, and local news. In Tinker's Cove news generally came from two sources: the town hall and the police and fire departments. Ted covered it all, sitting through interminable evening meetings of the school board, the finance committee, the zoning board of appeals, and the selectmen. Nobody knew more about town politics than he did. Whenever the police and fire departments were called, Ted was there, writing up the automobile accidents, chimney fires, and petty crimes that had been all that filled the log books until now.

The last violent crime in Tinker's Cove had happened in 1881 when a hired man killed Mrs. Flora Kenny with an ax he happened to be holding in a dispute over wages. He had been chopping wood at the time. Immediately overcome with remorse, he'd obligingly hanged himself in the apple orchard. At least, that's how the story went. Anyway, it had happened a very long time ago.

Ted had written a feature story about the Tinker's Cove ax murder, and Lucy had enjoyed reading it. It had seemed more like fiction than fact, until she'd stumbled on the grave of Flora Kenny, "Beloved Wife and Mother," in the cemetery one day last summer. Flora had been real, just like Sam and Barney. The difference was that Flora had been killed in a fit of temper. Whoever killed Sam and tried to Barney had been cold and calculating.

On the other hand, thought Lucy, pulling into the driveway, you couldn't be sure. Perhaps Barney *had* hit a patch of black ice. The road to Barrow's Light was notorious.

As she braked, she saw Bill's father carrying a load of suitcases and bags to his car.

"You're not leaving already?" Lucy protested.

"I'm afraid so. I've got work tomorrow, you know."

"Tomorrow's Monday. I'd forgotten. I was hoping we'd have a longer visit."

He grunted as he lifted a heavy suitcase. "We'll be back soon. Edna's got some crazy idea about cross-country skiing. Probably break her leg."

Bill senior stood back to admire his packing job. Even though his large sedan had a huge trunk, he prided himself on getting the bags stowed perfectly.

"It's just like walking," Lucy reassured him.

"At our age, even walking is risky," he complained. "One slip and you're out of commission with a broken hip."

"Excuses, excuses," Edna chided, advancing with a shopping bag of Christmas loot. "You're just lazy." She turned to Bill, taking the bag he was carrying for her. "He just wants to stay home and play with the VCR."

"We'll send you lots of videos, I promise, but we'd love to have you stay longer."

"I'm hoping I can pry him loose Presidents' Day weekend. I'll threaten him with the coat sales." Edna laughed and gave Lucy and Bill each a peck on the check.

They stood arm in arm, watching the salt-stained car disappear down the driveway. Feeling suddenly weary, Lucy leaned against Bill for a moment, luxuriating in the knowledge that he was there to support her.

"Tough night?" he murmured, wrapping his arms around her.

"Not too bad. What's up here?"

"Not much. The usual day-after-Christmas mess."

Entering the house through the back door, Lucy was relieved to see that her mother had the kitchen firmly in hand. She had just started the dishwasher and was wiping the counters.

"Did you have breakfast? There's some stollen," she told Lucy.

"I cooked a huge breakfast for Eddie, but I forgot to eat any myself. I'd love some stollen, and a big glass of milk. Don't bother, I'll get it."

"No, go on in and sit down. I'll fix it for you."

Lucy stepped carefully over the Christmas presents that were scattered across the floor and collapsed on the couch, propping her feet on the coffee table. Toby was too engrossed in his video game to do more than say, "Hi, Mom," but the girls shrieked and jumped up as soon as they saw her. They perched on either side of her and showed her their favorite new Barbie outfits. Lucy sipped her milk and chewed her cake, watching Bill as he cleaned out the fireplace. For once she didn't feel compelled to clean up the Christmas mess; she'd do that later. For now she was positively enjoying the disorderly house, her children, her mother, and, most of all, her husband.

* * *

Christmas week passed in a blur. The children were busy with visits to friends and excursions to the movies and the ice-skating rink. Lucy kept in touch with Marge, but the news was always the same. Barney's physical condition continued to improve, but he remained deeply comatose. Marge brought in newspaper articles that she thought would interest him and read them aloud; she even read *Peanuts* to him. She took in photographs of Eddie, and she played his favorite Jimmy Buffett and George Thorogood songs on a portable tape player, but he remained stolidly unreachable.

On New Year's Eve Lucy drove her mother to the airport. They went alone, partly because Lucy didn't want another long wait with the children in tow, but also because she wanted a chance to talk with her mother.

"How are you doing?" Lucy asked as they drove along the highway. "I don't want your polite answer, I want to know how you're *really* doing."

"Well, I don't like the way things are, but I'm all right."

"I was very worried about you when you came. You seemed so depressed."

"I almost didn't come," admitted the older woman. "I was afraid it would be too painful. But there's so much going on at your house that I forgot to worry."

"What do you worry about?"

"Everything! The car, the house, the furnace, the roof. I've never had to think about those things before. What if something breaks?"

"Just call the plumber or the mechanic," Lucy sensibly advised.

"But the expense," her mother protested.

"You've got plenty of money. I think you're really

worried about yourself—whether you can cope without Daddy."

"I miss him so much. I still expect him to walk through the door at five-thirty every night."

"I keep seeing men who remind me of him," confided Lucy. "I'll be in a parking lot and I'll see a man who holds his head a certain way, or who has a cap like Daddy used to wear, or a red-and-black plaid jacket. For a second I'll think it's him. Then I remember, and I feel so sad. It must be much worse for you." Lucy glanced at the shriveled figure beside her.

"It's awful. But I know I've got to pick up and get going. Maybe I'll volunteer at the Red Cross or something."

"That's a good idea," Lucy encouraged.

Helen managed a shrug and a wan smile. When it came time to board the plane, Lucy gave her an awkward hug and stood watching as her mother made her careful way through the gate, never turning to look back.

Later that night, Lucy and Bill went out to a movie, and on the way home they stopped at a package store and bought a bottle of champagne. The inexperienced babysitter hadn't been able to get the kids to bed, so they all sat together on the couch and watched TV, counting down as the ball dropped at Times Square. Lucy gave the kids tiny liqueur glasses of champagne, and they felt very grown-up as they drank a toast to the new year.

On New Year's Day Lucy, Bill, and the kids watched the Tournament of Roses parade and took down the Christmas tree. With the tree gone and the presents put away, the house suddenly seemed much bigger. Lucy was looking forward to Monday, when life would return to normal. Bill would go off to work, Toby and Elizabeth would ride the yellow bus to school, and she would drop Sara off at nursery school. Then she would take down the Christmas cards and decorations, she would clean out cupboards and drawers, she would prepare the house for the long winter ahead.

Chapter Nineteen

#8071 Deluxe sport watch is highly accurate and reliable for field and travel. Quartz crystal ensures it never needs winding. Date indicator and full sweep second hand, luminous dial for night readings. Nylon wrist strap, tan only. Specify man's or woman's model. $39.95.

The cleaning frenzy began as soon as Lucy had the house to herself. She scrubbed the bathroom, mopped the kitchen floor, and changed all the beds. She sorted through the kids' clothes and toys, bagging up the outgrown and tossing out the worn, torn, and broken. She took all the cushions out of the chairs and sofas and found crumpled foil candy wrappers, a small plastic Toto figure, and eighty-seven cents in change. She didn't know what to do with the Christmas cards, so she bundled them together and tucked them away in the bottom desk drawer. The washing machine and dryer hummed steadily in the background as she cleaned and tidied the old farmhouse. She tossed out last year's magazines, unearthed the lemon oil and rubbed the antiques until they gleamed, and replaced the battered old poinsettias with fresh house plants.

On Wednesday morning she was on her knees in the kitchen, emptying the cupboards so she could replace the lining paper. When the phone rang she rose awkwardly to her feet and stepped carefully around the pots, pans, and small appliances that were spread out on the floor.

Expecting the caller to be one of her neighbors, she was surprised when a deep male voice said, "This is Man for Hire."

"What?" said Lucy, noticing that there was quite a thick layer of dust on top of the wall phone.

"You answered my ad," the voice growled. "Man for Hire."

"Oh," said Lucy, realization dawning. "Man for Hire. How nice of you to call. And so punctually, too," she added, noting that the Regulator read precisely nine-thirty. "That's important, I think. Punctuality is desirable in this matter."

I sound like a fool, thought Lucy. This is harder than I thought. I've got to get to the point.

"I'll get right to the point," she said, unconsciously repeating herself. "The reason I need your services is that I'm not happy with my husband."

"That's not an unusual problem, ma'am," rumbled the voice. "If you employ me, you will find that I make every effort to satisfy. I never let my ladies down."

"You work only for women? Isn't that odd?" asked Lucy.

"I only swing one way, ma'am. If you want more variety, you'll have to get somebody else."

"Variety? What do you mean? I give you the picture, you do the job."

"Ma'am, you must be looking for a hit man. I provide other services."

"Oh," said Lucy, color rising to her cheeks. "I'm not interested in *that,* but thanks for calling."

She put the receiver back on the hook and stood looking at it as if it would suddenly leap off the wall and attack her. Then, holding her sides with both hands, she slid onto the floor, sputtering with laughter.

Pulling herself together, she checked the clock. Her conversation with Man for Hire had taken only a few minutes; it would be at least twenty-five minutes before the next call. What was his name? She couldn't remember. In fact, it seemed eons ago, almost another lifetime, that she and Barney had sat together at the kitchen table answering the ads in *Modern Mercenary.*

At exactly ten o'clock, the phone rang. Lucy took a deep breath, and while she waited for the second ring she rehearsed what she planned to say. She picked up the receiver and said, "Hello."

"Lucy, this is Dave Davidson. I didn't wake you up, did I?" As minister, Dave knew that a lot of the women in the parish who worked the night phones at Country Cousins took naps at odd times during the day.

"No, Dave, I'm up and about. But I am expecting an important call. Could I call you back later?"

"This will only take a minute." Dave spoke in quiet, measured tones. "Can you host the coffee hour on March twentieth?"

Lucy sighed. "I guess so."

"Good. I'll put you down. You'll get a reminder the

week before." His voice was very sincere as he added, "Thank you. Go in peace."

"Thank you," said Lucy, wondering how it was that whenever Dave Davidson asked her to do a favor, she ended up thanking him. She had no sooner replaced the receiver than it rang again. She snatched it up, reminded herself to calm down, and said cautiously, "Hello."

"Pest Control here."

"Thank you for calling. I have a job and I wonder if you'd be interested."

"Pest control's my business, ma'am," said the voice, chuckling.

"Well, the pest I want removed is my husband," said Lucy.

"It usually is." The voice sounded resigned. "It's sad, really. Marriage isn't what it used to be."

"I'm afraid I don't have any alternative. Divorce is out of the question."

"Of course. A direct route to poverty."

"Absolutely," Lucy agreed. "My husband has quite a lot of life insurance."

"How nice. You'll be able to maintain your current lifestyle. It's really a shame to spend all that money on hiring a professional when you could do it yourself."

"I haven't the faintest idea about how to kill someone," Lucy said indignantly. "That's why I want to hire you."

"There are definite advantages to doing it yourself," the voice informed her, sounding like a friendly hardware salesman. "Wives have so many opportunities; the average home is full of dangers that can be fatal to the unsuspecting husband."

"Really?" Lucy was incredulous.

"Absolutely. A slip in the bathtub, a short circuit in the hair dryer, cyanide in the Tylenol, there's even the bad mushroom, although that is a bit old-fashioned. If you would just give it some thought, I'm sure you could come up with a surefire method. After all, nobody knows him better than you."

"Is this what you advise all your clients?" demanded Lucy.

"Well," the voice admitted, "you're actually my first client."

"Then you aren't the man I'm looking for," said Lucy. "I'm looking for someone with experience."

"I understand," the voice said mournfully.

Lucy replaced the receiver, feeling a bit like Alice in Wonderland. Had she really had this conversation? "Curiouser and curiouser," she muttered to herself as she opened the undersink cabinet and got to work.

When the phone rang at ten-thirty, Lucy was sitting at the kitchen table, relaxing with a cup of coffee and a piece of toasted raisin bread.

"This is Bad Guy," announced the voice. "Have you been a naughty girl?"

"No, but I'm thinking of doing something very naughty," she said in a playful tone. "Are you interested?" This was sort of fun.

"I'm always interested when little girls are naughty," affirmed the voice. "I bring my own paddles, whips, and chains."

Lucy slammed the receiver on the hook and stood leaning on the counter, afraid her legs wouldn't support her. This was too much. And the worst part was that she couldn't tell anybody about it. Sue would love this. Lucy just couldn't believe these things really went on. Did they? Was it all make-believe? Did grown-ups really do this stuff? What was the world coming to? She wondered if she would ever be able to look at people in quite the same way.

When eleven o'clock came and went and the phone didn't ring, Lucy was relieved. Although the house was cleaner than it had been in months, every surface gleaming and twinkling in the bright winter sunlight, she knew it was largely an illusion. Decades' worth of dust was packed into every crack and seam, impossible even for the vacuum to suck out. She washed her hands and face, combed her hair, and carefully applied lipstick and eyeliner. Her face in the mirror looked the same as it had yesterday, but she felt different somehow. She remembered hearing as a teenager that once you lost your virginity it showed in your face. When she had finally gone all the way with an earnest second-string soccer player during freshman year of college, she was both relieved and disappointed that she couldn't see any change in her features. Grabbing her bag and keys, she decided to take Sara out for lunch at Jake's Donut Shop. It would be a treat for Sara, and she wanted to get away from the telephone for a while.

The next morning the phone rang promptly at ninethirty. No matter what she might think of the characters who advertised their services in *Modern Mercenary,* Lucy had to admit they were certainly punctual. They must consult their field watches frequently, she thought.

"This is Combat Veteran, answering your note," said the voice in the tone of one reporting for duty. "I am ready to go into action anytime, anywhere in the world. Asia, Africa, Latin America are all no problem for me."

"That's certainly good to know," Lucy said, impressed. "This job is in Maine."

"Maine! You must be crazy, lady. Maine in the winter! Poor tactics, extremely poor. Don't you know what happened to Napoleon in Russia?"

Lucy smiled as she replaced the receiver and pulled on a pair of rubber gloves. She reached for the oven cleaner, and got to work. Half an hour later she was closing the door on a spotless oven when the phone rang. The voice on the other end was warm and reassuring.

"This is Cool Professional, answering your letter."

"Terrific," said Lucy. "I'm looking for someone to kill my husband."

"I'll want fifty thousand dollars. Twenty-five up front, and twenty-five afterward. Cash. I don't wait for insurance payoffs. Send me his name and address, a picture, and his schedule."

"As simple as that?"

"Absolutely. Perhaps you'd like to think about it for a while?" he asked courteously. "Maybe you can work something out."

"No, I've made up my mind."

"Fine."

"Just a minute," said Lucy. "Would you answer just one question for me? Have you ever killed anybody in Tinker's Cove, Maine?"

"I've never even heard of Tinker's Cove," said the voice.

Lucy believed him. Just because he was a killer didn't mean he was a liar, too.

Chapter Twenty

#3167 Originally designed for runners' use in the winter months, these snow boots are lightweight and practical for everyday use. Uppers constructed of polyester fabric are breathable, warm, and guaranteed waterproof. Vibram soles provide excellent traction on ice and snow. Whole sizes only. Men's and women's, $69.95.

As she looked around the house, Lucy realized there was nothing left to do. Four days of steady work, fueled no doubt by post-holiday letdown and premenstrual hormones, had wrought a miracle. Call *Country Homes* magazine, she thought to herself, send photographers immediately. This will probably never happen again. As she wandered from room to room, admiring the handsome antiques she and Bill had collected over the years, the afternoon stretched emptily ahead of her. Sara had a play date at a friend's house and wouldn't be coming home. Lucy climbed upstairs to change out of her grubby cleaning clothes, thinking perhaps she would spend the afternoon checking out the after-holiday sales in Portland, and noticed the bags of outgrown clothes piled on the landing.

There were some nice things in those bags: warm footed pajamas, cozy sweat suits, winter jackets, and even a pair of hardly worn snow boots bought late last winter that Sara couldn't cram her feet into this year. Lucy hated just to toss those things in a Salvation Army bin; she tried to think of someone she knew who could use them. Unfortunately none of her friends had girls younger than Sara, and her playmates all wore clothes larger than the things in the bags. Then she remembered Lisa Young's little girl. Surely she could use those clothes. Her thoughts were interrupted by Bill's voice.

"Lucy, are you home?"

"What are you doing home this time of day?" she asked, bounding down the stairs.

"I'm looking for some lunch, woman. Where's Sara?"

"At Caroline's."

"You're alone? There are no kids?" Bill was like a bird dog catching scent of a hot trail.

"That's right," Lucy admitted.

"Thank you, God," he said, reaching for her.

"Sorry, Romeo. It's the first day of my period."

"Why do you have to sound so pleased about it?" complained Bill, dropping his arms. "What's for lunch?"

"Turkey soup—homemade." Lucy hauled a big enamel pot out of the refrigerator. "And tuna fish sandwiches."

"I guess you're not such a bad wife after all," Bill conceded. "So what're you going to do this afternoon? Curl up on the couch with the kittens and a mystery?"

"I thought I'd drop off those outgrown clothes down Bump's River Road."

"Bump's River Road? I don't want you going down there," said Bill.

"I've already been down there," Lucy said. "That's where I got the kittens." She picked up Mac, who had climbed up her pant leg following the tuna fumes, and scratched his head.

"Well, don't go there anymore. A lot of weird people live down there."

"They're not weird. They're just poor," Lucy said reasonably. "Look how well the kittens turned out."

"Those people live that way because they want to, Lucy. Nothing's stopping them from working like the rest of us. Now listen to me," he said, using his authoritarian father voice, "don't go down there. Understand?"

"Yes, Daddy," said Lucy, clearing the table. As she stood at the sink rinsing off the lunch dishes and putting them in the dishwasher, she watched Bill climb into his truck and drive off. She hated it when he treated her like a child. She *was* a woman, all grown up, the mother of three children. She managed all their money, she dealt with teachers and doctors. She was capable of making decisions for herself, thank you. Besides, she kept remembering that dark-haired little girl in her torn shirt. She was just the right size for Sara's outgrown things.

Lucy loaded the bags into the Subaru and started the engine. She'd be back in plenty of time to make supper.

It was a beautiful day for a drive. The trunks of the trees lining the road were almost black and contrasted sharply with the light dusting of snow that lay on the ground. Thanks to the bright sun and the mild temperature, the snow on the road had melted. Lucy whizzed by in her little station wagon, humming along with the radio and enjoying driving all by herself for a change. She

passed farms with snow-covered fields, the old farm-
houses with attached barns far outnumbering the new
houses on the road. As she drove farther from Tinker's
Cove the farms thinned out and the road was lined with
thick woods on either side.

The turnoff for Bump's River Road was just past an
old store and gas station. This was a genuine country
store that had made no attempt to pretty itself up for the
tourists; the faded signs on the outside advertised cut plug
tobacco and Nehi soda, but they were overlaid with
newer signs for the state lottery. A teenaged boy stood in
the doorway, his long hair hanging down either side of
his face and his snowmobile suit unzipped to the waist,
revealing his skinny chest. He watched as she turned off
the state road.

The day she had gotten the kittens she had been in a
hurry, intent on following the directions she had been
given, and she had not really paid attention to the scenery.
Today as she passed the worn-out, shabby homes surrounded by junk-filled yards, she was horrified. Up close,
in the unblinking winter sunlight, the houses looked
flimsy and unsubstantial. How would these people survive the cold winter? When she had lived in the city she
had grown used to seeing homeless people outside the
grocery store and the bank, and there were neighbor-
hoods she passed all the time on the train that she'd never
visit. In the city she had always been aware of poor people, but since she'd moved to Tinker's Cove she'd assumed that poverty was a city problem. In the country,
unless you went looking, you weren't likely to encounter
real poverty.

Pulling up in front of Lisa Young's place, she smiled at
the little girl sitting on the step, playing with a Barbie

doll. She was absorbed in make-believe, stroking the doll's bright yellow hair and talking to it in a high-pitched singsong voice. She didn't look up until Lucy spoke to her.

"Hi there. Is your mom home?"

The little girl disappeared inside and soon Lisa appeared at the door, wearing the same defensive expression Lucy remembered from her earlier visit.

"Do you remember me? I took the kittens before Christmas."

"Sure." Lisa stood in the doorway, the little girl clinging to her side.

"Well, I wanted to thank you. My kids really love the kittens, but that's not why I'm here," explained Lucy. "I cleaned out my daughters' closets, and I've got a lot of outgrown clothes that I think will fit your daughter. What's her name?"

"Crystal," said Lisa, still expressionless.

"I really think these will fit Crystal. Would you like to see?"

"Sure." Lisa shrugged and grudgingly followed Lucy to the car. Lucy put down the tailgate and began spreading out the garments, feeling like a saleslady as she pointed out the virtues of each item.

"This is really warm, isn't it cute?" she said, holding up an appliquéd bathrobe. "And this sweater used to be Elizabeth's favorite. She cried when it got too small." Lucy shook her head, neatly folding the sweater and replacing it in the bag.

"How much do you want?" asked Lisa.

"Nothing." Lucy was shocked. "I usually give things like this to a friend, but none of my friends have a little girl the right size. Couldn't Crystal use these?"

Lucy smiled at Crystal, who was fingering a bottle-green velvet dress with a lace collar and pearl buttons.

"Okay," said Lisa, picking up the bags. "Thank you kindly."

"You're very welcome. Can I help you carry them?"

"I can manage," said Lisa. Lucy watched her as she stepped up onto the sloping porch and went into the little cabin, closing the door firmly behind her.

Lucy turned and climbed back into the car. Do people know about this? she wondered as she turned the key and drove slowly down the muddy track. These people might as well be living in the nineteenth century, she thought, noticing that most of the houses had little outhouses behind them. How would Crystal adjust to school? How would she cope with flush toilets, bell schedules, and computers?

Deep in thought, Lucy hadn't been paying close attention to the road. But it was too late. She'd managed to sink all four tires in the slushy mud. She opened the car door and scouted for something to put under the tires to give her some traction. She saw a yard just a bit up the road that was filled with junk. She picked her way carefully along the muddy road, glad that she'd worn her waterproof boots.

There must be something here I can use, she thought, looking about for a few boards or pieces of plywood; even a flattened cardboard box would do. She glanced at the house that was in the center of this junkyard, but no one seemed to be home. She picked her way around a broken washing machine, past bits and pieces of automobiles and lots and lots of tires, and finally found a pile of old asphalt shingles. She was bent over, picking up a generous handful, when she heard a low growl. Turning around, she saw a large, shaggy brown dog coming toward her at top speed, teeth bared and ears flat.

She dropped the shingles, scrambled up a pile of building debris, and, reaching for the branch of a big old pine tree, pulled herself to safety with just seconds to spare. Panting from fright and exertion, she wrapped her arms around the trunk of the tree and rested her forehead against it. She was perhaps seven or eight feet from the ground. The dog had climbed up the pile of debris and was standing on his hind legs, barking frantically at her and snapping his teeth at her feet. She was safe enough since he couldn't climb the tree, but she sure couldn't go anywhere.

After a while the dog stopped barking and jumping. Instead, he stood on all fours, eyeing her patiently, prepared to wait. I've played this game before, he seemed to be saying to her. Every now and then he'd bark sharply, making her jump, and then he'd resume his patient wait. Lucy shouted for help, and the dog again began barking frantically and jumping up, nipping at her feet. Lucy looked hopefully at the house, praying that someone was home who could help her. Miraculously, the door opened and a large, fat man in overalls scrambled out holding a shotgun.

"Don't shoot!" Lucy shouted. "The dog's got me stuck in this tree."

She watched in horror as the man slowly and deliberately raised the gun to his shoulder and fired. Instinctively she crouched as the shot rang out. She saw the dog's legs go out from under him as he collapsed on the junk heap, whimpered once, and went still.

Perhaps the dog belonged to someone else, Lucy thought as she jumped down from the tree. Maybe it was a nuisance dog he'd been looking for an excuse to shoot. She advanced toward the man, smiling. He had smooth round cheeks and blue eyes and smiled back at her. Then he raised the shotgun to his shoulder. Lucy ducked behind a big old steel desk just as he fired off the second round.

Lucy peeked out from behind the desk, saw that he was busy reloading, and ran for more secure cover behind a big stump of elm.

"God," Lucy prayed, "don't let this be happening to me. Let me wake up, let it be a bad dream. Please. I know. Bill was right, I was wrong. Now, get me out of here." She cringed behind the stump, shaking violently as two more shots rang out. The man wasn't coming any closer, she saw. He was still standing in the same spot, reloading again. If only he'd stop smiling at her. Damn it, that smile was familiar. She just couldn't place it. Maybe he would run out of ammunition and give up. It would be getting dark soon; maybe she could creep away in the darkness. Maybe she'd die like the dog, shot by a smiling idiot.

"Harold, put that gun down," said a voice. "Harold, I mean it. This is an order. Put it down, right now."

Raising herself just enough so she could see over the stump, Lucy saw Lisa standing at the edge of the yard, pointing her finger at the man as if he were a naughty child. Obediently he dropped the gun and shambled off to the house.

"Is that all I had to do?"

"Yeah. You just gotta let him know who's boss. He shouldn't have a gun. Dunno why they let him have it. I can't believe he shot his dog. He'll be sorry when he realizes what he done. You okay?"

"I feel a little shaky," admitted Lucy. "My car's stuck."

"You can use those shingles," Lisa informed her, walking back toward her house.

"Thanks a lot, I guess," Lucy muttered, scooping up some shingles. She spread them in front of the car tires, and by accelerating very slowly and carefully in four-wheel drive, she got going again.

She felt guilty about leaving the shingles in the road, but she absolutely could not make herself climb out of the car. Maybe they'll help someone else, she thought. Keeping her foot firmly on the accelerator and willing the car forward with every ounce of energy she had, she finally made it up Bump's River Road and pulled onto the hard-top at the store.

"Al," she said, reading the tattoo on his chest, "I wonder if you'd mind answering a question for me."

She took a ten-dollar bill out of her wallet and fingered it. "There's a big old dumb guy down there, his first name's Harold. Do you know who I mean?"

"Sure, I know him," admitted the kid, his eyes on the money.

"What's his last name?"

"Higham. Harold Higham."

"Oh, really," Lucy said slowly. She knew she'd seen that smile before. "Well, thanks for the information," she said, passing him the bill. "I think I'll take one of those small bottles of brandy behind you."

Chapter Twenty-One

#1150 San-Sol sunglasses are known throughout the world for superior performance whether on the ski slopes or the beach. Polarized lenses reduce glare, block UV rays. $89.

L ucy got back in her car and sat for a few minutes, taking small, unsteady sips of the brandy. She was surprised to see that according to the digital clock it was only two-thirty. It seemed like an eternity since she'd left the house for Bump's River Road.

She turned on the radio and let the brandy do its work, spreading warmth through her body. Gradually her muscles relaxed and she stopped shaking; her teeth stopped chattering; all that remained of her fear was a hard rock in her stomach.

She didn't think she would ever forget Harold Higham's blank, smiling face as he'd raised the shotgun and aimed at her. Who was Harold Higham, she wondered, and what was the matter with him? How was he related to George? They certainly had a family resemblance, but that's where the resemblance ended. George's desk at Country Cousins was always neat and tidy, his navy blue blazer and gray flannel pants freshly pressed. She had just assumed he came from a solid middle-class background, but now she wasn't so sure. She screwed the cap onto the brandy bottle and dropped it into her purse, then put the car in gear and turned onto the state road.

As soon as she made the turn onto the highway, the bright sunlight made her wince. Instinctively, she pulled down the visor and groped for her sunglasses. She was driving right into the sun, and the visibility was very poor. The sun reflected off every bit of ice and smear on the windshield, and to make matters worse, the woods lining the road made deep shadows. She was terrified she wouldn't see a pedestrian or bicyclist in the shadows until it was too late.

A big pickup truck loomed suddenly behind her, tail-gating so closely that she was afraid to try to pull over to let it pass. Her nerves already raw, she clutched the steering wheel tightly and tried to maintain a steady forty miles an hour. Her eyes couldn't adjust to the changes in light and shadow as she tried to see the road ahead, keep track of the truck behind her, and check the speedometer.

I have to do something, she decided, and cautiously tapped the brake and turned on her left signal. To her relief the pickup backed off, giving her room to pull over to the side. The driver, a young fellow with his black Lab beside him on the passenger seat, honked and waved, and Lucy shook her head.

She was stopped, she realized, right in front of Miss Tilley's antique Cape Cod house. The little white clapboard house hugged the ground, anchored by a huge central chimney. It had been built more than two hundred years ago and was designed to stay warm even in the frigid winter winds. Impulsively Lucy turned into the driveway and marched up to the door. If anyone in town would know about Harold Higham, it would be Miss Tilley.

"Lucy, how nice to see you," she said, opening wide the solid pumpkin pine door. "I was just having some tea. Won't you join me?"

Lucy glanced at her watch. If she didn't stay long, she could still be home before the school bus.

"Thank you, I will. I'm awfully sorry about dropping in on you like this," Lucy apologized. "I have a question I want to ask you."

"I'm always glad to see you, Lucy," said Miss Tilley, leading the way into the cozy living room. Despite her age she had kept her height and her ramrod-straight back. "Lucy, do you know Emily Miller?" Miss Tilley indicated a tiny figure seated on a wing chair near the fireplace.

"Oh, dear, that fire has gotten low, hasn't it?" Miss Tilley threw another log on the fire and stirred it up with the poker. "There, that's better. Now, Emily, this is Lucy Stone. I think I may have mentioned her to you."

"Of course, Lucy Stone. It's very nice to meet you." Although she was tiny and frail, Mrs. Miller's eyes were bright. She seemed to have recovered her strength since the day of Sam's funeral.

"I really don't want to interrupt you," insisted Lucy. "I'll come back another day."

"Nonsense," said Miss Tilley in her old library voice. "Just sit down in that rocker, Lucy, and I'll freshen up the teapot."

Lucy smiled apologetically at Mrs. Miller and did as

she was told. Miss Tilley always had that effect on her; she did on everybody. Lucy didn't understand how she did it. Everyone in town knew her name was Julia Ward Howe Tilley, but Lucy had never heard anyone call her Julie, or Julia, or anything except Miss Tilley.

"Julia is so forceful," Mrs. Miller said, smiling.

Lucy's eyes widened, and she smiled politely at the old woman.

"I am awfully glad you stopped in. We have tea together quite often, and it's nice to have someone new to talk with."

Miss Tilley appeared in the doorway, carrying a loaded tea tray. Lucy watched as she stepped across a minefield of small, frayed antique rugs, but the older woman never missed a step. She sat down gracefully on a straight chair and, lifting a teacup in her left hand, poured a steady stream of steaming tea from the Royal Doulton pot she held in her right hand. She was seeing a perfect demonstration of a lost art, Lucy realized, feeling that she was taking part in some ancient ritual.

"Sugar?" asked Miss Tilley.

"No, thank you."

"Cream or lemon?"

"Lemon." Lucy leaned forward to receive the teacup and saucer and settled back in her chair, holding the fragile porcelain carefully. She still felt a bit shaky and was wondering how she could break the tranquil atmosphere with her rather awkward question.

"Lucy, you said you had something you wanted to ask me," said Miss Tilley, handing a cup to Mrs. Miller.

"I do." Lucy took a sip of tea. "I was wondering about a man named Harold Higham."

"However did you hear about him?" wondered Mrs. Miller. "He's not wandering around town, is he?"

"No. I, uh, I encountered him on Bump's River Road today."

"Whatever were you doing down there, Lucy?" demanded Miss Tilley.

Wondering how she had become the questioned instead of the questioner so quickly, Lucy replied, "I was just taking some outgrown clothes to a woman I know there."

"I thought playing Lady Bountiful had gone out of style years ago," Miss Tilley observed tartly.

Mrs. Miller cackled at her old friend's comment.

"You can't just forget those people," Lucy defended herself. "There's terrible poverty down there. If I can do something to help, what's the matter with that?"

"Well, from the look of you, I'd say your charitable impulses were resisted." Mrs. Miller chuckled.

"More than resisted, I'd say," hooted Miss Tilley. "They must have put up quite a fight."

Looking down, Lucy realized that her jeans were covered with mud and the pocket of her jacket was torn. She must be a sight, she thought, color rising to her cheeks. She laughed.

"Well, I can laugh about it now, but I was pretty scared. The car got stuck in mud, a vicious dog had me treed, and then Harold Higham shot the dog and took a few shots at me."

The two ladies clicked their tongues sympathetically.

"That's why I stopped by," Lucy continued. "I was wondering about Harold Higham. Is he related to George Higham?"

"He's his brother," said Miss Tilley.

"How can that be?" Lucy demanded. "They're so different."

"George is a remarkable man," said Mrs. Miller. "He's really his own creation. He pulled himself up by the bootstraps and walked right out of Bump's River Road."

"When he was a little boy he'd come to the library after school every afternoon. He'd settle himself in a little corner of the children's room and read there until closing time. Then he'd go walking off down the road, a tiny little fellow. I don't think they lived so far out of town then."

"No," agreed Mrs. Miller. "They lived in a ramshackle old house next to the Mobil station. It's gone now. It fell down. It was an awful place, a terrible firetrap. I used to worry about them, especially in winter. Lord knows what they used for heat."

"Probably a woodstove, set right on the floor, with a nice pile of newspapers and kindling kept handy right next to it."

"I'm sure you're right. It's a wonder it didn't burn down." Mrs. Miller shook her head.

"The father was a piece of work, I can tell you that."

"He was a dreadful man," Mrs. Miller agreed. "He used to lie on the porch steps, drunk as a skunk, throwing things at people who walked by. He called them terrible names, too."

"The mother died when George was about ten or so, I think," Miss Tilley remembered. "Poor woman was probably glad to go."

"She led a terrible life, between the husband and the idiot son."

"She might not have realized how terrible it was," observed Miss Tilley. "She wasn't very bright as I recall."

"Wasn't there something you could do?" Lucy asked. "Today it would be called child neglect, maybe even worse."

"People did try, but all they ever got for their efforts was a torrent of abuse from the father. Or worse. Just like you did today."

"How did George manage to do so well?"

"His teachers encouraged him, and I'd let him stay at the library. Other people took an interest in him. He was always different from the rest of the Highams."

"Maybe he's not so different after all," commented Lucy. "Thanks for the tea and the information, but I've got to go. The kids will be coming home from school."

"It's just as well you're leaving, Lucy. At four o'clock, we switch to sherry," said Miss Tilley.

"You can't imagine how decadent we can be," Mrs. Miller twinkled from her chair. "Fortunately, I don't drive anymore. Tom will pick me up and take me home."

"In a wheelbarrow," snorted Miss Tilley. "Lucy," she advised, "be careful. Curiosity is a fine and wonderful thing, but it can also be dangerous. Remember Madame Curie."

"I promise," swore Lucy, smiling, "from now on I will avoid radioactive materials. 'Bye."

Lucy caught up with the big yellow school bus on Red Top Road and followed it the rest of the way home. She put out a plate of cookies and glasses of milk for Toby and Elizabeth and sat with them at the big oak table.

Elizabeth was somewhat disgruntled; her best friend had played with someone else at recess. She consoled herself with a huge number of chocolate-chip cookies and then went off to play in peace by herself before Sara came home.

Toby only nibbled at his cookies, and Lucy instinctively asked him what was the matter.

"The Pinewood Derby is Sunday, Mom, and I haven't even started on my car."

"Well, you better get started."

"I don't know how."

"Let's look at it together."

Toby brought the little box to the table and took out the block of wood that he had to turn into a car. Lucy turned it over in her hands.

"What style car do you want to make? Have you got any ideas?"

"I want it to look like a Corvette."

Lucy smiled. "That's pretty ambitious. How about making some sketches. Then Daddy can help you cut it out tonight."

She ruffled his hair as he bent over the table, the pencil gripped tightly in his chubby hand. She smiled to see him concentrate so hard on his drawing, then went upstairs to change her clothes. It was time to get ready for work.

Chapter Twenty-Two

#5999 Remington .44-caliber revolver. Features a swing-out speed cylinder, double action with checkered hammer. Fixed-blade front sight with adjustable rear sight. Hammer block safety. Molded checkered wood-grain grip. Complete with molded carrying case. $134.95.

Lucy stared at the blank computer screen in front of her and hit the return key. The command bar on the top of the screen lit up, and she read, "Good evening, Lucy. Your rep number is 400L. Your total sales for tonight: $14.99."

"I hate it when it's slow," she announced to no one in particular.

"Me too," agreed Ruthie. "It's always slow after Christmas, but I've never seen it this slow."

"It's depressing with everyone gone, but I can see why they made the layoffs," admitted Lucy.

"I guess," Ruthie agreed. "I've been looking for another job."

"Really? Doing what?"

"Anything. I saw an ad for a ward secretary at the hospital in Portland, and I put my name in for customer service rep at Kmart. There's not much out there, but anything's better than this."

"I hope you find something, but, I'll really miss you," said Lucy, feeling bereft. "I miss the old gang."

Lucy's light went on, and she answered with the usual, "Country Cousins, may I help you?"

The voice that answered was clipped and very British. It was the expedition leader of a group planning to map the Andes.

"Never been done, up till now. Done properly, that is," explained the voice, which went on to order nine sets of polar underwear, nine Arctic Tundra parkas, nine pairs of Arctic Tundra pants, nine pairs of Glove-Mitts, and nine pairs of Sure-Tread boots, "guaranteed under all weather conditions."

"Do you need any camping gear?" asked Lucy.

"I'm afraid we do," complained the voice. "Lost an awful lot of stuff to a ycti in the Himalayas last spring."

"Really? I thought they were mythical."

"It's difficult to be certain," said the voice. "There's not much oxygen up there; men behave strangely in extreme circumstances."

"I suppose they do," agreed Lucy. "Now, what do you need?"

She placed orders for nine down-filled mummy bags (guaranteed to maintain body temperature to -20 degrees), five two-man mountain tents, five flame-glo camp stoves, and a case of pressurized fuel canisters.

"Anything else? Socks, for example?"

"Good show," said the voice. "You can never have too many socks on an expedition."

"That has been my experience," said Lucy, thinking of last summer's camping trip to Mount Desert Island.

"I'll take thirty-six pairs of your very best socks."

Lucy smiled as she typed in the order—the socks alone, she figured, would come to nearly three hundred dollars.

"Do you want a total?" Lucy asked.

"Not really. We'll just let the Royal Geographical Society worry about that," confided the voice. "How soon can I expect the shipment? We're scheduled to leave on February first."

Lucy worked out the details for the geographer and smiled as he rang off with a very British, "Cheerio."

"Wow," said Ruthie as Lucy hit the return button and saw her total was now nearly ten thousand dollars.

"Boy, that was something that doesn't happen every day. That man was outfitting a nine-man mountain-climbing expedition. I think I'll call Ted Stillings. Maybe he'll put it in the paper."

"Might as well," agreed Ruthie. "There's nothing else going on."

Lucy stood up and stretched, dug her change purse out of her bag, and headed for the break room, where the pay phone was located. She got a diet Coke from the machine and dialed Ted's number.

"Ted, Lucy Stone here at Country Cousins. I think I've got a scoop for you." She gave him the details of the order, and he promised to write it up for the paper.

"That's a cute story, Lucy," he said. "Thanks."

"Pam told me you've been following Barney's accident. Do they know any more?" asked Lucy.

"Only that something caused the car to go right through the guardrail. Fortunately, it got caught in some trees. If he'd been a little farther along, it would have gone right into the water."

"Do the police know what caused him to go over?"

"There were tire marks showing that he swerved. Something made him swerve, but they don't know what. If he doesn't come to, they may never know."

"What about the crime lab?" questioned Lucy.

"They did send stuff to be analyzed. They won't have the results for a couple of weeks, anyway. Hey, don't you read the paper?" demanded Ted.

"I do when I have the time," Lucy said guiltily. "Which reminds me, I'd better get back to work."

She hung up and, walking out to the hallway, stood reading the bulletin board and finishing her soda. There was a strict policy forbidding liquids near the computers, and she didn't want to risk angering George.

Where was George tonight? she wondered. She hadn't seen him at all, which was unusual. In fact, peering down the dark tunnel of hallway that led to the executive offices, she didn't think any of the managers were in the building tonight.

Lucy took a last swig of soda and walked slowly down the hallway. All the offices were dark. She stood for a minute outside George's door, then impulsively reached for the knob.

It turned, and immediately she snatched her hand away and jumped back. She hadn't expected the door to be unlocked. She stood in the hallway for a minute, then slipped into the office, closing and locking the door behind her. She flipped on the wall switch and stood for a moment blinking in the brightness. Then she went over to the window and pulled down the shade.

Quickly she worked her way around the small room. She pulled out file drawers and felt behind the files; she peered into a decorative vase. She even checked the wastebasket. She couldn't have said what she was looking for, but when she opened the desk drawer and saw a black revolver, she was sure she'd found it.

She glanced around quickly to make sure she hadn't disturbed anything, switched off the light, and slipped out into the hallway. Her heart was pounding as she walked back to her desk. Whatever had possessed her to do such a thing? What if she'd been caught? What could she have said?

Sitting down at her desk, she realized how foolish she'd been. She jumped when Ruthie asked her if Ted had liked the story.

"I think so. We talked for quite a while; I was asking about Barney. Did I miss anything?" Lucy hoped her nervousness didn't show.

"Mrs. Murgatroyd in Sioux Falls is not happy with the Dipsy-Tipsy bird feeder her son gave her for Christmas."

"No?" asked Lucy. "Why not?"

"The squirrels still get the bird seed," Ruthie told her. "She wants to return it for a refund."

"And what did you tell her?" asked Lucy.

"Just pack it in the original carton, if possible, and include the original invoice, please," recited Ruthie. "We will be happy to refund the entire purchase price. At Country Cousins, we're not happy unless you are."

"Very good," said Lucy. "What time is it?"

"Almost nine."

"Only nine?" Lucy was incredulous.

"Sorry. Want to balance my checkbook for me?"

"No. I guess I'll make up my grocery list."

Lucy thought her shift would never end. By the time the clock buzzed at one A.M. she was exhausted, twice as tired as she would have been if she'd been busy.

As she drove home along the dark, lonely roads, she kept thinking of Barney, driving along a similar country road on Christmas night. Had a shot suddenly exploded into the darkness, causing him to jump reflexively and swerve right off the road, through the black emptiness and into the trees? Had George fired that shot?

Lucy pulled the car up as close to the house as she could and ran straight into the kitchen without pausing to look, as she usually did, at the night sky.

Reaching the safety of the kitchen, she leaned against the door for a moment, panting, and then turned the lock.

Tiptoeing upstairs, she checked to make sure the kids were safely asleep. Reassured, she went back downstairs and heated some milk for herself. She knew she'd have a hard time getting to sleep.

As she sat at the kitchen table, sipping her hot milk and whiskey, Lucy tried to relax. But no matter how hard she tried, she couldn't control her thoughts. She kept thinking of the ugly black gun in George's drawer, and poor Barney, his car spinning out of control and plummeting through the darkness to the rocks below.

Chapter Twenty-Three

#4263   Handmade by a native Maine craftsman, this earthenware jam pot is decorated with a charming blueberry design. Complete with wooden spoon. $18.

In Maine the winter sun is very bright, and on Friday morning it poured through the kitchen windows, turning the oak table into a golden pool. The three children were sitting with their backs to the window; the morning sun seemed to give them halos. Lucy was not impressed.

"Eat your oatmeal," she advised them.

Bill bounced into the room, humming a little tune, and poured himself a cup of coffee. He sat down at the table and took a spoonful of sugar, spilling some on the table.

"Do you know you always do that? Whenever you fix your coffee, you spill a little sugar. I'm always wiping up after you," Lucy said meanly.

"Gee, I didn't realize. I'm sorry," said Bill, raising an eyebrow and reaching for a corn muffin. He broke the muffin open with a knife, scattering crumbs on the table as he buttered it liberally. Then he compounded the mess by dropping a large blob of marmalade on the table.

"Look what you're doing!" said Lucy. "Haven't you ever heard of plates!" She picked up the muffin and plopped it on a plate, then carefully wiped off Bill's patch of table. "I have to do everything," she complained. "I work until one in the morning and then nobody helps. You just make messes and leave them for me to clean up."

"You're right," placated Bill. "I just wasn't thinking. We'll all try harder to be nice to Mommy, won't we, guys?"

The children nodded solemnly. They were wisely keeping silent this morning.

"Tell you what, Lucy. I'll leave a little late and drop Sara off at preschool for you. How's that?"

"It's no good," Lucy grumbled. "I have to go out anyway."

"Oh? I was thinking you might like to have a second cup of coffee and some time to yourself. Maybe read the paper? Have a relaxing bath? Take some Midol?"

"I have to take Marge to the hospital."

"Oh," said Bill in the tone of one who sees light dawning.

"Don't say it," Lucy warned. "You think I'm just irritable because I hate going to the hospital. That might be true, but you have to admit you're awfully messy."

"I know," admitted Bill. "But you usually don't mind."

"I do mind. You're going to have to try harder. I can't work and do all the housework, too."

"Of course not," Bill agreed. "I solemnly swear I will change my ways from now on. I will faithfully strive hence forward to be neat and clean, especially at certain times of the month." Then he added, "You don't have to see him, you know."

"I can't just drop Marge off and go shopping or something." Lucy was horrified.

"You could. You hate tubes and things, you know you do."

"Well, I'll just have to be brave. He's a friend."

"Marge would understand."

"I'd hate myself."

Bill nodded and picked up his plate and mug. He carried them over to the sink and rinsed them. Then he placed them carefully in the dishwasher.

"Do I pass inspection, Sergeant?"

Lucy laughed. "Get out of here."

An hour later she was waiting in her car outside Marge Culpepper's house. The engine was running, the radio was playing, and she was tapping the steering wheel nervously.

Marge climbed in beside her, squeezing her large self onto the small bucket seat.

"You can slide the seat back—it will give you more room."

"You can't be serious about this seat belt, Lucy. Nobody has a waist this small."

"Toby does." Lucy smiled. "He's a stick. How's Barney?"

"The same." Marge sighed.

"What do the doctors say?"

"Well, they say there's more brain activity. That means he could wake up pretty soon. But I don't know. He looks just the same. He's hooked up to all sorts of machines. It's been an awful long time."

"Less than two weeks," Lucy said.

"Seems like forever," said Marge. "I don't know how I'd have managed if it wasn't for Dave."

"Dave Davidson?" Lucy was surprised.

"Yeah," said Marge. "To tell the truth, I never really liked him a whole lot before. I guess I thought he was kinda cold, but he's really given me a lot of support. He drives me to the hospital, and talks with me about Barney. He even talks with the doctors for me."

"Hmm," said Lucy. "How's Eddie doing?"

"Pretty good." Marge sighed. "He spends a lot of time with his friends. I haven't brought him to the hospital. I didn't want him to see Barney like this."

"Is he all ready for the Pinewood Derby on Sunday? Did he get his car made?"

"He's been ready for a while. In fact, he and Barney finished up the car on Christmas Eve."

"He's way ahead of Toby. He's still got to paint his and put on the wheels. He wants to paint it the Cub Scout colors—blue and yellow."

Marge chuckled softly, then fell silent. Now and then Lucy tried to make conversation, but Marge didn't seem interested in chatting, so Lucy gave up. All too soon they arrived at the hospital. Together they walked through the automatic doors and down the long maze of hallways to the intensive care unit.

"Do you want some time alone with him?" asked Lucy.

"No. Actually, I'm supposed to meet Dave in a few minutes. You go on in. He always enjoyed your company. I'll be over at the chapel."

Standing alone outside the door, Lucy wondered what Marge meant. Surely she didn't think that Barney . . . that she and Barney were more than friends, did she? But Marge had always been completely straightforward, never one for double entendres, Lucy thought to herself, and pushed open the door.

Barney's room was bright with sunlight and full of flower arrangements; a young nurse was bustling around straightening the sheets and checking the indicators on the machines that flanked the bed. All of which served to distract Lucy—for a few minutes at least—from the figure lying there. When she finally did look at Barney, she was startled to see that his eyes were wide open. Unseeing, it seemed, but wide open.

"His eyes are open," said Lucy.

"That's right," said the nurse. "He opened them yesterday. He's also been moving his arms and legs."

"Is that normal?" asked Lucy.

"Oh, yes. Actually, they're signs of progress. He's coming closer to consciousness. One of these days someone will walk through the door and he'll say 'Hi' just as if he'd never been unconscious."

"Really?" asked Lucy.

"Really." The nurse smiled. "Isn't that right, Barney? There's more going on in that coconut of yours than people realize, isn't that so?" She spoke to Barney, looking directly into his eyes.

"Can he hear you?" Lucy was doubtful.

"We think so," said the nurse. "People who come out of comas tell us that there's a long period during which they can see and hear others but can't speak themselves. He's making excellent progress, and the doctors think he'll begin speaking any day now. I'm just going to put the radio on, and then, I'll get out of here. If you need anything, ring the call button."

"Okay," said Lucy, taking off her coat and sitting on the orange plastic chair the hospital provided for visitors.

"So, you can hear me, Barney. At least I hope you can. Well, I don't know where to begin."

She looked cautiously at Barney's face but found his open eyes unnerving. A tube snaked out of his nose, an electrode seemed to be glued to a shaved patch on his skull, and an IV machine blinked at the head of his bed. A bag of yellow fluid hung from the bed rail; Barney had been catheterized. Lucy immediately averted her gaze, turning back to his face.

"Poor Barney, this is a hell of a mess. They say you're doing real well, though. Poor Marge is so worried about you, and Eddie, too. He's a good kid, Barney, and he really misses you.

"Oh, shit. You know all this stuff. I know you're working hard to get well as fast as you can."

Unable to sit any longer, Lucy got to her feet and paced back and forth between the window and the door. "I've been getting some phone calls lately, Barney. The mail-order murderers all called." She couldn't keep from smiling.

"Boy, was that a stupid scheme." Her face got red as she remembered the phone calls, and she looked at Barney to see if there was a response. But he seemed the same as before.

"If I'd been interested in weird sex, those guys were more than willing," she continued. "But I don't think any of them killed Sam Miller. Only one of them seemed like a real professional killer." She shrugged. "I guess it was a silly idea.

"Barney . . ." Her voice rose. "If you could just tell me

what happened the night of the accident, it would be an awful big help. What made you swerve? A gunshot? A bright light? I have an idea," she said, dropping her voice and leaning closer to him.

She looked up, startled, as the door opened and a tired-looking Marge entered the room, along with Dave Davidson. The three of them stood awkwardly together in the small room.

Lucy smiled. "Hi, Dave."

He nodded but didn't speak to her, and Lucy thought briefly of Mr. Shay, the minister of the church she had attended as a child. Mr. Shay had been a round, jolly man who made everyone feel at ease. Dave Davidson was tall and thin, and he had a permanent slouch. Through years of counseling sessions he'd developed the habit of helpful listening and rarely initiated a conversation himself. Lucy had no doubt that this technique was useful in helping troubled souls focus on their problems, but it did little to smooth the course of social exchange, especially in uncomfortable situations in places such as hospital rooms or even in the vestibule after church services. Dave's attentive gaze always reduced Lucy to profound speechlessness, and as he himself did little but proffer his limp white hand, Lucy routinely scooted past him after church on Sundays.

As she stood there today she felt the familiar urge to flee. But first she had to tell Marge the good news.

"Marge, look! Barney has opened his eyes. The nurse says one of these days he'll just start talking as if nothing happened. Isn't that great?"

Marge and Dave didn't react with the joy she had expected. In fact, they seemed to be waiting for her to leave. Lucy was only too happy to oblige.

"I think I'll get some coffee. You can find me in the coffee shop whenever you're ready."

"Thanks, Lucy."

"See you downstairs," Lucy said as the door swung shut. But she couldn't help wondering why Marge wasn't as overjoyed about Barney as she was.

Chapter Twenty-Four

#1005 Tater Chips are made from native Katahdin potatoes grown in Maine. Carefully sliced and kettle-cooked in 100% soybean oil, these chips are favorites everywhere. Three pounds in a decorative tin, $5.99.

Lucy stood for a moment looking at the door that had just been closed so firmly; then she shrugged and began walking down the corridor to the elevator.

The snack bar was bright and cheery; it was staffed by volunteers, mostly retirees, who enjoyed playing waitress one or two mornings a month. The food was delicious and reasonably priced. Lucy treated herself to an egg salad sandwich, something she loved and rarely bothered to make. Taking her tray, she sat down at a table in the corner and ripped open the little bag of potato chips that came with her sandwich. From her table she had a clear view of the hospital lobby and as she ate, she enjoyed watching the passing parade.

She wasn't surprised when she saw Ted Stillings come

into the snack bar. He checked in frequently at the hospital for the "Hospital News" column in *The Pennysaver.* Seeing her wave, he came over to her table, carrying his roast beef sandwich and chocolate shake.

"Hi, Lucy. You here to see Barney?"

"It was my turn to bring Marge." She brightened. "The doctors say he's making excellent progress."

"That's great news." His long, solemn face lit up in a big smile and he scratched his crew cut thoughtfully. "That accident of his is driving the cops crazy. They've gone over that cruiser with a microscope, but they can't find any sign of tampering or mechanical failure. They just can't believe Barney would go over the cliff there by accident, he knew the road too well."

"Black ice?"

"He would have allowed for it and known what to do. He'd gone to all the special cop driving classes. They all say he was a terrific driver." Ted leaned forward and lowered his voice. "Lucy, do you think he might have tried to kill himself?"

"No, not Barney. On Christmas night? You can't be serious!" Lucy exclaimed.

"It's a possibility," insisted Ted. "People do commit suicide, you know." He took a big bite of pickle. "It'd be a hell of a story. I could use a hot story right now."

"I thought Sam Miller's murder was a big story for you."

"It was. My original article got picked up by *The Boston Globe* and *The New York Times.*" Ted offered this news shyly, much as Toby might show her a paper his teacher had marked "A."

"That's terrific! Congratulations!" Lucy was genuinely excited for Ted.

"It was great," said Ted. "I thought it would be a nice opportunity for me. I love Tinker's Cove and all, but I'm a little tired of small-town news. All those meetings. Last night I was at the school committee until midnight. They couldn't decide if they should cut the late bus or not. They debated for hours. I can't help wondering if I'd like a big-city paper more. I was hoping the Sam Miller story would develop into something." He shrugged. "But it never did. Nobody knows who killed Sam Miller, or why."

"I think I do," said Lucy. "And I think the same person tried to kill Barney." She sat back and waited to see his reaction.

Ted was skeptical. "Tell me more."

"Well, the person I'm thinking of had motive, means, and opportunity. Isn't that what a suspect has to have? My suspect has all three."

"Go on."

"This person is very ambitious. He comes from a very poor background, but he educated himself and got a good job at Country Cousins. I think he realized he'd gotten as far as he was going to go as long as Sam Miller was in charge. Appearances counted a lot with Sam—just look at his wife and his car—and he'd never let this man crack the inner circle. On the other hand, the guy I suspect is good buddies with Tom Miller. His chances are much better with Sam gone."

Ted smiled. "What about means?"

"A piece of hose? That's not hard to come by. And this man does have a gun—I checked. He could have fired a shot and startled Barney so he went over the cliff. I think the way these crimes were done, kind of at arm's length, goes along with this guy's personality."

"I'm beginning to think you might be on to something."

"And he had lots of opportunity at Country Cousins. He saw Sam all the time. And he doesn't have a family, at least not a family that would miss him if he was out Christmas night."

"You're talking about George Higham," said Ted, putting down his chocolate shake.

"You think he did it, too." Lucy was excited.

Ted shook his head. "George was one of the first suspects. The police investigated him thoroughly. They decided he couldn't have done it."

"Why?" Lucy demanded.

"I forget exactly," said Ted. "I think he was someplace else and could prove it."

"That doesn't prove a thing," insisted Lucy. "He probably arranged an alibi. I'm surprised Horowitz fell for it."

"Horowitz is a pro," Ted reminded her. "He knows what he's doing."

"If I could find some link between George and Barney, if I could show that Barney was so dangerous to George that he had to kill him, they'd have to investigate George again, wouldn't they?"

"Hang on a minute, Mrs. Stone. This is real life. You have a husband and kids. If he did kill Sam and tried to kill Barney, he's very dangerous. You'd better mind your own business."

"You sound just like Bill."

Ted chuckled. "It goes with the territory. The worst thing about getting older is that I sound just like my father. It hit me one day. I was telling Adam to take out the garbage and I suddenly realized I'd had the exact same conversation—from the other side—thirty years ago. He stood and picked up his tray. "I've gotta go. Paper goes to press this afternoon and I wouldn't want to leave out Mrs. Reilly's gall bladder operation."

"Last week, *The Times . . .*" sympathized Lucy.

"This week the hospital news," Ted finished for her. "Don't remind me." He paused. "You know, Lucy, I think I will stop by the barracks and have a word with Horowitz. It might be worth taking another look at George."

"Really?" Lucy brightened.

"You never know. If you're right, it'd be a hell of a story. Say hi to Bill for me."

Lucy watched Ted cross the lobby and disappear through the doors. A few minutes later Dave Davidson appeared, alone. Lucy's eyes followed him as he paused for a moment and felt his hair with tentative fingers. Other people ran their hands through their hair, they tossed their heads, they tucked a lock of hair behind an ear, thought Lucy, but Dave Davidson explored his. Evidently reassured, he continued on his way to the parking lot. A few minutes later a flustered-looking Marge Culpepper appeared. Lucy waved to her and was horrified to see Marge burst into tears.

Chapter Twenty-Five

*#5109 Fine Irish linen handkerchiefs are appreci-
ated by those who still value quality. With hand-
crocheted lace trim and blue forget-me-not
embroidery. Set of two. $10.*

"Gosh, Marge," said Lucy, taking her by the elbow
and leading her to a seat in the lobby, "I don't
usually have this effect on people. Loved by one and all,
that's me, or at least it was before this morning."

"Oh, Lucy," moaned Marge, dissolving into a fresh
torrent of tears.

Lucy patted her hand, supplied her with a clean hanky,
and murmured, "There, there," until Marge's shoulders
gave a little convulsive shudder and she wiped her eyes
for the last time.

"I'm sorry," she said, smiling apologetically. "It's just
that I don't know what to think anymore."

"What do you mean?" asked Lucy. "Barney's getting
better. All you have to do is wait and hope. You'll have
him back any day now. That's what the nurse said."

"But Dave says it's not right to let him suffer."

"What?"

"Dave says if Barney had made a living will, he wouldn't have to go through this. He says it's inhumane. No one should be hooked up to machines, to suffer endlessly, when there's no hope."

"Maybe he's right when there's no hope. But there's plenty of room for hope in Barney's case," Lucy said with what she hoped was cheerful encouragement.

"Dave says there isn't. He's seen this before, he says. It's just a cruel hoax that the doctors and hospitals play on families so they can collect weeks and weeks' worth of medical insurance."

"Dave said that? When?" questioned Lucy.

"All the time," Marge wailed. "He's been wonderful to me. I don't know what I would have done without him. He's spent so much time with me and Barney. But now he says it's time to say good-bye."

"He's going away?" Lucy was puzzled.

"Lucy, I can't talk about this here." She indicated the busy lobby. "Let's talk in the car."

Back in the car, heading for Tinker's Cove, Marge sat quietly and chewed her lip. Lucy was determined to get her talking again. She was sure Marge had discovered the key to Barney's accident.

"Marge, what did Barney do before the accident? Did he call anyone or go anywhere? Do you remember anything that would help?"

"No," Marge remembered. "It was Christmas. We opened presents, we ate turkey. That's all. It was just a regular family Christmas." Marge's voice began to tremble, so Lucy changed the subject.

"But Dave's been real helpful?" Lucy looked over her shoulder, checked the mirrors, and accelerated onto the highway.

"He's been real nice, and I feel like I owe him a lot. Whenever I turn around he's there, ready to help me. He says he'll help me do it."

"Do what?" Lucy asked.

Marge looked around her. She took a deep breath and lowered her voice. "He says that I must summon all my courage and—" She stopped, staring down at her hands in her lap.

"And what?" Lucy asked impatiently.

"And pull the plug," whispered Marge.

"He wants you to pull the plug on Barney?" Lucy couldn't believe it. She braked and pulled the car off the road, bouncing on the rough surface. As soon as the car stopped, she turned and faced Marge. "He wants you to pull the plug on Barney?" she demanded.

"He says it's the only thing to do. That Barney is suffering. That his spirit wants to be free. That people in his condition want to die. They're not afraid. They see a long dark tunnel with a light at the other end. A warm radiant light of shining peace. Barney wants to get there more than anything, and we're holding him back. He says I must let him go. I must set him free."

Marge's voice droned on. This was a lesson she had heard so often, she knew it by heart. That she didn't accept it as true was clear from her tone, but she was also obviously afraid of disobeying her teacher.

"Nonsense, Marge. Barney's not your pet pigeon. He's a man who loves you and Eddie and wants to get back to you as soon as he can. He's coming back, Marge. I'm not kidding. I saw his legs twitch like crazy when the radio said the Celtics lost at the Garden last night."

Marge laughed weakly. "Oh, Lucy, you do have a knack for making people feel better. I'm so glad you were here, or I might have done something terrible."

"I don't think so," said Lucy.

"Oh, yes. I was really weakening. I almost did it today."

"Well," Lucy said, "you might have unhooked something, but it wouldn't have killed Barney. Those machines are just monitors. He's breathing on his own. I guess Dave didn't realize that."

"You mean—even if I had pulled the plug, it wouldn't have mattered?" asked Marge.

"Well, it might have set off some alarms, but it wouldn't have killed him," Lucy reassured her. "My father was on a life-support machine, so I know. Now, we've got to get back home. I'm going to have to pay extra at Sara's preschool as it is." She paused, choosing her next words carefully. "Marge, if I were you, I'd try to avoid Dave for a few days. He's probably sincere and all, but Barney's getting better. Believe me."

"I don't know who to believe anymore. It's been so long, Lucy. I just want Barney back. I miss him so much."

Lucy glanced anxiously at Marge but was relieved to see she wasn't crying, just sitting quietly. "So do I. We'll really miss him at the Pinewood Derby. Last year he did such a good job as announcer."

"He really hammed it up, didn't he?" Marge recalled, smiling.

"The boys loved it. He made it sound just like a real car race. What's Eddie's car like?"

"It's pretty sharp. Bright red, with a black bumper. Some idea of his. Last year his car broke and he didn't get to finish. He thinks the bumper will help."

"That is a good idea. What did he use? Foam?"

"No, a little strip of rubber. Barney got it from Dave's wife, Carol. He remembered she used some on that sculpture she put in the front yard."

Lucy laughed. "That thing is ugly, isn't it?"

"Sure is. And she gets a lot of money for those things," said Marge.

"When they sell," observed Lucy. "Who would buy one?"

"Marcia Miller did," Marge said. "Dave said she's a real fan of her work, and got her placed in a gallery in Boston. I guess they're friends."

Lucy pulled up in front of Marge's house and waited patiently as Marge hauled herself out of the little car.

"Thanks, Lucy. Thanks for everything."

Lucy gave her a cheery good-bye wave, then checked her watch and sighed. It was already one thirty, and the meter was running over at Kiddie Kollege. She shifted the car into gear and turned onto Main Street, the most direct route to the preschool. As she passed the church and the rectory beside it, she glanced at the piece of black sculpture Carol had placed on the front lawn. Impulsively she pulled the car over and stopped in front of it.

The sculpture was made of automobile parts—at least Lucy assumed the odd metal forms came from automobiles. As she studied the sculpture, she could make out two human forms: a muffler and a transmission made one, a piece of twisted fender the other. The whole piece had been spray-painted black, and a length of sturdy black hose wound the two figures together. Lucy decided she'd better take a closer look at the hose.

She turned off the ignition and climbed out of the car. She slipped as she scrambled up the steep, grass-covered bank, and as she got back to her feet the sculpture loomed over her. The piece generated a sense of pain and anguish that made Lucy uneasy. She paused to read the handwritten label that had been placed at the base of the statue and then jumped back as if she'd been bitten. "Bondage of Love," it read.

Lucy leaned forward to examine the hose, reaching out and wrapping her fingers around it. It felt just as she expected it would. For now there was no doubt that she had tried to pull a piece of the exact same hose from Sam Miller's car window.

Carol worked in an old barn behind the house, and that's where Lucy went, her ankle smarting. She didn't want to go, but she had to talk to Carol. Things were beginning to add up, and she didn't like the way her thoughts were headed.

The big barn door was unlatched and yielded to her hand with a noisy scrape. She stepped into the dark and waited a moment for her eyes to adjust. She looked toward the loft window, and there she saw Carol's limp body, swaying slightly, silhouetted by the bright afternoon sun.

Chapter Twenty-Six

#3335 Magnetic slate is a copy of the slates used by students in one-room schoolhouses but can be affixed to the refrigerator and used as a note board. A useful memory jog. $12.

"This is getting to be a bad habit, Mrs. Stone," said Lieutenant Horowitz as he sat down opposite Lucy at Marge's kitchen table. He made an odd snorting noise; he was obviously enjoying his little joke.

Lucy narrowed her eyes at him and took another swallow of the sweet tea Marge had brewed for her. After making her gruesome discovery at the rectory, Lucy had driven right back to Marge's house and called the state police. Horowitz and a team of investigators had arrived in a matter of minutes. Now the team was already at work gathering evidence at Carol's studio, and Horowtz was questioning Lucy.

"Now, Mrs. Stone, why did you stop at the rectory?" Horowitz had his notebook out and was ready to record her answer.

"Because of the hose. The hose on the sculpture. No. Wait. Because Marge told me that Dave was trying to get her to pull the plug on Barney. That didn't seem right to me, and then she said Barney got a piece of hose from Carol and I wondered if it was the same hose used to kill Sam Miller. And it was." Lucy leaned her head on her hand. She'd never felt so tired.

"Davidson wanted Mrs. Culpepper to pull the plug on Barney?" asked Horowitz.

"That's right," said Marge. "He's been after me for weeks. Keeps telling me it's cruel to keep him alive when there's no hope. I believed him, too, until Lucy told me Barney's getting better. The nurse told her. Dave had talked to the doctors for me. . . ." Marge's voice trailed off. "I thought he was helping me," she whispered.

"What about the hose, Mrs. Stone?"

Lucy snapped to attention. "The hose. I stopped to look at the sculpture, and there was some black hose on it. I wondered if it was the same hose that was used to kill Sam Miller. It was."

"So Dave Davidson killed Sam Miller?"

"I think so," Lucy said.

"And tried to kill Barney," added Marge.

"Why?" said Horowitz.

"It's all in the sculpture." Lucy sighed. "Dave was having an affair with Marcia Miller."

Horowitz and Marge exchanged a glance.

"Run that by me again," said Horowitz.

"Just look at the sculpture. It's called *Bondage of Love,*" explained Lucy. "It's two figures, Dave and Marcia, in an embrace. They're bound together by the hose, by the fact that Dave killed Sam. Jealousy, hate, it's all there," Lucy said matter-of-factly. "It's a public proclamation by Carol that Dave was having an affair with Marcia Miller and killed her husband. He'll never be free of her. That's why Carol hanged herself."

"You got that out of the sculpture?" Horowitz was skeptical.

"Why else would she use all those auto parts?" asked Lucy. "Cars were Davidson's weapon of choice."

"Barney saw them together," Marge said flatly. "He didn't think there was any hanky-panky, of course. He wouldn't, with Dave being a minister and all. But he did say to me once that Marcia Miller must be a lot more religious than anyone realized because he saw her leaving the church so often on Tuesday afternoons." Her face was a study in disbelief.

"Tuesday afternoons?" exclaimed Lucy. "In the church?"

Marge nodded. Horowitz pursed his lips and made a note. Lucy stifled an ever-growing urge to laugh hysterically.

"They sure fooled me," confessed Marge. "They fooled everybody. Not an easy thing to do in a town like this."

"They didn't fool Sam," said Lucy. "If he hadn't been so smart, he'd probably still be alive."

"The problem is that all this is hearsay and rumor. I can't see that sculpture convincing a jury," observed Horowitz. "In order to get a conviction these days you've got to have everything on videotape. Whispering in your ear isn't a crime, Mrs. Culpepper."

"He's there with Barney!" remembered Marge. "I left him there at the hospital! He's alone with Barney—I've got to get back there!"

"Maybe you can get him on tape after all," said Lucy dryly.

Chapter Twenty-Seven

#8795 Havahart trap is the humane way to dispose of nuisance animals such as skunks and raccoons. The trap confines but does not harm the animal so it can be released back to its proper environment. 100% rustproof steel construction. Small, $40; medium, $55; large, $75.

"Lucy, I'm so scared I don't think I can stand it. I'm afraid I'll pee in my pants," Marge said with a moan, clutching Lucy's hand. The two were in the backseat of a cruiser, speeding down the highway to the hospital in Portland.

"I know," agreed Lucy. "He's a killer. He killed Sam Miller, and he almost succeeded in killing Barney. I hope we're in time."

"How am I going to pretend I don't know he's guilty? I keep thinking about Carol—he doesn't even know his own wife is dead."

"Just try to forget. Make believe it's yesterday. Dave's

just the minister of your church, trying to help you make a difficult decision."

"I don't think I can. My stomach's killing me. I think I have to throw up."

"Here, suck on this," said Lucy, giving her a broken candy cane she found in the bottom of her purse. "You need a little sugar." Seeing Marge so shaken and white-faced, she continued, "You've got to pull yourself together, Marge. This is the only way that they can make a case against Davidson. Barney won't be safe until he's put away."

"I know. I guess I've always been a little bit afraid of him," admitted Marge. "The minister, you know, like a teacher but with God backing him up."

"I don't think God's on his side anymore. Besides, I'll be there for you. And Horowitz, and probably half the state police. All you have to do is be yourself."

Marge took a little quivering breath and squared her shoulders as they pulled up in front of the hospital. A trooper helped them out of the car, and they hurried through the door and into the lobby. When the elevator doors opened a nurse met them and led them to the room next to Barney's, where Horowitz was waiting for them.

"Okay," he told Marge. "Everything is set. There's a video camera in the room, and a tape recorder, too. You'll be under observation at all times. My men"—he indicated two state troopers in the room—"are only a few steps away. You're absolutely safe, and so is your husband. All you have to do is make Davidson incriminate himself. He has to tell you to kill him, or he has to take some action that would kill Barney. Do you understand?"

Marge's eyes were enormous, her mouth tiny as she nodded.

"Okay. You go on in the room and wait for him. We'll have him paged."

"Good luck." Lucy smiled and patted her hand. "You can do it."

Lucy watched as Marge left the room, then reappeared on the video screen. Horowitz and the two uniformed state police officers stood behind her, also watching the screen.

"I have two men dressed as orderlies in the hall," said Horowitz. Just then, they heard the public address system call for Reverend Davidson to go to room 203, and Horowitz said, "Now we just have to wait."

Cool and self-contained as always, she stood watching the video monitor. To Lucy the scene on the screen looked like something from a daytime soap opera. There was the hospital room filled with flowers and cards. There was the bed surrounded with blinking and beeping pieces of machinery. There was the patient lying still, unconscious.

They watched as Marge settled herself on a chair next to Barney's side. They saw her take his hand in her own and stroke it gently. They heard her soft words as she greeted him. Still unconscious, he showed no reaction to her presence but lay peaceful and still, defenseless as a napping baby.

Marge looked up sharply, and suddenly Dave Davidson appeared on the screen. She stood up awkwardly as he embraced her.

Watching the screen, Lucy shivered. How could evil be so self-effacing and mild-mannered? She preferred the directness of Cool Professional to the hypocritical helpfulness of the minister. The men around her tensed. One officer was nervously fingering a walkie-talkie, and the other stood by the door with his pistol in his hand. They were ready to spring the trap.

"This is a sad business," said Davidson, withdrawing from the embrace and patting Marge mechanically on the back.

"Well . . ." Marge sighed. "His condition never changes. I'm afraid this will go on for years."

"I've seen that happen. It's a terrible thing to watch." The minister shook his head mournfully. "Now he's still robust and peaceful, but not for much longer, I'm afraid. As the weeks and months go on, he'll gradually deteriorate. You'll see him getting thinner and thinner. He'll curl up into a fetal position. His hair will become dry, his skin coarse and white. His eyes and cheeks will sink and he'll look like a corpse, but they won't let him go. The doctors, these scientists"—he spat out the word—"will keep him alive no matter how hopeless his condition. It's a living hell. You will suffer watching him, and make no mistake, he will be suffering, too. His spirit is yearning to be set free."

Even on the screen Lucy could sense the intensity and magnetism of Davidson's appeal.

"He's not afraid," crooned the minister in Marge's ear. "He wants to be released, to climb a sunbeam and join the angels."

Marge's eyes shone with faith and desire. "What must I do?" she asked.

"It won't be hard," he assured her. "All you have to do is unplug the equipment." He dismissed the battery of machinery with a wave of his hand. "Then Barney's soul will slip away. He will find the peace that passeth all understanding."

"Will you help me?" asked Marge. "Will you stay with me?"

Lucy saw a flicker of hesitation cross Davidson's face, but then he murmured, "Of course."

"Thank you," whispered Marge. "I think I'm ready. Should we do it now?"

"Yes," said Davidson, taking her hand and leading her to the outlet behind the bed. Lucy stood transfixed as she saw Dave push Marge's hand toward the plug.

"Just unplug it," Davidson whispered. "Nothing simpler."

He placed Marge's hand on the plug and wrapped her fingers around it. Covering her hand with his, he pulled. The machinery sighed, and suddenly the room was deathly quiet.

Lucy realized she was holding her breath and gasped for air. Horowitz hissed, "Go." The officer with the walkie-talkie spoke into it. "Now. Grab him."

They rushed from the room, and Lucy watched as they reappeared on the screen. "David Davidson, I am arresting you for the attempted murder of Barney Culpepper. You have the right to remain silent . . ."

Lucy went to the doorway and watched as they led Davidson, handcuffed, down the long hospital corridor. Entering Barney's room, she saw that Marge had already replaced the plug. She put her arm around her shoulders and stood with her, watching Barney's chest rise and fall.

"It doesn't seem to have done him any harm, but I think I'll call the nurse just to be sure," said Marge. She had just bent to ring the call button when Barney's eyes flew open. She jumped back in shock.

"What's going on here?" Barney demanded.

Chapter Twenty-Eight

#3076 Surprise mugs. These white stoneware mugs have a surprise on the bottom for good little boys and girls who finish their cocoa. Specify frog or kitten. $6.50.

"Of course they were having an affair," said Emily Miller, her white head bobbing and her blue eyes twinkling over her teacup.

Her ancient friend, Miss Tilley, nodded. "I said so all along, if you remember."

"It was certainly a surprise to me," Lucy confessed.

Once again she was having tea with the two old friends, and this time she was dressed for the occasion. She was wearing a brand-new blouse and sweater she'd bought at the Country Cousins January overstock sale. Her ankles were clamped together neatly, a linen napkin was perched on her knees, and she was using her very best manners. In fact, she felt rather like a child at an adult party, a sensation she was doing her best to overcome.

"No, I didn't know, and I don't think most other people did, either. I was sure George Higham did it," she admitted, taking a sip of tea and nearly choking on its odd, smoky flavor.

"It's Lapsang souchong, dear. Perhaps you'd like something milder?" inquired Miss Tilley.

"Oh, no, this is fine. In fact, I rather like it," Lucy insisted bravely.

The two old women exchanged a glance.

"I've always thought you had possibilities, Lucy Stone. You always chose such eclectic reading material," remembered Miss Tilley. "Now, do tell us all about that dreadful afternoon." She settled back in her chair and took a sip of tea, rolling it over her tongue and savoring it.

"I'd taken Marge to the hospital to visit Barney," Lucy began. "She told me that Dave Davidson was encouraging her to pull the plug on Barney. He kept telling her that Barney would never recover, and that the kindest thing to do would be to end it. It made me suspicious because the nurses told me Barney was getting better."

"How is he doing, Lucy?" asked Mrs. Miller.

"He's doing wonderfully. Every day he's stronger and remembers more. I will never forget how he came out of that coma. One minute he was unconscious, and the next he was wide awake, demanding to know what was going on. It was amazing."

"Of course, if the Reverend Mr. Davidson had had his way, it would have been very different," Miss Tilley added tartly. "Such a wicked man."

"I always tried to avoid him after church," confessed Lucy. "I never liked him. He made me uneasy. Of course, I never thought he was a murderer until I saw the sculpture."

"Carol's sculpture? That did surprise me," said Miss Tilley.

"The sculpture? I never did like her work, either," observed Lucy.

"No, no, dear. Not the sculpture. So original. No, the way she hanged herself. I would have expected her to react differently. I rather liked her, you see. She didn't behave the way a minister's wife is supposed to. She never went to church; she had a career of her own. I admired that. I was very disappointed to hear she'd killed herself."

"True grit," commented Mrs. Miller. "She didn't have it."

Mrs. Miller certainly had grit, thought Lucy. She would never let anyone see her grieve for her son.

Grief, like love, was private.

"Well, it must have been pretty devastating," said Lucy. "First her husband had an affair with Marcia; that would be awful for any woman. And then she figured out he'd murdered Sam, and almost murdered Barney. It would be pretty hard to take, especially if she loved him."

"Young people are so romantic," Mrs. Miller said.

"I wouldn't call this romantic," said Miss Tilley. "Not in the true sense of the word. I would call it maudlin."

The other women nodded automatically. After forty years as a librarian no one argued with her about facts. Or definitions.

"What about the sculpture? How did it make you realize Davidson was the murderer?" asked Miss Tilley.

"The black hose. Carol had wrapped it all around the sculpture. It was the same hose Dave used on Sam's car." Lucy dropped her voice. She hated talking about Sam with his mother.

"A public declaration of his guilt?" Mrs. Miller asked

a little shakily. Lucy was reminded again that this must still be hard on her.

"I think so," she said. "Barney had stumbled on the hose when he mentioned to Carol that he needed something for Eddie's car. The Cub Scouts are having the Pinewood Derby this month—you know, they race little wooden cars that they make themselves. Well, Barney was looking for some scraps of rubber to make a bumper for Eddie's car. Knowing Carol was a sculptor and apt to have bits and pieces around, he asked her if she had something he could use. When she gave him a bit of black rubber hose, he recognized it as the same hose that was used on Sam Miller's car. Barney was going to take it to the police lab the day after Christmas, but he never made it. Dave must have realized Barney had the evidence that could convict him, and decided he had to get rid of him. He parked out near the point, and when Barney came round the bend he turned on his high beams. Barney swerved right off the road."

The two women clicked their tongues. "I wonder how many of the Ten Commandments he actually broke," Miss Tilley mused. "Definitely the seventh, and the sixth, of course."

"He was covetous, and he lied," Lucy added.

"And Marcia certainly became more important than God to him. She had that effect on a lot of men, including Sam, I'm sorry to say." Mrs. Miller helped herself to another piece of banana bread.

"He did remember the Sabbath," said Miss Tilley, determined to be fair. "And I must say I never heard him swear. That's more than many Christians can claim."

Lucy and Mrs. Miller chuckled.

"I don't know what he can expect in the next life, but I

hope he will be punished in this life." Mrs. Miller smoothed the napkin in her lap.

"Oh, yes. Detective Horowitz told me they have an airtight case. Carol left a detailed suicide note, and of course they videotaped him trying to convince Marge to pull the plug."

"And you saw the police arrest him?" asked Miss Tilley.

"How did he react? When he knew the game was up?" Mrs. Miller sounded serious.

"He seemed angry," Lucy reported. "He didn't say anything, but he looked furious."

"I hope he's punished," said Mrs. Miller. "I hope he doesn't get off on some sort of technicality."

"I don't think he will," said Lucy. "What about Marcia? And your grandson? Will they come back?"

"I don't think so. She's living in Paris. She writes to me, you know. I think Tinker's Cove was a bit tame for her. I may visit them this summer."

Lucy smiled at her. The resilience of this old woman amazed her. She reached for a piece of banana bread, chewed it thoughtfully, and, sipping her tea, she observed the two old women. Miss Tilley with her large, strong features covered with a tough netting of wrinkles, her long white hair drawn up in a bun; and Mrs. Miller, with a round face just like a dried apple-head doll and her carefully curled and blued hair. In the life of Tinker's Cove they were forces to be reckoned with. As ardent conservationists they had been instrumental in creating the Tinker's Cove Conservation Trust. Miss Tilley had spearheaded the local literacy program, and she was a frequent contributor to the letters column in *The Penny-saver*. Together the two women acted as a collective conscience for the town. They were vital, strong women who were interested in the world around them.

Lucy thought of funerals she had attended where all the women of her generation were in tears, their faces bleak and uncomprehending, their knuckles white as they clutched crumpled tissues. Death was unbelievable to them, an assault on everything they worked so hard to maintain.

The older women, Lucy had noticed, never seemed as distressed. They rarely cried but sat silently through the service, gathering in small groups afterward to comfort each other. When it was time to speak with the bereaved they knew what to say, while Lucy and her friends could only babble clichés such as "Call me if there's anything I can do."

She had always admired the acceptance and assurance of these women; she had hoped that in time she would grow to be like them.

She thought of her mother. Her mother had never accepted death the way these women did. Although she was in her sixties, the death of her husband had left her as raw and hurt as if she were a young bride. Her mother had never developed the self-protective detachment so many older women grew.

Lucy wondered what life held for her and how she would cope. Would she maintain her naiveté and her vulnerability, as her mother had, or would she turn into someone as wise but as cynical as Miss Tilley?

"We've been keeping an eye on you, Lucy." Miss Tilley interrupted her thoughts.

"Yes, you seem . . . well, interesting," agreed Mrs. Miller. "You're not afraid to get involved."

"My husband wouldn't agree with you," observed Lucy. "He's always telling me to mind my own business."

"Oh, husbands," Miss Tilley said dismissively.

"I'm afraid I'd better be getting back to mine. He's watching the kids today." She stood up reluctantly and said her good-byes. But as she drove home she kept thinking of the two old women.

Pulling into the driveway, Lucy was surprised not to see any sign of the kids. Maybe Bill had gotten a video for them, but she thought they really ought to be outside on such a nice day. As she opened the front door, she didn't hear the TV, and she was surprised when Bill met her in the kitchen.

"Where are the kids?" she asked him.

"Your friend Sue took them over to the new playground in Gardner."

"She did? Why'd she do that?"

"Well, she's your best friend, and she thought you might enjoy a little time alone with your husband."

"I don't suppose you had anything to do with that," Lucy said, smiling.

"I might have," said Bill, slipping his arms around her waist.

Lucy raised her face to his and was rewarded with a long, loving kiss.

"Oh, Bill," said Lucy. "If I let you have your way with me, will you respect me afterwards?"

"I hope not," said Bill, leading her upstairs.

CHRISTMAS
COOKIE MURDER

Chapter One

28 days 'til Xmas

"I'd rather die."

Judging by her determined expression and her firm tone of voice, Lucy Stone was pretty sure that her best friend, Sue Finch, had made up her mind. Still, ever the optimist, she couldn't resist trying one last time.

"Oh, come on," pleaded Lucy. "It won't seem like Christmas without it."

"Nope." Sue shook her head and shoved a piece of overpriced lettuce around her plate with a fork. "No cookie exchange this year."

The two friends were having lunch at the Chandlery, the toney bistro in the Ropewalk, the newest mall in Tinker's Cove. The Ropewalk had once been exactly that, a nineteenth-century workshop complete with a long, narrow alley used for twisting hemp fibers into rope for the clipper ships that once sailed all over the globe from their home port in Tinker's Cove, Maine.

Long a ramshackle eyesore on the waterfront, it had recently been restored, and local craftsmen had moved in, creating what the developer called "an exciting retail adventure with a seafaring ambiance."

Today, the day after Thanksgiving, the Ropewalk was packed with Christmas shoppers and Lucy and Sue had had to wait thirty minutes for a table. When their salads finally came they were definitely on the skimpy side— the kitchen was obviously running low on supplies. The two friends hadn't minded; the demands of juggling homes and careers made it difficult for them to spend time together, and they were enjoying each other's company.

"It's not like it was, well, even a few years ago," said Sue. "Then we were all in the same boat. We all had little kids and plenty of time on our hands. People snapped up the invitations and brought wonderful cookies." A dreamy expression came over her face. "Remember Helen's baklava?"

"Do I ever," said Lucy, who had a round face and a shining cap of hair cut in a practical style. She was casually dressed, wearing a plaid shirt-jacket and a pair of well-worn jeans. "It was like biting into a little piece of heaven." She paused and sipped her coffee. "Whatever happened to her?"

"She moved away, to North Carolina, I think," said Sue, who provided an elegant contrast to her friend in her hand-knit designer sweater and tailored flannel slacks. "And that's exactly my point. A lot of the old regulars have moved away. And things have changed. Getting together to compare recipes and swap cookies isn't as appealing as it used to be."

"It is to me," said Lucy. "I've still got a family to feed, and they don't think it's Christmas without cookies. Lots of different kinds. I don't have time to bake five or six batches. And to be honest, I don't want to have that many cookies around the house." She bit her lip. "Too much temptation. Too many calories."

"I know," Sue said with a sigh. "With the exchange you just had to bake one double batch."

"But you ended up with twelve different kinds, a half dozen of each." Lucy started counting them off on her fingers. "Your pecan meltaways, my Santa's thumbprints, spritz, gingerbread men, Franny's Chinese-noodle cookies, shortbread, and Marge's little pink-and-white candy canes. . . ."

"Marge probably can't come this year," said Sue, with a sad shake of her head. "The lumpectomy wasn't enough, and they've started her on chemotherapy. She feels lousy."

"I hadn't heard," said Lucy, furrowing her brow. "That's too bad."

"I thought you newspaper reporters thrived on local gossip," teased Sue, referring to Lucy's part-time job writing for the weekly *Pennysaver*.

"Actually, I'm so busy covering historic commission hearings and stuff like that, I never have time to call my friends." She smiled at Sue and glanced around at the restaurant, which was festively decorated with artificial pine garlands, ribbons, and gold balls. "This is fun—we don't get together enough. So what else is new? Fill me in."

"Have you heard about Lee?"

"Lee Cummings? No. What?"

"Well," began Sue, leaning across the table toward Lucy, "she and Steve have separated."

"You're kidding." Lucy was astonished. Lee and her husband, dentist Steve Cummings, had seemed a rock-solid example. They went to church together every Sunday, and Steve had coached his daughter's T-ball team.

"No." Sue's eyebrows shot up. "Apparently Steve is finding marriage too confining. At least that's what Lee says."

"She tells you all this?"

"Oh, yes. And more. Every morning when she drops Hillary off at the center." Sue directed the town's day-care center, located in the basement of the recreation building. "It's all she can talk about. Steve did this. Steve did that. His lawyer says this. My lawyer says that. The latest is who's going to get the stove."

"They're arguing over the stove?"

"I think it's a Viking," explained Sue, with a knowing nod. "But that's just the beginning. They're also fighting over the books and the CDs and the china and the stupid jelly glasses with cartoon characters."

"So you think they're going to get a divorce?"

"It sure looks that way."

"And that's all she talks about?"

"Yeah. And if I have the cookie exchange, I'll have to invite her, and if she comes, she'll turn the whole evening into a group-therapy session. Trust me on this."

"I can see that's a problem," admitted Lucy, picking up the check. "Come on. Let's get out of here. When the going gets tough, the tough go shopping."

* * *

Leaving the restaurant and entering the shopping area, the two friends joined the throng that was flowing past the gaily decorated craftsmen's booths. It was crowded, but people were in good humor, aided by the Christmas carols playing on the sound system.

"Tra la la la la, la la la la!" warbled Lucy, unable to resist singing along. "Isn't it nice to hear the carols? They always take me back to my childhood."

"You'll be sick of them soon enough," grumbled Sue. "You know which one I hate? That one about the little drummer boy. Talk about insipid!"

"You're really having an attack of Grinchitis, aren't you?" asked Lucy, stepping into a booth filled with baskets of potpourri. "Look at these," she said, picking up a package of three padded hangers. "And they smell so good. Do you think Bill's mom would like them?"

"Sure."

"Are they enough? It's kind of skimpy for a Christmas present."

"Add some drawer paper, or sachets," suggested Sue, as a smiling salesclerk approached.

"They're handmade, and filled with our unique blend of potpourri," said the clerk, with an encouraging nod.

Lucy examined the price tag, and her eyes grew large.

"I don't know," she said, hesitating. "What if the scent clashes with her perfume?"

"You wouldn't want that," agreed Sue, who loved to shop but rarely paid full price, preferring to keep an eye out for sales. She could spot a markdown a mile away.

Lucy gave the clerk an apologetic little smile, and the two left the stall. In the walkway outside, Lucy grabbed Sue's arm.

"Did you see the price?" uttered Lucy. "Thirty-five dollars for three hangers. I can't afford that."

"You're not the only one," said Sue glumly. "I don't think this is going to be a very happy Christmas season. Money's too tight."

"Isn't it always this time of year?"

"This year's worse," said Sue, pausing to examine some handcrafted wooden picture frames. "I've never seen it so bad. I've already gotten a restraining order, and it's only Thanksgiving."

"Restraining order?"

"Yeah. The moms at the center get them when the dads and boyfriends start acting up. There's always one or two during the holidays, but I've never had one quite so early."

"But the economy's supposed to be booming."

"Not for some of the families using the day-care center. I keep hearing about the lobster quota."

"The state had to do that, or there won't be any lobsters left," said Lucy. "They have to protect the breeding population. I wrote a story about it for the paper."

"I know," agreed Sue, replacing the frame and moving on to the next booth. "But a lot of people in this town depend on lobsters for a living. They're really taking a hit."

"Hi, Franny!" exclaimed Lucy, waving to the woman in the next booth. "I didn't know you'd gone into business."

Franny Small, a fiftyish woman with tightly permed hair, beamed at them proudly from behind a display of jewelry.

"Well, you know, the hardware store finally closed—couldn't compete with that new Home Depot. I was cleaning out the place, and I didn't know what to do with all the bits and pieces—you know nuts and bolts and stuff like that—and then I had this idea to make jewelry. And well, here I am."

"This is hardware?" Lucy looked more closely at a pair of earrings.

"See—that's a hex nut. But these are my favorites— they're dragonflies made from wing nuts. The wings are copper screening."

"Look at that, Sue. Aren't they great?"

"They're wonderful," exclaimed Sue, "and only ten dollars. I'm going to buy a pair to put in Sidra's stocking."

Sidra was Sue's daughter, recently graduated from college and now working as an assistant producer at a TV station in New York.

"That's a good idea," said Lucy, thinking of her own teenage daughter. "I'll get a pair for Elizabeth. She'll love them."

"Do you want them gift-wrapped? I use the old brown paper and string from the store—it kind of completes the look."

"Sure," said Lucy. "Thanks."

"So, Sue, when is the cookie exchange?" asked Franny, as she tore a sheet of paper from the antique roller salvaged from the hardware store. "I want to be sure to mark my calendar."

Sue groaned and Lucy explained. "She says she isn't having it this year."

"That's too bad," said Franny, neatly folding the paper so she didn't have to use tape, and tying the whole thing together with a length of red-and-white string. "Why not?"

"It just didn't seem like such a good idea—I didn't

really know who to invite. So many of the old regulars have moved away, and Marge is sick, and . . ."

"Can't you invite some new people?" asked Franny brightly.

"Yeah, Sue," said Lucy, pulling out her wallet. "How about inviting some new people? You must know a lot of nice young moms from the day-care center."

"I'd love to make some new friends," said Franny, giving them their change and receipts. "I don't have much time for myself, what with making the jewelry and running the shop here. I've really been too busy to socialize. I've been looking forward to the cookie exchange for months."

"I knew this was coming," protested Sue. "New people! You don't understand. These young moms aren't like we were. They don't cook! They buy takeout and frozen stuff. Remember when I invited Krissy, the girl who owns that gym? She brought rice cakes! Somehow she didn't get the idea of a cookie exchange at all."

"They were chocolate chip rice cakes," said Lucy, grinning at the memory.

"Put yourself in their shoes," said Franny, earnestly. "It must be very hard to raise a family and keep a job—don't know how these young girls do it all."

"With a lot of help from me," muttered Sue. "It isn't just day care, you know. It's advice, and giving them a shoulder to cry on, and collecting toys and clothes and passing them on to the ones who need them."

"You do a fantastic job," said Lucy.

"You do," agreed Franny, turning to help another customer. "But I hope you won't give up the cookie exchange. I'd really miss it."

Lucy gave her a little wave, and they turned to investigate the pottery in the next booth. Lucy picked up a mug, running her fingers over the smooth shape. Then she looked at Sue, who was examining an apple-baker.

"There's no way around it. You have to have the cookie exchange. People are counting on you. It wouldn't be Christmas without it."

Sue's dark hair fell across her face at an angle, and Lucy couldn't see her expression. She hoped she hadn't been too persistent, that she hadn't pushed Sue too hard. She really valued their friendship and didn't want to jeopardize it. When Sue flicked the hair out of her eyes, Lucy was relieved to see that she was smiling.

"You're right, Lucy. It wouldn't be Christmas without the cookie exchange. But it doesn't have to be at my house. Why don't you be the hostess for a change?"

"Me?" Lucy's eyebrows shot up

"Yup." Sue pointed a perfectly manicured finger at Lucy. "You."

Chapter Two

16 days 'til Xmas

Sue had been right, thought Lucy, pushing open the kitchen door and surveying the mess. Agreeing to host the cookie exchange had been a big mistake. It was almost five o'clock, the guests were due at seven, and she hadn't had a chance to do a thing with the house.

She'd been tied up at *The Pennysaver* all day; she'd spent the morning writing up an interview with Santa, instead of eating lunch she'd dashed out to the Coast Guard station to photograph the guardsmen hanging a huge wreath on the lighthouse and then had gone to the weekly meeting of the Tinker's Cove board of selectmen. The selectmen had been unusually argumentative, which made for good copy, but she wouldn't have a chance to write it up until tomorrow morning, just before the Wednesday noon deadline.

Congratulating herself on her foresight for baking the DeeLiteful Wine Cake ahead of time, she shrugged off her coat and dropped her notebook on the pile of papers covering the round, golden oak kitchen table. It consisted mostly of financial-aid applications for her oldest child, Toby. He was a high school senior and was applying to several high-priced liberal arts colleges.

He wouldn't be able to go unless he got financial aid, and she had to fill out the complicated forms before January 1, the date recommended by the school guidance office. The thought of the forms was enough to make her feel overwhelmed—how was she supposed to know what their household income would be next year? Bill was a self-employed restoration carpenter, and his earnings varied drastically from year to year. So did hers, for that matter. Ted, the publisher of *The Pennysaver*, only called her when he needed her. She usually worked quite a lot in December, and in the summer months, but things were pretty quiet in coastal Maine in January and February.

First things first, thought Lucy, scooping up all the papers into a shopping bag and stuffing it in the pantry. She had to come up with something for dinner, and the sink and counter were covered with dirty dishes.

She opened the door to the family room, and spotted her sixteen-year-old daughter, Elizabeth, stretched out on the couch with her ear to the telephone.

"Elizabeth!" she yelled. "Say good-bye and get in here."

Then she pulled a big stockpot out of the cupboard and filled it with water. She was setting it on the stove when Elizabeth floated in.

"I wish you wouldn't yell when I'm talking to my friends," she complained. "It sounds so low-class."

Lucy gave her a sideways glance. This was something

new, she thought. In the past, Elizabeth had concentrated on outraging her parents, insisting on cutting her dark hair into short spikes and threatening to get her nose pierced. Now, Lucy noticed, the black oversize sweater and Doc Martens were gone, replaced by a shiny spandex top with a racing stripe down the side and a pair of sneakers with blue stripes. Her hair was combed into a smooth bob.

"What's with the new look?" asked Lucy.

"Styles change," said Elizabeth, with a shrug. "So what did you want me for?"

"Would you please do something with those dirty dishes? That's supposed to be your responsibility. It's not fair for me to work all day and come home to a messy kitchen."

"It's not my fault," said Elizabeth, demurely folding her hands in front of her. "Toby didn't clean out the dishwasher. It's full, so I had no place to put the dirty dishes."

"Elizabeth, I don't have time for this." Lucy bent down and pulled a can of dusting spray and a rag out from under the sink. "The cookie exchange is tonight; I have a dozen friends coming at seven. So do whatever you have to do, but get this mess cleaned up."

"Okay," said Elizabeth, in a resigned voice. "But it's not fair."

Lucy sighed and charged into the dining room, intending to give the table a quick wipe with the dust cloth. Unfortunately, it was covered with Toby's college applications.

"Toby!" she hollered, aiming her voice in the direction of the hall staircase. "Get down here!"

"He can't hear you. He's got his earphones on," advised eleven-year-old Sara, who was doing homework in the adjacent living room. "What's for dinner?"

"Spaghetti," said Lucy, gathering up the applications and stuffing them in the sideboard. "Be a sweetie and make the salad?"

"Do I have to?" groaned Sara. "I don't feel very good. I think I might be getting my period."

"Really?" asked Lucy, with a surge of interest. "Do you have cramps?"

"No," admitted Sara, who was anxiously awaiting the day when she would join her friends who had already begun menstruating. "I just feel bloated."

"Well, that's probably the stuff you've been eating all afternoon. There's enough dirty dishes in the kitchen to have fed an army. Now scoot and get started on that salad. I've got company coming tonight."

"All I had was yogurt," sniffed Sara, pushing open the door to the kitchen.

"And cereal, and a peanut butter and jelly sandwich, and about a gallon of milk," added Elizabeth, whose head was stuck in the dishwasher. "You're going to get fat if you don't watch it."

"Well, that's better than . . ." began Sara, but the door shut before Lucy could hear the end of the sentence.

Finishing up in the dining room, Lucy flicked her dust cloth around the living room, plumped the couch cushions, and headed for the family room. There she found her youngest child, Zoe, deeply absorbed in a coloring book.

"What'cha doing?" asked Lucy, giving her a little pat on the head.

"Homework."

"I didn't know they had homework in kindergarten, even all-day kindergarten."

Lucy sent up a quick prayer of thanks for the all-day

kindergarten program, which had just begun that year. It made it possible for her to work because Zoe now came home on the school bus with her older brother and sisters.

"Let me see that," said Lucy, taking the book. She was amused to see that Zoe had neatly written her name in the upper left-hand corner of the picture, just as she had been taught in school. "Very nice letters."

"The *z* is hard," said Zoe, very seriously.

"You got it perfect," said Lucy. "Now, would you do me a big favor and set the table for supper?"

"Sure, Mommy."

Lucy sighed. If only they would stay this sweet and agreeable throughout adolescence.

"Thank you, honey," she said, watching fondly as Zoe trotted into the kitchen.

She quickly straightened up the untidy newspapers and magazines, and scooped up a few stray glasses and dishes and carried them into the kitchen.

"How's the salad coming?"

"All done."

"Great. You can help Zoe set the table, okay? Elizabeth, here's some more stuff for the dishwasher and . . . " Lucy stopped in the middle of the room and slapped her hand to her head. "What am I doing?"

"Dinner," reminded Elizabeth.

"Right. Dinner. Did I defrost the hamburger?" She peered in the refrigerator. "No. Of course not." She pulled a package out of the freezer, unwrapped it, and dropped it in the frying pan with a clunk.

"What? No meatballs?" It was Bill, home from work.

"Not tonight." She tilted her cheek up for a kiss and smiled at the tickly feeling from his beard. "I'm kind of frantic, actually," she explained, pushing the meat around with a spatula. "I had to work all day, and the cookie exchange is tonight."

"I thought Sue did that," said Bill, hanging up his coat on the hook by the door.

"I got drafted this year."

"Well, it's a worthy cause—Christmas cookies!" Bill was settling down at the half-set kitchen table, with a cold beer in his hand.

"Since you feel that way, do you mind finishing up this sauce?" Lucy glanced nervously at the clock on the wall above the stove. "I'd like to set out the party refreshments in the dining room."

"Sure thing." Bill took the spatula from her, and Lucy scurried into the pantry, pulling out the ladder and climbing up to take the cake box off the top shelf. She carried it into the dining room and lifted off the top, expecting to see the festively decorated Dee-Liteful Wine Cake she had stored there.

Instead, she saw that only three-quarters of the cake was left.

Clenching her fists, she marched up the kitchen stairs and threw open the door to Toby's room.

"How could you?" she demanded, pulling off his earphones.

Startled, Toby looked up.

"How could I what?"

"You know what! Eat my cake!"

"What cake?" muttered Toby, grabbing for the earphones.

"The one with sprigs of holly and red candied cherries that was on the top shelf of the pantry." Lucy's arms were akimbo, and she was drumming her fingers against her hips.

"Oh, that one," said Toby, biting his lower lip. Then his face brightened as he turned on the charm. "It's pretty good, Mom."

"Flattery isn't going to get you out of this, buddy," said Lucy, implacably. "What were you thinking? I made a cake and decorated it for you to enjoy all by yourself?"

He lowered his head. "I'm sorry, Mom. I shouldn't have done it. But I was so hungry. It's all this pressure with the college applications and everything."

"Give me a break," muttered Lucy, disgusted. "I'm gonna get you for this—I don't know exactly how, but you'll pay."

She thumped down the front stairs to the dining room and got a knife out of a drawer, cutting the cake into neat slices and arranging them on a plate. She opened a package of holiday napkins, unfolding one and laying it over the sliced cake and arranging the rest on the sideboard, along with her sterling-silver dessert forks and teaspoons, her best china plates and cups and saucers.

Stepping back, she glanced around the room. It wasn't as lavishly decorated as Sue's house, but it was festive. A bowl of holly sat on the sideboard, little electric candles stood on the windowsills, and there was a crystal bowl filled with silver and gold Christmas balls in the middle of the now gleaming mahogany table. She took a deep breath and went from window to window flicking on the candles. She dimmed the overhead chandelier and went into the kitchen to see how dinner was coming.

Bill was just setting a big pot filled with noodles and sauce on the table when Lucy pushed open the kitchen door and slipped into her seat next to Zoe. With impeccable timing, Toby thundered down the back stairs and thumped into his chair.

"Hey, did you hear?" he began, in an effort to deflect her attention from himself. "Richie got into Harvard."

"He did?" Lucy stopped, serving spoon in midair. "How does he know already?"

"Early decision," said Toby, passing the salad bowl.

"Bob and Rachel must be so pleased," said Lucy, wishing that she felt a little more pleased with her own son.

"I bet it costs a pretty penny to go there," said Bill, taking a piece of Italian bread and passing the basket to Lucy.

"I think they're all about the same," said Lucy, busy buttering her bread. "Thirty thousand."

"I just don't get it," complained Bill. "When I went to college it was fifteen hundred a year, and that was everything. Tuition, room and board, the whole shebang. I had a five-hundred-dollar scholarship, and Mom got a part-time job to pay the rest."

"Well, I've got a part-time job," said Lucy. "But I sure don't make thirty thousand dollars. Most people around here don't even make that with a full-time job."

"What's the matter with the state college? That's what I want to know," demanded Bill, turning toward Toby.

"I'm applying there, too," said Toby, shoveling a big forkful of spaghetti into his mouth. "But my guidance counselor says I should try some of these other schools, too."

"I think we'll qualify for financial aid," said Lucy, hoping to ease the tension that was building up between father and son.

"Well, frankly, before I break my butt trying to pay for

a fancy education for the young prince here, I'd like to see a little more initiative, if you know what I mean." Bill gestured angrily with his fork. "His room's a mess, if you let him he'll sleep until two or three in the afternoon, and when he borrows my truck he always brings it back with an empty gas tank."

Toby didn't respond, but kept his head down, steadily scooping up his spaghetti.

"You know what I did today?" said Lucy brightly, changing the subject. "I interviewed Santa Claus!"

"The real Santa Claus?" Zoe was skeptical.

"I think so. It was the Santa at the Ropewalk. It didn't seem polite to ask for his credentials."

"I don't suppose you need a driver's license for a sleigh and reindeer, anyway," observed Elizabeth, who was the proud possessor of a learner's permit.

"What did he say?" asked Zoe.

"Well, he said it's very warm here, compared with the North Pole."

Bill chuckled. "The North Pole is probably the only place colder than here."

"That's exactly why I don't want to go to the state college! I want to get out of this freezing cold place where there's nothing to do," exploded Toby, who had been on a slow simmer. He threw down his napkin and marched out of the room.

"I wish you wouldn't be quite so hard on him," said Lucy.

"I wouldn't have to if you didn't spoil him, now would I?" said Bill.

"So, Sara, how was your day?" asked Lucy, determined to get through the meal with some semblance of civility.

"We had an assembly. A man came who used to be a drug addict. He told us how he ate food from garbage cans and . . . "

"Drugs are terrible," said Lucy. "What made him decide to give them up?"

"Well, he had really hit bottom. He was lying with his face in a pool of vomit . . . "

"Do you mind? We're having dinner," complained Elizabeth.

"Well, Mom asked. I'm only telling what he said."

"I think we get the idea," said Lucy, glancing at the old Regulator clock that hung on the wall. It was almost six-thirty, she had to get a move on. "You girls can clean up and have some frozen yogurt for dessert. I've got to change my clothes."

Hauling herself up the steep back stairway took every bit of energy that Lucy had. She had to concentrate to lift her feet from one step to the next. It had been a long day, she thought, but she wasn't usually this tired. No, it wasn't tiredness, she realized; it was depression.

She pushed open the door to the room she shared with Bill and flicked on a lamp. It was peaceful up here; she could just barely hear the girls' voices in the kitchen downstairs as they squabbled their way through the dishes.

The dormered room was spacious and uncluttered. The dresser tops were neatly organized, a rocking chair in the corner held only a needlepoint cushion and the wood grain of the blanket chest gleamed in the lamplight. The bed was neatly made, covered with a white woven bedspread.

It looked so inviting, thought Lucy. It wouldn't hurt to

stretch out for a minute or two, just to put her feet up and rest her eyes.

Falling back on the pillows, Lucy stretched her arms and legs and made a conscious effort to relax. She tried to push the dark clouds from her mind and to think of the enjoyable evening ahead. But instead, she kept replaying Bill's voice. His tone had been so antagonistic, calling Toby "the young prince." What was that all about?

Sure, Toby was lazy and liked to sleep late on weekends. And he was messy, but no more so than his friends. But, to give him credit, he was a pretty good kid. He got all As and Bs in school, he had been captain of the soccer team this fall and he'd scored an impressive 1450 on his SATs.

With that package and any luck at all, thought Lucy, feeling her spirits brightening a little, he would get into a really good college. Oh, probably not Ivy League like Richie, but he could certainly get into one of the top twenty liberal arts colleges. Which would it be? He had shown interest in Amherst and Williams, and of course there were Bates and Bowdoin and Colby right here in Maine.

Wasn't it lucky, she thought, that she had a new car. A fire had totaled her old Subaru wagon, and she had a spiffy new model. It would look great with a classy college decal on the back window. Of course, she thought, with a little pang of jealousy, her sticker wouldn't be quite as prestigious as Rachel's Harvard sticker. But then, Rachel had to put her sticker on a very elderly, rusty Volvo.

She suddenly felt much better, she realized, hopping off the bed. She'd talk to Bill and find out what was bothering him. But down deep, she knew, he wanted the best for Toby just as much as she did.

Lucy opened a drawer and took out a bright red sweatshirt with a huge Santa printed on the front. Just looking at the ridiculous thing made her smile; it had been a gift ftom Zoe last Christmas. There weren't too many occasions that it was suitable for, but it would be perfect for the cookie exchange. She took off the plain blue sweater she'd been wearing and pulled on the sweatshirt, added a pair of Christmas ball earrings and gave her hair a quick brush. She was ready.

She bounced down the front stairs, sending up a quick plea to the Spirit of Christmas Present: Please let my cookie exchange be a success.

Chapter Three

Still 16 days 'til Xmas

Of course it would be a success, she thought, smoothing her sweatshirt nervously as she checked the living room and dining room one last time. The holiday decorations were festive, and Bill had even laid a fire for her in the living room fireplace. She took one of the long fireplace matches out of its box and lit it, bending down to set the fire alight. Then she lit the candles on the mantelpiece and on the sideboard, and switched off the brightest lamps. Studying the effect, she nodded in satisfaction. In candlelight, the odd stains and worn spots disappeared, and the rooms looked quite lovely.

She only saw two storm clouds on the horizon: Lee Cummings's separation and Richie's acceptance at Harvard. But thanks to Sue, she knew all about Lee's tendency to monopolize the conversation with her separation. If that happened, resolved Lucy, she would just have to change the subject, firmly. The cookie exchange wasn't a group-therapy session, no matter what Lee might think. And Sue would help out, too. In fact, she'd promised to come early.

As for the matter of Richie, well, Lucy suspected that his early acceptance at Harvard might have put quite a few maternal noses out of joint. Andrea Rogers was particularly competitive; she had been ever since Toby and Richie and the other boys had all been on the same Little League team. Thank goodness Marge had said she was coming, having completed her first round of chemotherapy. She was so down-to-earth and unpretentious, and could be counted on to express her genuine happiness for Richie's success to his mother, Rachel. With Marge on hand the natural competitiveness of the group would be kept in check.

Pushing open the kitchen door, Lucy saw that Sara was almost finished wiping the counters.

"Thanks, sweetheart," she said. "You did a really good job."

"No problem, Mom. Oh, Elizabeth said to tell you that the upstairs toilet is clogged up again."

"Oh, no. That's all I need tonight."

"Want me to tell Dad to fix it?"

"No. Not now." Lucy knew that Bill's plumbing projects tended to get very messy indeed. "He'll have to take it apart, and that means turning off the water. Listen, just do me a favor and ask everybody to use the downstairs toilet, okay?"

"Do we have to? I hate having to be polite and talking to your friends. Mrs. Orenstein always wants to know what books I've been reading and Ms. Small pinches my cheeks."

"Use the back stairs. You won't have to talk to them then."

"Okay, Mom."

The doorbell rang just as Sara disappeared up the stairs and Lucy looked at her watch. Only six-fifty. It was probably Sue, keeping her promise to come early to help out. But when Lucy opened the door she recognized Stephanie Scott, one of the young mothers from the day-care center Sue had suggested inviting.

"Hi, Steffie. You're the first. Come on in."

"I hope you don't mind that I came a little early," said Steffie, carefully maneuvering her tray of cookies through the door. "Tom—that's my husband—he asked me to bring some MADD pamphlets. But I wanted to make sure it was OK with you, so I thought I'd better get here before everybody else."

"Mad pamphlets?" asked a puzzled Lucy, taking the cookies and leading the way to the dining room. She lifted the foil and peeked, nodding with satisfaction at what looked like old-fashioned mincemeat cookies.

"Right," said Steffie, with a nod that made her perky short blond hair bounce. "Mothers Against Drunk Driving. They have a campaign this time every year to cut down on holiday accidents."

"These look yummy," said Lucy, setting the cookies down on the table.

"Just an old family recipe, they're quick and easy," said Steffie, slipping out of her coat and handing it to Lucy. She began digging in her enormous leather shoulder bag. "Now, about the pamphlets—I thought we could just put them out next to the cookies."

Lucy regarded the handful of brochures doubtfully. "I don't think . . ."

"Oh, but nobody could object, could they?" asked Steffie earnestly. "After all, we're all mothers, and this is from *Mothers* Against Drunk Driving. And Tom, that's my husband, tells me they are doing an absolutely fabulous job. He's a police lieutenant, and he has the utmost respect for MADD. He says they're one organization that is really making a difference."

Steffie's blue eyes were blazing and she was speaking with all the zeal of a true convert. Lucy felt a little prickle of resentment. This was her party, after all. Steffie had no business promoting her agenda in Lucy's house.

"It's certainly a worthy cause . . ." began Lucy, intending to firmly reject Steffie's offer, but realizing in mid-sentence that there was no way she could decently refuse. She could hardly argue in favor of drunk driving. What was she going to say that wouldn't sound irresponsible? She realized she was trapped, and began to think she really didn't like Steffie all that much.

The phone rang just then, and Lucy seized on the opportunity to avoid the issue. "Fine," she said, with a dismissive wave of the hand, reaching for the receiver.

"Lucy, this is Marge."

Oh, no, thought Lucy, watching as Steffie began arranging her pamphlets on the table. She can't come.

"Hi. How are you doing?"

"Not so good—that's why I'm calling." Marge spoke slowly, as if even talking on the phone was an effort. "I'm sorry, but I just can't make it tonight."

Lucy had known this might happen, but she was still disappointed.

"That's too bad . . ." she began, passing the coat back to Steffie and pointing her to the coat closet.

"I know. I was really hoping I could come. I got the candy cane cookies all made, and Sue's going to pick 'em up and bring 'em. But I guess making the cookies used up all my energy. I'm beat now."

Lucy hoped it was the effects of the chemotherapy that was making Marge feel bad, and not the cancer, but she didn't know how to ask.

"I heard you're having a rough time with the chemo."

"You can say that again. If I can just survive the treatment, I'll have this thing licked," she said, with a weak chuckle. "At least, that's what they tell me."

"You hang in there," said Lucy. She thought of Marge's husband, Police Officer Barney Culpepper, and her son, Eddie, who was Toby's age. "Barney and Eddie need you."

"I know they do," replied Marge, with a little catch in her voice. "They've been terrific, you know. Hardly let me do a thing in the house. They keep saying I've got to save my energy to fight the cancer."

"They're right. You concentrate on getting well. I'll make sure you get your cookies. I'll bring them over one day this week."

"That'll be great. Thanks, Lucy."

What rotten luck, thought Lucy, slowly replacing the receiver. Marge was barely forty and the rumors around town were that her prognosis wasn't good, but she was fighting with every ounce of strength she had.

That's all you can do, thought Lucy, who feared every month when she examined her breasts that she'd find a lump.

"That was Marge Culpepper," Lucy told Steffie by

way of explanation. "Her husband is on the police force, too."

"I think I've heard Tom mention his name."

"Well, Marge can't come tonight. She's been having chemotherapy and doesn't feel very well."

"Cancer?"

Lucy nodded. "I have a few things to do in the kitchen, so why don't you make yourself comfortable? I'll be right back."

She hurried into the kitchen, where she set up the coffee-pot and filled the kettle with water for tea. Then she filled the sugar bowl and creamer and carried them out to the dining room, setting them on the sideboard along with the cake. Turning toward the living room, where Steffie was perched on the couch and leafing through a coffee-table book, Lucy thought it was about time for Sue to show up. After all, Steffie was her friend.

As if by magic, the doorbell rang just then.

"Come on in," cried Lucy, welcoming reinforcements in the form of Juanita Orenstein and Rachel Goodman. Juanita's little girl, Sadie, was Zoe's best friend.

"Before I forget—congratulations, Rachel. Toby told me all about Richie."

"Thanks, Lucy," said Rachel, glowing with maternal pride. "I can still hardly believe it myself, and I was the one who encouraged him to give Harvard a try."

"You never know unless you try," added Juanita, sagely.

"What? What's happened?" asked Steffie, joining the group in the hallway.

"Oh, where are my manners?" Lucy rolled her eyes. "Let me introduce Steffie Scott. This is Rachel Goodman—her son was just accepted at Harvard—and . . ."

"Harvard!" shrieked Steffie, sounding like one of the hysterical winners in a Publishers Clearinghouse commercial. "That's fantastic!"

Lucy and Juanita's eyes met. Lucy raised her eyebrows, and Juanita gave a little smirk.

"Actually," said Rachel, whose glow of pride had been replaced with a blush of embarrassment, "the best part is having the whole application process over with. I'm so glad he decided to try for early decision—now he doesn't have to worry and can enjoy his senior year."

"Well, I've been reading up on this," said Steffie. "My son, Will, is only three, but it's never too early to start planning. And the experts say that early decision definitely increases your chances at the top schools."

"Does it really? I didn't know that," said Rachel. "Actually, Richie's grandfather went to Harvard, and I think that had more to do with his admission than anything else."

"Really?" asked Steffie, her eyes round in surprise. "I didn't know they took Jews way back then."

For a moment the women stood in shocked silence. Then Rachel spoke. "You're probably right, though I'm sure it's nothing they're proud of today. And anyway, it was my dad who went, and he's not Jewish. My maiden name is Webster. For the record, Bob's folks are Jewish, but I have to confess we don't really practice any religion at all." She chuckled. "On Sunday mornings we walk the dog and read the paper."

"I didn't mean to give the wrong impression," said Steffie, realizing she'd made a blunder. "It doesn't matter to me what religion you are. Can I help you with those cookies?"

Hearing a knock, Lucy opened the door. As she suspected, it was Franny, who preferred a quiet rap to the gong of the doorbell.

"It's just me and Lydia," she said, with a nod toward her friend, kindergarten teacher Lydia Volpe. "I hope I parked OK. I didn't want to block anybody in." She was looking anxiously over her shoulder.

"She's parked fine," said Lydia, with a shrug. "I kept telling her."

"I'm sure it's fine. Let me take that," said Lucy, reaching for the cookie tin Franny was clutching to her bosom.

"Just the same old Chinese noodle cookies—I'm not much of a cook and you don't have to bake them. You just melt the chocolate and add the noodles and peanuts and drop them on waxed paper. I could never make pizzelles like Lydia—I don't know how she does it. They seem so difficult."

"Not really," said Lydia. "Trust me. I'm not really a good cook—not like my mother."

"Well, I'm sure they're both delicious. As always. My kids love them. It wouldn't be Christmas without them."

"You're sweet to say so, Lucy," said Franny, idly picking up one of the pamphlets.

"If we brought mudpies, Lucy would find something nice to say," joked Lydia.

"Don't the cookies look good this year? Don't tell me you made this cake, Lucy. It looks delicious," said Franny.

"Mmm, it does," agreed Lydia. "Now what can we do to help?"

Lucy looked up as the door flew open and Pam Stillings and Andrea Rogers sailed in.

"Would you be dears and bring in the coffee? The pot's in the kitchen. And the tea water ought to be ready, too."

"Be glad to," said Lydia, as she and Franny headed for the kitchen.

Lucy went to greet the new arrivals.

"We didn't ring the bell—we figured you'd have your hands full," announced Pam, who was married to Lucy's boss at *The Pennysaver,* Ted Stillings.

"Well, come on in and make yourselves at home. You know where everything is."

"I made my usual decorated sugar cookies," said Andrea, handing a basket to Lucy. Her eyes were bright, and her color was high. Lucy wondered if she had a fever.

"Are you feeling OK?" she asked in a concerned voice.

"Who me? I'm fine," said Andrea, avoiding Lucy's eyes and looking around the hallway to the rooms beyond. "Doesn't everything look wonderful? I'm so glad you decided to continue the cookie exchange. It's such a wonderful tradition."

"How many years, Lucy?" inquired Pam.

"It must be sixteen, anyway," guessed Lucy.

"That's right. I think Adam was still in diapers when I came for the first time."

"And Tim hadn't even begun playing baseball, yet," said Andrea, who always thought of her son's growth in terms of his progress in the sport. "Remember Little League? Wasn't that fun?"

"It sure was," said Lucy, winking at Pam. Their sons hadn't shown much talent for baseball, and they mostly remembered the games as opportunities for the boys to make humiliating mistakes. Andrea, however, had afforded everyone a great deal of amusement as a one-woman cheering section for Tim.

"I always knew baseball would pay off for Tim," continued Andrea. "And it has. You know quite a few scouts were interested in him last season, and we got a call from the athletic director at Maine Christian University this afternoon." Andrea's voice was rising and had become quite loud. "He got a full scholarship—tuition, room and board, even a little spending money. Isn't that fantastic?"

"Congratulations! That's great news," said Lydia, appearing in the doorway with the pot of coffee. "My little kindergarten grads are doing well. Did you hear about Richie?"

"What about Richie?" asked Andrea, narrowing her eyes suspiciously.

Here we go, thought Lucy.

"He's going to Harvard. Early decision," announced Lydia.

"No! That's great," said Pam, hurrying off to congratulate Rachel. "Good news for a change! Local boy does good!"

Andrea, of course, hadn't taken the news quite as well. To her way of thinking, Tim was tops. She didn't mind other kids being successful, she just didn't like them to outdo Tim. And while Maine Christian University was undoubtedly a fine school, it couldn't compare with Harvard.

"My that coffee smells good," said Andrea, with a little sniff. "I'd love a cup."

"You must be so proud of Tim," said Lucy, steering the conversation back to Andrea's favorite subject. "He was on the All-State team last year, wasn't he?"

"And he won the batting title last year and was voted

MVP by his teammates," recited Andrea, looking a little happier..

"He was always a little firecracker," said Lydia, who had long ago trained herself to remember only her students' positive attributes.

Confident she was leaving Andrea in good hands, Lucy left the group in the dining room and went into the living room to invite the women gathered there to take some refreshments.

"There's cake and coffee in the dining room—and I wouldn't dilly-dally," she said. "There's a pretty hungry crowd in there."

"I'm so glad you did this, Lucy. It's such a nice Christmas tradition," said Rachel, who was leaning back in a wing chair with her feet propped on a footstool. "But I can sure understand why Sue thought it was time to take a break. Is she coming?"

"I've been wondering the same thing," said Lucy. "She's supposed to, and she's bringing her new assistant at the center, Tucker."

"Tucker's wonderful," said Steffie, rising to her feet and joining the general drift toward the dining room. "Will just adores her."

As they passed through the hallway the doorbell rang and Lucy stopped to open it, expecting to see an apologetic Sue standing on the other side. Instead, she saw Lee Cummings.

"Just what I need," she muttered to herself. "The woman scorned, the soon-to-be divorcée from hell." She pasted a bright smile on her face. "Hi, Lee. I'm so glad you could make it."

"Me too, Lucy. For a while I didn't think I was going to be able to come. I was waiting for Steve, that weasel. I mean, to hear him talk he absolutely adores the girls, and I'm the evil witch who keeps him from them. But when it comes to taking care of them for one single evening, where is he? He forgot all about it. I had to call all over town, and I finally tracked him down at the donut shop." She paused for breath and shook her head. "I hope he chokes on them. I hope the cholesterol clogs up his blood vessels and he has a stroke and lies there paralyzed for days and nobody finds him until he rots. And when they find him the rats will have been chewing on him . . . "

"These cookies look really good," said Lucy, taking a platter covered with plastic wrap from her.

"It's the most wonderful recipe," said Lee, hanging up her jacket on the hall coat tree. "They taste great and believe it or not, they're low fat and have hardly any sugar. They're actually good for you."

Lucy raised a skeptical eyebrow. Lee took her role as the wife of a dentist very seriously, and was known for using recipes that were good for you but didn't necessarily taste very good.

"Sounds like a miracle."

"It really is—oh, Lucy, do you mind if I just run upstairs to use the loo?"

"Of course not," said Lucy, mentally crossing her fingers. So far, the plumbing seemed to be holding up but she didn't want to risk any disasters. "Please use the downstairs powder room instead. Do you know where it is?"

"Sure thing."

Lee dashed off through the kitchen, while Lucy added her platter of cookies to the others on the table. It was filling up, Lucy saw with satisfaction, surveying the array of homemade baked goods. The women had packed the cookies in sandwich bags, each holding six cookies, and a few had decorated them with bright holiday ribbons and stickers. The table was so crowded, in fact, that Steffie's little brochures had disappeared from sight.

"So, what's it like to be the proud mother of a genius?" asked Lydia, striking up a conversation with Rachel. "You must be so proud of Richie."

"I am," admitted Rachel. "But I was proud of him before we got the letter, too."

"You don't have to be modest," said Lydia, "Harvard is the top American college, after all."

"There are plenty of other good schools, too," said Pam, who was growing tired of hearing about other people's kids. "Adam wants to go to Boston University, or maybe Northeastern."

"MCU's awfully good, too," said Andrea. "Especially if you have a full scholarship like Tim does."

"And a lot of kids can't take the pressure at a place like Harvard," continued Pam. "They crash and burn."

"That's right," added Steffie. "There's a lot of alcohol abuse at those fraternities. Was it Harvard? Maybe it was MIT. I'm not sure which, but I remember reading that a freshman died from alcohol poisoning."

"That was MIT," said Lee, joining the group. "But I don't think Harvard's much better. It certainly didn't do much for Steve, I can tell you that."

There was a sudden commotion as Rachel dropped her coffee cup, shattering the cup and saucer and spilling the coffee on the rug, "Oh, I'm so sorry, Lucy," she said, dropping to her knees and attempting to clean up the mess with a holiday napkin.

"Here, let me take care of that," said Lucy. As she knelt beside Rachel, she saw that tears were filling her eyes. "It's nothing . . . " began Lucy, reaching for more napkins. "We spill stuff all the time—why do you think I'm having this little do by candlelight?"

Rachel giggled, and Lucy gave her a quick hug. She didn't think for a minute that Rachel was crying over spilt coffee; she had been upset by her friends' meanness.

"Don't pay any mind," whispered Lucy, taking the sponge Franny was offering her. "They're just jealous."

"Oh, I know. But I've really had to bite my tongue tonight, let me tell you. Especially with Andrea," hissed Rachel, picking up the broken pieces of china and handing them to Franny. "To listen to her, you'd never know Tim isn't quite the paragon she wants everyone to think he is."

"He isn't?" Lucy was definitely interested.

"No. He was arrested last week for driving under the influence. He's in big trouble."

"My goodness," said Franny

"How do you know?" asked Lucy.

"They hired Bob to defend him." Bob, Rachel's husband, was a lawyer.

Rachel's hand flew to her mouth as she rose to her feet. "Don't tell anybody, okay? I'm not supposed to know about this—client confidentiality and all that."

"Your secret's safe with me," said Lucy, now standing and scanning the table for the brochures. She finally found them under Franny's Chinese noodle cookies. Making sure no one was watching, she lifted the plate and scooped up the brochures, wadding them into a ball along with the sodden napkins. Then she turned, intending to throw the whole mess into the kitchen garbage.

"Oh my goodness, Lucy," said Lee, suddenly appearing at her elbow. "Who brought those awful Chinese noodle cookies? Can you imagine making something as unhealthy as that in this day and age? What could she have been thinking? Those things are full of saturated fat and all sorts of preservatives. Talk about empty calories!"

Lucy looked across the table toward the sideboard, where Franny was refilling the teapot, and saw her hurt expression.

"Oh, I don't know," said Lucy, catching Franny's eye. "I can't resist them myself—and it's only once a year."

That's right, she told herself. Christmas only comes once a year, thank goodness. And with any luck, she'd never have to have this blasted cookie exchange again. How could she have forgotten? It was the same thing every year. Somebody always went home with hurt feelings. Of course, this year looked to be something of a record in the hurt-feelings department. It was all Sue's fault, she decided. If she'd gotten to the party on time, she could have helped keep the combatants apart. As it was, if she didn't arrive soon, thought Lucy, blood would probably be shed.

In the kitchen, Lucy tossed the pamphlets into the bin under the kitchen sink. The last thing she wanted was for Andrea to see them; remembering her swollen eyes when she arrived, Lucy was sure she was enormously upset about Tim's arrest. All that bragging about the MCU scholarship was her way of putting on a brave front.

Of course, nobody was more competitive than Andrea when it came to kids. As much as Lucy sympathized with her, and dreaded finding herself in the same situation, she couldn't help feeling just the teeniest bit that Andrea was getting her just deserts.

Lucy was far too superstitious ever to brag about her children; the most she would do was modestly accept a compliment on their behalf. That wasn't Andrea's way.

Ever since Tim caught his first Wiffle ball, gently lobbed by his father, she had hailed him as a superb athlete. Her friends had listened patiently through the years as she had provided a play-by-play narration of his achievements. In his mother's eyes, Tim could do no wrong. He was perfect. He was, thought Lucy, too good to be true.

Returning to the dining room, Lucy poured herself a cup of coffee and propped a slice of cake on the saucer. Then she followed the group into the living room, where they had settled to enjoy their refreshments. Lee was making the most of this opportunity to reap her friends' sympathy by making sure they all knew the details of Steve's latest transgressions.

"He told his lawyer that there's no reason for me to get the stove because I never lifted a hand to cook a home-cooked meal in the entire seven years we've been married—can you believe it?"

Receiving clucks and murmurs of sympathy from the group, she continued. "I mean, we entertained at least once a week and I thought nothing of whipping up beef Stroganoff or coq au vin for his dental-society colleagues and their incredibly boring wives, not to mention chicken wings and homemade pizza—with sun-dried tomatoes, I might add—for his annual Super Bowl bash. This stuff didn't all just appear, you know. I spent hours cutting and chopping and stirring and sweating over a hot stove the very stove he says I never touched. Can you believe it?"

"It's funny. If people don't do something themselves, they don't understand how much work it is," said Pam. "Ted doesn't have a clue about housework. I'm sure he thinks the rugs vacuum themselves while I lie on the couch all day watching soap operas."

The women chuckled and nodded in agreement.

"Don't even mention rugs," moaned Lee. "You know my beautiful Kirman, the one my parents gave us for a wedding present?"

"He wants that?" asked Lydia.

Lee nodded, and the women sighed and shook their heads in dismay.

"That's terrible," said Juanita.

"I'd tell him exactly what he could do with it," said Pam.

"Well, he's not going to get it," said Lee. "I'm going to make sure of that. That's why I went with the Boston lawyer. He says he always goes right for the jugular!"

"And I bet he charges Boston prices, too," said Rachel, who was standing next to Lucy.

"Like the hair-dye commercial says, 'I'm worth it,'" said Lee, defending her choice. "Besides, I have my girls' futures to think of, too."

This was received with another murmur of approval, and Lee paused to take a bite of cake.

Rachel turned to Lucy. "She's making a big mistake," she whispered. "A local lawyer like Bob would try to get them to reconcile, or at least work out an amicable agreement. That would be a lot better for the kids, believe me."

Lucy nodded in agreement. She tended to think people were often too quick to opt for divorce and didn't consider the consequences, especially for the children. "I don't know—even if she gets everything she wants, she isn't going to be able to keep the same lifestyle. Whatever he makes, now it's got to support two households instead of one."

"That's right," said Rachel. "Except for a handful of very wealthy people, divorce is a one-way road to poverty."

"Yoo-hoo," halloed Sue, sailing through the front door. "Sorry I'm late . . ."

"It's about time you got here," complained Lucy, who had been wondering if Sue had abandoned her.

"Nice shirt—and so subtle, too," joked Sue, blinking at Lucy's bright Santa sweatshirt. "I would have been here hours ago except my battery died. So, how's it going?"

"Touch and go," said Lucy, with a little shrug. "No fatalities—yet."

"I'd say you're doing great," said Sue. Then, raising her voice, she announced, "Now, listen everybody. I know you can't wait to start grabbing cookies but I want you to meet someone. This is Tucker Whitney, my new assistant at the center."

Tucker, Lucy saw, could be trouble. She was a strikingly attractive twentysomething. Tall and slender, she had long, naturally blond hair.

"Hi, Tucker," chorused the group, without much enthusiasm. Realizing she was no longer the center of attention, Lee decided to pour herself a second cup of coffee.

"Hi, everybody," said Tucker, smiling broadly. Although she was the youngest person there and didn't know most of the others, she was one of those rare people who are comfortable wherever they go.

She turned to Lucy and indicated the stack of platters and tins in her arms. "What should I do with these? I hope I made enough. Sue didn't tell me how many to bring so I have these twelve dozen but if you need more, I've got another six dozen in the car."

"Oh, my goodness. You didn't need to do all that," said Lucy. "You only needed to bring six dozen."

"Oh, well, you can keep the extras," said Tucker. "Sue

told me you've got four kids." She looked around at the house, obviously impressed. "You're so lucky. Someday I want to have a big family and a house just like this."

Lucy started to protest politely, but changed her mind. "You're right. I am lucky. Thanks for reminding me. Sometimes I take too much for granted."

"Don't we all," said Tucker. "Now, I hope everyone likes these cookies. It's a new recipe I got from a magazine, and it sounded too good to be true. They're supposed to be low in fat and sugar . . ."

"That can't be!" exclaimed Lee, glaring at Tucker from the other side of the table.

"Well, that's what it said," insisted Tucker.

"They're the same as my cookies!" Lee pointed an accusing finger at Tucker. "You stole my recipe!"

Tucker didn't reply, she just shrugged her shoulder apologetically.

Lucy felt a little bit like a firefighter, rushing to put out yet another flare of temper.

"It just goes to show that good recipes get around," she said. Out of the corner of her eye she saw Toby heading upstairs, looking like a young man with a mission, but before she could remind him to use the downstairs bathroom she was distracted by Tucker's request to borrow something to put her cookies in.

"I didn't think to bring an extra container," she confessed.

"Not a problem," said Lucy, pulling a bread basket out of the sideboard and giving it to her. "Don't mind Lee," she added. "She's involved in a messy divorce."

"I know. Her little girl, Hillary, comes to the day-care center. She talks about it a lot. She's pretty upset about Daddy leaving home."

"That's too bad," responded Lucy automatically, her attention drawn to the living room.

There, as if in slow motion, she saw Franny approaching Andrea, holding out something. Oh my God, she thought, realizing that Franny, dear, well-meaning Franny, had saved one of the MADD pamphlets and was intending to give it to Andrea. No doubt expecting her to be grateful for this show of concern.

Lucy immediately started across the room, hoping to intercept Franny before the exchange could take place. In her haste, her foot slipped out of her loafer and she began to fall. She caught herself by grabbing the doorjamb and quickly shoved her foot back into the shoe.

"What is this? A joke?" exclaimed Andrea, glaring at Franny.

Lucy hurried to explain. "Steffie brought these pamphlets. Her husband is   "

"I know exactly who her husband is," hissed Andrea.

"Well, if I'd known about Tim, I never would have let her put the pamphlets out. And as soon as I heard, I threw them away. I'm sure Franny was only trying to be helpful."

"That's right," sniffed Franny.

To Lucy's dismay, Steffie joined their little group and placed her hand on Andrea's arm.

"It's very normal to feel angry about Tim's arrest, but it's for his own good," she said. "My husband has seen too many terrible accidents where kids, kids like Tim, have been killed. Isn't it better for him to learn that drinking and driving is unacceptable? I mean," she continued with the bright certainty of the mother of a blameless three-year-old, "I would much rather spend a morning in court with Will than a night in the emergency room."

"Well, I wouldn't be so confident, if I were you," said Andrea, pulling her arm free of Steffie's grasp. Her voice rang out shrilly, and the other women dropped their conversations and turned toward her.

"I know what you're thinking, all of you," continued Andrea, her eyes flashing with anger. "You're all positive that something like this will never happen to you because you're good mothers. It's only bad mothers whose kids get in trouble. And you've done everything right. You've cooked dinner every night. OK, so once in a while you order pizza, but that's as bad as it gets. Right?"

Pam and Juanita chuckled nervously.

"You don't let the kids watch too much TV—it's not good for them. And you don't let them eat too many sweets because you want them to have strong teeth. You go to church every Sunday, and you make sure the kids go to Sunday School."

Franny dabbed at her eyes, which were filling with tears.

"Most of all, you've been good examples. You don't drink and drive, and your kids would never dream of doing it. Oh, no. You've spoken with them and told them that if they need a ride home, they should call you. No matter what the time. You'll get them, no questions asked. Right?"

A few heads around the room nodded, including Lucy's. She and Bill had had that very talk with Toby just a few weeks ago.

"Well, you know what?" demanded Andrea, who was shaking with rage and shame. "I am a good mother. I've done all those things. And my son was arrested. The lawyer tells me he'll have a criminal record for the rest of his life. So don't be so sure it can't happen to you."

Stunned, the women were silent, staring at Andrea, who was wiping tears from her face. Nobody seemed to know what to say. Realizing she had a social disaster on her hands, Lucy hurried to Andrea, proffering a napkin printed with holly. She gave her a little hug and turned to face the group.

"Come on, everybody. It's time to swap those cookies. Remember, you can only take a half dozen of each kind. Okay?"

The women picked up the empty baskets and cookie tins they had brought and formed a loose line that wrapped around the table. Only Andrea remained in the living room, being consoled by Tucker.

"Have you ever seen anything like this?" cooed Juanita. "The cookies this year are better than ever."

"They're absolutely wonderful," agreed Pam.

"I don't know how I'm going to keep them hidden until Christmas Eve," confessed Lucy. From upstairs, she thought she heard the sound of the toilet flushing. Then she remembered Toby, hurrying upstairs with an especially purposeful expression. She held her breath, willing the aged pipes to cooperate, just this once.

"We have ours on Christmas Day with hot cocoa," said Pam, counting six Chinese noodle cookies into a sandwich bag.

"I take mine to my folks' house," said Lee. "We always have Christmas with them."

Lucy reached across the table to take some of Tucker's cookies when she felt a drop of water on her hand. She looked up and, horrified, saw the dining room ceiling beginning to sag, the plaster bulging with water.

"I felt a drop," said Lee. "Lucy, I think you have a leak . . . "

Lucy was standing openmouthed, transfixed by the sight of the bulging plaster bubble growing even larger.

"Quick! Pick up the table!" ordered Sue, taking in the situation. "We can carry it . . . "

The women hurried to obey, struggling to lift the solid mahogany table Bill and Lucy had bought at an estate sale. But as Lucy watched, the drops of water began coming faster and faster, rapidly forming a trickle that in only a few moments more became a stream. Finally, just as the women were beginning to shift the heavy table, the plaster let go. It fell on the cookie-covered table with a thump, followed by a deluge of water that poured onto the table and then cascaded onto the floor, splashing everyone.

"Wow," said Sue, wrapping an arm around Lucy's shoulder and giving her a squeeze. "You sure know how to give one heck of a party."

Chapter Four

15 days 'til Christmas

Wednesday morning, it took every bit of Lucy's willpower to drag herself out of bed. All she wanted to do was to pull the covers over her head and forget everything—especially the cookie exchange.

Once the flooding started, time had seemed to switch to slow motion. She remembered the horrified faces, and the polite assurances that "it didn't matter one bit, we had a wonderful time, anyway" as the women departed, leaving her to face the sodden mess. Franny had offered to help clean up, but Lucy had sent her on her way, preferring to handle it herself.

Bill had helped, holding a big trash bag open for her so she could dump the ruined cookies into it. It almost made her cry, thinking of all the work the soggy cookies represented, all those expensive ingredients gone to waste.

She groaned, turning over and burying her face in her pillow.

"You've got to get up," said Bill, nibbling on her ear.

"I don't want to."

"Tough," said Bill, whacking her bottom with a pillow.

Lucy didn't get up, she burrowed deeper under the covers, but she knew she was just postponing the inevitable. Bill was right. She had to get up. She had to get the lunches made and the kids off to school, then, she had to go straight to *The Pennysaver* and write up the selectmen's meeting in time for the noon deadline. Ted was counting on her. She rolled over and got out of bed.

"Thanks, Lucy, you did a real nice job with this," said Ted, after he had given the story a quick edit. He scratched his chin and smiled slyly. "I guess the real story was your cookie exchange. Pam said you had quite a flood."

"Don't remind me," said Lucy, buttoning up her coat. "I've never been so embarrassed in my life."

"These things happen to everyone," said Ted. "Don't forget the kindergarten Christmas party on Monday, okay."

"I'll have it for you Tuesday," promised Lucy.

She took his nod as a dismissal and left the office, scowling at the cheery jangle of the bell on the door. Crossing Main Street to her parked car, she consulted her mental list of things to do. She could pick up a few presents, she could tackle the Christmas cards, she could get started on Zoe's angel costume for the Christmas pageant . . . the list went on and on.

Nope, she decided, shifting the list to a mental "do later" file. Right now, she needed some tea and sympathy. She climbed in the car and started the engine, driving down the street to the rec building.

Sue's reaction, when she looked up from the sand table where she was helping two little boys build a racetrack for their Matchbox cars, was not what Lucy had hoped for.

"That was some party last night," said Sue, giggling. "If you could have seen the look on your face when the water started dripping—I never saw anything so funny in my life."

"Well, I'm glad somebody had a good time." Lucy plopped herself down in a child-sized chair. She glanced around the room, where another boy was busy building a tower of blocks and a group of little girls were playing in the dress-up area, and asked, "Where's your helper?"

Sue shrugged her shoulders. "No phone call, no nothing. It's a heck of an inconvenience. I had to call the moms of the three infants and have them make other arrangements. You know, I really thought Tucker was different. Mature. Responsible." She shook her head. "Sooner or later, they all revert to form. She's only a kid, after all. I don't know what I was thinking."

"I don't know. I was pretty impressed with her. She was the life of the party, until the party . . . "

"Died a watery death?"

"It needed to be put out of its misery, believe me."

Lucy watched as Sue put an arm around one of the little boys and began gently stroking his stomach.

"Take it easy, Will," she coaxed. "Just relax."

Will's narrow chest, however, continued to rise and fall rapidly under his OshKosh overalls.

"Is that Steffie's Will?" Lucy asked, putting two and two together.

"Yup. This is my friend, Will, and this is Harry," said Sue. "Boys, this is Mrs. Stone."

"Glad to meet you," said Lucy, reaching across the table and shaking their hands. Harry smiled brightly at her, but Will, intent on his struggle to breathe, only gave her a glance.

Sue pulled an inhaler out of her pocket and he obediently took a puff, and then another.

Lucy glanced at Will, raised her eyebrows, then shifted her gaze to Sue. "You know it was Steffie who brought the MADD pamphlets. I got rid of them as soon as I heard about Tim, but Franny must have saved one. I know her intentions were good, but Andrea didn't see it that way."

"That woman"—Sue tipped her head toward Will— "must be a fanatic. Why would you bring something like that to a party? I mean, you could very well have served wine. That would've put the kibosh on things."

"It really threw me when she showed up with the darn things. I didn't know what to do."

"I don't know what else you could have done, under the circumstances." Sue pushed a little red car along in the sand, following the road Harry was making with his toy bulldozer. "And to tell the truth, I feel badly for Andrea, but Tim's gotta learn, too. This isn't the first time he's been driving drunk; it's just the first time he got caught."

Lucy nodded thoughtfully, watching Will. He looked as if he could use another puff on the inhaler, but she knew it was too soon. Elizabeth had asthma, and Lucy had often helped her manage an attack.

"Lee didn't help matters much, either," said Lucy. "You were right about her, All she can talk about is how badly Steve's behaving. And what was that about Tucker stealing her cookie recipe?" Lucy looked puzzled. "I didn't understand that at all."

Sue snorted. "She isn't worried about her cookie recipe, believe me. She's afraid Tucker is stealing her husband." Sue paused, and put a comforting arm around Will's shoulder. The little boy's eyes looked huge under his bangs. "Steve's been dating Tucker. She told me all about it last night."

"Ohhh," said Lucy, "now it makes sense." She reached across the table and gently pinched Will's chin, but he didn't look at her. He was entirely focused on his struggle to breathe and was beginning to panic. "I don't like the look of this," said Lucy. "I think he needs a nebulizer."

Sue nodded. "Can you stay here, until I get back?"

"No problem." Lucy noticed Will's eyes were beginning to roll up into his head. "You better hurry. Get your coat." She picked up Will and carried him over to the cubby area, where the coats were kept, and began zipping him into his jacket.

Sue grabbed her coat and yanked open a desk drawer, pulling out Will's emergency file. She took out a card and tucked the manila folder under her arm.

"Notify his folks, okay?" she told Lucy, handing her

the card. "They can meet me at the emergency room."
Then she scooped up the little boy and hurried off.

Lucy took a quick head count on the remaining kids.
Harry, she saw, had gone to join the little boy who was
playing with blocks. Two of the girls had moved into the
toy kitchen, and Hillary Cummings was piling stuffed
toys into a doll carriage. Everything seemed under control, so she sat down at Sue's desk to phone Steffie.

Looking at the number printed on the card, Lucy hesitated and let her fingers play with the numbered buttons
on the keypad. After last night, she didn't really want to
talk to Steffie. Her conscience took over, however, before
she could decide if her reluctance was due to anger with
Steffie or embarrassment over the leak, and she punched
in the number.

Listening to the phone ring, she thought about the frail
little boy Steffie seemed to have such high hopes for. Finally, the phone was answered; it turned out to be a bank
in the next town, Gilead, and she was connected to
Steffie.

"Of course. You couldn't call my husband," sighed
Steffie, when Lucy explained the situation.

"I didn't think of that," said Lucy, remembering the
police station was just around the corner. She flipped
over the card. "Actually, yours is the only number we
have."

"I can't believe this," fumed Steffie. "As it happens,
I'm in a very important meeting, and I can't leave right
now. I'm sure Will's in good hands at the cottage hospital."

"Do you want me to try your husband?" asked Lucy,
somewhat stunned. She couldn't imagine reacting as

Steffie had, but then, she hadn't tried to juggle a demanding career with motherhood.

"Never mind," snapped Steffie. "I'll get there as soon as I can, but I'm at least ten miles away."

Well, thought Lucy, replacing the receiver, at least Will is with Sue and she won't leave until his mother shows up.

Realizing it might be a while before Sue returned, Lucy went around the room, chatting with each of the children. She suspected they might be concerned about Sue's sudden departure, and she wanted to introduce herself and let them know that she would be taking care of them. Then she spotted a tray with a pitcher and a plate of cookies, and realized it was well past snack time.

As soon as she placed the tray on the table, the children came running and jostled for seats.

"Wow, you guys must be hungry," said Lucy, pouring cups of apple juice for them. "There's plenty for everyone."

She sat down with them and played a name game. The first child said his name, Justin, and the second child had to say Justin's name and add hers, Hillary. The third child, Emily, had to say the other names in order: Justin, Hillary, Emily.

Lucy was last, and she pretended to have a terrible time remembering all the names. The kids thought she was hilarious, and had a rollicking good time laughing at a stupid grown-up. Finally, when everyone had finished their snack, she recited the names in proper order and sent the kids over to the cubbies to put on their jackets so they could all go out for some fresh air. While they did that, she cleared up the snack things and gave the table a quick wipe.

By the time she joined them, the kids had done a pretty good job with their coats. She knelt down and helped them with zippers and buttons, and made sure they had their mittens on. Then she slipped into her own coat and led the little line over to the door. She was just about to open it, when Officer Barney Culpepper's face appeared in the glass window.

"Hi, Officer Culpepper," she said, opening the door. "What can we do for you today?" She assumed he was there for one of the many safety programs he presented at local schools—maybe bike safety, or stranger danger. So did the kids, who clustered around him, demanding to see his walkie-talkie. But today Officer Culpepper wasn't smiling, his St. Bernard jowls were drooping and he looked very grim.

"Go on outside, children. It's playtime," said Lucy. "Officer Culpepper will be back another day."

"What's the matter?" asked Lucy, fearing that his wife, Marge, had taken a turn for the worse.

"Where's Sue?" Barney looked through the doorway. "I need to talk to her."

"At the hospital. Will Scott had an asthma attack. Can I help you?"

"Maybe." Barney took off his blue cap and scratched his brush cut. "I probably shouldn't tell you but, heck, it's gonna be all over town soon enough, anyway." He held the cap in his hands and shifted his weight from one foot to the other. Finally, he spoke. "Tucker Whitney was killed this morning. A neighbor noticed her front door was open and called 911. The responding officer found her dead, inside the house."

Lucy collapsed against the door frame, feeling as if

she'd been punched in the stomach. "I can't believe it. I just saw her last night."

"It's terrible." Barney shook his head.

Lucy's mind was in a whirl, trying to understand how a healthy young girl like Tucker could be dead. "Was it an accident?"

"Doesn't look like it. They're not saying anything until the medical examiner is through, but it sure looks like murder."

"How?" Lucy asked in a small voice.

"She was strangled. At least that's what they think."

"Oh my God." Lucy closed her eyes and leaned against the doorjamb. Then, hearing a shriek from the play yard, she was reminded of her responsibilities.

"Justin, Matthew—one at a time on the slide, please," she said, struggling to keep her voice level.

She looked up at Barney, blinking back tears. "I just can't believe it. Who would do such a thing?"

Barney shook his head sadly. "It's early, still. I don't know if they have any suspects, yet. I came to see if she had an address book or anything like that here—they didn't find anything at her place."

"I don't know. I think she used the desk by the window. You can look around."

"Thanks, Lucy. I'll be out of your way in a minute."

"No problem."

Shoving her hands in her pockets, Lucy strolled out to the play area. It wasn't too cold, maybe thirty-five degrees, and it was bright and sunny, but Lucy felt chilled to the bone. The kids didn't seem to mind the cold one bit. The boys were scrambling up the ladder and shrieking as they went down the slide, a couple of the girls were bouncing on plastic horses fastened to sturdy springs.

Two others were going up and down on the seesaw. It all seemed so normal. A typical day at the day-care center. Maybe it was, she thought, finding comfort in denial. Maybe she'd imagined the whole thing. Barney hadn't come, and Tucker was still alive.

"Thanks, Lucy," came Barney's voice, from over the fence. She turned and saw him, tipping his hat at her. "I'll be on my way now."

She lifted her hand to wave and a dark wave of grief overwhelmed her, like clouds rolling in and blotting out the sun. She sat down on a bench and watched the children play, but they seemed very far away, and their voices were muffled. It was only when she heard the steeple bell at the community church tolling the noon hour that she realized it was time to go inside for lunch. Otherwise, she didn't know how long she might have sat there.

Chapter Five

To the children, the bells meant it was lunchtime. Shrieking, they ran for the door and tumbled inside.

But to Lucy, they sounded like funeral bells, tolling the years of a life that was far too brief. Distracted, she went through the motions automatically, helping the children hang up their coats in the cubbies and telling them to wash their hands. Used to the routine, they were soon sitting at the table, waiting for Lucy to get their lunches out of the refrigerator and bring them to the table.

They thought it was hysterical when she gave Justin's blue lunch box to Harry; everyone knew Harry had a Power Ranger lunch box. Their laughter roused Lucy, and she reluctantly returned to the here and now, letting go of Tucker's death for the time being.

"Are you sure the Power Ranger lunch box is Harry's?"

she teased, peeking inside. "I see Oreos—I think it must be mine."

All the children laughed, except Harry, who appeared a bit anxious.

"Oops, I forgot," said Lucy, slapping her hand to her head. "I didn't bring any lunch today. This must be Harry's!"

With a big sigh of relief Harry took the box and opened it up. Like the other children he began arranging the contents on the table in front of him.

Lucy went into the kitchen to get the milk and grabbed a few graham crackers for herself. After she poured the milk she sat with the children, nibbling on the crackers. She noticed that they all followed the same pattern: first they ate their cookies and fruit, after a lively trading session in which one fruit roll-up went for a box of raisins and two Vienna fingers, then they took a bite or two out of their sandwiches and discarded the rest.

Lucy was tidying the table, sighing over the waste, when Sue returned without Will.

"They wanted to keep him for a while, to make sure he isn't coming down with something, and I was afraid I'd never get away," complained Sue, "but his mother finally showed up. She had to cancel 'two very important meetings, mind you.'" Sue was a good mimic, and copied Steffie's officious tone perfectly. Lucy almost smiled.

"Hey, what's the matter?" prompted Sue. "You look as if something awful's happened."

"Barney came by with some bad news," began Lucy, wishing there was some way to soften what she had to say. "Tucker's dead."

"What?" Sue didn't believe what she heard.

"It's true. She was found dead this morning. A neighbor noticed the front door was open and called the police. Barney came here looking for an address book, so they can notify her family."

"Was it an accident?" Sue was struggling to understand.

Lucy shook her head. "They think she was strangled," she said, her voice breaking.

"Oh my God." Sue collapsed on a little chair, her long, elegant legs splayed out at an awkward angle.

Noticing the increase in the volume of the children's voices, Lucy turned her attention to them. Two of the girls were fighting over the bride's veil in the dress-up corner and Justin and Matthew were crashing toy wooden cars into each other.

"Okay, quiet down," she said, rising to her feet and giving Sue's hand a little pat. "It's time for a story."

Back in the familiar groove of their daily routine, the children gathered on the rug in the corner and sat cross-legged. Lucy settled herself in the rocking chair and opened the first book that came to hand. Afterward, she couldn't have said what book it was, but it held the kids' attention. Then, knowing the drill, they unrolled their mats and settled down for quiet time. Lucy popped a cassette of soothing music into the tape recorder and went back to Sue.

"Can I get you some tea? Something to eat?"

Sue didn't respond, so Lucy put two mugs of water in the microwave to heat and raided the graham-cracker box once again. Hearing the ding, she dropped tea bags into the mugs.

"Drink this," she urged Sue.

Sue took the mug with shaking hands. "I just can't believe this. I was with her yesterday."

"I know." Lucy sipped her tea. "You know what I was thinking last night, when I was talking to Tucker? I was thinking how wonderful it would be to be young again and have my whole life ahead of me."

Sue shook her head. "It's not fair. She loved life—she had so much enthusiasm. Once I asked her if she didn't get depressed sometimes, and you know what she said? She said she woke up every morning convinced that the day held something wonderful for her, and it was up to her to find that beautiful thing. It might be a smile from one of the kids, or a postcard from a friend, or a kitten . . . " Sue's face crumpled as she dissolved into tears.

Lucy wrapped an arm around Sue's shoulder and let her cry, grateful they were hidden from the children's view by a bookcase. Raffi's gentle voice drifted across the room. Finally, Sue's shoulders stopped heaving, and she wiped her eyes with a tissue.

"I'm sorry, Lucy. I don't know what's the matter with me. It must be the shock."

"You don't need to apologize. You have a right to grieve." Lucy wondered who else would be grieving for Tucker and remembered Barney's visit. "You know, Barney was looking for an address book but I don't think he found anything."

"She had a bright pink agenda—you know, calendar, address book, your whole life wrapped up with a Velcro flap." Sue sniffled and reached for another tissue.

"How big was it?" asked Lucy, going over to Tucker's desk. The top was bare except for a plant, a small pink mitten, and a picture of a smiling middle-aged couple. Lucy picked it up for a closer look. Tucker had inherited her coloring from her mother, but her smile came from her dad.

"About like this." Sue described a ten-inch square with her hands. "It was chunky, a couple of inches thick."

"It wouldn't fit in a pocket?" Lucy replaced the picture and slid the center drawer open. It was empty, except for a clutter of pens and pencils in the tray designed for them. Pulling open the top drawer on the side, Lucy noticed Sue had joined her.

"No, it was pretty big." Sue peered in the drawer. "She'd only been here a few months. She didn't have time to accumulate much."

The drawer held only a bottle of Advil and a spare pair of panty hose.

"What brought her here?" asked Lucy, pulling open the middle drawer and lifting out a sweater.

"She'd finished two years of college and wanted a break. Her folks said OK, as long as she did something useful. I almost fainted when she walked in one day, answering the help-wanted ad. I never expected to get anyone with her qualifications, not for what we pay. But she said she didn't need much money, she was living in her parents' summer house on the coast road."

Lucy raised an eyebrow. Smith Heights Road overlooked the cove and was lined with enormous, gray-shingled "cottages" belonging to wealthy old-line families who summered in Tinker's Cove but lived in New York, Washington, or Philadelphia. Among them were a cabinet secretary, a prominent pediatrician whose name had become a household word, and the celebrated talk-show hostess, Norah Hemmings. Others were CEOs or lawyers or investment bankers.

In the bottom drawer Lucy found a well-worn pair of loafers, a handful of college catalogs, and a guide to hiking trails.

Sue picked up one of the catalogs and fanned the pages. "She was thinking of changing her major—she wanted to concentrate in early childhood education. I warned her it was a bad career move—low-paying, not respected—but she said she didn't care. She said she loved working with kids." Sue closed her eyes and took a deep, quavery breath. "She said she'd never been happier."

Sue bent down to replace the catalogs in the drawer and gently shut it. When she stood up, her eyes were glistening.

"No sign of the agenda, here. And I know Barney didn't take it. I would've noticed."

"She usually carried a gym bag. She took a tai chi class after work. That's probably where it is. We don't need it, anyway. I have next-of-kin information on her emergency card." She sighed. "I can't let them nap forever. I've got to get them up. Would you call the police station for me?"

Lucy nodded. Sue stood up, then sat down, propping her elbow on the desk and resting her head in her hand. "Damn—I've got to find someone to replace Tucker." She rubbed her eyes. "At Christmastime, no less."

"Don't panic. I can help out some. And I bet there are plenty of young moms who could use some extra Christmas cash."

"We'll see." Sue didn't seem convinced. She got back up and, walking slowly, went over to the bookcase and clicked off the tape recorder, reaching her hands high over her head. "C'mon, kids. It's time to get up—let's see you all give a big stretch."

While Sue led the children in their wake-up exercises,

Lucy went to the phone and dialed the police station, asking for Barney.

"Did you find what you were looking for?" she asked.

"Nope. Not a thing."

"Sue says she had a pink agenda, one of those organizer books, and she kept it in her backpack."

"I'll pass that along, but I'm pretty sure they would have found it if it was there."

"Well, I can give you the information on her emergency card," said Lucy, pulling out the file folder and opening it up. "Mr. and Mrs. John Whitney," she read, trying very hard not to think of the smiling couple in the photograph on Tucker's desk.

"Thanks, Lucy," said Barney, when she had finished.

"Who's going to call them?" asked Lucy. "Will it be you?"

"I hope not." Barney sighed. He had knocked on too many doors late at night, bringing bad news. "I sure hope not."

"Me too," said Lucy, feeling a surge of anger as she replaced the receiver. It was bad enough the murderer had taken Tucker's life, but whoever it was had done more than that. So many people would be affected: the little children in the day-care center who had come to trust and love Tucker; Sue would not only have to cope with her own grief, but she would have to find a new assistant; the police officers would have to struggle with their own emotions as they investigated the case. Everyone in town would be touched by this violent death in some way. Women who had walked alone at night without giving their safety a thought would now look uneasily over their shoulders. At home, they would be extra careful to make sure the windows and doors were locked at night. Children would be warned not to talk to strangers. No one would be able to rest easy, Lucy realized, until the strangler was caught.

She refiled Tucker's emergency folder and snapped the cabinet shut, making a little vow to herself. Tucker's murderer would be found and punished.

Chapter Six

14 days 'til Xmas

The next morning, after Bill had left for work and the bus had carried the kids off to school, Lucy found herself alone in the house. Usually she enjoyed these few quiet early morning moments, sitting down at the kitchen table with a second cup of coffee and planning her day. She reached for her calendar and opened it—Christmas was only two weeks away, she realized with a shock, and her shopping was far from done. She still only had one present for Elizabeth; the earrings, and didn't have the slightest idea what else to get her.

Lucy pushed the calendar away. It might be December, all right, but it sure didn't feel like Christmas. Not with Tucker dead. Things like that shouldn't happen. Young girls shouldn't die, but it was especially cruel when it happened this time of year.

Tucker had a mother and father who had undoubtedly been making their own Christmas plans. Her father perhaps looking forward to a game of indoor tennis with his best girl, or maybe even a skiing trip. Her mother had probably been fussing over what to buy her for Christmas, just as Lucy was worrying about what to give Elizabeth. Or perhaps she had found just the right present and had tucked it away, carefully wrapped in jolly holiday paper.

How did people stand it, wondered Lucy. How did they manage to go on living after losing a child? Worst of all for Tucker's parents, thought Lucy, was the fact that she had been murdered. It would be hard enough to accept the loss of a child in an accident, but how did you deal with the knowledge that somebody had killed your precious daughter on purpose?

Unable to sit still any longer, Lucy pushed the chair back and stood up. She reached for the sponge and began wiping the counter, pacing back and forth the length of the kitchen. She tossed the sponge in the sink, spotting a gaily decorated tin that had gone unnoticed in the ever-present clutter, tucked away on top of the cookbooks.

Curious, Lucy opened it up and found a carefully arranged assortment of cookies from the cookie exchange. Puzzled, she furrowed her brow. Finally the light dawned. Someone, probably Franny, had put them aside for Marge.

No time like the present, thought Lucy, as a plan took shape. She'd been intending to visit Marge, anyway, and now she had a good excuse. And since Marge was married to Barney, she might have some inside information on the police investigation.

* * *

"Barney didn't have much to say about it," said Marge, straightening the scarf she was wearing to hide the effects of the chemotherapy. She was lying on an aging plaid Herculon couch, with her shoulders propped on a pile of cushions. "I think it upset him, her being so young and all. And anyway, the state police handle all the homicides."

"I know," said Lucy, taking a seat in the rocking chair. Somehow it seemed presumptuous to sit in Barney's big recliner. "But they use the local manpower, too. For routine things like questioning neighbors, running background checks. Did Barney happen to mention who's in charge of the investigation?"

Marge's expression brightened. "He did mention Lieutenant Horowitz, I think. He's usually the one they send."

Lucy recognized the name. Her most recent encounter with the lieutenant had been the year before, when she was a member of the library board of directors and there had been some trouble.

"He's very thorough," said Lucy, remembering that Horowitz had even considered her a possible suspect. "I wonder if they have any suspects yet? You know, I heard she was involved with Steve Cummings."

As she spoke, Lucy suddenly realized that Steve was the most likely suspect. The husband, or in this case, boyfriend, always was.

"That nice dentist?" Marge raised her eyebrows.

"That nice dentist walked out on his wife and two adorable little girls," said Lucy. "Lee was pretty upset with Tucker at the cookie exchange."

"I don't blame her," said Marge. "Though by rights

he's the one she should be angry with. And what's a man of his age doing with a young girl like Tucker anyway?"

"That seems to be the fashion nowadays. I guess it's some sort of status symbol to have a young girlfriend." It was that very generation gap, thought Lucy, that could cause problems in a relationship. Problems that could lead to murder.

"Nothing new about that," sniffed Marge. "It must be awful hard on their kids. Little girls, you said?"

"Hillary and Gloria. Gloria goes to school with Zoe, and Hillary's in the day-care center."

Marge clucked her tongue. "I suppose she has to work now that they're separated, but I don't see why these young mothers can't spend a few years at home with their little ones."

"They all have careers," Lucy said, remembering little Will's asthma attack the day before. "You know, I was helping Sue at the center yesterday, and Will Scott got sick. Sue had to take him to the emergency room, but when I called his mother she acted as if it was all a big inconvenience. She told me I should have called her husband."

"I guess I'm old-fashioned," said Marge, with a shrug. "I was raised that you never bothered a man at work. When Eddie broke his leg, I took him over to Doc Ryder. When the water heater broke and flooded the cellar, I was the one who called the plumber and got it fixed. Barney never knew what happened 'til it was all over and done with."

"Steffie's not like that, that's for sure," said Lucy. "But she takes an interest in Tom's work—she's real active in Mothers Against Drunk Driving."

"Now that's something I don't hold with," said Marge,

lifting a glass of water from the coffee table and taking a long drink. The table was filled with the clutter of illness: pill bottles, a heating pad, information pamphlets, and instruction sheets. "A man's work is his own business. Barney did his job, and I do mine. 'Course now it's different because I'm sick, but I always used to have a nice hot dinner on the table and a smile on my face when he came home from work. But I don't bother him about what he did or who's in trouble. If he wants to talk about it, fine, but I don't press him. It's hard enough being a cop, but he only has to do it forty hours a week. The rest of his time is his."

"It is a hard job, isn't it? After all, people don't call the police when everything's going great."

"That's for sure," agreed Marge. "But just between you and me it's worse than ever now that Tom Scott is the big cheese in the department."

Lucy couldn't help smiling. She hadn't heard that expression in years. "What's the problem?"

Marge shrugged. "Tom's got all these ideas about how Barney should improve his outreach program."

"Really?" Barney was the department's safety officer, and through the years Lucy had seen most of his presentations at the school. "He does a great job, and the kids love him. That bike-safety obstacle course, where he sets up the real traffic light, they all look forward to that. He always does it the first day after spring vacation."

Marge's face softened. "Barney loves it, too. You know, he made all those signs and the traffic light—spent one whole winter down in the cellar, building all that stuff." She sighed. "Traffic safety, stranger danger, all that's old hat according to Tom. He wants more antidrug and anti-alcohol education."

"For kindergarten?"

"Can't start too young, I guess. Gotta scare 'em straight. At least that's what he tells Barney."

"Gee, whatever happened to childhood innocence? We used to try to protect kids."

"That's what Barney says, but Tom's given him these curriculums he's supposed to use. Big, thick books." She glanced at the recliner, where a special pocket held the TV remote. "Barney's not much of a reader."

Lucy chuckled, recognizing the truth of Marge's statement.

"Actually," continued Marge, leaning forward, "I'm kind of worried. The more Tom leans on Barney, the more Barney resists. I'm afraid he's gonna snap and do something he'll regret. If he lost his job, I don't know what we'd do. We really need the medical insurance." She touched the scarf, reassuring herself that it hadn't slipped. "The surgery, the treatments, it's all very expensive."

"I wouldn't worry. Barney's got lots of seniority. I don't think they could fire him."

"I'm not worried about that, Lucy. I'm worried that he'll quit."

"He wouldn't do that—I can't imagine him as anything but a cop. It's what he is." Lucy patted her chest. "It's part of him."

"He keeps threatening. . . ."

"I think he's just talking." Lucy hoped it was true; she knew how vital medical insurance was. She and Bill had been unable to afford it themselves until the Chamber of Commerce set up a plan for members who were self-employed, like Bill. Before that, a case of pneumonia one winter had forced them to depend on food stamps and a loan from Bill's parents. Bill had only lost a few weeks of work, but the hospital had demanded payment and threatened legal action.

"Hey, did you hear about Richie?'" asked Lucy, eager to switch to a more positive subject. "He got into Harvard."

"That's wonderful," enthused Marge, relieved to have a new topic of conversation. "Of course, he's always been a bright boy. What are Toby's plans?"

"He says he's interested in several colleges, but he's being awfully lazy about the applications."

"Who can blame him?" Marge rubbed her forehead and Lucy suspected she was getting tired. "I tried to help Eddie, but I couldn't manage it."

This was news to Lucy. She had thought Eddie would probably get a job after high school or join the armed forces. "Where's Eddie applying?"

"Culinary school. He wants to be a chef."

Lucy was impressed. "That's a good idea. He's worked at the Greengage Café for a couple of summers, hasn't he?"

"He loves it. But he says he has to go to culinary school to be a chef."

"Maybe I could help," offered Lucy. "The boys could work on their applications together. It might be just what Toby needs to get his done, too. Eddie could come over one day next week."

"That'd be great, Lucy. You could help him with the essay part since you write for the paper and all."

"I'll do what I can." Lucy checked her watch. "I've got to get going. I've got a list of errands a mile long."

"Thanks for coming, and thanks for the cookies." Marge nodded at the tin on the coffee table.

"Is there anything I can get you before I go?"

"No, Lucy, I'm fine."

"You take care now," said Lucy, giving Marge a quick hug before she left. Then, heading downtown, she thought about their conversation.

She sympathized with Marge, but she also knew that under the leadership of Chief Crowley, whose health had been declining for years, the Tinker's Cove Police Department had settled into a long slumber. Maybe Tom Scott would bring some much-needed vigor to the department.

Then, rounding a corner, she drew up short, noticing Steve Cummings's dental office. Acting on impulse, she pulled into the drive and parked in the small parking area behind the building. She hadn't gotten much information from Marge. Why not question her prime suspect directly?

As she made her way up the neat brick path to the door she tried to think of an excuse for seeing the dentist. Have her teeth cleaned? Dr. Cummings probably had a dental hygienist who handled that chore, and, besides, she would probably have to make an appointment. A cleaning was hardly an emergency.

Could she claim she had a toothache? A really bad one that needed emergency attention? The idea made her uneasy. If Steve Cummings had murdered Tucker, she hardly wanted to put herself at his mercy in a dental chair.

No, she would have to try a different approach. By the time she pulled on the door she had a plan.

"Do you have an appointment?" inquired the woman behind the desk. She was a rather heavy, middle-aged woman with brass-colored hair cropped in one of those upswept styles that was supposed to make a woman of a

certain age look younger. It made this woman look like a
Marine drill sergeant, thought Lucy.

"No, I don't. I'm from *The Pennysaver*, you know, the
newspaper?"

The woman's face hardened. "We don't advertise," she
said. "It's a matter of professional ethics."

"Oh, no. I'm not selling advertising. I write for the
paper. I'm Lucy Stone."

The drill sergeant was not impressed with this information.

Lucy smiled, and plunged ahead, improvising as she
went.

"Actually, I'm working on a feature story. We're asking prominent citizens, you know, people our readers will
recognize, what they want for Christmas. It's kind of a
man-in-the-street thing, with kind of a new twist? It'll
only take a minute of the doctor's time."

"I don't think so." The drill sergeant shook her head.
"In fact, Dr. Cummings has cut back his schedule today.
He's only seeing a few patients whose treatment can't be
delayed."

"Could you just ask him for me?" persisted Lucy. "In
my experience, most of the people we interview for stories like this are pleased and flattered by the attention."

"I don't think that would be the case here." The receptionist's tone was flat.

"You never know. He might be upset if he learned
you'd sent me away," suggested Lucy. "It's good publicity, and it's free. . . ."

Just then the door behind the receptionist's desk
opened and Dr. Cummings appeared in his white jacket,
followed by an elderly woman who looked a bit dazed.

"Ruth, I want you to make another appointment for Mrs. Slade here. Preferably next week." He handed a chart to the receptionist and quickly consulted a clipboard, then turned to Lucy. "Mrs. Green?"

"Oh, no," Lucy said quickly, before the receptionist could get her two cents in. "I'm Lucy Stone, from *The Pennysaver*."

She watched his face closely, looking for a reaction, but Steve Cummings wasn't giving anything away. He looked the same as always, a thirtysomething professional with thinning hair and wire-rimmed glasses, except that today his eyes looked tired.

"I'm doing a feature story about Christmas, and I'd just like to ask you a few quick questions, if you don't mind?"

"Sure. Come on in."

Lucy followed him, making a point not to look at the receptionist. She knew looks couldn't kill, but she wasn't taking any chances.

He led her into a small office, with a large desk. He seated himself behind it, and Lucy took a chair.

"It's just a man-in-the-street sort of thing," she began, letting her hands flutter in front of her. "I'm supposed to ask various important people, you know, people our readers will recognize, what they want for Christmas. You can be as serious or as funny as you want to be. And, of course, I have to take your picture."

She bent down to fumble in her purse for her notebook, all the time keeping an eye on Dr. Cummings. He leaned back in his chair, folding his arms behind his head.

"What I want for Christmas, eh?" He sighed, and a shadow seemed to pass over his face. Then he focused his eyes on her. "There's something I always wanted, ever since I was a kid, but I never got. My parents didn't think it was appropriate: a G.I. Joe doll. They didn't approve of dolls for boys, but I'm telling you, they made a big mistake. I saw one at an antique show not long ago, and it was worth a bundle."

Lucy smiled and scribbled down his quote. Actually, she thought, this could turn out to be a good idea for a story. But before she left, she had another question she wanted to ask. She pulled her camera out of her bag and waved it apologetically in front of her face.

"Now's the tough part. I have to take your picture."

"Go ahead. Shoot."

She glanced around the room. "You're against the window—that doesn't work. Could you stand against the wall?"

"Oh, sure." He got up and moved into position, straightening his jacket and smiling.

"You know, I really lucked out with this assignment. I was afraid I'd have to cover that murder," volunteered Lucy, from behind her camera.

"That was a terrible thing," said Steve. His smile was gone. He looked as if he was going to cry.

"Oh, I'm sorry," said Lucy, lowering her camera. "I didn't know you knew her."

"Only slightly." Steve's expression became guarded. "But I have a wife and two daughters. I don't like the idea of something like this happening in Tinker's Cove."

"I'm surprised to hear you say that." Lucy smiled mischievously at him. "I was at a party with Lee a few nights ago, and it didn't sound as if she would mind if you were murdered one bit."

He gave a hollow chuckle. "I guess that's par for the course. We're separated, you know, but hopefully we'll work things out."

"Hopefully." Lucy raised the camera again. "Now think of those two beautiful daughters of yours." His face brightened, and he smiled; Lucy snapped the photo.

"Thanks so much for your time," she said, starting to pack up her camera and notebook, when the door flew open.

The receptionist was clucking nervously, like a hen spying a hungry dog on the other side of the fence. No wonder, thought Lucy, recognizing the man behind her: Lieutenant Horowitz, the state police detective.

"I was just leaving," said Lucy, heading for the door.

"Good idea," said Horowitz, making eye contact with her. "This is the last I want to see of you, Mrs. Stone. Do you understand?"

Lucy hastened to reassure him. "Yes. Yes, I do. I'm gone. You won't see me again."

"I hope not." Horowitz pulled his long upper lip down, and pressed it against his bottom lip. It made him look a little bit like a rabbit. Then he turned. "Dr. Cummings, I have a few questions for you. . . ."

So, great minds think alike, thought Lucy, pushing the door open. She wasn't the only one who suspected Cummings. Pausing for a moment on the stoop, she surveyed the scene. Not only did she recognize the detective's gray sedan, but two cruisers were also parked on the street in front of the office. Horowitz had brought reinforcements.

She slung her shoulder bag up over her arm and started down the path to her car. What she wouldn't give to hear Horowitz's questions.

But as she started her car, she couldn't help harboring a few doubts. Somehow, Steve Cummings just didn't seem like a murderer to her.

Chapter Seven

As she headed downtown to the dry cleaners, Lucy tried to sort through her confusing thoughts. Logically, she knew Steve was the obvious suspect—boyfriends and husbands accounted for the great majority of murdered women. Her instincts, however, told a different story. Steve had seemed friendly and open, he hadn't seemed like a man with a death on his conscience. And even if all the terrible things Lee said about him were true, which Lucy doubted, there was no question that he adored his little girls. She couldn't forget the way his face had brightened when she told him to think of Hillary and Gloria when she snapped his picture.

Lucy pulled into a free parking space and picked Bill's good sport coat off the passenger seat. She sat there, holding it in her lap, wondering if she could really trust her feelings about Steve. Murderers, she knew, didn't come with handy identifying marks on their foreheads. Mostly, they were ordinary people who had snapped for one reason or other: sweet-faced young babysitters who had shaken a crying baby a bit too hard, frustrated boyfriends whose anger had gotten out of control, battered wives who hadn't seen any other way out.

Just because Steve seemed like a perfectly nice guy didn't mean he couldn't have murdered Tucker. Lucy didn't have access to the evidence, she didn't know what Lieutenant Horowitz had found at the crime scene. All she had to go on was her gut feeling, and that didn't count for much in a court of law. She sighed and opened the car door.

Inside the little shop, with its strong chemical scent, Lucy had to give her name and phone number.

"I thought I knew most people in town," said the clerk, with a little sniff.

"We're not regular customers," explained Lucy, taking the little pink slip. "Most of our clothes go in the washing machine."

As she pushed open the door and headed back to the car, she decided to pay a visit to the person who knew Steve best: Lee. It wasn't as if she was getting involved in the case, she told herself. Not at all. She had a very good reason for stopping in the decorating shop where Lee worked. Since Bill was going to have to repair the dining-room ceiling, anyway, they might as well freshen the room up with some new wallpaper.

Captain Crosby Interiors occupied one of the big old houses on Main Street, in fact, it had been occupied briefly by Captain Elisha Crosby after his marriage to the lovely Betsy Billings. Local legend had it that he kissed Betsy good-bye one fine February morning in 1886, promising to return by Christmas with a hold full of China tea, and was never heard from again.

Nowadays, the fine old house was an ideal setting for the shop, which sold fabrics and wallpapers. Lee had worked there part-time for years, mostly as a hobby, but had switched to full-time after the separation.

When Lucy entered, Lee was busy with a customer so she gave her a little wave and settled herself down with the wallpaper books. As she flipped the pages, she tried to think of a graceful way to bring up her questions about Steve. After all, just because Lee wasn't very happy with him these days didn't necessarily mean she would welcome the idea that he was a suspect in a police investigation.

As it happened, however, Lucy didn't have to find a way to work the murder into the conversation after all. Lee couldn't wait to talk about it.

"Lucy!" she exclaimed, after her customer had left. "Did you hear about Tucker?"

"Isn't it terrible," murmured Lucy.

"You won't find me shedding any tears for that little hussy," declared Lee. "If you ask me, she got what she deserved. I don't know if you knew, but she'd been trying to steal Steve away from me."

"I'd heard something like that," admitted Lucy. "Was it serious? I mean, do you think Steve was planning to marry her?"

Lee snorted. "That little snippet? I don't think so. Not that she wasn't trying. And it wasn't just Steve, either. She was doing her darnedest to turn Hillary against me."

Lucy's chin dropped. "What do you mean?"

"At the day-care center. She always made a huge fuss over Hillary. Big hellos and good-byes, even hugs and kisses. It was a bit much, if you ask me. Oh, I know you're not supposed to speak ill of the dead, but this is one death that couldn't have happened to a nicer person."

Lucy was glad she was already sitting. If she hadn't been, she would definitely have needed a chair. Lee's attitude would have knocked her off her feet.

"Aren't you worried that the police might suspect Steve?" she asked.

"Steve?" Lee thought this was hilarious. "Are you kidding? He couldn't even drop a lobster into a pot of boiling water. I always have to do it."

Lucy looked at her curiously, and Lee gave her head a shake.

"Listen to me, going on like this. You didn't come in here to talk about my marriage. What can I help you with? Wallpaper?"

"For the dining room. Since we have to fix the ceiling anyway, I thought we might as well do the whole room."

"Good idea! I have just the thing. It would be beautiful in your house."

Lee pulled a book out from beneath the counter and set it in front of Lucy. With a flourish, she revealed a bright Oriental design featuring enormous, brightly colored peacocks.

"Isn't that gorgeous? That blue! And the green and the pink. Go for it, Lucy. People are so afraid of color. It's a big mistake when it can bring life and excitement to your home."

"I was thinking of something more . . . beige," said Lucy.

"Beige?" Lee was disappointed.

"Maybe a stripe," suggested Lucy.

"I've got it." Lee pulled out another book. "Wainscoting! That way you can have your cake and eat it, too. Color on the bottom of the wall, something light and airy above."

"That's a good idea," admitted Lucy, intrigued.

"It would be nothing at all for Bill to put up a little bit of molding."

"It would really dress up the room. I'll think about it. Can I take the book?"

"Sure." Lee drew closer and lowered her voice. "Don't tell anybody I told you this, but I can probably do something for you on the price. We have a big sale after Christmas, anyway."

"Thanks, Lee. I'll get back to you as soon as I can."

"There's no rush. Take your time."

Lucy couldn't swear to it but she thought Lee was humming a happy little tune as she saw her to the door.

"Have a nice day, now, you hear."

As she walked down the pathway to her car, Lucy was so deep in thought that she didn't notice Lieutenant Horowitz approaching.

"I seem to keep running into you," he said, eyeing her with disapproval. "And I don't think it's a coincidence. I'm beginning to suspect that you're conducting your own investigation of Tucker Whitney's death."

Lucy looked up, startled. "I'm sorry. What did you say?"

"I said I think you ought to mind your own business instead of poking your nose into an official police investigation, that's what I said."

"Oh, I'm not. . . ."

"Don't give me that," growled Horowitz. "I know what you're up to, and I'm warning you that you could be breaking the law."

Lucy smiled sweetly, and held up the wallpaper book as proof of her innocence. "Buying wallpaper is against the law?"

"No, Mrs. Stone. There's no law against buying wallpaper, but there are plenty of laws about obstructing justice."

"Well, I happen to be interested in wallpaper," said Lucy, allowing a self-righteous tone to creep into her voice.

"Right," muttered the lieutenant, brushing past her and pulling open the door to the shop.

Lucy continued on her way to her car, checking her watch as she went. It was later than she thought, she realized, thinking guiltily of the long list of Christmas errands she hadn't done. With only two weeks left until the holiday she'd wasted an entire day running around town looking for information, and she didn't even have the comfort of knowing she'd made any progress. The sun was already setting, a giant red ball sinking behind the stark, black silhouettes of the bare trees, and she had more questions about Tucker's murder than she'd had that morning when she set out. All she'd managed to accomplish, she realized, was to antagonize Lieutenant Horowitz. Now, the kids were home from school and she had to get home, too, and put that roast in the oven if they were going to have it for supper.

Chapter Eight

13 days 'til Xmas

Today was another day, another chance to tackle that list of errands, resolved Lucy as she started the car on Friday morning. If she didn't get anything else done, she definitely had to get the Christmas cards mailed. Then she had to go to the bank, get gas and groceries, and stop at the church to pick up Zoe's angel costume for the Christmas pageant.

As she drove down Red Top Road and turned toward town and the post office, she remembered that she only had a few dollars in her wallet. She turned and was driving down Main Street, approaching the rec building on her way to the Seamen's and Merchants' Bank, when a huge Ford Expedition suddenly pulled out in front of her, directly in her path.

Lucy slammed on the brake and held on to the steering

wheel for dear life, narrowly missing a collision. As she watched, horrified, the Expedition almost tipped over as the driver made a sharp turn into the narrow street. For a second or two it was only on two wheels, then the driver gained control and it righted itself. As it sped down the street past her, Lucy got a clear view of the operator. It was Lee.

Making a quick decision, Lucy flipped on her blinker and turned into the rec-center parking lot Lee had just exited. She must have just dropped Hillary off at the day-care center; maybe Sue would know what was going on.

"I haven't got a clue," said Sue, who was on her knees struggling to unzip Hillary's jacket. "Mommy was in a hurry this morning, wasn't she?"

After a few more tugs the zipper opened, and Hillary shrugged out of her jacket and ran across the room to join Emily at the toy stove.

Sue examined the zipper, fingering the place where the fabric was torn.

"I don't know what's going on, but this obviously wasn't a good morning for Lee. She just shoved Hillary through the door and left, never said a word."

"She was driving like a maniac when she left here. Almost ran right into me."

Sue shook her head. "Maybe she's finally realized that Steve's a suspect in the murder. Last night Horowitz paid me a visit and all his questions were about Tucker's relationship with Steve."

"He's the obvious suspect. Obvious to everyone except Lee."

"Oh, I don't know. It seemed to me that he and Tucker were more good friends than anything else. Tucker told me she liked him and all, but she thought he was too old for her. She said it was like dating her father!"

"Maybe Tucker wasn't serious, but Steve was," suggested Lucy. "Sounds like a motive to me."

"Could be." Sue glanced around the room, making sure the children were all behaving themselves.

Lucy took the cue. "I've got to go—have a nice weekend."

"It doesn't look too good right now. Tucker's parents are coming to make funeral arrangements—the service is going to be on Monday night—and they want to meet with me."

Sue's expression was grim, and Lucy knew she was dreading the meeting.

"Will you be all right? Do you want me to go with you for moral support?"

"Thanks, Lucy," said Sue squeezing her hand, "This is something I have to do alone. I'll be all right."

"Okay. Call me if you change your mind."

Back in the car, Lucy tried to sort out her thoughts. From what Sue said, it seemed that Steve was definitely the prime suspect. Horowitz had questioned him, he'd questioned Lee, he'd even questioned Sue about Steve's relationship with Tucker.

Lucy tried not to think about how likable she'd found Steve, she tried not to think about how happy Lee had been to have Steve all to herself again, she tried not to think about little Hillary and Gloria. Whatever was going to happen was out of her hands. If Horowitz had the evidence, there was no doubt he would arrest Steve Cummings.

All weekend, Lucy followed the newscasts. She tuned

in while she drove Sara and Zoe to their friends' houses on Saturday, she listened to the radio while she cooked supper that night. On Sunday morning she was so eager to see the paper that she went out to the plastic tube that stood by the road in her slippers, even though there were two inches of snow. Her feet got cold and wet, but she didn't learn anything new. Police were reported to be continuing the investigation, but there were no new breaks in the story.

On Sunday afternoon, she and Bill left the kids home and went to the mall in Portland to finish their Christmas shopping. Bill was happily humming along to a favorite Clapton tune when Lucy switched the radio to the all-news channel.

"Why'd you do that?" he asked.

"I keep waiting to hear if they've arrested Tucker's murderer," she explained.

"I'm sure they'll break in with an announcement if that happens," he said, switching back to the local music station. "Why don't you just sit back and enjoy this rare opportunity to be alone with me? I'm your favorite husband, after all."

"Okay," said Lucy, laughing, and temporarily shelving her intention to talk to him about Toby. "It's just you and me and a very long shopping list."

At the mall, Lucy couldn't help thinking that Bill looked a little out of place in the trendy juniors shop, refugee from the granola wars in his beard and corduroy slacks, topped with a plaid flannel shirt and a bulky down jacket. He surprised her when he pointed to a sparkling spandex T-shirt and suggested they buy it for Elizabeth.

"That?" Lucy raised her eyebrows doubtfully. To her, it looked sleazy. Besides, it was overpriced at thirty-nine dollars.

"She'll love it," he said, nodding positively. "I saw something just like it on MTV. And it's on sale."

He was right, Lucy realized, spotting a sign indicating the whole rack was one-third off.

"That makes it . . ." She furrowed her brow as she figured the math.

"About twenty-four dollars."

"Okay." Lucy pulled the shirt from the rack.

Now, on Monday afternoon, as she tucked tissue paper around the shirt and arranged it in the box, she couldn't help smiling fondly. That was the thing about Bill. He kept surprising her. Married for almost twenty years, and he hadn't lost the power to amaze her. That itself was astonishing, she thought, picking up the ringing phone.

"Oh, Lucy," wailed Sue. "It was awful."

"What was?"

"Tucker's parents came."

Lucy sat down on the bed, remembering how worried Sue had been on Friday afternoon. It seemed like eons ago.

"That must have been sad. Were they real emotional?"

"That was the worst part. They're terribly polite, you know, and very stiff-upper-lip and all that. But you could tell they were all ripped up and torn inside. They should have been beating their breasts and sobbing, but instead they were telling me they didn't want to intrude and would only take a minute but they did want to gather up Tucker's belongings and by any chance, if it wasn't too much trouble, could I tell them a little bit about her work at the center?"

"What did you say?"

"What I told you. That she really seemed to enjoy her work and that I don't know what I'll do without her." Sue paused. "They wanted to know if she'd seemed troubled or anxious—they really seemed to want to know about that."

"Of course they would."

"I couldn't bring myself to tell them anything about Steve—I just said I hadn't noticed anything wrong. I should have noticed something, shouldn't I?"

"Don't blame yourself," said Lucy. "What could you have done? You didn't even know about Steve until she told you on the way to the cookie exchange."

"If only she'd confided in me sooner. I could have advised her, warned her to be careful. I don't know."

"Well, Steve is the last person you'd think to warn her about," said Lucy, matter-of-factly.

"You think it really was him?"

"I'm not convinced, myself, but I think it's just a matter of time until he gets arrested. What I can't figure out is what's taking the police so long."

Sue was silent for a minute. Finally, she spoke. "Well, at least then the Whitneys will know what happened to Tucker. They say that the trial brings a sense of closure to the victim's family."

"I wish I believed that," said Lucy, remembering Tucker's bright presence at the cookie exchange. "I don't think parents ever get over the death of a child. Oh, they go on living, but they're never the same. It's like they're walking wounded."

"You're right." Sue's voice was so sad that Lucy struggled for some way to console her.

"You gave her something wonderful, you know. You gave her the job at the center and she discovered her vocation—that she wanted to work with kids. She loved working at the center, everybody says so. And she was perfect for it. She was bright and happy and full of energy." Lucy paused, hearing the kids arriving home from school in the kitchen downstairs. "That's how I'm going to remember her. Now, I've got to go. It sounds as if the Mongol hordes have found the refrigerator."

"I better let you go, then." Sue sniffled. "Thanks for everything, Lucy. Talking to you really helped."

"Anytime. Now, for my next challenge: preventing World War III."

In the kitchen, Lucy found Eddie and Toby with their heads buried in the refrigerator. Elizabeth was perched on the counter, legs crossed, doing her best to catch Eddie's eye. Sara was prying open a yogurt carton, not having bothered to remove her coat, and Zoe was precariously balanced on a kitchen chair, trying to reach the cookies in the cabinet high above the stove.

"Hi, Eddie," began Lucy. "Elizabeth—off the counter. Zoe, don't climb on chairs, it's dangerous. Sara, hang up your coat. Toby, reach that bag of gingersnaps for me."

Lucy set out a plate of cookies and poured big glasses of milk for the boys. Elizabeth didn't want any; she fled from calories like a vampire avoided the rays of the sun. Sara took the yogurt into the family room and Zoe renewed her efforts to scale the kitchen cabinets, this time looking for the chocolate syrup.

Lucy pried her loose and joined the boys at the kitchen table, planting Zoe in her lap.

"So, are you going to work on those college applications today?" she asked. She turned her gaze on Toby. "As I remember, you owe me one, and today's a good day to make good."

Toby grimaced and popped a cookie in his mouth. Eddie shifted his bulky frame in the chair and leaned back, brushing his crew cut with his hand. Lucy was struck yet again by how much he resembled his father, Barney.

"You don't want to be a cop, like your dad?" Lucy realized she had spoken without intending to.

Eddie's face reddened; he looked uncomfortable. "Nah," he finally said, reaching for another cookie.

"He just likes to eat—that's why he wants to go to cooking school." Toby punched Eddie's shoulder.

Lucy shook her head. They might be bigger, she thought, but they behaved just like the little Cub Scouts who used to cluster around her kitchen table every week.

"Did you bring the applications?"

Eddie nodded and pulled a thick sheaf of papers from his backpack.

"Well, it looks as if you guys have your work cut out for you. Why don't you get started—just jot down some ideas for those essays. I'll see how you're doing in about half an hour, OK?"

"Sure thing, Mom," said Toby, pulling his own pile of papers toward him and opening the top folder.

"Call me if you get stuck," she said, heading downstairs to the washer and dryer.

* * *

From time to time Lucy peeked in the kitchen and saw the boys bent over the table, apparently deeply immersed in the applications. When she noticed it was beginning to get dark, she decided to ask Eddie to stay for dinner. But when she went into the kitchen she found the boys had disappeared, leaving the papers behind. Leafing through the printed forms she saw that only the most basic questions had been answered; there was no sign of any progress on the questions that required essays.

"January 1. These are due January 1," she muttered to herself, looking out the window.

There was no sign of the boys in the yard, so she checked the family room and went upstairs to peek in Toby's room.

"Have you seen Toby?" she asked Elizabeth, who was reclining on the couch in the family room and flipping through channels with the remote. "By the way, don't you have any homework?"

"Nope. Tomorrow is 'Smart Kids, Smart Choices.'"

"What's that?"

Elizabeth pulled a wad of folded paper from her pocket. "Don't read the back, OK?"

"Scout's honor," said Lucy, carefully prying the layers apart and studying the Xeroxed notice.

"Smart Kids, Smart Choices," she learned, was made possible by the Tinker's Cove Police Department and the PTA. This traveling troupe of reformed alcoholics and drug abusers, none older than twenty-five, would present a "hard-hitting, graphic account" based on their own experiences. The rest of the morning would be spent in discussion groups and in the afternoon the entire school population would work together to create message murals that would be displayed in the halls.

"This is taking all day?" asked Lucy "What about French and chemistry and algebra and . . ."

"Oh, Mom," groaned Elizabeth in a world-weary voice. "If they actually taught us chemistry, we'd probably just cook up our own drugs. That's what they think, anyway."

"Well, maybe if they taught you some solid reasoning skills, they wouldn't have to indoctrinate you and you could figure out for yourselves that drinking and using drugs isn't very smart."

"Interesting, Mom," said Elizabeth. "Very interesting." She studied her fingernails, which were painted light blue. "But hopelessly retro."

"That's me. Hopelessly retro,"agreed Lucy, who had received a solid prep-school education and could still conjugate her Latin verbs, even if her inability to comprehend percentages had been the despair of the entire math department. She resolved to call the principal for a little chat, in which the school's declining SAT scores would definitely be mentioned.

Failing to find the boys in the house, Lucy concluded that they must be outside. She stood in the kitchen doorway and yelled for them. Their heads popped out from behind the shed, only to disappear immediately.

What are they up to? she wondered, pulling on her jacket. She marched across the yard, straight to the shed.

"What are you guys doing? Are you smoking?" she asked, suspiciously.

This last was met with gales of laughter. Laughter that didn't stop, but rolled on, eventually forcing the boys to clutch their stomachs and sides. There was also a sweet, familiar scent in the air.

"Pot!" exclaimed Lucy. "You've been smoking pot!"

Suddenly Toby's odd behavior made sense, including the disappearance of her Dee-Liteful Wine Cake.

"Shhh, Mom. Not so loud." Still shaking with laughter, Toby put a finger over his mouth to caution her.

"I can't believe it!" She shoved Toby in the direction of the house. "How stupid are you? Don't you know you could get in big trouble?"

Eddie and Toby glanced at each other and dissolved into giggles.

"Where did you get it?"

"It's all over the school, Mom," said Toby. "You can get whatever you want."

"You can? Like what?"

"Uppers, downers, heroin, crack . . ."

"Crack!"

"Yeah, Mom. Crack."

"You've actually seen crack?"

"Well, no," admitted Toby. "But I've heard about it."

"And who's the person who's got all this stuff?"

Now the boys weren't giggling. Their glance was an agreement not to reveal any names.

"Okay, okay," said Lucy, backing off. She shook her head. "Boy, your dad isn't going to like this."

"Mom—you're not gonna tell Dad, are you?"

"Of course I am. And Eddie's dad, too."

"You can't do that, Mom," begged Toby. "Dad's already pissed off at me."

"And my mom's sick and all—this'll kill her," added Eddie.

Lucy took a deep breath. "Okay," she finally said. "I won't tell anybody, but you have to promise not to do this again. Ever. OK?"

The boys nodded.

"Now, inside. I'm going to make some coffee."

It was all she could think of that might counteract the effect of the marijuana and return the boys to their normal state. Not that they seemed to be out of control. They were content to sit at the table, watching her scoop instant coffee into mugs with bemused expressions on their faces.

"I can't believe you're this stupid," she hissed at them. "Especially after what happened to Tim Rogers. He got himself into a mess of trouble, and you could, too, if you get caught with marijuana."

She poured hot water into the mugs, set them in front of the boys, then made one for herself.

"And you've wasted the whole afternoon," she couldn't help adding, glancing at the unfinished applications. "Don't you want to get this over with and get those damned things in the mail?"

Toby shrugged and shoveled several spoonfuls of sugar into his mug. "I don't know, Mom. I don't know if it's worth it."

"What do you mean?" Lucy was puzzled. "You have wonderful opportunities ahead of you." She glanced at Eddie. "Both of you. You're lucky you have families that will help you get the educations you want."

"Dad's not so keen," said Toby, stirring his coffee.

"My dad isn't either," admitted Eddie.

"That's not exactly true," said Lucy, with a flash of insight. "They just don't want to admit that you're growing up."

Toby sook a slurp of coffee. "Really good, Mom. Reeelly good. Taste it, Ed."

Eddie gulped down half a cup and smiled. "Yeah, man. Good."

Lucy sighed. "Well, I guess you're not going to finish these today." Lucy gathered up the papers.

"What's the point?" asked Toby. "Look what happened to Tim."

"Yeah," agreed Eddie. "He trained all year long. Made All State and MVP. And then they took away his scholarship. Over nothing."

"He lost his scholarship? Because he was arrested?"

"Bastards took it back," fumed Eddie.

Lucy was seized with the desire to grab the two boys by the scruffs of their necks and knock their heads together. Instead, she counted to ten. Then she spoke.

"You don't get it, do you? Tim broke the law, that's why he lost the scholarship. He got drunk and he drove the car and he got caught. It's nobody's fault but his own. Get that straight."

But looking at them, she knew they didn't believe her. To them, Tim was just proof that the harder you tried, the more you had to lose. Therefore, you might as well not try in the first place.

Finishing her coffee, she revised her earlier opinion of "Smart Kids, Smart Choices." Maybe it wasn't such a bad idea after all. It certainly couldn't hurt, she thought, watching as the boys finished off the last of the ginger-snaps.

Chapter Nine

"You'll ruin your appetites." Lucy couldn't help saying it, even though she didn't think it mattered much to the boys whether they had room for dinner or not.

Dinner, she realized with a start. She'd forgotten all about it. She had to get the chili cooking, and then she had to do something about getting Eddie home. Normally, Toby would drive him home in her car, but she couldn't let him do that while he was still feeling the effects of the pot. She would have to do it herself.

"I'm really angry with you," she told Toby. "Now I have to rush to get dinner made because I have to drive Eddie home. I can't believe you boys are so inconsiderate, so irresponsible."

"Don't mean to be, Mom," said Toby, brushing away a

tear. He was clearly coming down from his high, ready to wallow in depression.

"Get out of here," said Lucy, losing patience. "I'll call you when I'm ready to go."

The boys thumped up the back stairs to Toby's room, and soon Lucy heard the repetitive thumps of a rap CD. Scowling to herself, she pulled a pan out of the cupboard and began browning a couple of pounds of ground turkey. While it cooked, she chopped up some onions, then added them to the meat along with some chili powder. She dumped in a few cans of beans and tomatoes, gave the whole mess a stir and covered the pot, setting the heat on low. Then she went in the family room to assign one of the girls to watch the pot.

Before she could ask Sara to keep an eye on the chilli, Toby and Eddie thundered into the room.

"You can't stop us, we're so tough we'll drop ya . . ." they cited together in rap style, hunching up their shoulders and leaning forward, stepping from side to side in unison.

"Mom, Eddie and Toby are acting weird," said Sara.

"They're just fooling around," said Lucy.

"Toby was crying—I heard him." The expression on Sara's round little face was serious. "And they ate all the cookies."

Lucy didn't know what to say. She certainly didn't want to give Sara the true explanation for the boys' mood swings and extraordinary appetites.

"They're worried about getting into college," she finally said, glancing at the dancing duo. "Stress can make you do strange things. Listen, Peanut. I have to get some milk, so I'm going to take Eddie home. Will you watch the chili for me? Give it a stir now and then and if it looks like it's cooking too hard, just turn the stove off. OK?"

"OK, Mom."

"C'mon, boys—it's time to go." Lucy herded the two gangsta rappers out of the family room and into the kitchen, where she handed them their jackets.

"Have you got all your stuff?" she asked Eddie.

"Yeah, I think so," said Eddie, taking his backpack from her.

She was sure he didn't have a clue. In fact, neither did Toby. The two were standing in the kitchen, waiting to be told what to do next.

"Car."

They nodded and shuffled out the door. She followed, shaking her head. It must be true, she thought. Pot today must be stronger than it was when she was in college. She'd smoked it a few times herself back then, but she didn't remember it having much of an effect.

Getting the seat belts fastened seemed to be quite beyond both boys so Lucy helped strap them in. Just like when they were little, she thought. Only then they were cute; now they were really beginning to get on her nerves. She climbed in behind the wheel and started the car. Her favorite classical radio station came on and the boys groaned, so she switched to WRPP, their favorite, to pacify them.

A song, or something like a song, was just ending, and the five o'clock news was next. After a string of commercials for cars, soft drinks, and a record store, they heard the familiar voice of deejay Fat Fred.

"We start tonight's news with a live report from Tinker's Cove, where state police have arrested dentist Steve

Cummings, charging him with the murder of Tucker Whitney last Wednesday. State Police Lieutenant Horowitz made the announcement just moments ago."

Lucy's right hand left the steering wheel and rested on her lips, she used her left hand to pilot the car down the driveway and on to Red Top Road. As much as she expected this. turn of events, it still shocked her. She listened to the sound bite with Horowitz's voice.

"The swift conclusion of this investigation was possible largely due to the efforts of the Tinker's Cove Police Department; in particular the crime-scene management of Lieutenant Tom Scott made possible the preservation of crucial evidence."

Then it was back to Fat Fred, who said Dr. Cummings would be arraigned in superior court the next morning.

Wow, thought Lucy. She'd never known Horowitz to share credit for an arrest. Wasn't Barney always complaining that while the local cops did much of the grunt work in criminal investigations the state police always acted as if they'd done everything?

"Say, man, isn't that your dentist?" Toby asked Eddie.

"Whuh?"

"Who's your dentist?" persisted Toby.

"Dr. Cummings." Eddie gave him a big. smile, revealing massive blocks of gleaming tooth enamel. "He's OK, for a dentist."

"Yeah, right. He just got arrested for murder."

"No way." Eddie shook his head.

"Way, man," said Lucy. "Way."

When Lucy got home, she found Bill sniffing a gallon container of milk.

"Sara said you went out to get milk, but we have this and part of another. Is there something wrong with it?"

"Uh, I guess I didn't see it," said Lucy, realizing she had been caught fibbing.

Just then, Toby shuffled into the kitchen, muttering under his breath. Bill glanced at him curiously.

"Actually, I forgot all about the milk. I came straight home because Toby said he was feeling kind of sick."

Lucy attempted to make eye contact with Toby, and jerked her head toward the stairs.

"I think you'd better go lie down. Right, Toby?"

"Whuh?"

"Lie down. I think you have a little fever. You'll feel better when you wake up."

Much to her relief, Toby disappeared up the back stairway. Bill watched him go, then turned to Lucy.

"Is something going on that I ought to know about?"

"I don't think so," said Lucy, checking on the chilli. She lifted out a fragrant spoonful. "Here, taste this. Tell me what you think."

She held the spoon and Bill took a bite.

"Mmmm."

"Mmmm good or mmmm needs something?"

"Mmmm good."

Hearing a clattering sound, Lucy and Bill turned toward the stairs. Toby staggered back into the kitchen and plopped himself in one of the chairs.

"When's dinner, Mom? I'm starved."

His eyes were abnormally bright. Lucy noticed and so did Bill. He bent down and studied them.

"Are you on something?" he asked suspiciously.

"Nah, Dad."

"I think he has a little fever," said Lucy, making a show of placing her hand on Toby's forehead.

Bill planted his feet in the middle of the kitchen and stared at Lucy. Then he turned his gaze on Toby. He shrugged and reached for his jacket.

"I'm not a fool," he said, and walked out the door.

Dinner, without Bill and with Toby's odd behavior, was an experience Lucy was only too happy to forget. It was almost enough, she decided as she slipped behind the wheel of the Subaru, to make Tucker's memorial service seem an attractive prospect.

But not quite enough, she decided, when she took her seat in a pew at St. Christopher's Episcopal Church. Bending her head, she recited the Lord's Prayer in an effort to focus her thoughts. She was here to remember Tucker, not to fret about her own problems at home.

She raised her head and listened to the organ music. There, in the front row, she saw a well-groomed couple accompanied by two teenage boys with shining caps of blond hair. Tucker's parents and her brothers. She hadn't realized Tucker had two younger brothers. Tears sprang to her eyes, and she screwed them shut, covering them with her hand.

When the tears stopped coming Lucy reached in her pocket for a tissue and wiped her eyes.

"Tough, isn't it?"

Lucy looked up and saw Sue taking the seat next to her. She nodded, and Sue took her hand. Sue's face, Lucy saw, was wet with tears, and she passed her a clean tissue.

I hope I brought enough, thought Lucy, realizing that

the service was going to be a tearful affair. But if she was honest with herself, she thought, she couldn't be sure if she was crying for Tucker or for herself

How could Toby be so thoughtless? So irresponsible? Didn't he know that whatever he did affected the whole family? What about the girls? They deserved a brother they could be proud of. And what about her and Bill? Didn't Toby know how much they loved him, how much they wanted him to be successful and happy? She looked at the Whitneys, bereft of daughter and sister. But people didn't have to die to be lost. Drugs could take away a beloved child just as surely as any murderer. Lucy tightened her fists, making her knuckles white. She wouldn't let that happen to Toby she promised herself. She would do whatever she had to do.

Her eyes fell on Tom and Steffie Scott, sitting together a few rows down. Maybe she should tell Tom about Toby. He'd know what to do.

She considered the idea. It would be such a relief to get the whole thing out of her hands. To pass it on to somebody who dealt with these problems every day. But was Tom the right person? What if he arrested Toby and he ended up in jail?

Lucy found herself shaking her head. She needed to slow down, she decided. Of course she was upset. But this was the only time she'd known Toby to use drugs. For all she knew, it was the first time. And it was only pot. It wasn't as if Toby was a drug addict; she'd been overreacting.

Tomorrow the whole school would be participating in "Smart Kids, Smart Choices." Maybe it would help Toby understand what a dangerous game he was playing. Lucy watched as Barney and Marge made their way down the aisle, taking seats near Tom and Steffie and the other police officers.

It wouldn't hurt to wait a bit, she decided, as the organ music stopped. And in the meantime, she could let Barney know she was concerned about the drugs in the high school without going into any specifics. After all, she would see him tomorrow at the kindergarten Christmas party. With that settled, she turned her attention to the service.

"Tonight," began the priest, "we are gathered together to celebrate the life of Tucker Whitney . . ."

Much to Lucy's relief, Bill was asleep when she got home. After the heartbreaking memorial service she really didn't want to get into an argument with him. She knew she ought to tell him about the marijuana, but she also didn't want to go back on her word to the boys. It was an impossible position, and she knew it. She never should have promised to keep it a secret.

The next morning was much too busy for any kind of serious talk—she had to pack lunch and make breakfast and, as it happened, Bill had an early meeting with a drywall contractor. The only bright spot, she thought as she hurried through her morning routine so she wouldn't be late for the kindergarten Christmas party, was that Toby didn't seem to be suffering any lasting effects from yesterday's experiment with illegal substances. Still, as she parked the Subaru outside the elementary school, she was determined to talk to Barney about the easy availability of drugs in the high school.

She was rushing up the stairs to the school, fumbling in her shoulder bag for her camera and reporter's note-book, when she ran straight into Lee Cummings.

"You're the last person I expected to see today," said Lucy, blurting the words out before she thought and then feeling horribly embarrassed. "That came out all wrong, Lee. What I meant to say is that I know this must be an awful time for you."

"I'm here for Gloria," she said in a subdued voice. "I know a lot of the kids have probably heard about Steve's arrest. I'm trying to keep things as normal as possible."

"It must be hard on the girls," began Lucy, as they walked down the hallway to the kindergarten classroom.

"You have no idea," said Lee, biting her lips. "What really hurts is that we'd decided to get back together."

Lucy raised her eyebrows in surprise.

"It's true. Steve and I talked when I got home from the cookie exchange, and he admitted he'd been a jerk and said he just wanted for us all to be together as a family again." She sighed. "I guess it'll be a while before that happens."

They had reached the kindergarten room, but before Lucy could push open the door Lee stopped her.

"Lucy, you've solved a few crimes in the past. You could figure out who really killed Tucker. Would you do it? Would you help Steve?"

Lucy's mouth dropped open. "Gee, I don't know. . . ."

"You could do it. Say you will. Please."

"Oh, Lee, I'm not on the police force. I don't know what evidence they've got, but Horowitz sounded pretty positive at that press conference that he had the right man."

"But they don't, don't you see? Steve was coming back to me. He was done with Tucker."

Lucy groaned inwardly. "Don't *you* see? That could be his motive. Maybe Tucker didn't want to let him go. Maybe they fought and he got angry and ended up killing her."

"Well, Lucy, if you think that, you sure don't know Steve. He'd never hurt anybody, he's really committed to healing. Back when a lot of dentists were refusing to treat patients with AIDS, it was just never an issue for him. He never turned anyone away, not anybody, even if they couldn't pay."

Lee pulled the door open and marched into the class-room. Lucy followed, wondering if she had a point. She wondered if the police really had a case against Steve or if they'd simply arrested the most obvious suspect.

"Welcome to our classroom," said Lydia Volpe, indi-cating Lucy and Lee with a nod. "There are chairs in the back of the classroom."

Lucy searched the room for Zoe and found her sitting beside her best friend, Sadie Orenstein. Gloria, Lee's lit-tle girl, was just behind them. Lucy gave them a smile and a little wave as she took her seat. As she expected, there was no sign of Barney yet. He would make a sur-prise appearance as Santa Claus after the children fin-ished presenting the songs and fingerplays they had been practicing for weeks. Of course, all of the children knew what to expect, thanks to older brothers and sisters. The Christmas party was a Tinker's Cove tradition, and local merchants generously donated toys and books for Santa to distribute. Lydia made sure that Santa knew in advance which children weren't likely to have very lavish Christmases at home so especially nice gifts could be given to them.

As always, the program was adorable, and Lucy had no trouble filling a couple of rolls of film with cute pictures. Ted often said you couldn't have too many photos of dogs and children in a community newspaper so she was sure he'd be pleased with her work.

Finally, when the children got to the last line of "Up on the rooftop, ho, ho, ho," the door flew open and Barney made his entrance, dressed in a Santa Claus suit that was beginning to look a bit worse for the wear, his familiar face hidden behind an elaborately curled, enormous fake beard.

"Ho, ho, ho!" He roared, and the children erupted into giggles and screams and jumped up and down with excitement. A few bolder children, children Lucy suspected didn't get much attention at home, wrapped their arms around his massive, treelike legs and hugged him.

"Children." After twenty years in the classroom, Lydia's voice commanded attention, and the children quieted down. "If you will take your places; I believe Santa may have some presents *for good boys and girls.* Is that right, Santa?"

"Yes, it is, ho, ho, ho. I have a pack filled with presents for *good little boys and girls.*" Barney turned his back, showing the bulging sack he was carrying.

There was a mad scramble as the children ran for their desks, anxious to get their presents as soon as possible. When it was quiet, Barney seated himself and plunked his sack down between his legs. Then he pulled out a long list, unrolling it with a dramatic flourish.

"Jason Adams."

Jason, a little boy with a huge gap in his front teeth,

jumped to his feet and ran up to Santa. Barney fumbled in his bag and presented him with a festively wrapped, flat package. Jason hurried back to his seat and began opening it. Every eye was on him. When he finally got it unwrapped he shrugged philosophically.

"It's a coloring book," he said. "With crayons."

Nobody seemed very impressed. They turned to Barney, waiting to see what the next present would be.

"Susanna Barlow," said Barney, pulling out another package that looked very much like the first. He gave it to Susanna, a little girl with freckles and long braids.

Lucy happened to know Susanna's grandmother, Dot Kirwan, who worked at the IGA. Dot was the first to admit she shamelessly spoiled her first grandchild, and Susanna was an expert at opening presents. She ripped the paper off in no time, revealing another coloring book and crayons. Scowling, she clumped back to her desk and mashed the wrapping paper into a ball.

The children began to fidget in their seats, growing restless. It was one thing to sit quietly, anticipating a terrific present like a Barbie doll or a soccer ball, but it was very hard to sit still for what they were all beginning to suspect was only a coloring book and a box of six no-name crayons.

"Justin Diggs."

As soon as Lucy heard the name she knew Barney was in trouble. Justin lived out on Bumps River Road in a hardscrabble neighborhood where the tired houses were surrounded with cars that didn't go and appliances that didn't work. This was probably going to be his only Christmas present, and he had been expecting something good.

"Justin, go and get your present from Santa," prompted Lydia.

Justin stayed put at his desk. "I don't want no coloring book. My brother got a Mighty Morphin Power Ranger last year. I want somethin' like that."

Lydia glanced at Barney, whose Santa beard didn't begin to hide his unhappiness, and took swift action.

"Santa, would you mind distributing the presents to the children? That would be quicker, I think, and the mothers can begin setting up the refreshments."

Taking his cue, Barney went from desk to desk passing out the coloring books. He kept up a brave front, issuing lots of ho-ho-hos, but Lucy knew his heart wasn't in it. He loved playing Santa and hearing the oohs and aahs and squeals of delight when he passed out the presents, and this year there were only a few polite thank-yous.

When the refreshments had been served and the children were busy licking the icing off their cupcakes, she approached him.

"What happened? No donations this year?"

"I had to refuse 'em. Orders from the top."

"What?"

"Lieutenant Scott. He said it wasn't appropriate for the safety officer to act like the Salvation Army. Told me to give out antidrug coloring books instead."

Lucy picked up one of the coloring books that had been abandoned on a nearby desk and flipped through it. When she got to the outline of a hypodermic needle with a big X through it she groaned and put it back down.

"My word," she said, shaking her head. Her first impulse was to sympathize with Barney, but then she remembered Toby and Eddie's little experiment with pot the day before. "Maybe Tom Scott is on the right track after all. . . ."

She was interrupted by Lee.

"Barney Culpepper, I have to talk to you."

"Fire away," said Barney, with a sigh.

"Maybe Santa could continue this conversation outside," suggested Lydia. "I think it's time to wrap things up."

A quick glance around the room was enough for Lucy. The little natives fueled by sugary treats, were getting restless.

"I hope you have recess next," she told Lydia.

"Are you kidding? Today is double recess." Then she raised her voice, making an announcement to the class. "Children, I'm afraid Santa has to go back to the North Pole now. What do you say?"

"Thank you, Santa," chorused the little girls and a few boys.

"Thanks for nothing, Santa," grumbled Justin. This was met with hoots of approval by the children.

"Merry Christmas, everyone!" roared Barney, turning and striding out of the room. A quick exit was definitely his best option.

Lucy hurried down the hall after him, determined to share her concern about the drug situation at the high school, but she didn't catch up to him until he was outside, by his cruiser, pulling off the Santa outfit.

"Hey, you're going to blow your cover," she joked.

"I think it's blown," he said, rolling the red suit into a ball and tossing it into the trunk.

"You know, what I started to say inside is that this antidrug campaign may not be such a bad idea, I think it's really needed." She took a deep breath and forged ahead. "From what I hear, the high school is full of illegal substances."

Barney snorted. "Stop the presses," he said.

"What do you mean?"

"Lucy, this isn't exactly news, you know. The whole town's full of the stuff." He shook his head. "I've never seen it so bad."

That wasn't quite what Lucy expected to hear. Nevertheless, she plunged on. "Well, if it's true, then isn't it important to educate the kids about drugs so they'll know not to use them?"

Barney threw up his hands in dismay and stood facing her, arms akimbo. "Let me tell you something, Lucy. All that education stuff sounds good in theory, but you know what, it doesn't work. The only thing that does work is keeping the drugs out, cutting off the supply. And as long as the only way a lobsterman can make a living is by bringing 'em in, well, we're not gonna be able to keep the drugs out. Too much money in 'em, and a man who's having trouble feeding his family or making the payment on his boat isn't gonna say no."

"I guess you're right."

"You know it." Barney pulled his heavy belt, complete with gun holster, out of the trunk and strapped it on. "Maybe there is something you could do, though."

"What?" Lucy asked eagerly.

"It isn't just drugs, you know. The kids especially get into trouble with booze. You know about Tim Rogers?"

Lucy nodded.

"Well, we're having a sting operation. Richie Goodman is going to try to buy booze, and if they sell it to him, we're gonna issue warnings. It could make a good story for the newspaper."

"Sure. Just let me know when, okay?"

"Deal." Barney slammed the trunk shut and pulled open the car door, but he wasn't quick enough to avoid Lee, who had followed them out of the school.

"Barney, I've got to talk to you," she demanded, grabbing his arm. "You know Steve's innocent, don't you?"

"We-e-ll," began Barney, looking more than ever like a worried St. Bernard. He shook his head dolefully. "I gotta tell you, it doesn't look good for Doc Cummings."

"They've arrested the wrong person, I'm telling you," insisted Lee.

Barney nodded sympathetically. "I know how you feel, but they've got some pretty convincing evidence."

Lucy leaned closer. "What is this evidence?" she asked.

Barney scratched his chin underneath the fake beard. "Fibers, skin cells, a gum wrapper."

"A gum wrapper? They're accusing my husband of murder because of a gum wrapper?" Lee was incredulous.

"Sugarless," said Barney. "With fingerprints."

Certain he'd clinched the case against Cummings, he climbed into his cruiser and drove off, leaving Lee and Lucy on the sidewalk.

"Because it's sugarless gum, it has to be a dentist?" Lee's voice dripped with sarcasm.

"He did mention fingerprints," said Lucy.

Lee dismissed that evidence with a wave. "Listen, I know Steve Cummings better than anyone, and I say, sure, he's a two-timing bastard and a lying, cheating son of a bitch and I wouldn't trust him with another woman as far as I could throw him, but he's no murderer!"

Chapter Ten

As she started the Subaru, Lucy couldn't help smiling. This was more like the Lee she knew. Outspoken, outrageous—you had to love her.

Lucy's next stop was the photo shop, where they promised to develop her film right away. Then she was off to *The Pennysaver* to write up a story about the Christmas party.

This was going to be a bit sticky—Ted was expecting a happy holiday feature about cute little kiddies receiving gifts from Santa. But that wasn't what really happened at the party. She didn't want to embarrass Barney, but she had an obligation to tell the truth.

The jangle of the bell and the sharp scent of hot lead that still lingered years after the linotype machines had been removed always had the same effect on her: It was something akin to the reaction a racehorse has to the sound of the trumpet. She sailed past Phyllis, the receptionist, giving her a wave, and plopped herself down in the chair Ted kept relatively clear for his visitors.

"I think I've got something . . ."

"Santa Claus is a fake?" asked Ted.

"Well, kind of. Something like that might work for a headline," said Lucy, ignoring his sarcasm. "There were an awful lot of disappointed little kindergartners at the school this morning. They all got antidrug coloring books instead of the usual gift bonanza. Barney said it was a policy decision by the lieutenant. I think it might be a significant story, considering the town's drug problem."

Ted considered her pitch.

"I dunno. Somebody must have donated those coloring books. We don't want to insult them. After all, Santa Claus did come, and the kids did receive gifts. Some readers might think the kids are just ungrateful."

"You know that's not true," argued Lucy. "Those coloring books are the only gifts some of those kids are going to get this Christmas, and they were expecting real presents, just like in the past."

"I know." Ted chewed on a pencil.

"And Barney says all this drug education is a lot of nonsense anyway. He says the town is full of drugs because of the lobster quota."

Ted pushed his chair away from the antique rolltop desk he had inherited from his grandfather, also a small-town journalist, and laughed.

"Lucy, this is not the *Washington Post* or the *New York Times*. We're a small-town weekly that depends on local advertisers. It's bad enough we have a young girl murdered by the local dentist, but now you want me to print that the town is full of drugs, too? Believe me, I hold my breath every time we get a press release from the state police drug task force—and so far, I've been lucky. Nobody from Tinker's Cove has been arrested. And believe me, this is one issue I'm not going to touch until I have to. If a handful of lobstermen are bringing in drugs to pay off their mortgages and keep shoes on their kids' feet, well, who am I to start pointing fingers? Folks around here have always done what they had to to get by."

"I get your point," said Lucy, holding her hands up in surrender. "It's smiling faces and ho-ho-hos all around."

At her desk, she flipped through the press releases Phyllis had collected for her, looking for possible future stories. Nothing looked very interesting, the annual holiday bazaar at the Community Church, a Christmas dinner for people who would otherwise be alone sponsored by Alcoholics Anonymous, and a batch of used-clothing and used-book sales. Barney's sting operation, a community taking care of its children, beginning to look better all the time. She picked up the phone and dialed the police station, intending to ask Barney for the date and time.

"Lucy?" Barney sounded defensive. "I can't talk about the Christmas party."

"I know. Don't worry. Ted wants a heartwarming holiday story, and that's what he's going to get."

"That's a relief." Barney expelled a great sigh—it sounded like a tornado on the telephone.

"This is off the record," she began, sensing that now that he was no longer worried about looking like the Grinch in the newspaper he might be more talkative than usual. "You know how convinced Lee is that Steve is innocent? She asked me to look into it and . . ."

"Oh, no." Barney cut her off. "Don't do that, Lucy."

"I wasn't intending to." Lucy was quick to tell him,

her voice rising in pitch. "But I just wanted to know—for my own peace of mind—are you guys sure you've got the right man?"

"'Fraid so." Barney lowered his voice. "I tell you, Lucy, morale around here is pretty high. Never been higher. You heard about Horowitz? Congratulatin' the department? That's never happened before. And you know why? Because the guys from the fire department, the EMTs would be all over the place before we could secure the scene. Chief Crowley knew it was no good, but he'd just say, 'What can you do? Ya gotta try to save the victim, even if the victim's beyond saving.' But now the lieutenant's in charge, it's different. This one was by the book and whaddya know? It worked. We're not the Keystone Kops anymore."

Lucy looked up as Phyllis deposited the packet of pictures on her desk.

"I don't think people thought you were Keystone Kops."

"Believe me. We took a lot of grief from the state police, even the cops in other towns."

"I didn't know that." Lucy ran her finger under the flap to open the packet. "So, what about the evidence that was so carefully preserved? What was it?"

"Oh, I dunno. Crime-scene experts took care of that. There were fibers, I guess. All that microscopic stuff. And the gum wrapper, o' course, with Cummings's fingerprints."

Lucy pulled out the pictures and saw Steve Cummings's smiling face looking up at her. She'd forgotten all about taking his picture on Friday. Now, she remembered telling him to think of his girls. The trick had worked; she'd caught him looking particularly attractive.

"What about time?" she asked. "That kind of physical

evidence could have been left anytime, and everybody knows he was seeing her."

"Nah," protested Barney. "They have ways of dating it. Plus, Cummings doesn't have an alibi for the time of death on Thursday morning. Shoulda been at his office, but he wasn't."

"Oh." The longer Lucy looked at Steve's picture, the less she thought he'd murdered Tucker.

"That's how you build a case, you know," said Barney, sounding rather pompous. "Bit by bit. In the end, it all adds up."

Lucy suspected he was reciting something he'd heard, perhaps a lecture by the lieutenant on the proper handling of evidence.

"Well, thanks a lot, Barney. I feel better. But it's still hard to believe Steve Cummings could do something like that."

"See, that's where amateurs go wrong," said Barney. "You think a person's innocent because you know them, and they're nice. From what I hear, Ted Bundy was a heck of a nice guy, a real charmer, but he killed a bunch o' women, didn't he? Nope, you can't trust people, but you can trust the evidence."

Lucy chuckled. "Okay. I give up. Now, when is that sting operation?"

"Lemme see." Lucy could hear rustling paper. "It's Thursday night. Is that good for you? Seven o'clock."

"Great." Thursday night gave her almost an entire week to write the story before the next Wednesday deadline. Plus, it would be a heck of a lot more interesting than that dismal dinner. "See you then."

She hung up and studied the photo of Steve Cummings. She had taken it under false pretenses and the last thing she wanted was for Ted to run it with the story about Steve's arrest, so she quickly tore it into small pieces and tossed it into the trash. She turned her attention to the pictures of the children, writing brief captions for the best ones. Then she quickly typed out a few paragraphs about the party, focusing on the children's songs and the refreshments provided by the mothers. She played Santa's arrival up big and played down the presents. When Ted read it he was pleased as punch.

"Just one question . . ." he began, exercising his editorial prerogative, as Lucy answered the ringing phone.

She held up one finger, indicating she would be with him in a minute.

"*Pennysaver,* this is Lucy."

"Thank God you're there!"

"Sue?"

"Can you come over? I'm desperate!"

"Right now?"

"Yes. It's Will. Another attack. I've got to take him to the clinic."

"Okay. I'm on my way."

Lucy expected to find the day-care center in chaos when she got there, imagining small figures running around and shrieking at the top of their lungs. All was quiet, however, when she pulled open the door. Connie Fitzpatrick, one of the teachers at Kiddie Kollege, the nursery school that was also housed in the rec building, had settled the children down for their nap.

"Hi, Lucy," she whispered. "Sue says they rest for at least a half hour, but if they fall asleep they can go 'til one-thirty."

Lucy nodded and Connie tiptoed out, leaving her in charge. She hung up her coat and checked on the children, who were lying on floor mats. Her buddies Harry and Justin were sound asleep, and Emily seemed ready to drift off. Hillary, Lee's little girl, was lying on her back, holding up a stuffed toy and whispering to it.

Lucy caught her eye and held her finger to her lips, warning her to be quiet. Hillary rolled over on her tummy, hugging the little bear and sticking her thumb in her mouth.

Continuing her circuit of the room, Lucy felt a bit nonplussed. She had expected to have to cope with a difficult situation but everything was under control. She looked out the window for a few minutes, then went over to Sue's desk, looking for something to read.

She picked up a magazine and sat down in the rocking chair. But somehow she couldn't get interested in whether she should "Take the Plunge! Go for the Gold!" and color her hair blond. As for "Paint Your Way Out of the Box!," well, her house was hardly a suburban box and, while the dining room definitely needed work, she didn't think she was interested in knocking even more holes in the plaster for an antique look and applying a faux marble finish.

She dropped the magazine in her lap and leaned back, closing her eyes and intending to relax, but it was no good. Her eyes refused to stay shut, and her legs twitched. She needed to move. She got up, stretched, and walked back to the window. She stayed there for a few minutes, doing squats to relieve the tension in her legs. Then she replaced the magazine on Sue's desk and stood for a moment at Tucker's.

It was now bare; her parents had taken her things. Lucy pulled out the chair and sat down. With nothing better to do, she opened the shallow center drawer; releasing the bitter smell of unfinished wood. As she expected, the drawer was empty, as were all the others. But when she tried to close the big bottom drawer it wouldn't go all the way in.

Getting down on her hands and knees, Lucy pulled the drawer out and peered behind it. Something was stuck in the space behind the drawer. She reached in and felt a plastic-covered book of some kind. The missing agenda, she thought, with a rising sense of excitement.

She pulled it out, discovering the bright pink, chunky day planner Sue had described. No wonder they hadn't been able to find it; as long as it remained upright, there had been enough room for the drawer to close. It was only when it fell on its side that it blocked the drawer.

Lucy set the agenda on the desk and replaced the drawer. Then she sat down once again and held the agenda, smoothing it with the palm of her hand. Should she open it? Some people used agendas like diaries, recording intimate details of their lives. Tucker, Lucy guessed, wasn't like that. She probably used her agenda as a calendar, so she wouldn't forget meetings and appointments.

It wouldn't hurt, thought Lucy, to take a peek. If it seemed personal and private, she could stop. But when she leafed through the lined pages she found only the briefest notations. On the day she died, Lucy discovered, Tucker had been planning to get a haircut at five-thirty.

Curiously, Lucy leafed through the pages preceding her death. They were mostly blank. The cookie exchange was noted, as was an oil-change appointment. And Tucker had planned something for Sunday, but Lucy wasn't sure what. In her clear, precise block printing she had written three letters: A, M, and C.

What did that mean, wondered Lucy. Was she planning to meet somebody? Somebody with the initials AMC? Who could that be? And when? Tucker had not written down any time, which seemed odd.

Unless, thought Lucy, it was such an important meeting she didn't have to. Her parents coming, perhaps? Or a serious boyfriend. Those weren't Steve's initials, that was for sure.

Not Steve, thought Lucy, struck with a horrible realization. Not Steve's, Lee's. Aurelie Mabelline Cummings. Lucy mouthed the words, silently. Then she picked up a pencil and wrote the initials on a scrap of paper: A. M. C.

Lucy's eyes fell on little Hillary, now sound asleep on her mat. She had the awful feeling she was looking at a motive. Just how far would Lee go to get Hillary and Gloria's daddy back? Lee had made no bones about the fact that she hated Tucker; could she have killed her?

Seeing Sue's face in the glass window of the door, Lucy rolled the paper into a ball and tossed it into the wastebasket. Her first impulse was to get rid of the initials; she wasn't ready to think about this now.

"Hiya," she whispered. "How's Will?"

"Better." Sue sighed: and sat down in the rocking chair without taking off her coat. "I'm exhausted."

"Racing off to the clinic with a sick child will do that to you," observed Lucy.

"It's really not fair," complained Sue. "If his folks weren't in denial about this whole thing, and if they started treating Will's asthma, I wouldn't have to go through this every other day."

"The doctor will talk to them."

Sue shrugged. "That's the problem with the clinic. It's a different doctor every time."

Lucy looked at her watch. "I have to go."

Sue nodded. "Thanks for helping out."

"No problem. Oh, by the way. I found Tucker's agenda. It was stuck behind a drawer."

"Always the detective." Sue smiled at her.

"I was bored." Lucy blushed.

"I'll send it to her folks."

Lucy nodded, relieved. That took care of that problem. "Thanks," she said, and hurried out to her car.

Today, she definitely wanted to be home when the kids got home from school. Considering yesterday's happenings, she didn't trust Toby and wanted to keep an eye on him. She also knew she had to tell Bill about the marijuana, and figured things would go better if she broached the subject after he'd had his favorite dinner: meat loaf.

She was in plenty of time, as it turned out. The Regulator clock in the kitchen read two o'clock when she got home, giving her at least an hour before the kids would arrive. Plenty of time to fix herself a belated lunch. But when she opened a cabinet to get a clean glass, she noticed the light on the answering machine was blinking. She punched the button and listened, while she poured herself a glass of milk.

"Mrs. Stone, this is the Tinker's Cove High School.

Please report to the assistant principal's office before the end of the day."

"Toby," groaned Lucy, replacing the milk container and slamming the refrigerator door shut. She took the glass of milk with her, to drink on the drive. She was pretty sure she would need nourishment to face what was coming.

Chapter Eleven

Calls involving the assistant principal never meant good news. The principal saved all the good news for himself; he issued all the congratulations and honors, leaving the assistant principal, Mr. Humphreys, to handle disciplinary matters.

It was ironic, thought Lucy. Toby had always had a blameless disciplinary record. But just as he was applying to colleges and would need faculty recommendations, of course now was the time he chose to get himself into trouble.

What had he done? It hit Lucy like a semi speeding down Red Top Road at ninety miles an hour. He had gotten caught with pot.

Her stomach twisted itself into a knot, and she regretted the milk she'd gulped while speeding along. A drug offense meant he was in big trouble. She struggled to remember the official school policy, clearly stated and sent home at the beginning of the school year with every student in the Tinker's Cove High School student handbook. If only she'd read the damn thing.

A detention or suspension wouldn't be so bad, but she had a horrible feeling that the school also took it upon itself to report drug offenses to the police. That could mean Toby would be charged with a crime. Could they send him to jail? With all those murderers and thieves and rapists. Not in my lifetime, vowed Lucy, determined to defend her child no matter what. Toby may have done something wrong, but he still had rights, and she was going to make sure he exercised them.

Stupid, stupid idiot, she muttered under her breath as she parked the car in front of the school, marched up the sidewalk and down the hall to Mr. Humphreys's office. She yanked the door open angrily and stopped dead in her tracks. It wasn't Toby sitting on the bench in Mr. Humphreys's anteroom, it was Elizabeth.

"What happened?" asked Lucy, sitting beside her. She felt completely off-balance. This wasn't what she had expected at all.

"I was only trying to help." Elizabeth was so angry her entire body was tense.

"Tell me the whole story."

"This girl named Chantal was having an asthma attack, and I gave her my inhaler."

"Did it work?"

"Yeah. She's fine." Elizabeth was picking at the brown paper cover on a thick history textbook. It was filled with multicolored doodles and scribbles and was beginning to tear at the corners.

"So what's the problem?" Lucy didn't get it.

"Ah, Mrs. Stone. You're here." Mr. Humphreys was a tall man with a little potbelly. He had a wispy blond mustache and had trouble keeping his thick eyeglasses up where they belonged. They kept sliding down his oily nose. "Why don't we all come in my office and discuss this?"

Elizabeth rolled her eyes and got to her feet, sighing as she stood up. It was the official teen sigh, a protest against the stupidity of adult rules and regulations.

Lucy flashed her a warning glance and stepped into the office. Elizabeth followed, and Mr. Humphreys shut the door behind them. He oozed across the room and seated himself behind his desk, giving them a little smile. Lucy felt itchy all over.

"Ah, Mrs. Stone. I'm afraid what we have here is a very regrettable situation. Elizabeth was found in possession of a prescription drug, and she distributed it to a fellow student."

"It's my asthma inhaler, and I gave it to Chantal because she couldn't breathe and was turning blue." Elizabeth spat the words out.

"But the problem is that students are not allowed to carry prescription drugs without a note from the doctor. I checked with Mrs. Irving, the school nurse, and it seems you are not authorized to carry an inhaler. There is no doctor's note in your file."

"Surely that's a technicality," said Lucy. "I can tell you that Elizabeth has asthma and her allergist has prescribed medication, including inhalers. She is supposed to carry one all the time in case she needs a quick fix." Ooh, she thought to herself, that didn't sound good.

"That's very well and good, Mrs. Stone, but Elizabeth neglected to request a drug authorization form from Mrs.

Irving and did not have the form completed and returned by the doctor. She is in clear violation of school policies. But what disturbs me even more is that she *distributed* a potentially dangerous drug to another student." Mr. Humphreys pursed his lips and fixed his eyes on Lucy, peering over his thick horn-rims.

"Now, Mr. Humphreys, you know as well as I do that there's a big difference between sharing an inhaler and selling crack cocaine. I'm sure Elizabeth was only trying to help—the girl was having trouble breathing."

"That's right!" interjected Elizabeth. "Mom, Chantal was really in trouble. Her fingernails were turning blue."

"Elizabeth has had attacks herself and has been taught to manage them," said Lucy. "It sounds to me as if she did exactly the right thing."

"Is Elizabeth a doctor?" Mr. Humphreys inquired sarcastically. "Is she qualified to prescribe drugs? I think not."

"Of course not," said Lucy, trying very hard to remain polite. "But only a handful of drugs are used to treat most asthma cases, and the inhalers are clearly marked by color. Kids who have asthma all know that the yellow inhaler is for emergencies. Considering Elizabeth's excellent academic record and the fact that she's never been in trouble before, I think you ought to make an exception in her case."

Mr. Humphreys made a tent of his fingers and slowly shook his head from side to side. "Mrs. Stone, our school board has adopted a zero tolerance policy toward drug use. That means there are absolutely no exceptions. That's what zero tolerance means. I don't think there is anything to be gained by continuing this discussion. Elizabeth clearly violated school policy as stipulated in the handbook. She will be suspended for two weeks and a report will be forwarded to the police department." He gave a little nod. "You can expect the police will want to conduct a thorough investigation."

"That's not fair!" Elizabeth was on her feet.

Mr. Humphreys glared at her from his seat. "Two weeks suspension plus one day, for disorderly behavior."

"Come on, Elizabeth." Lucy wrapped an arm around her shoulder and led her out of the office. "Let's get out of here."

As soon as they were in the hallway Elizabeth completely lost control. She jumped up and down in fury and shook her head, the sleek sophisticated hairdo began to fray as clumps of hair worked loose.

"Come on, baby. You can do that at home. In fact, I'll join you. But now we've got to get out of here before they call the cops on you."

"Mom, this is so unfair! I saved that girl's life. I did. She was in real trouble, and the teacher, it was a substitute, wouldn't let her go to the nurse's office and kept telling her to stop making a scene. If I hadn't given her my inhaler, she would have passed out for sure."

"I know you did the right thing." Lucy hugged her. "I'm proud of you. I'll always be proud of you. And we'll figure this thing out. In the meantime, look on the bright side," she said, pushing open the school doors. "You don't have to come back for two weeks."

Elizabeth shrugged and thumped down the steps in her clunky platform shoes.

Behind them, inside the school, Lucy heard the bell ring. She quickly followed Elizabeth to the car, hurrying to stay ahead of the flood of students that would soon come pouring out of all the exits.

The car was blocked in by a line of school buses, so Lucy and Elizabeth couldn't leave. They sat, watching as a steady stream of students flowed down the steps and onto the buses, keeping an eye out for Toby. When they spotted him, Lucy honked and Elizabeth stuck an arm out the window and waved.

"Hi, Mom. What are you doing here?"

"Elizabeth got suspended."

Toby's eyes almost popped out of his head, but he quickly recovered and climbed in the backseat, forgoing the usual argument about who was going to ride in the front seat.

"Good going, Lizzie. You were probably tired of being on the honor roll, anyway."

"Shut up," growled Elizabeth.

"Be nice, children," said Lucy, easing into the flow of traffic as the school buses began moving. As they inched along, Lucy replayed the meeting with Mr. Humphreys in her mind, deciding the whole thing was ridiculous. Ridiculous, she thought, and dangerous. She didn't like it one bit.

Neither did Bill when he heard the whole story at dinnertime.

"Elizabeth, it serves you right. This whole thing could have been avoided if you'd simply followed the rules and gotten a note from the doctor," he said, taking a big forkful of meat loaf and mashed potatoes. "But, frankly," he added, glowering at Toby, "you're not the one I thought would get in trouble for drugs."

Just then the phone rang, and he got up to answer it.

When he returned to the table, he looked a bit shame-faced.

"That was Mrs. Williams, Chantal's mother. She said she wanted to let us know how much she appreciated Elizabeth's quick thinking. She's convinced Elizabeth saved Chantal a trip to the hospital."

Later, while the kids did the dishes, Lucy and Bill remained at the table, drinking their coffee.

"What do we do? Do we fight this?" asked Lucy.

"I don't get it," said Bill. "From what Mrs. Williams said Elizabeth ought to be a hero. Instead, she's suspended. It's crazy."

"Mr. Humphreys said he's referring it to the police." Lucy furrowed her brow. "Maybe I should call Barney."

"Wouldn't hurt," agreed Bill. "And in the meantime, I'm going to have a talk with Toby, *mano a mano*. He's got to understand that if he keeps messing around with pot, he could get in real serious trouble."

He cocked an eyebrow and grinned at Lucy, and for a moment he reminded her of the college kid she'd fallen for so many years ago. A college kid who never passed along a joint at a party without taking a toke.

Chapter Twelve

7 days 'til Xmas

When Lucy arrived at the police station on Thursday night to cover the sting operation she felt a bit uncomfortable. After all, until now no member of the family had been in trouble with the authorities. Tom Scott immediately put her at ease.

"I received that report from the school concerning Elizabeth, and I don't see anything for my department to investigate—she didn't break any drug laws." He gave her a big smile. "You ought to be proud of her—her quick thinking probably saved that girl an ambulance ride."

"That's a big relief," said Lucy, smiling as Barney and Richie Goodman entered Scott's office. Lucy had known Richie ever since he was a baby, but she was always surprised by how quickly kids grew up. She could have sworn he'd grown a foot since she last saw him. He was at least six feet tall, a lean, good-looking boy with a thick mop of curly brown hair.

"Now, Richie here is going to try to buy alcohol from license holders in the town," explained the lieutenant. "He's obviously underage—he's seventeen and the legal age is twenty-one. Richie, will you tell Mrs. Stone here what your instructions are?"

Richie looked embarrassed, but he spoke right up. "I'm supposed to ask for a bottle of beer, and if they sell it to me I'm supposed to bring it out to Lieutenant Scott. If they ask me for ID, I'm going to say that I don't have any."

"That's right. We want to do this thing fair and square," said the lieutenant. "Right, Culpepper?"

Barney shrugged and nodded. "Right."

Lucy didn't think he sounded very enthusiastic.

"Now, just to make it absolutely clear that we're not planting any alcohol on innocent license holders, I'm noting on the record of this operation that Richie does not have any alcohol concealed on his body. Do you want to pat him down, Mrs. Stone?"

Richie was blushing furiously.

"I think I'll leave that to Barney," said Lucy.

Barney quickly checked Richie's pockets and confirmed that except for a wallet and car keys they were empty.

"We're off, then," said the lieutenant, grabbing his blue jacket from the coat stand in the corner.

They all piled into a cruiser: Barney was driving, and the lieutenant sat next to him in the front seat. Lucy and Richie were in the backseat. Lucy got out her reporter's notebook and uncapped her pen.

"Is this the first sting the department has conducted?" she asked.

"As far as I know," answered the lieutenant. "Officer Culpepper's the one to ask—he's been here a lot longer than me."

"It's the first," agreed Barney, sounding glum.

"Liquor stings have proved to be effective community policing—a lot of departments are trying them," said Scott, turning to face Lucy. "It lets licensees know that we're really serious about enforcing the drinking age. And that's a message we want to get out now, with the holidays just around the corner."

"If Richie is able to purchase beer, what will you do? Will you charge the license holder?" Remembering Ted's reluctance to offend the business community, Lucy hoped not.

"This time we're issuing warnings," said Scott. "And, of course, we're hoping that having this written up in the paper will also act as a deterrent. No community businessman wants bad publicity."

Lucy squirmed in the uncomfortable seat. She didn't like the feeling that she was being used to punish local businesses.

Tom Scott seemed to sense her discomfort and hastened to reassure her.

"This is kind of a personal crusade for me," he said. "When I first started out in police work I felt the same way a lot of cops do—that my time and energy were best used to fight serious crimes. I tended to ignore minor violations in order to concentrate on cases that involved bodily harm or violence—muggings, bar fights, things like that. Remember, this was in New York City, where there are a lot more crimes against people and property than there are here."

He paused a moment, and when he resumed his voice was strained.

"That all changed for me one night when I got a call to a motor-vehicle accident—a car had hit a light pole. This was in a section of the precinct where we were rarely called. A very nice residential area in the Bronx called Riverdale with fancy homes, lots of trees and grassy lawns, not exactly mean streets, if you know what I mean.

"Well, when I got to the scene I found a brand-new Mustang. . . ." Scott paused to swallow, as Lucy scribbled his story down in the notebook word for word. "I knew it was bad. Entire front end was gone, like it had disintegrated under the force of the impact. When I got to the car the windows were open, and I could smell the alcohol."

He sighed and shook his head.

"It was too late. There was nothing I could do. Two kids, both dead. All dressed up in their prom clothes. He was wearing a tux, she had on a long dress. Her flowers— white roses—were still on her wrist."

He paused, working his teeth.

"That night I had to stand on two doorsteps, ringing the bell, knowing that the people on the other side of the door were never going to be the same after I delivered my news. It was then I decided that I'd had enough. I promised myself I was going to do whatever I had to do to stop this, this epidemic of alcohol abuse that is killing our young people."

In the front seat, Barney pulled a huge, white handkerchief out of his pocket and blew his nose. In the backseat,

Lucy finished writing just as they pulled up in front of Mrs. Murphy's liquor store. She glanced over at Richie and saw his Adam's apple bob as he swallowed.

"Are you ready?" asked Scott.

"Ready as I'll ever be," answered Richie, climbing out of the car.

The others remained in the cruiser, watching as Richie approached the brightly lit store. He pulled open the glass door and went in. They could observe him through the plate-glass windows as he walked over to a cooler and chose a bottle of beer, which he carried to the counter.

The clerk, an older man with gray hair, shook his head.

"That's Jim Murphy—he knows the business," said Barney, a note of satisfaction in his voice.

Tom noticed and looked at him curiously. "If I didn't know better, I'd think you're hoping this sting is unsuccessful," he said.

"Well, we all hope that, don't we?" asked Lucy. "That means that the laws are being obeyed in our town."

"Except for one fact," said Tom. "We know they're not. Since I came here last summer we've arrested thirteen juveniles for operating under the influence."

They looked up as Richie pulled open the door and got in the car. "Mr. Murphy knows me," he said, apologetically. "Maybe I should have worn a disguise or something."

"That's okay, son," said Scott. "We've got plenty more to try."

But as the evening wore on, Richie continued to be unsuccessful. He wasn't able to buy a single beer. Wherever he tried, in the town's three liquor stores, in the grocery store, even in the roadhouse out near the highway, he was refused.

"Are you sure you're doing exactly what I told you to do?" Tom finally asked him, when he returned empty-handed from the Bilge, a bar down by the waterfront that was a favorite with fishermen.

"Yeah," said Richie. "I just go up to the counter and ask for a Bud. I mean, I don't make any conversation or anything. Should I?"

"Nah," grunted Scott.

"Maybe if he wore my hat," he volunteered, as they pulled up in front of Richard's Fine Wines. He pulled a navy blue watch cap out of his pocket and jammed it down on his head. But the hat didn't fool the clerk, who asked to see his identification. Richie was despondent when he returned to the car. "He offered to sell me a Coke."

"Well, that's it," said Barney, checking his clipboard. "That was the last one on the list."

"I don't understand it." said Tom as they drove back to the police station. "I never heard of a liquor sting that didn't net any violators."

"Well, you probably wouldn't," said Lucy. "It's not much of a story if nobody gets caught."

"Are you going to write it up for the paper?" he asked as Barney parked the car.

"Sure. I've spent a lot of time on it already. Besides, Ted likes to print good news whenever he can, especially if it puts his advertisers in a good light."

Tom picked right up on the cue. "It's not often in law enforcement that you have such a satisfying outcome," he said, speaking slowly so she could get every word. "It's gratifying to know that the department's efforts to enforce the legal drinking age are working and that our young people cannot purchase alcohol in Tinker's Cove. And I want to express a special word of thanks to Richie Goodman, who volunteered his time tonight."

Lucy got it all down, and climbed out of the ear.

"Thanks for inviting me along," she said, shaking Tom's hand. She turned to Richie, who was standing beside her. "Do you have a ride home?"

"Yeah," he said, stuffing his hands in his pockets and striding off toward his car.

"He's a good kid," said Barney, nodding his approval.

"Maybe too good," mused Tom. "Maybe I should have gotten a kid who had more street smarts."

"This is a small town," said Barney. "Everybody knows everybody. The kids probably go a few towns over where nobody knows them. Maybe we should try a joint operation with the Gilead P.D."

"It's a thought," admitted Tom. "Or maybe we could just try not to tip off the storekeepers in advance."

Under the lights that illuminated the parking lot Lucy could see Barney's face redden. "Nothing like that happened," he said.

"If you say so," said Scott, replacing his cap on his head and marching into the building.

"Barney, you didn't do anything like that, did you?" asked Lucy, as she watched the lieutenant stride off.

"No, damn it, but I was sure tempted. I don't like this kind of stuff. It's awful close to entrapment, if you ask me. I'd rather wait for somebody to commit a crime, and then arrest them. I don't like to trick 'em into it."

"Police do undercover operations all the time. It's perfectly legal."

"Well, that don't make it right." Barney planted his cap on his head and shifted his belt. "You know what he wants me to do now? I'm supposed to put a box out on the desk when I visit the schools and tell the kids they can write me a note about anything that's bothering them. Like maybe if their big brother is smoking pot or something like that. And I'm supposed to tell the kids it's just between them and me and nobody will get in trouble. But that's not true. The lieutenant here wants me to pass on suspected violations to the school authorities, and by law, they have to report drug use to the police."

"Do people know about this? Maybe I should write a story."

"Oh, I wouldn't do that if I were you," said Barney, waggling his finger at her. "Your daughter has come to the attention of the department—you wouldn't want her investigated, now, would you?"

"Tom said everything was okay, that he was dropping the whole thing."

"And he will," said Barney, giving her a wink, "as long as you do things his way."

Barney was way off base, thought Lucy, as she drove home. She had Tom's word that he wasn't going to investigate the inhaler incident any further. There was nothing to investigate, for that matter. There was no law against helping a person in distress, Tom had said so himself. He'd said Elizabeth should be congratulated for her quick thinking.

Poor Barney was under a lot of stress. He was no doubt worried sick about Marge. This was no time for him to have to adjust to a whole new way of doing things at work. After all, Barney had been on the force for twenty years or more, working the whole time for Chief Crowley. It was no wonder he was having trouble accepting the lieutenant's ideas about community policing.

But even Barney had admitted that the lieutenant was getting results—hadn't he bragged to her about the department's success in preserving the evidence that nailed Steve Cummings?

The lieutenant certainly seemed to know what he was doing, thought Lucy, as she turned onto Red Top Road. And he was truly committed to his job. She remembered how his voice had cracked with emotion when he described finding the young couple dead in the crash, how he couldn't forget the flowers on the girl's wrist. White roses.

What a tragedy, she thought, blinking back tears. And it would make a great lead when she wrote about the sting for *The Pennysaver*. She pulled into her driveway and braked, turning off the ignition. This was one story she couldn't wait to write.

Chapter Thirteen

6 days 'til Xmas

"**G**reat story, Lucy," said Ted, after he finished reading her report on the sting operation.

Lucy had been so eager to write it that she'd gone into *The Pennysaver* office first thing Friday morning, way ahead of deadline.

"You don't think I went over the top?"

When she had been writing the story, Lucy had been carried along in a rush of creative energy. Now that it was finished, she was beginning to have second thoughts. Maybe she should have taken the time to make a few phone calls to New York to check the accuracy of Scott's account.

"No. Great detail, especially the white roses."

Lucy felt better; Ted was a lot more experienced in the news business than she was.

"Our advertisers will love it," he continued. "Good news for once."

"I knew you'd say that." Lucy took a deep breath and plunged in. "Do you think maybe we're getting a bit too concerned about the advertisers? I mean, it seems to come up an awful lot lately."

"Damn right it does. Adam wants to go to BU—do you know how much that costs? Frankly, this paper makes a pretty thin profit as it is, and I can't afford to alienate any advertisers right now. Not if Adam's going to get a college education."

"You'll get financial aid."

"Not enough—I've done the calculations. And a lot of that aid is probably going to be student loans, which I'd like to avoid if I can. I don't want Adam starting out with a huge debt burden."

"That worries me, too," admitted Lucy.

"The good news is that revenues are ahead of budget this month, thanks to that new Ropewalk mall. They've placed a lot of holiday advertising with us."

"That's great," said Lucy. "Ho, ho, ho!" She shrugged into her coat and buttoned it up. "I'll see you Monday."

In the car, she turned on the radio. The local station was also getting plenty of ads; as she drove she heard commercials urging her to celebrate the holiday season in a variety of ways: with specially decorated Dunkin' Donuts packed in festive jars, with a new car from Fat Eddie and his "happy, holiday elves" who were practically giving away the new models in a burst of Christmas spirit, and with a "luxurious," meaning expensive, outfit from the Carriage Trade. And if the stress of the season was getting her down, a public service announcement informed her she could call the Samaritans for counseling.

If she were honest with herself, she thought, it did seem as if a gray cloud of depression was following her wherever she went these days. It was partly a reaction to the forced jollity of the Christmas season, but she was also struggling to cope with Tucker's murder and Steve's arrest. And if that weren't enough, she was anxious about the kids. Toby's experiments with pot and his lackadaisical attitude about the college applications, not to mention Elizabeth's suspension. This was not the Christmas she had hoped for.

She had intended to stop by at Miss Tilley's to deliver a Christmas present, but in her present mood she wasn't sure it was a good idea. When she got to the corner of Miss Tilley's road, however, she found herself flipping on the turn signal and accelerating. Through the years she had found there was nothing like a conversation with Miss Tilley to put things in their proper perspective.

Julia Ward Howe Tilley, who allowed only a sadly diminished number of contemporaries to call her by her first name, was the first person who befriended Lucy when she and Bill had moved to Tinker's Cove. Then the librarian at the Broadbrooks Free Library, Miss Tilley had noticed Lucy's interest in mysteries and began saving the new titles for her. As they grew to know each other, Lucy had come to appreciate Miss Tilley's tart wit and no-nonsense attitude. Now that she was retired and steadily growing frailer, Lucy tried to stop by for a chat as often as she could.

Rachel Goodman opened the door when Lucy

knocked. After her auto accident a few years ago, Miss Tilley arranged to have Rachel help her with meals, housekeeping, and driving.

"Hi, Rachel," said Lucy, as she took off her coat. "You'll be reading about your son in the paper next week."

"Nothing bad, I hope," said Rachel, hanging it up in the coat closet.

"No. You should be proud. He did a great job on that liquor sting."

Rachel grimaced. "He didn't want to do it, but he didn't feel as if he could refuse. Richie thought that if he said no, the lieutenant would think he was in the habit of buying booze illegally."

It occurred to Lucy that both Stones, Steffie and Tom, definitely had the knack of putting people on the spot.

"Come to think of it, he did seem a little uncomfortable, but I figured it was just part of being seventeen."

Rachel shook her head. "No. He didn't like the idea of tricking people and getting them in trouble. Plus, he does have a bit of a guilty conscience, I think. Now that he's got his acceptance from Harvard, he's come down with a wicked case of senioritis. He's been spending a lot of time with Tim Rogers, and I don't think they're memorizing Bible verses." She lowered her voice to a whisper. "Frankly, I don't know why the police are so concerned about underage drinking—the real problem at the high school is drugs, if you ask me."

Lucy would have loved to share her own thoughts on this subject, but was interrupted.

"Who are you talking to?" Miss Tilley asked in a quavery voice from the next room. "I thought I heard Lucy Stone."

Lucy went into the living room, where Miss Tilley was seated in an antique Boston rocker next to the fireplace, with a bright crocheted afghan across her knees, A small fire was burning on the hearth. Lucy gave her old friend a quick peck on the cheek and presented her with a foil package wrapped with a bright red bow.

"What is this?"

"Scottish shortbread. Elizabeth made it!"

"What a clever girl."

"Not that clever, I'm afraid," said Lucy, seating herself on the camelback sofa. "She's been suspended from school."

"I can't believe it," said Rachel.

"It's true," said Lucy, telling them the whole story. When she had finished, Miss Tilley clucked her tongue.

"Zero tolerance sounds like a good policy for people who have zero common sense and zero intelligence. You tell Elizabeth she did the right thing, and she shouldn't hesitate to do it again. Goodness sakes, rules are made to be broken."

Lucy chuckled. "It's nice to hear you say that. I was beginning to have doubts myself."

"But what about school?" asked Rachel. "Two weeks is a long time. Won't she miss a lot of classwork?"

"Toby gets her assignments for her and she's been keeping up at home. It's kind of nice having her around the house, actually. She's been doing a lot of baking and has started making herself a dress to wear on Christmas."

Rachel shook her head. "It seems like she got a rum deal to me. I'll ask Bob to give Mr. Humphreys a call. He's been known to become a bit more tolerant when he's faced with legal action. The school committee hates to pay legal bills." She stood up. "How about some tea to go with that shortbread?"

When Rachel had gone into the kitchen, Miss Tilley leaned forward and tapped Lucy's knee with her bony hand.

"Elizabeth's not the only one who's being treated unfairly—what do you think about poor Dr. Cummings?"

Lucy shrugged. "Lee asked me to see if I could find out anything, and I talked to Barney—he says it's pretty much an open-and-shut case. They're certain he did it."

"Nonsense. Steve Cummings has been taking care of my teeth for years. . . ." She pulled back her lips and tapped her yellowed incisors. "I still have all my own teeth, I'll have you know, and that's thanks to Dr. Cummings. I ask you, do you really think a man who has the patience to put up with an old horror like me would even think of committing murder? It's just not in him. He's a kind, good man."

"You only know him professionally," argued Lucy. "He's no saint. He left Lee and the girls and he was dating Tucker, who was only half his age. Isn't it possible the situation got out of hand, and he lost control and killed her?"

"This doesn't much sound like the Lucy Stone I know," observed Miss Tilley, taking a cup and saucer from Rachel. "What's happened to that inquisitive mind of yours? Since when did you start swallowing the official line?"

Stung, Lucy took a consoling sip of tea. Miss Tilley sure had a way of getting right to the heart of the matter. Wishing she knew the answer, she delayed by taking a bite of shortbread.

"When it seems the only logical conclusion," she finally said, but she had the uneasy feeling that Miss Tilley was right. Lately, it seemed to her, she'd been spending a lot of energy avoiding facts that didn't fit rather than trying to work out the truth for herself.

"Actually," she found herself saying, "I do have another theory about Tucker's murder—-but it's so awful I haven't even been able to think about it."

"What is it?" asked Rachel. Both she and Miss Tilley were leaning forward in their chairs, eager to hear.

"Well, I found Tucker's agenda—it had been missing. It turned out it was jammed behind a drawer in her desk at the day-care center. There wasn't much in it, but there was a notation the Sunday before she died. Apparently she'd had a meeting with Lee."

"You think Lee killed her?" Rachel's hand flew to her mouth. "I can't believe it. Besides, that was Sunday. Tucker wasn't killed until Wednesday morning."

"What if Lee met with Tucker on Sunday and begged her to give up Steve and Tucker refused," argued Lucy. "That would give Lee a strong motive to kill her, wouldn't it? She was desperate to get back with Steve. You saw how she treated Tucker at the cookie exchange."

Rachel bit her lip.

"The female of the species is more deadly than the male." Miss Tilley nodded with satisfaction. "I knew it couldn't be Dr. Cummings."

"It can't be Lee, either." Rachel shook her head. "Think of those two little girls. What would happen to them?"

"I know," agreed Lucy. "Hillary and Gloria. That's why I don't even want to think about it."

"Their father could take care of them if she went to jail." Miss Tilley snapped off a piece of shortbread and popped it in her mouth. "I think you should go straight to the police with this information. Where's the agenda now?"

Lucy's and Rachel's eyes met. "It's gone. Sue sent it to Tucker's parents."

"That doesn't matter. The police should consider all the evidence. You have a responsibility to tell them."

Lucy shook her head. "A minute ago you were telling me to think for myself. Well, I don't think anything would be gained by making Lee the subject of an investigation. If Steve is really innocent, well, it will undoubtedly come out at the trial, and he'll be acquitted."

"You'd leave the innocent little girls in the hands of a murderer?" Miss Tilley was shocked.

"Well, if she did murder Tucker, it was only because she was desperate to save her family," said Lucy. "Besides, I don't have any real proof—just a theory. This time I'm going to mind my own business."

"Let the police earn their salaries, that's what Bob always says," advised Rachel.

"Well," snorted Miss Tilley. "I can only say how glad I am that I remained a single lady. Marriage apparently has a terrible effect on one's morals."

"And it only gets worse when you become a parent," added Lucy darkly.

As she drove home, Lucy listened again to the steady barrage of holiday commercials. She tried to change the station but it didn't make any difference whether she listened to 102.9 or 107.5 or 98.8—it was all buy, buy, buy. Disgusted, she reached to turn it off, but paused when she heard the familiar strains of one of her favorite carols.

As she sang along, she remembered that the community carol sing was that night. They'd go, she decided, the whole family. It was just what they needed to restore their Christmas spirit.

Much to her surprise, everyone was agreeable when she presented her plan at the dinner table. Sara and Zoe loved any excuse to sing Christmas songs, Elizabeth was tired of being stuck at home, and Toby saw an opportunity to socialize with his friends. Even Bill agreed to give up an evening of channel surfing.

"There's nothing good on TV on Friday, anyway," he said.

Bill and Lucy took the Subaru, along with the younger girls, while Toby drove the truck, with Elizabeth for company. He hoped to hook up with his friends, in which case he would need his own transportation home.

"Behave yourself," Bill warned, as he handed over the keys.

A light snow was falling when their two-car caravan arrived in town, and Christmas lights were twinkling on most of the houses. A Christmas tree had been placed on the porch roof of the general store, and a bonfire was burning brightly in the parking area out front. A crowd of people had already gathered and were singing, accompanied by Stan Pulaski, the fire chief, on the trumpet.

"We three kings of Orient are . . ." was one of Lucy's favorites and she joined in eagerly. She knew the words by heart, but the kids didn't; somebody passed them a sheaf of paper with the lyrics.

This was what Christmas was really all about, thought Lucy. Neighbors and friends gathered to enjoy old songs, raising their voices together to celebrate the season. She looked from face to face, familiar faces lighted by the glow of the bonfire, and felt a warm sense of fellowship. It was wonderful to be in this place at this moment, she thought, placing her hand in Bill's.

The general store faced the town green, an open space with grass and a few trees that afforded the carolers a clear view of the little town: the main street lined with stores, all decorated with Christmas lights, and beyond, the harbor, where some of the fishing boats had also been trimmed with holiday lights. The restored Ropewalk stood next to the fish pier, its unique shape outlined with strings of twinkling white lights.

Stan had played the first few notes of "Silent Night" when a sudden explosion rocked the ground they were standing on. Everyone looked up, there was a collective intake of breath. Flames were shooting from one of the narrow windows of the Ropewalk.

Lucy saw Stan running toward the firehouse, clutching his trumpet to his chest. A few others, volunteer firemen, also ran to help. Moments later the scream of sirens filled the air as the fire engines roared out of the station and tore off down the street. The rest of the carolers stood rooted in place; watching in horror as the flames grew larger and smoke began to billow into the night sky.

Chapter Fourteen

Suddenly, they were all running down Main Street toward the fire. Everyone wanted to see the spectacle; it was the biggest thing that had happened since the sardine cannery fire some twenty years ago.

"This is history being made right here," Lucy heard one man tell his son. "You look and don't forget and you'll have something to tell your grandkids."

All Lucy could think about, as she ran along with the crowd, were the people inside the mall. With less than a week left to Christmas it must have been packed with shoppers. She remembered the clutter of stalls and the narrow walkways, not to mention the aged wood. It had all looked most attractive, but Lucy wouldn't have wanted to be inside it in a fire. It wouldn't take much smoke to turn the old building into a death trap.

Holding tight to Zoe's hand, Lucy followed Bill, hurrying to keep up with him. Toby had run ahead with his friends, Elizabeth had also joined a group of high schoolers. Sara ran along with her father.

No one had had time to set up barricades, but the crowd didn't advance past the edge of the Ropewalk parking lot, where the fire trucks were parked and the volunteer firemen were laying hose. There, you could smell the smoke and feel the heat of the flames that had now spread from a single ground-floor window to several more, including some on the second floor. People were streaming from the exits, holding scarves and handkerchiefs to their soot-blackened faces. Lucy spotted Franny and ran up to her, first making sure that Bill had a firm hold on Zoe's hand.

"Are you okay?" she asked.

Franny coughed and nodded in reply.

"Can everybody get out?"

"I think so." Franny dabbed at her eyes. "It's dinnertime, so there weren't too many people, yet. Frank Crowell, he's the manager, raised the alarm and told people to go to the exits. Do you see him?"

Lucy and Franny scanned the faces of the people in the crowd looking for Frank, who was instantly recognizable because of his flamboyant handlebar mustache.

When they failed to see him, Franny began asking who had seen him last.

"He was behind me," said a woman Lucy recognized. She had a stall selling stained-glass suncatchers and lampshades that she made herself. "I heard his voice, telling everyone to keep moving."

"Did he get out?"

"No. I saw him go back," added a tiny woman with

curly white hair, who was clutching her Ropewalk shopping bag as if it were a life preserver. "He got us to the exit and then he turned back." She shook her head. "I don't know why."

Hearing this, Franny ran up to Chief Pulaski, who was giving orders through his megaphone. Lucy followed, but couldn't hear what Franny was saying over the din of the sirens and the throb of the pumper truck's diesel engines. She saw Pulaski shake his head, mouthing something to two new arrivals, volunteer firemen who were pulling on their gear. Lucy caught a glimpse of a head of thick red hair just before one of the men put on his helmet.

By now, huge flames were leaping from the Ropewalk windows, bathing everything and everyone in a flickering red light. Now and then there was a popping noise; someone said it was window glass exploding from the heat of the fire. The parking lot was filled with fire trucks, hoses snaked everywhere, and in the distance sirens could be heard as fire companies from the neighboring towns of Gilead, Smithfield, Hopkinton, and Perry answered the call for mutual aid.

Lucy watched as the two firefighters lowered their face shields and vanished into the burning building. The last thing she saw was the reflective letters on the backs of their coats. They had the same name: Rousseau.

"Why aren't they pumping any water yet?" she asked Bill.

"It takes time to lay hose," he said, as water started streaming from two, then three hoses. "Here it comes."

"Finally." Lucy was clutching herself, her arms across her chest. She was holding her breath, waiting for the two Rousseaus to emerge from the building.

They finally did, holding an unconscious figure between them, just as flames began to erupt from the roof and everyone had given them up for lost.

EMTs rushed up with oxygen and a stretcher, and police officers began setting up sawhorse barricades, pushing everyone back to the sidewalk on the opposite side of the street.

Moments after the street had been cleared, a ladder track began moving very slowly along it, stopping so hoses could be shifted to minimize the damage of the heavy truck rolling over them.

"They'll never be able to save it," said Bill, and Lucy realized he was right. The firefighters were now spraying water on neighboring buildings, the harbormaster's office, and a row of shops that included Jake's Donut Shack, a real estate office, and a T-shirt shop. "This street's so narrow the buildings are awfully close together," he said. "It'll be a miracle if the whole block doesn't go."

As she watched, Lucy began to make out the faces of people she knew. Rachel's husband, Bob, was one of the volunteer firefighters, so was Hank Orenstein, Juanita's husband. When a ladder was extended from one of the fire trucks to the roof of the Ropewalk, Lucy gasped to see Hank begin climbing it.

"What's he doing?" she asked Bill.

"Trying to vent the fire, I think. He's going to try to break a hole in the roof."

"Oh my God. What if he falls?" Hank and Juanita's daughter Sadie was Zoe's best friend.

"He'll be careful." Bill put an arm around her shoulder.

"I hope so." Lucy watched as Hank leaned from the

ladder and swung his fire ax, she took a breath and choked on the smoke. What must it be like up on that ladder, so close to the fire? She could only imagine the heat.

The street was now running with water, the red-and-yellow flames were reflected in the wet surface. The fire-fighters' faces were gleaming with sweat; she saw one man lean against an engine, his chest heaving as he mopped his face. An EMT approached him, offering an oxygen mask, and he took it.

All at once, it was too much for Lucy. She couldn't watch anymore. It wasn't just a spectacle, something to see. Real people's lives were going up in smoke. She thought of all the individual craftsmen who had opened shops in the Ropewalk, all the labor they had put into making and marketing their wares. The Ropewalk was supposed to offer a new chance to people in the economically beleaguered town, now all those hopes and dreams were going up in smoke. Lucy turned away.

"I can't watch anymore," she said to Bill.

"Are you going home?" he asked.

It was tempting. Their house was far from the fire. She could take a bath, make herself a snack, even go to bed with a book.

"No." She shook her head, watching as several more firefighters collapsed against the ambulance, waiting for their turn at the oxygen. Down the street, the clean, white light from the IGA's plate-glass windows caught her eye.

"I'm going to get some food and drink for the men—they need nourishment and fluids," she said.

Bill nodded and hoisted Zoe up onto his shoulders, where she perched like a little monkey. Lucy hurried down the street relieved to get away from the overwhelming sights and sounds of the fire.

When she approached the store, she saw the cashier, Dot Kirwan, standing in the doorway, arms folded across her chest, watching from a distance.

"That's a real shame, that is," she said, nodding grimly.

"All that work, all those high hopes," agreed Lucy.

"Don't tell me you're doing your Friday night grocery shopping," said Dot. "I haven't had a customer since the sirens went off."

"I thought I'd get some juice and stuff for the men— they've been at this for quite a while and they look like they need to refuel."

"Why didn't I think of that?" Dot grabbed a cart and pushed it over to the dairy case where she started filling it with gallon jugs of fruit punch and cartons of orange juice.

Lucy took another cart and wheeled it to the bakery aisle, where she grabbed boxes of doughnuts and loaves of bread. A few aisles over she found big jars of peanut butter and jelly and added them.

"Ring this all up—I'll use my charge card, OK?"

"I don't think so," said Dot, raising her eyebrows. "Joe can take it off his taxes as a charitable donation." Joe Marzetti was the owner, but Dot really ran the store. "I'll just get a knife or two and we'll be off." She hurried over to the deli counter and grabbed some sandwich spreaders; as an afterthought she grabbed a package of paper cups.

Pushing the cart back down the street toward the burning Ropewalk, Lucy felt better. At least she was making herself useful. The policeman at the barricade pushed the sawhorse aside when he saw them coming and they rolled their carts next to the ambulance. Dot passed out the juice while Lucy made sandwiches, using the child seat of the cart as a work surface.

Up close, she saw the toll the fire was taking on the firefighters. One man's helmet rolled onto the ground and she bent to pick it up, shocked to discover how heavy it was as she handed it back to him. Underneath their heavy slickers the men were sweating, and their faces were blackened with soot. Just walking in their heavy rubber boots and coats had to be an effort, and many of the men. were also burdened with tanks of air. Yet they scrambled up the ladders and hauled hoses around, never hesitating when they were given an order.

"I hate it when there are fires down here," said one tired firefighter. "The whole town could go up."

"We're earning our pay tonight," said another, tilting back his head and gulping down a quart of orange juice.

"How much do you make?" asked Lucy, handing him a sandwich.

"A hundred and fifty dollars a year," he said, with his mouth full of peanut butter. "We're basically volunteers. One of the last volunteer companies in the state."

"You're doing an amazing job," said Lucy. "Who were those guys who went into the building?"

"That was Rusty and J.J.—disobeying the chief, like usual."

"It's gonna go—all clear!" she heard someone yell and looked up. The hose crews began moving back, individual firefighters ran for safety as the huge front wall of the building began to fall. There was a huge crash and a spray of glowing red cinders rose and fell, showering those closest to the blaze.

The firefighters moved back in, pouring water onto the

remains of the building. Nothing was left of the Rope-walk but a smoldering heap. Some of the fire companies began to pack up their equipment, preparing to leave.

Surveying the scene, Lucy was struck by the unfamiliar new shape of the waterfront, the space formerly occupied by the Ropewalk was now vacant, revealing a view of the harbor beyond. The neighboring buildings had all been saved, but it would have to wait until morning to learn if they had been damaged.

Ted approached her. "Can a reporter have a sandwich?"

"Sure," said Lucy, spreading peanut butter on a piece of bread for him. "Some story."

"Not the kind I like to write," said Ted, taking a big bite of his sandwich.

"Do they know how it started?"

"Not yet."

"Any word about the manager, Frank Crowell?"

He shook his head.

She turned away. She'd had enough, she was bone tired, she wanted to go home.

"Lucy, can I help?" It was Franny.

Lucy remembered how proud Franny had been of her jewelry shop in the Ropewalk, how excited she'd been about having her own business. "I'm so sorry for you," she said, enfolding her in a hug.

Franny shrugged. "I was pretty lucky. I hadn't moved my workshop into the Ropewalk, yet. All my supplies and equipment are still at home. All I had there were finished pieces, and frankly, I'd sold most of them. I didn't lose much at all." She blinked a few times. "Most of the others weren't so fortunate. I don't know what they're going to do. They've lost everything, and they're going to have to start over from scratch." She paused a moment. "If they can."

Lucy nodded. "Well, Dot should be back soon. She went to make some coffee for the guys who'll be here all night."

"Here you go," said Franny, slapping a sandwich together for a very small firefighter from a neighboring town. The firefighter yanked off his helmet and two braids tumbled down; Lucy realized he wasn't a he at all.

More power to her, thought Lucy, as she said good-bye to Franny and rejoined Bill and the girls. Not, of course, that she'd want her girls to become firefighters. The work was too hard and too dangerous. Then she remembered Tucker. Nothing was safe, it seemed.

"Let's go home," she said, wrapping her arms around Bill and resting her cheek on his chest.

He gave her a squeeze. "You bet."

Chapter Fifteen

5 days 'til Xmas

Lucy was headed out the door on Saturday morning to do her grocery shopping when the phone rang. It was Ted with an assignment.

"The volunteer firefighters are meeting on Monday night—can you cover it?"

"Sure." Lucy checked her calendar and wrote in the time of the meeting. "Are they handing out awards or something? Should I take my camera?"

Ted snorted. "Definitely take your camera, but it's not about awards. Several firefighters have been charged with stealing from the fire. The meeting is to decide what the organization is going to do—they might go on strike in protest."

"Whoa." Lucy couldn't believe what she was hearing. "This is the first I've heard about this. Explain."

"Can't. I don't have time. I've got to be at a press conference in five minutes. Stop by the office later today, OK?"

"OK."

She had almost made it to the door when the phone
rang a second time. This time it was Mr. Humphreys from
the high school.

"Ahem, Mrs. Stone," he began, clearing his throat several times.

Whatever he had to say was apparently stuck in his
craw. Finally, he managed to get it out.

"I had a conversation with your legal representative
yesterday, and I think I may say it was most enlightening
and informative. And as a result of that conversation,
Elizabeth's suspension has been reduced and she will be
welcome to return to school on Monday."

Lucy resisted the impulse to crow. "That's very good
news," she said. "Thank you for calling."

In the car, she flipped on the radio just in time to hear
the nine o'clock news report. Ted was right. Four volunteer firemen had been arrested and would be charged with
larceny at the Ropewalk fire: Russell Rousseau, Jean-
Jacques Rousseau, Fred Childs, and George Paxton. Paxton was also the captain of the volunteer force, next in
line of command after the chief, Stan Pulaski. All four
men had been released on bail pending their arraignment
Monday. Tinker's Cove police were expected to release
more details later this morning.

The station promised a "six-pack"—six songs without
a commercial—but Lucy couldn't have told you what
they were. She was hardly listening; her mind was occupied by this disturbing news.

Last night she had been at the fire and witnessed first-hand the heroism of the volunteer firefighters, especially the Rousseau brothers. Everyone in town understood the risks involved in fighting fires, and Tinker's Cove citizens were proud of the volunteer firefighters. The force was one of the last volunteer departments in the state. Most of the neighboring towns had been forced to switch to paid, professional forces, but interest in Tinker's Cove remained high and the chief never short of volunteers. Members of the department marched in the Fourth of July parade, afterward they held a huge picnic and invited the whole town to watch as they competed in contests of skill such as ladder races and obstacle courses. The most popular, especially if the weather was hot, was to see who could hit a target with water from the fire hose. It was funny to watch people struggle with the hose, which seemed to have a life of its own. Kids and women were usually knocked off their feet; only the strongest men could control the jet of water that shot out of it.

Why would such public-spirited men as the volunteer firefighters steal from a fire? She'd never heard of such a thing, but could understand them taking souvenirs like a sign, perhaps a brick or a unique bit of woodwork. It would be something to keep, a reminder of the night the Ropewalk burned. But that could hardly be called theft, she thought, except by the strictest moralist.

Lucy knew that many people in Tinker's Cove had been seafarers for generations, and weren't above picking up a loose bit of flotsam or jetsam and claiming it for their own. When she and Bill were first married they had found a wooden cable spool washed up on a beach and rolled it home, where they had used it as a table for years. Most anything that washed up was considered free for the taking, except for lobster traps. They were left for their owner to reclaim; you could get shot for taking somebody else's lobster trap.

Turning onto Main Street, Lucy gasped at the sight of the burned Ropewalk. Nothing of the building remained except for a huge heap of burned wood; the paint on the neighboring block of stores had blistered, and the roof shingles had curled with the heat. It was amazing that the firefighters had been able to save the stores—even the church across the street was black with soot. The street in front of the Ropewalk had been closed off with yellow tape; water used to fight the fire had frozen overnight, making it too slippery for traffic.

Lucy took the detour, straining her neck to get a last look as she made the turn and headed for the IGA.

While she waited in line at the checkout, she listened to Dot chatting with the woman ahead of her.

"It doesn't surprise me in the least bit," said Dot, as she passed the cans and boxes through the scanner. "My oldest boy, he was on the Tinker's Cove force for years but then he went professional over in Gilead. He's an EMT and all; he got trained when he was in the army.

"Well, Joe told me, one of the reasons he wanted to go pro was that he didn't like some of the stuff the volunteers were doing." She paused to find the UPC code on a box of cat food. "I swear, sometimes they hide these darn things. Anyway, Joe said, the attitude was that they could take whatever they wanted because the insurance company would be paying for it all anyway." Dot's eyebrows shot up. "And I told him that was a lot of poppycock because we'd all end up paying higher insurance rates.

There's no such thing as a free lunch, that's what I told him."

Soon Dot had the woman's groceries bagged, and she turned to Lucy.

"Seems like I'm seeing an awful lot of you," she said.

"I can't seem to stay away," agreed Lucy, with a smile. "Last night was quite a night, wasn't it?"

"One I wouldn't care to repeat, thank you," said Dot, reaching for a bag of apples and smoothing the plastic so the scanner could read the price code.

"Last night I thought those men were heroes, and today I hear on the radio that they're bums—I can't figure it out," Lucy said.

"In my experience, most men are a little bit of both, if you know what I mean." Dot leaned across the counter. "But I can tell you this much. If Chief Crowley was running things down at that police station, this would have been taken care of, and nobody would have been the wiser."

"What do you mean?"

Dot shrugged. "He mostly turned a blind eye, figuring that the firemen deserved whatever they could salvage— it isn't like they get paid or anything. If somebody complained or something, he would have them return the stuff. It all would have been taken care of without making people look bad."

"That's true," chimed in Andrea Rogers, who had stepped up to the checkout behind Lucy. "Chief Crowley would never have brought charges against Tim. He would have given him a talking-to and brought him home, figuring his parents would take care of it. Now they've got this zero tolerance policy." Andrea twisted her lips into a smirk. "It's supposed to be zero tolerance for drugs and booze, but I think it really means zero tolerance for kids."

Lucy nodded in agreement, she was a sadder and wiser woman after Elizabeth's experience.

"I think you've got something there. Has Tim gone to court yet?"

"Not 'til January. Bob says they'll probably put him on probation and make him take an alcohol education course, plus he'll be stuck with a conviction." Andrea sighed. "Every time he applies for a job or renews his driver's license or whatever, he'll have to check the yes box."

"Look on the bright side," said Lucy. "The way things are going, he'll have plenty of company. What about next year?"

"MCU doesn't want him anymore, that's for sure. We're thinking of sending him for a thirteenth year at Wolford Academy. He can play there and hopefully he'll get recruited by another college."

"That's a good idea," said Lucy, watching as Dot rang up the last of her order.

"That'll be one fifty-four and thirty-one cents."

"Ouch," said Lucy, reaching for her wallet.

At *The Pennysaver,* Lucy found Ted hunched over his desk, tapping away at his keyboard. She plopped down in the chair he saved for visitors, not bothering to move the clutter of press releases that had accumulated there.

"Listen, Ted. I'm not sure this firefighter story rates page one. From what I heard at the IGA this morning, this is nothing new. The firemen have taken stuff in the past, and Chief Crowley just turned a blind eye on it unless he got a complaint. Then he'd make them return the stuff, but he didn't bring charges or anything. Tom Scott's new on the job; he doesn't understand about small towns."

Ted looked up and Lucy saw he looked like someone who hadn't been getting enough sleep. She also thought he looked terribly sad, showing none of the excitement he usually felt when working on a big story.

"I hate this story," he confessed. "These men risk their lives, they get up out of warm beds in the middle of the night to put out fires and pry people out of crashed cars, and they don't get paid a penny. Do I care if they take some souvenirs from a fire? Do I care if they help themselves to some fire-damaged stuff that's going to get thrown out anyway? I don't give a damn, and that's the truth. But I've got to cover it because it's already been on the radio and Tom Scott held a big news conference this morning and invited media from all over New England. Goddamn *Globe* was there."

He dropped his hands in his lap and shook his head. "What really gets me is that I'm the only one who's going to mention what this is really about—and only a few thousand people are going to read me and hundreds of thousands are going to read the story Scott's hand-fed to everybody else. It was slick, let me tell you. Piles of merchandise, stacked up on tables, for all to view. Gold and silver jewelry. Rare coins. Everything all polished up. Even a couple of stained-glass lamps. Worth thousands of dollars, or so he said."

"I had no idea. I thought it was a couple of bricks or something like that."

"Nope. You gotta hand it to the boys. They made quite a haul. But that's not the story, not really. Because it wasn't the shopkeepers who complained—I've been calling them, and they have nothing but good things to say about the firefighters. They all say their businesses were total losses anyway. Nope. You know who filed the complaint. The Gilead fire chief."

Lucy was beginning to understand. "And Gilead is a professional force."

"Right. And they're asking for a raise at the town meeting this year. . . ."

"And they don't want to have to explain why folks in Gilead have to pay for something folks in Tinker's Cove get for free," interjected Lucy.

Ted nodded. "And if the volunteers go on strike, which is what they're threatening to do, they'll look even worse, and the voters will get disgusted. This is the end of the volunteers, I'm telling you. When this is over, Tinker's Cove will have a professional fire department. It's the end of an era."

He paused, studying his hands, then raised his head.

"Thanks for covering the meeting for me. I hated to ask, but the kids' Christmas concert is Monday night, and Pam says I have to go."

"No problem," said Lucy.

Chapter Sixteen

3 days 'til Xmas

As soon as Lucy opened the door to the fire station she heard the rumble of the men's voices. She nodded at the dispatcher and went past his desk into the common room, where CPR classes and training sessions were held. The last time Lucy had been there was when she covered the rabies clinic last spring; then the big room had been filled with assorted dogs and cats, and their owners and the conversation had been friendly as people chatted about their pets.

Tonight, the mood was much different. The gathered firefighters were angry and sullen. Lucy could feel the tension when she entered the room, and it made her pause. The only thing that kept her from turning and fleeing was the knowledge that Ted was counting on her to cover the meeting.

Heads turned and people stared at her; someone snickered and she realized she was the only woman in the room. Dot had been right on the mark when she said the Tinker's Cove Volunteer Fire Department was a men's club. "She writes for the paper," she heard someone say, and the word was passed through the room. Lucy felt uncomfortable under the gaze of so many men and looked for a familiar face. She was relieved when she spotted Bob Goodman, Rachel's husband, and Hank Orenstein sitting in the back. There were empty chairs next to them so she approached them.

"Hi, Lucy," Bob said with a smile. "Sit yourself down."

Bob was a tall, lean man with wire-rimmed glasses. He was the only man in the room who was wearing a suit.

"Thanks. For a minute there I felt a bit unwelcome. This doesn't seem like a very friendly group. And thanks for calling Mr. Humphreys. Elizabeth went back to school today."

Bob nodded. For a lawyer, he was remarkably taciturn.

Raised voices and the crash of a chair falling caught their attention, and Lucy glanced nervously around the room.

"Are these guys always so rowdy?" she asked.

"They're not so bad when you get to know them," said Hank. "They're just a little upset."

Hank was shorter and heavier than Bob, with a round face and a beard. He ran a cooperative that sold heating oil and energy-saving devices at discount prices.

"Do you think they'll really strike?" asked Lucy.

"Might," said Bob.

"A lot of them want to," said Hank. "At least the ones I talked to today. They feel like those boys are getting a raw deal."

"Ted says it was an awful lot of stuff—worth thousands of dollars." Lucy kept her voice low; she didn't want to be overheard.

Hank snorted in disgust. "Those boys were just plain greedy."

Bob nodded. "This time they went too far."

"What do you mean?"

The two men exchanged a glance, then Hank broke the silence.

"So, how's Bill doing? Is he keepin' busy this winter?"

"Bill's fine. And you don't have to worry that I'm going to quote you in the paper. Anything you say is off the record. Promise. But I sure could use some background information, and from what you were saying and from what I've been hearing around town it seems like there's been an unofficial policy that it's okay to salvage stuff from fires. Is that true?"

Hank bent closer to Lucy and spoke very softly. "Yeah. I'd say that's true. The boys only get a small stipend—a hundred fifty dollars a year 'cause it's a volunteer force. And you know what the economy's like in this town. And now with the lobster quota, well, a lot of the guys are really hurting. If they see something they can use, or sell, they're not going to walk away from it. Chief shoulda put a stop to it a long time ago, if you ask me. At first, they didn't take much, but when he never said anything it started to escalate. It's really gotten out of hand."

"So you think Tom Scott did the right thing?"

"Now I didn't say that." Hank's face reddened. "It could have been handled differently. There was no cause to put those boys in jail overnight."

"It wasn't necessary," added Bob. "They all have families in this town; they weren't going to go anywhere."

Lucy nodded, aware that the meeting was beginning. A huge man, still wearing his bright yellow fisherman's waterproof pants pulled up over a ragged sweatshirt and a plaid flannel shirt, was banging on a table with a gavel, calling the meeting to order.

"Quiet down," he roared, his droopy mustache and the bristly whiskers on his chin making him look a little bit like a walrus. "None of us wants to be here all night, so let's get started."

"Who's that?" asked Lucy.

"Claw Rousseau—he owns the lobster pound out on Cove Road," whispered Hank.

"That's the same name as two of the men who were arrested. . . ."

"His sons, Rusty and J.J."

"And he's president of the volunteers' association?"

Hank nodded, and Lucy wrote it all down in her notebook. This could get interesting, she thought.

"This meeting has been called at the request of some of the members," said Claw. "In fact, I have here a petition signed by more than two thirds of the members calling for the department to go on strike until criminal charges against four of our members have been dropped."

"I move we strike," called out a voice. "Let's vote and get it over with. The Pats are playing Dallas tonight."

This was greeted with raucous laughter.

"Hold your horses," said Claw. "We gotta do this by the rules. First, we gotta have discussion. Who wants to go first?"

Before Claw Rousseau could choose one of the men who had raised his hands, a middle-aged man with a white beard got to his feet and took the floor.

"This isn't right," he began. "What the hell's going on

in this town? Here we have four fine young men, willing to risk their lives in order to help other folks, being treated as if they were common criminals. What we have here is a crime all right, but the crime isn't what Lieutenant Scott thinks it is. The crime is taking our good men, they hadn't even had a chance to get out of their gear, and throwing them into jail. That's the crime, and we've gotta let them know that we're not gonna take it. You can't throw us in jail and then expect us to come runnin' to save your ass when you've drove into a 'lectric light pole or put a pot on to cook and forgot all about it and all of a sudden the place is goin' up in smoke. Ain't gonna happen."

The men cheered and stamped their feet in approval, and several jumped to their feet to speak.

"Who was that?" asked Lucy.

"Mike O'Laughlin," said Hank. "He's always got something to say."

"Got a big mouth," added Bob, leaning back in his chair and crossing his arms on his chest. He seemed to be enjoying himself.

"He's right!" said a thirtyish man in jeans and work boots. "I say we strike 'til the charges are dropped. Let those guys in Gilead cover for us—make 'em earn their fat salaries for a change."

The crowd greeted this with hoots of approval.

"A strike's the only thing that'll teach 'em," said another.

Lucy recognized Gary from the gas station, where he worked as a mechanic.

"I mean, we drop everything when that siren blows, we never hesitate for even a second and we never know what we're gonna face. Last year, Jack Perry and Bill

Higgins went to the hospital. Jack had burns and Bill broke his ankle. What do they get for their pain? A big fat nothing. Don't get me wrong. We're all volunteers here, and that's the way it oughta be. People helpin' people. But don't we deserve a little appreciation? A little consideration? That's all we're asking for, and we're gonna get it or they're not gonna get their calls answered."

This also was met with noisy approval. But when Claw recognized Stan Pulaski, the fire chief, the crowd fell silent. Lucy could almost feel the men bristling as he began speaking.

"I know how upset you all are," he began, "and I know how proud you all are to be a volunteer force. But if we go on strike, how are people supposed to have confidence in us? They'll say you can't depend on a volunteer force, and next thing you know we'll be a call force taking orders from a bunch of college-educated strangers who're getting paid to tell us what to do. I think a strike's a bad idea."

"The chief is right," said Claw. He spoke slowly, and his words had weight. "The people of this town have faith in us, that we will answer their calls for help. They trust us and depend on us; we can't let them down."

A sullen silence followed his words. A few of the men looked a bit ashamed of themselves; others were clearly angered.

"Whatsa matter, Chief?" demanded one young man. "What happened to sticking together, like you always say? We gotta work together, isn't that what you're always telling us. Well, we gotta stick behind Rusty and J.J. and the others."

Lucy followed his pointing finger and recognized the two brothers, sitting along with two others who she assumed were the other men who had been charged with stealing. They shifted uneasily in their seats as their fellow firefighters cheered and applauded. After giving vent to their emotions for several minutes, the men quieted down and a single voice was heard.

"Those men broke the law." It was Tom Scott, speaking from the doorway.

His entrance wasn't greeted with boos, as Lucy expected. Instead, the men seemed subdued, like a classroom of kids who had lost control when their teacher left the room only to scurry back to their desks when she returned. He strode to the front of the room, where he stood next to Claw Rousseau.

"I know you're angry about the arrests," he began, holding his official blue hat in his hands. "Maybe it'll help if I clear some things up. First of all, I want you to understand that nobody in this town is above the law."

This drew some chuckles from the firefighters, but Scott wasn't fazed.

"Second, I want you to understand that I respect what you do. You fellas are willing to put your lives on the line for your neighbors, and that's a fine and noble thing to do.

"Finally, the district attorney has informed me that he is open to a plea bargain in this matter and is prepared to be lenient."

Scott turned to face Claw and extended his hand. Claw hesitated a moment and then grasped it; Scott pulled him close in a bear hug. From the crowd, there were murmurs of approval as well as mutters of discontent. Claw banged his gavel and called the meeting to order once again.

"There's a motion before us," he said. "We've gotta vote. All in favor, that means a strike, raise your hand."

Tom Scott remained beside him, watching as he counted the votes.

"I count nineteen in favor."

Listening closely, Lucy thought she sensed a note of relief in Claw's voice.

"What does it take? Two-thirds?" she asked Bob.

He nodded. "They don't have the votes."

"Opposed?" called Claw. "A no vote means no strike."

Hank and Bob were among those who raised their hands.

"I count sixteen. The motion fails. No strike." Claw disregarded the angry epithets uttered by some of the thwarted strikers. "Any other business?" He banged down the gavel. "Meeting adjourned."

Lucy got to her feet and tried to make her way to the front of the room to get a comment from Claw. He was already engaged in discussion with several of the firefighters, so Lucy turned to Tom Scott instead.

"Are you pleased with the vote?"

Tom thought for a minute, weighing his words. "I think this is the best possible outcome to an unfortunate situation. A few of the firefighters made a mistake, and that's being addressed by my department and the justice system. I think it's to the credit of the volunteers that they understand their responsibility to the town."

"A majority voted to strike," Lucy reminded him. "Do you think there will be friction between your department and the firefighters in the future?"

"There's no room for petty squabbles in this business," said Scott. "We're public servants, and we work together."

Lucy wrote as fast as she could, but when she looked up to ask her next question she saw that Scott had walked away and was approaching the firefighters who had been charged with theft. The crowd of supporters gathered around them dissipated as he drew near.

Lucy watched as the four men huddled around Scott, wishing she dared to attempt to overhear their conversation. Instead, she wove her way through the scattered groups of firefighters and greeted Claw.

"Lucy Stone, from *The Pennysaver*. Do you mind if I take your picture?"

Claw shrugged and Lucy produced her camera. When the flash went off there was a moment of silence, then the buzz of conversation resumed. She snapped the shutter a few more times, then tucked the camera away and pulled out her notebook.

"Are you happy with the vote?"

"Like everybody else, I can go home tonight and know that if I need help, help will be there."

"What about the men who were charged? Two of them are your sons?"

Rousseau's face sagged and Lucy thought he must be older than she had guessed at first, probably closer to sixty than the robust fifty she had noted in her book. "At times like this you have to have faith," he said.

His answer took her by surprise. She had expected him to defend his sons, or at the very least to point out their heroism at the fire.

"Thank you," she said, and put away her notebook. She didn't want to bother this clearly troubled man any further.

Chapter Seventeen

L ucy never worried about going out by herself after
dark in Tinker's Cove, but tonight she was unpleas-
antly aware of her vulnerability as she left the fire station and crossed the parking lot to her car. A group of
firefighters had followed her out of the building, and although she could hear their gruff voices and heavy foot-
steps, she couldn't see them without turning her head.
She didn't want them to think she was nervous about
their presence, so she kept her eyes forward and tightened her grip on the car keys she held ready in her hand.

As soon as she got inside the car she locked the doors,
feeling slightly ridiculous as she did so. She rarely bothered with the locks, but tonight she felt uneasy.

She started the car and carefully backed out of her
parking space, then drove slowly across the lot to the exit.
There she pulled to a stop and looked right and left to

make sure the road was clear; she was ready to pull out when her eyes were suddenly hit with a bright glare. A pickup truck had pulled up behind her and its headlights were set so high that they beamed straight into her mirrors and the bright light bounced directly into her eyes. She squinted, trying to avoid the glare and pulled out. She actually never saw the oncoming car; only the blare of the horn and the screech of brakes as it swerved into the opposite lane to avoid a collision gave her any indication of the danger she had been in.

Her heart was pounding and her hands were shaking as she proceeded slowly down the road. The truck was still close behind her, and the glare was so strong that she was practically blinded, even after she flipped the rearview mirror. She considered pulling over and letting the truck pass, but she knew that probably wasn't a good idea. After all, they were in a passing zone, and there was little traffic. There was no reason why the driver of the truck couldn't pass her if he wanted to. Lucy suspected he was harassing her on purpose and was afraid that if she stopped, he, whoever he was, would pull up right behind her and she would be at his mercy. She didn't really have any choice but to keep going, hoping that her tormenter would eventually grow impatient with her slow speed.

After following her for a mile or so, that's exactly what happened. She heard a roar as the truck accelerated, then zoomed past and raced off down the road. A glance in the rearview mirror explained everything—a police cruiser had apparently scared off her pursuer and was now following her.

She didn't know whether to be relieved or worried; expecting any moment that the blue lights would flash, signaling that she should pull over. That didn't happen, however, and it was only a few moments later that she made the familiar turn onto Red Top Road and finally reached her own driveway; the cruiser paused at the edge of the road and waited until she was safely inside the house before pulling away,

Secure in her kitchen, Lucy let out a sigh of relief as she unzipped her parka and hung it among the other coats and jackets that crowded the row of hooks beside the door. She missed its warmth—Bill had turned down the heat before going up to bed and the kitchen was chilly—and rubbed her arms briskly. Realizing she was too keyed up to go to sleep, she poured a mug of milk for herself and set it in the microwave to heat. She stood, watching the seconds count down, and tried to sort out her emotions.

She should have felt grateful for the police escort, she supposed. It was most likely Tom Scott in the cruiser, she thought. He had probably seen the men following her after the meeting and had decided to keep an eye on the situation. Thanks to his intervention the firefighters had stopped harassing her and she had gotten home safely. He had saved her from goodness knows what unpleasantness, and she owed him a big debt of gratitude.

The microwave beeped, and she took out the milk and sat down at the table, wrapping her hands around the warm mug. Any proper person would be dashing off a thank-you note, she thought, but she didn't feel grateful at all. She was angry, she realized. She was furious that she had needed protection and even madder that Scott had presumed to provide it.

She had lived in this town for nearly twenty years and had managed to get along without police protection until now, and she wasn't sure she had really needed it tonight.

Her followers had probably just been teasing her; maybe they hadn't even realized the blinding effect of the truck's headlights.

After all, Tinker's Cove was the sort of place where people never locked their houses. Nobody bothered to lock a car, either, and lots of people even left their keys in the ignition when they parked on Main Street. There were occasional crimes of violence, like Tucker's murder, but they were usually the consequence of emotions gone awry, intimate relationships poisoned by jealousy or alcohol or unemployment, not street crimes like you'd expect in a big city.

It was odd, she thought, that she had never felt the least bit unsafe in Tinker's Cove until now. When Chief Crowley was in charge, the letter of the law had been taken rather lightly, but somehow it had worked, or at least it seemed to.

Now, the attitude was zero tolerance. There were no excuses, no exceptions. It didn't matter if you were an honor student helping another student or a kid supplying drugs to your classmates, you were treated the same. And firefighters who had risked their lives were treated like common criminals. Nowadays nobody winked at a minor transgression, nobody trusted their own judgment, everybody got treated the same.

Except they didn't, realized Lucy, taking a sip of the hot milk and grimacing. It tasted awful. She got up and went into the pantry, looking for some vanilla to flavor it. She didn't find any vanilla but she did find a bottle of brandy she had bought to make eggnog. She poured a dollop in her mug and added a spoonful of sugar. Much better, she decided, as the soothing drink flowed over her tongue.

Zero tolerance might be the official line, she thought, but Mr. Humphreys had backed down soon enough when he had been threatened with legal action. Tom Scott had backed down, too, and offered a plea bargain when the firefighters had threatened to strike.

Lucy finished her drink and set the mug in the sink. Then she stretched, enjoying the sensation of warmth and relaxation the drink had induced. She flipped off the kitchen light and tiptoed up the stairs, ready to go to bed. But when she slipped in beside Bill and closed her eyes, listening to Bill's regular breathing, punctuated by an occasional snore, she couldn't clear her mind for sleep. Disturbing thoughts kept flooding in.

First there was the fire. The huge flames breaking through the Ropewalk roof, the sweaty faces of the firefighters caught in the revolving beams from the emergency lights on top of the trucks. That was how she remembered the fire, but she knew that she didn't have the whole picture. While she had been watching all the activity in the front of the building, something else had been going on in the back, where some of the firefighters had been carrying off valuables. She struggled to reconcile the two images: the brave heroism taking place in the front and the sneaky thievery going on in the back.

Then she saw Claw Rousseau's tired, lined face. Unlike Andrea, he didn't make excuses for his boys or try to defend them. Why not, she wondered. She would have expected Claw to be intensely loyal to his sons. She thought of the panic she felt when she got the call from the high school, and the anger she still nurtured in her heart against Mr. Humphreys. If she felt this strongly about the school's disciplinary policy, why wasn't Claw furious with Scott? Was he really able to set aside his own feelings? Had he truly been willing to sacrifice his sons for the general welfare of Tinker's Cove?

Maybe the emotional ties between parents and their children grew weaker as the children grew older; after all, Claw's "boys" must be well into their thirties. Lucy rolled back onto her other side and pressed her fanny against Bill spoon-style. Somehow, she didn't think so. She thought of the Whitneys, devastated by the loss of their grown child. She thought of herself, determined to send Toby off to college where he would do what? Get drunk? Try drugs?

Lucy rolled over and rearranged the pillow. Toby didn't have to go to college to try drugs; drugs were readily available in Tinker's Cove. Barney knew it, Ted knew it. What had he said? That he was grateful he hadn't had to report any arrests in Tinker's Cove.

Why not, wondered Lucy. There were plenty of arrests in neighboring towns; the court report in the Portland daily was full of them. Why weren't drug offenders and dealers getting arrested in Tinker's Cove? Lucy thought of the fire, the heroism out front, and the thievery that was going on behind the scenes. She thought of Main Street, the picture-perfect New England town where people didn't bother to lock their doors but where high-school kids were getting illegal drugs.

And she thought of Tucker, supposedly killed by a jealous lover. Except the lover hadn't been all that jealous, from what she'd heard. And Tucker hadn't really seemed like the sort of girl to encourage attention from a married man twice her age.

Lucy flopped onto her back and stared at the ceiling, gray in the dim light from the hall night-light. Above its smooth blankness, she knew, was a jumble of wires and insulation, a century's worth of dust, insect colonies and, no doubt, families of mice. Tinker's Cove was the same, she thought, a quaint little fishing town with a drug problem.

Under the covers, Lucy shivered and stared at the clock. It was almost two. She had to be up at six, and she had a long day ahead of her. She was going to get to the bottom of this; she was going to find out what was really going on, and a good place to start would be to take another look at Tucker's murder. She snuggled down deeper under the covers and pressed her body against Bill's. She closed her eyes and matched her breathing to his. She slept.

Next thing she knew it was morning. She woke feeling tired and a look in the mirror wasn't reassuring; her eyes were puffy, and she suspected it was going to be a bad hair day. In the kitchen, Zoe was singing Christmas carols and pouring milk into a bowl already overflowing with Cheerios.

"For Pete's sake, Zoe, watch what you're doing," she grumbled, pouring herself a cup of coffee.

"Who's Pete?" chirped Zoe.

Lucy gave her an evil look.

"Well, I see we have lots of Christmas spirit this morning," said Bill.

"Ho, ho, ho," growled Lucy, hanging on to her coffee mug as if it were a life preserver.

Bill studied her, then sighed. "I'll make the lunches," he said.

"Thanks." Lucy fought the impulse to rest her head on the table and took a swallow of coffee.

* * *

After a shower and two more cups of coffee Lucy felt almost human. Ted didn't even look up when she arrived at *The Pennysaver,* just grunted and told her he needed the story on the meeting ASAP.

"And make it short," he said. "Space is going to be tight this week."

Lucy took him at his word and tapped out six inches of copy, reporting the results of the vote and adding a quote or two representing the differing points of view expressed at the meeting. It was still early when she left the office, so she decided to head for the gym. If she hurried she could catch Krissy's ten-thirty workout. Lord knows, she could use it, but what was more to the point, hadn't Sue told her that Tucker took a tai chi class after work?

"Hi, Lucy," Krissy greeted her, annoyingly pert in a high-cut orange leotard. "You look as if you've got the holiday blues."

"I'm trying my damnedest to get some holiday spirit, but it's awfully hard this year, with the murder and the fire and all."

Keeping up her spirits never seemed to be a problem for Krissy, who had opened the Body Works a few years ago. Even her ponytail bounced, as if it were full of energy, but her face was solemn as she nodded in agreement.

"I know. I just can't believe that creep killed Tucker. . . ." Her gaze wandered to some other clients who were coming through the door, and she raised her voice a few decibles. "You've come to the right place. We'll warm you up, stretch you out, work those muscles and finish up with a relaxing cooldown. You'll feel like a new person when we're done."

"Can I talk to you after class?" asked Lucy as she handed over her five dollars.

Krissy nodded grimly and Lucy gave her hand a squeeze, then headed for the locker room.

When the session was over, Lucy had to admit that although she didn't feel exactly like a new person, she did feel like a much-improved version of the old one as she headed down the carpeted corridor to Krissy's office.

Krissy was on the phone, but she smiled at Lucy and pointed to a chair. "I'm on hold—I'm trying to get airplane tickets. All of a sudden I have this irrational urge to go home for Christmas."

"Good luck," said Lucy.

"Yeah. You're right." Krissy put the receiver back in its cradle. "I'll never get tickets this close to Christmas." She rolled her eyes. "I don't know what I was thinking. My family is completely screwed up. I swore I'd never go through another holiday with them, and here I am, ready to spend top dollar to fly to Jersey City just so they can tell me how worthless I am. I think I'll stay here, and have Christmas with Earl."

Earl was Krissy's black Labrador. Pictures of his progress from puppyhood to maturity were plastered all over her office walls, and Earl himself was sound asleep on a futon in the corner.

"Earl's good company," said Lucy.

"The best," affirmed Krissy. "Don't tell him, but I got him a new collar and a squeaky toy for Christmas. Plus a case of tennis balls."

"Mint-flavored?"

"I thought about it, but I decided he really likes them kind of dirt-flavored, and the mint might interfere with the proper aging process."

Lucy laughed. "So Earl is the man in your life these days?"

"You know it." Krissy shook her head. "Face it. There's not much night life in a town like this, except the video store." She sighed. "I really miss Tucker. We had some good times together." Krissy stared at a point above Lucy's head and blinked furiously.

"I didn't realize you were such good friends," said Lucy.

"Well, you know how it is in a small town like this. There aren't that many young, single women. We met here and we hit it off right away. She was such a sweetheart— why'd he have to do it? What a bastard."

"Maybe Steve didn't do it," said Lucy slowly.

"He did it all right," said Krissy. "You wouldn't believe what an unattached woman goes through in this town."

Lucy looked puzzled.

"Tucker loved to dance, you know? So one night we went out to this bar, Scalliwags, they've got live music there on weekends. It's kind of a dump, but we thought what the hell. So we're having a great time dancing with these guys but they get the wrong idea. They think that dancing with them means you want to bear their children, you know what I mean?"

Lucy knew. "Is that what it was with Steve? That he wanted more than she wanted to give?"

Krissy shrugged.

"He just doesn't seem to me like the kind of guy . . ." began Lucy.

Krissy snorted. "They're all the same, believe me. And they're all available—it's just their wives don't know it."

Lucy chuckled. "Don't want to know, is more like it." She paused. "But I heard that Steve and Lee were getting back together."

"Maybe. That doesn't change the fact he was sniffing around Tucker like Earl used to do to the lady dogs before his trip to the vet."

"Okay. I give up. Steve's a worthless scum, but I still think there's a big difference between acting like a hound dog and killing somebody." She scratched her chin. "You know, an awful lot of drugs have been coming through town lately. . . ."

Krissy made her eyes round, pretending to be shocked. "No way."

Lucy continued. "I was just wondering if Tucker might have got involved somehow, got in too deep or something."

"Whoa." Krissy held up her hands to protest. "Are you kidding? Tucker wouldn't touch drugs with a ten-foot pole. Do you know who her father is?"

Lucy shook her head.

"He's a big shot in the Department of Justice, I mean way up there. Just under the attorney general, I think. Anyway, he's head prosecutor for all the federal drug cases."

"I had no idea."

Krissy nodded. "'Just say no' is like a religion in that family."

"Yeah, but, look at yourself. Kids don't always agree with their parents."

"Tucker did. Believe me. She used to say she didn't see why people couldn't just get high on life. Nature, the woods, skiing, sailing, she used to come back from those AMC hikes all excited about the trees and the clouds, for Pete's sake."

Lucy wondered if she'd heard right. "AMC hikes?"

"Yeah. You know, Appalachian Mountain Club. Tucker was a member."

So that was what the notation in Tucker's agenda meant, thought Lucy. She hadn't met Lee that Sunday before she'd died, she'd gone for a hike.

"Does anybody else around here belong? Anybody I could talk to?"

"Sure. Witt's actually the president, I think."

"Witt?"

"He teaches kick boxing." Krissy glanced at her watch. "That reminds me. It's time for me to kick butt."

"Kick butt?" asked Lucy, standing up to go.

"That's what I call it. It's a class for women who want to tighten and firm their bottoms. We have it at noon so the working gals can come."

"Oh." She walked down the hall with Krissy. "I hope you and Earl have a merry Christmas."

"We're gonna do our best," said Krissy, as she pulled open the gym door. Lucy peeked through the door, wondering if she knew anybody in the class and recognized Steffie Scott. She tried to catch her eye, but Steffie was too absorbed in her thoughts to notice her.

Lucy paused in the entryway, studying the bulletin board as she zipped her parka, looking for the class schedule among the clutter of posters and announcements. There, under a notice advertising an amateur performance of *The Nutcracker* she saw a bright yellow sheet of paper announcing AMC hikes every Sunday at one o'clock. Next to it was the schedule: Witt's kick-boxing class was at three-thirty on weekday afternoons.

Swinging her gym bag over her shoulder, Lucy headed for the car. She'd get some lunch and do some last-minute shopping, she decided, and then she'd try to catch Witt before his class.

Chapter Eighteen

The backseat of Lucy's car was filled with bags of goodies and stocking stuffers when she returned to the Body Works at twenty past three. She hesitated for a moment in the vestibule, wondering how to approach Witt, when she saw a young man in exercise clothes coming out of the office with a sheet of paper in his hand. He stopped at the reception desk and started to poke around in a drawer, obviously looking for something.

Lucy walked over to the desk and he looked up. "Can I help you?" he asked.

"I'm looking for Witt."

"That's me," he said, with a lopsided smile.

Lucy smiled back. Witt had the easy manner of someone who was comfortable with himself and knew he could handle pretty much any problem that came up. He wasn't very tall and at first glance seemed rather stocky, but he was all muscle.

"I'm interested in these AMC hikes," she began. "Can you tell me anything about them?"

"Sure," he said, opening an Altoids tin and plucking a thumbtack out of the assortment of paper clips and other small, useful items it contained. He held up the paper for her to see and walked over to the bulletin board, bouncing on the balls of his feet as he went.

"See, this is the schedule. We have a different hike every Sunday." He rearranged the papers on the bulletin board and made a space for his new notice, then turned to Lucy. "There's no charge or anything, but we kind of encourage people to become AMC members if they become regulars."

"That's fair enough," said Lucy, noticing that his eyes were very blue indeed. "I think a friend of mine was a member—Tucker Whitney?"

"Yeah." He looked down, studying his hands. He swallowed and Lucy saw his Adam's apple bob, a little bulge in the middle of his size 18 neck. "That was too bad."

"Did you know her well?"

"Just from the hikes. She almost always came." He seemed to be choosing his words carefully. "It's not going to be the same without her."

"I know." Lucy's voice was gentle. "I wish I'd had time to get to know her better."

He sighed. "I know what you mean."

Something in his tone made Lucy wonder if he'd had hopes of a serious relationship with Tucker.

"So, what do you do on these hikes?"

"Hike, you know. Follow a trail. Some people take

photographs or look for birds." He looked over her shoulder and smiled at one of his students. "Go on in—I'll be with you in a minute."

Lucy felt she was running out of time. "How many people go?"

"Sometimes just two or three, if the weather's really nice we might get eight or nine."

"And that Sunday before she died?"

"Five or six, I think." He nodded at a pair of students who were signing in at the desk. "Tucker was late that day. We waited a good forty-five minutes for her. Usually we wouldn't do that, but nobody wanted to start without her."

Lucy lowered her voice. "Did she seem the same as usual? I mean, could she have been stoned or something?"

"Tucker?" His voice was sharp, and those blue eyes seemed to bore right through her.

Lucy felt she had to defend her question. "I heard some things."

"About Tucker?" His tone implied she couldn't have been more wrong.

Lucy shrugged.

"That's ridiculous. Who told you that?" He looked as if he'd like to smash a fist into whoever had suggested Tucker might have used drugs.

"Maybe I got it wrong," said Lucy.

"You sure did. Look, I've got to go. The hike's at one, if you want to come."

"Thanks." Lucy started to go, then turned around and called after him. "Did she say why she was late?"

Witt whirled to face her, the movement was quick, and

he was perfectly balanced. "She said she took a wrong turn." Then he vanished into the gym.

Lucy checked the bulletin board for the old schedule, and found it under a notice advertising a slightly used set of barbells.

According to the schedule, that Sunday the group had hiked in the conservation area near Smith Heights Road.

That was funny, thought Lucy, as she headed back to her car. Tucker had summered on Smith Heights Road for her entire life—how could she make a wrong turn that would delay her for forty-five minutes?

As she started the car, she considered taking a quick spin out along Smith Heights Road to the conservation area, to see where Tucker might have made her wrong turn. A look at the dashboard clock told her she didn't have time, today. She had a family waiting and a Christmas tree to trim.

The Stones always set up their tree on the last day of school before Christmas vacation, usually the day before Christmas Eve. Nobody quite knew how or why the custom began, but through the years it had taken on the weight of tradition. Now, it was absolutely unthinkable to put up the tree on any other day.

When Lucy arrived home, Bill and Toby had already brought the tree in and set it in its stand and Toby was perched on a stepladder, arranging the strings of lights. Bill was carrying in the boxes of ornaments, Sara was busy digging out the Christmas CDs, and Zoe was a small ball of excitement.

"Hurry, Mom. It's time to trim the tree."

"So I see. But we can't start hanging the ornaments until Toby finishes putting on the lights."

"He's almost done," insisted Zoe, ignoring the coils of wire and bulbs covering the family-room floor.

"Why don't you help Sara find the music?"

"Okay, Mom."

Having distracted Zoe for a moment, Lucy hurried upstairs to hide the bags of stocking stuffers she had bought earlier. That done, she stood outside the room Elizabeth shared with Sara and knocked on the door. The frantic drumbeats of alternative rock told her Elizabeth was inside.

"What?" Elizabeth called out in answer to Lucy's knock.

"We're trimming the tree. Don't you want to help?"

"Do I have to?"

"Don't you want to?"

There was a long silence. "Not really."

Lucy poked the door open and peeked in.

"Is everything OK?" asked Lucy. "Are they giving you a hard time at school?"

"Nah. School's cool." Elizabeth was standing in front of her mirror, considering her appearance.

From the pile of clothes on the bed, Lucy guessed she was trying on outfits. Personally, she didn't think the black fishnet stockings really went with the silky, pink sheath, and the chartreuse sweater was really a mistake.

"Whaddya think?" Elizabeth turned, cocking her hip.

"What's the occasion?" asked Lucy.

"Nothing, really." Elizabeth ran her hands through her hair, making it stand up in short spikes.

"You look fine," said Lucy, starting down the stairs.

Under her breath she added, "Just don't think you're leaving the house looking like that."

Elizabeth called after her. "Did you say something, Mom?"

"Nothing."

In the kitchen, Lucy found Sara filling a plate with cookies from the cookie jar.

"Good idea. I think I'll make some cocoa, while we wait to get started." Lucy got out a pot. "Is something bothering Elizabeth?"

"Woomph," said Sara, her mouth full of cookie.

"Would you mind repeating that?" Lucy measured cocoa and sugar and dumped them into the pot, then added a quart of milk.

"Lance."

Lance and Elizabeth had been close friends, but this fall Lance had gone away to a private boarding school.

"What about Lance?"

"Susie Macintyre told Elizabeth that he's home for Christmas, but he hasn't called her yet."

"Oh."

Lucy set the pot on the stove and turned the burner on. She got a spoon out of a drawer and began stirring the mixture, so it wouldn't stick to the bottom. When it was ready she poured the hot chocolate into mugs, set them on a tray and carried it into the family room.

Zoe, she saw as she entered, hadn't been able to resist opening the boxes of ornaments. She'd already unwrapped some of her favorites and had lined them up on the coffee table.

Lucy set the tray down beside them and picked one up. It was a little baby, sleeping in a crescent moon.

"That's Elizabeth's," she told Zoe. "From her first Christmas."

"It's beautiful."

"Yes, it is." Lucy sat down on the couch and took a bite of cookie. She wanted Elizabeth to hang the ornament on the tree, just as she had every year until now. "Why don't you see if she'll come down and hang her ornament?" she suggested.

Happy to have an important errand, Zoe ran off.

"Cookies and cocoa," announced Lucy, noticing that Sara was making quite a dent in the cookies. "Better come and get some before it's all gone!"

"I think I'll get a beer," said Bill, heading for the kitchen.

"In a minute," said Toby, reaching for the last string of lights.

Sara had already polished off her mug of cocoa when Zoe returned.

"She said to save it for her. She'll be down in a while."

"Where's Elizabeth?" asked Bill, sitting beside her and tilting back his bottle of beer.

"Sulking in her room."

Lucy watched as Zoe carefully lifted the mug of hot liquid to her lips and took a swallow. "Mmmm," she said, and licked her upper lip with her tongue.

Just then a blast of organ music came from the stereo and a famous choir began singing "Venite Adoremus." Tears sprang to Lucy's eyes as she was overwhelmed with a flood of jumbled emotions from all the Christmases past, and for a brief moment she wanted to be a little girl once again, standing in the candlelit, pine-scented church, holding tight to her father's hand.

"Well, let's get started," she said, opening one of the

boxes of ornaments and lifting out a bright red ball. She carried it over to the tree and placed it on a branch.

Soon the floor was covered with tissue and newspaper wrappings, and the tree was filling up with decorations. Ordinary glass balls, special ornaments collected on family vacations, pinecones and seashells the children had gathered and coated with glitter when they were little, and a small but precious collection of antique German glass ornaments that had somehow survived scores of clumsy fingers and hundreds of Christmases.

Lucy was watching as Zoe hung one of the very oldest, a glass fish so old that the paint had become translucent, when the phone rang. Zoe immediately lost interest in the ornament and turned toward the phone, ready to race Sara and Toby to answer it. Lucy quickly snatched the ornament from her, letting out a sigh of relief as she twisted the bit of wire that served as a hook securely onto a high branch.

This time, Sara won the dash for the phone. "Elizabeth!" she shrieked. "It's Lance!"

Disappointed the call wasn't for them, the other children turned back to trimming the tree. In a few minutes, Elizabeth joined them. Ignoring everyone's curious glances, she picked her ornament off the coffee table and hung it on a branch.

"Is it OK if I go out for a while?" she asked, casually.

"Lance asked her out!" Zoe was fascinated by the whole idea of romance and dating.

"Is that true?" asked Lucy. "What are your plans?"

"Just to hang out," Elizabeth murmured, nervously twisting a strand of hair.

"That's unacceptable," said Bill, decisively placing a candy cane on the end of a branch.

"What do you mean?" demanded Elizabeth.

"Well, this is a family night," began Lucy.

"You mean I can't go?"

Lucy looked to Bill for support.

"I don't mind if you go out," he said. "You haven't exactly added a lot to the occasion so far. But I don't want you hanging out in some car at the end of a dark lane. And you certainly can't go looking like that. Put some slacks on."

"Dad!" Elizabeth was indignant.

"Well, I don't think you should go out at all," insisted Lucy. "Why not invite Lance to join us here, decorating the tree?"

"Oh, Mom," groaned Elizabeth, then ran out of the room. They could all hear her thumping up the stairs in her platform shoes.

"That went well," said Bill, facetiously, as he reached up and set the star on the top of the tree.

"She'll sulk in her room all night," said Lucy.

"Not a problem for me," said Bill, pleased to have thwarted one of his daughter's suitors. "How about I call for some pizza?"

"Great idea." Lucy wrapped her arms around his waist and hugged him.

Elizabeth declined to join the rest of the family for their pizza supper, but that didn't stop the other kids from enjoying their treat. When every scrap of pizza was gone, and the room had been cleared of papers and ornament boxes, Bill switched on the tree and turned off the lamps. They all stood for a moment, admiring the lighted, decorated tree.

"It's magic," sighed Zoe.

"It's the best one ever," said Sara.

"Neat," said Toby.

Later, while everyone was watching Christmas videos on TV, Lucy slipped upstairs to talk to Elizabeth. She found her sprawled on her bed amidst most of her clothes, talking on the phone. On the bookcase, her little pink TV was playing.

Lucy stood, not knowing where to start. Why couldn't she take better care of her clothes, instead of leaving them draped all over? Why was she always, always on the phone? And why was the TV on, when she obviously wasn't watching it?

Lucy reached out to switch it off, but was caught momentarily by the drama. It was an old black-and-white gangster movie, with actors she didn't recognize.

"He's gettin' to be a problem," growled one gangster, talking around a huge cigar.

"What do you want?" Elizabeth was glaring at her from the bed.

Lucy wanted to sit beside her, to hug her, but there was no place to sit. "I just wanted you to know that Daddy and I only want what's best for you."

"Yeah? Well, why won't you trust me? All I wanted to do was spend some time with my friends," demanded Elizabeth.

"He's not goin' along with the program," commented another gangster, a small fellow with a wizened face.

"That's why," said Lucy, pointing to the TV. "I trust you to do what's right, but I don't trust all your friends."

"I can take care of myself," insisted Elizabeth.

"He knows too much. We gotta rub him out." It was the gangster with the cigar.

Stunned, Lucy sat down on the bed, staring at the TV.

Elizabeth reached out and turned it off, and the picture shrank to a little, bright dot.

Suddenly, Lucy knew why Tucker had been killed. She had been a good girl, a girl her parents trusted not to get into trouble. And she hadn't done anything wrong herself, but she had seen something she shouldn't have, probably during that forty-five minutes she was supposedly lost before the hike. She had known too much. And that made her dangerous to somebody. Her innocence hadn't protected her, it had made her vulnerable.

"Mom, are you OK?"

Lucy nodded, and pulled Elizabeth close to her.

Chapter Nineteen

1 day 'til Xmas

Lucy had just slipped the chocolate cheesecake into the oven and was starting to make lunch for herself and the girls, Toby having been recruited to act as Bill's gofer, when she realized she was ready for Christmas. The long month's preparations were done. The cards and packages had been sent, the presents had been bought and wrapped, the house decorated and the tree trimmed, the refrigerator and pantry were stocked with holiday treats.

"Do you girls have any plans for this afternoon?" she asked, as they gathered around the kitchen table to eat tuna fish sandwiches and tomato soup. "Zoe, you've been invited to go to Sadie's house to make gingerbread men."

"Cool," said Zoe, prompting Lucy to raise an eyebrow. They sure grew up fast these days.

"I'm supposed to go ice-skating with Jenn," said Sara. "Mrs. Baker said she'd pick me up at one."

"That sounds like fun, what about you, Elizabeth?"

"Lance wants me to go over to his house to go swimming."

"Isn't it kind of cold for swimming?" Lucy took a bite of sandwich.

"They got an indoor pool."

Lucy choked on a bit of tuna fish that went down the wrong way. "An indoor pool?"

She knew Lance's mother, Norah Hemmings, better known as the "queen of daytime TV," was a wealthy woman, but this was definitely a first for Tinker's Cove.

"Yeah, he's invited a bunch of us to come over and hang out. I can go, can't I, Mom?"

"Only if you bring back a complete report," specified Lucy. "Sue will want to know all the details."

"Deal."

It was one-thirty when Lucy pulled into Norah Hemmings's driveway, after dropping Zoe at the Orensteins'. True enough, she saw that a large addition with huge French windows had been added to the back of the big mansion on Smith Heights Road. Norah's house now dwarfed the neighboring houses, including Corney and Chuck Canaday's, which stood next door.

"Dad's going to pick you up on his way home, around four."

"Why don't I just call, instead," suggested Elizabeth.

"No way, Jose," said Lucy, firmly nipping that idea in the bud. "And listen. If I hear the slightest rumor that anything went on here that shouldn't have, you can count on being grounded for the rest of vacation. Understand?"

"Oh, Mom," groaned Elizabeth, as she climbed out of the car. "You can trust me."

"Right," muttered Lucy to herself, as she turned the car around in the spacious driveway.

As Lucy drove past one impressive house after another, all with spectacular ocean views, she couldn't help wondering why anybody would want to live here year-round. A bone-chilling wind came right off the ocean, she could feel it pushing against the Subaru. And the ocean wasn't much to look at on a gray day when you couldn't tell where water ended and sky began. In the distant sky she could see two herring gulls. One, an immature brown one had a fish, she could see silvery flashes as it struggled to break free. The other, a mature white-and-gray bird, was darting at the younger bird, trying to make him drop his prize. The brownish gull held on stubbornly, but the fish finally wriggled free and fell through the air, only to be scooped up by the more experienced bird, who flapped off in triumph. The yearling gull complained against this injustice. His harsh, hollow call echoed in Lucy's ears as she passed a mailbox marked WHITNEY.

Acting on impulse, Lucy braked and stopped the car. She looked at the house, a big old wooden box ringed by a generous porch, no doubt filled with chintz-cushioned wicker chairs in the summer but now bare and empty. Long window boxes had been filled with geraniums, now black stumps shriveled by frost. Lucy shuddered, thinking of Tucker all alone in that big, hollow house.

She drove on down the road, surprised to come upon the conservation area only a quarter mile or so from the

Whitney house. Once again, Lucy thought it unlikely that Tucker had lost her way, as she had told her fellow hikers. She had summered in that house for her whole life; she must have known about the conservation area.

Saying she was lost must have been an excuse. Something must have delayed her, and it must have been something she didn't want to talk about. Something she felt she had to cover up. What could it be?

Lucy looked up at the Whitney house, and realized it was built on an outcropping of rock that sct it up highcr than the neighboring houses. In fact, it was so high that someone standing in one of the upstairs windows would have a clear view out to sea, looking right over the roofs of the houses on the other side of the road. From there, Lucy realized, Tucker could see the boats coming and going from Tinker's Cove, and with a pair of binoculars she could probably see the big freighters farther out at sea on their way to Halifax.

What if Tucker had seen something out of the ordinary, as she looked out of those big windows, thought Lucy. What if whatever it was she saw made her so curious that she went to investigate? Reaching to the end of Smith Heights Road, Lucy was about to turn out onto the main road when she noticed a well-worn dirt road branching down toward the water. Impulsively, she decided to see where it led. After all, she had no other responsibilities this afternoon. It was hers to spend as she liked.

The Subaru bounced along, rocking from side to side and crunching through icy patches, for a few hundred feet. Then the road opened out and Lucy found herself looking at a cluster of metal buildings. A small sign read ROUSSEAU'S LOBSTERS.

Nobody seemed to be around, there were no cars or trucks, so Lucy turned off the ignition and got out of the car. A blast of cold wind blowing off the water hit her, and she shivered, pulling up the hood of her parka and stuffing her hands in the pockets as she began walking across the yard to the dock. This wasn't at all what she expected a lobster pound to be; she had somehow imagined the lobsters would be kept in some sort of pen or corral in the water. But there was nothing like that, only a dock with a hoist at the end, for unloading the boats. The holding pens must be in the metal buildings, she decided, so the workers could stay relatively warm and dry. Reaching the end of the dock, she stood a minute, scanning the empty cove. The wind rattled the line on the hoist; it creaked as it swung back and forth. Realizing her teeth were chattering, she turned to go back to the car and saw she had company. A pickup truck was now parked next to her car, and two men were coming towards her.

Recognizing Rusty and J.J., Lucy gave a wave and a big smile, but they didn't smile back.

"What are you doing here?" demanded J.J., when they were within earshot.

"I was looking for lobsters," improvised Lucy. "For Christmas dinner."

Rusty and J.J. exchanged uneasy glances.

"Isn't that what the sign says? Lobsters?" asked Lucy, cocking her head.

The two men were standing opposite her, blocking her path to the car, a situation Lucy wasn't entirely comfortable with. In fact, she would have been a lot happier in her car, speeding back home. Snooping around suddenly didn't seem like such a good idea.

J.J. shook his head, and a lock of curly dark hair fell across his forehead. "We only do wholesale," he said.

"Yeah," agreed Rusty, scratching the orange stubble on his chin. "And with the quota and all, we don't have any extras."

Lucy shrugged her shoulders. "Well, that's too bad. I guess I'll have to try someplace else."

Much to her relief the two men courteously stepped aside, clearing the path to her car.

"Merry Christmas," she said, reaching for the door handle, when she heard the sound of a boat motor. They all looked up as a boat approached the dock, then turned abruptly as a red pickup truck sped into the yard and stopped suddenly, brakes squealing. The driver-side door flew open and Claw jumped down and ran toward them.

"What's going on?" he demanded, pointing a stubby finger at Lucy. "What's she doing here?"

"She wants lobsters," J.J. explained. "I told her we only sell wholesale."

"Don't you know who she is?" Claw was looking past them, out to the dock. "She's that newspaper reporter. From the meeting the other night."

Rusty looked over his shoulder to the dock, where a man was tying up the boat. "Is that true?"

"I write for the paper," began Lucy, as Claw began running to the boat, waving his arms. "Mostly features, you know, soft stuff. In fact," she extemporized, checking her watch. "I'm supposed to interview Mrs. Santa Claus— to get the behind-the-scenes story—and I'm a little late. So, Merry Christmas to you and your families."

Determined not to look back no matter what happened she grabbed the handle and pulled the car door open. Stepping next to her, Rusty slammed it shut.

"I think the old man wants to talk to you," he said, roughly grabbing her arm. Before she could protest, J.J. had her other arm and they were dragging her toward one of the buildings. A door was opened, and she was roughly thrust inside. "You wait here," he said, and the door slammed shut.

"You can't do this to me," she screamed. Nobody answered. The door remained shut. Lucy looked around. She was in a dim, chilly room with a concrete floor. Light came through translucent plastic panels on the roof, and she could make out big vats lined up in rows. She peered in the nearest one and saw a few dozen lobsters resting on the bottom.

She stood there, looking at them, wondering how she could have been so stupid. She had retraced Tucker's steps all too well, only to be trapped herself. Whatever Tucker had found had gotten her killed. Lucy was determined that wasn't going to happen to her. She began exploring the room, looking for a way to escape.

It only took minutes to discover that there were no windows and only the one door. She turned the knob, but it was locked. She looked up at the roof, wondering how solid the light panels were, when she heard voices approaching. When a few minutes had passed, and the door didn't open, she pressed her ear against the crack, hoping to hear what they were saying.

"I don't like this business. We should never've locked her up. Now what are we gonna do with her? Say, gee, sorry about that, don't tell anybody, and we'll let you go. *Joyeux Noël* and all that?"

Sounds good to me, Lucy thought hopefully.

"What else could we do?" It sounded like J.J. "The

stuff's coming in and we've got a newspaper reporter right here. . . ."

Lucy's breath caught. She could hardly believe what she had heard. They really were dealing in illegal drugs.

"Let me tell you," continued J.J. "There's something wrong with this picture, and what's wrong is that broad being here."

Lucy felt her cheeks redden.

"No, what's wrong with this picture is that we ever got involved in the first place." That was Rusty, Lucy thought, straining to hear every word. "We're in so deep, how're we ever gonna get out?"

Lucy saw a dim ray of hope. Maybe she could convince them that tossing her in with the lobsters or whatever they planned to do with her would only make things worse. She heard the rattle of keys and stepped back from the door just in time.

It opened, and Claw entered, followed by his two sons.

"What's your name?" he asked.

"Lucy Stone. I live in town with my husband and four children. They're probably wondering what's keeping me."

Claw nodded. "You tell me, what exactly brought you out here?"

"Lobsters—for Christmas." Lucy decided to stick with her story. "Do you treat all your customers like this? Lock them up?"

Behind Claw, J.J. was smiling. "Sorry about that. It's just that, well, you heard about this quota?"

"Yeah, that's it," said Rusty. "We've got too many lobsters. We're way above quota. And you're not gonna tell anybody about it, because I'm gonna give you some of these lobsters. That makes you guilty, too, right?"

"Right." Lucy watched as J.J. picked up a wooden

stick with a hook on the end and went over to the tank. He began pulling out lobsters and putting them in a burlap sack, and she felt a huge sense of relief. She was actually going to get out of here.

"How many you want?" he asked.

"Just one," she said. "Like a dollar to seal a contract."

"Nah," said Claw. "You said four kids. Give her six, six nice ones. For Christmas dinner."

"Thank you so much." Lucy took the sack. "Believe me, I won't say a word about this to anyone."

"Not even Mrs. Santa Claus?" Claw's eyes gleamed mischievously.

"Not even her."

Claw opened the door for her. "Rusty, those are heavy. You carry them for the lady."

"I can manage," protested Lucy, to no avail. Rusty insisted on escorting her to her car. He opened the door for her, and carefully placed the sack of lobsters in the back.

"Safe home," he said, before he slammed the hatchback down.

Her hands were shaking so badly Lucy could hardly get the key in the ignition. When it finally slipped in and turned, and the car started, she felt tears streaming down her face. It was as if she had been given a wonderful gift, a gift she didn't deserve, and she felt humble and thankful and guilty and incredibly lucky all at once. She shifted into gear and lifted her foot off the brake, and began slowly turning the car around toward the driveway. She pressed her foot on the gas, accelerating toward the drive, when a police cruiser suddenly appeared, blocking the way out and leaving her with no choice but to slam on the brakes.

Chapter Twenty

When Tom Scott emerged from the police cruiser Lucy had mixed emotions. She didn't really want the Rousseaus to get in trouble, but she couldn't condone drug dealing, and that was what she suspected they were up to.

She gave Tom a big smile and a wave, expecting him to move his car when he saw who she was, but that didn't happen. He only gave her a glance and went straight over to Rusty and J.J. Lucy figured the best course of action was to stay in her car, continuing the pretense that she was only there to pick up some lobsters.

She didn't even turn her head to observe their discussion, she wanted to make it clear she was minding her own business, but she could see them in the rearview mirror. Scott was clearly the one in charge. She could tell from J.J.'s and Rusty's bowed heads and restrained gestures that they were not challenging him, but that was to be expected. Nobody argued with a cop, not even at a traffic stop, unless they wanted to get into more trouble. So she sat and waited for Scott to move the cruiser.

The men finally appeared to finish their discussion and Lucy watched as Tom walked across the yard toward the two cars, expecting him to finally move the cruiser and wave her on. Instead, he stopped next to her and yanked the door open.

"Out," he said.

"What's this all about?" she asked, unfastening her seat belt. "I'd really like to get home with my lobsters."

"You're not going anywhere," he said, roughly turning her around and shoving her against the car. "Hands behind your back."

Lucy had seen enough movies to know that that meant she was about to be handcuffed. She turned her head, and started to protest.

"I said, hands behind your back," growled Scott.

Reluctantly, she obeyed and discovered that being handcuffed was a lot more uncomfortable than it looked, especially if you were wearing a bulky parka. The next step, she supposed, was to be placed in "the cage" in the back of his cruiser. But instead, Tom pulled her in the other direction, toward the lobster pound office, where she was thrown into a hard, wooden chair. Her upper arm, which had taken the brunt of the impact, felt sore and bruised.

"Don't move," he warned her.

Confused and frightened, Lucy nodded.

He opened the door to leave, but stepped back as an enraged Claw Rousseau came charging in.

"What do you think you're doing?" Claw bellowed at him. "This is my place! You got no business here!"

Scott grinned at him. It wasn't a very nice grin, thought Lucy, trying to make herself as small and inconspicuous as she could.

"You know how it works. You're behind." Scott shook his head. "The retirement fund's not growing the way it's supposed to. You missed last month, you haven't paid anything yet this month. What's going on? I thought we had a deal."

"We've got a deal." said Claw, looking nervously past Scott to Lucy. "You'll get it, don't worry. But you've got to let her go. She doesn't know anything about this."

Scott glanced at Lucy, and she cringed in the chair. "You know who she is? She's a reporter. She's been snooping all over town."

Claw raised his hands to protest, but Scott cut him off.

"Look, right now, she's my problem. I'll take care of her."

Lucy swallowed hard. That didn't sound good. She strained to hear as Scott lowered his voice and led Claw across the room, toward the door.

"You've got problems of your own. I just picked up some interesting information on the radio—a couple of your associates from Boston have been spotted on the turnpike. They might be headed here, you think?"

The door flew open again and Lucy jumped in spite of herself. The thumping in her chest slowed when she realized it was only Rusty and J.J.

"Did you hear?" Claw's tone was urgent. "The guys from Boston are coming here."

Rusty looked stricken, as if he'd been punched in the heart.

"They want Russ Junior," he said.

J.J. wrapped an arm around his smaller brother's shoulder.

"We'll take care of 'Ti Russ," he said. "We'll put him on the boat, send him up the coast. These guys are city boys. They won't find him."

Lucy struggled to follow their conversation. 'Ti-Russ, she knew, was short for Petit Russ, Rusty's son. She remembered him as a sturdy little fellow on Toby's youth soccer team. He'd be in high school now, she thought.

"That's no good." Rusty's eyes were wide. "They don't find Russ, they'll kill us, or our wives and kids. Burn down the house—they don't care. They just want to send a message." He buried his head in his hands. "I can't believe he was so stupid, what he got us into."

"He's a kid. Kids are stupid." Claw shrugged. "We'll get the money; they'll go away."

Lucy remembered Toby and Eddie refusing to tell her who was dealing drugs in the high school. Now she had a pretty good idea that it was 'Ti-Russ. What had he done? Helped himself to part of a shipment, shorting the buyer and putting his whole family in peril?

"So where are we gonna get the money?" demanded Rusty, his voice breaking.

"Take it easy," said Scott. "It's under control. The drug task force is onto them—it's just a matter of time before those guys are out of the picture. You lie low, keep your young entrepreneur under wraps for a while. Go on, get started. Get on out of here." He glanced at Lucy. "I'll take care of Miss Snoopy."

The three men seemed to confer silently for a moment,

then Claw nodded, and they shuffled out of the room. Not one of them looked at her.

Left alone with Scott, Lucy's situation hit her with a thudding certainty. She knew way too much. Scott was going to kill her, just as he'd killed Tucker.

Chapter Twenty-One

Not if she could help it, she vowed to herself. She was going to get out of this. Nobody, especially a mealy-mouthed hypocrite like Tom Scott, was going to wreck her family's Christmas. She glanced around frantically, looking for something, anything. The drug task force was supposed to be in the area. If only she could draw their attention somehow, anybody's attention, maybe she could save herself. She needed time, and the only way she could think of getting it was by keeping him talking.

"You sure had me fooled," said Lucy. "I never would have picked you for Tucker's murderer."

She was surprised to find her voice strong and steady. At that moment she wasn't afraid of Tom Scott; she was disgusted by him. He had come into town under the banner of zero tolerance for drugs and alcohol, and he even had his wife passing out Mothers Against Drunk Driving pamphlets. While he was mouthing sticky sentiments about the tragedy of teen drunken driving deaths he was turning a blind eye on the drugs that were pouring into town and collecting kickbacks. Retirement fund. She snorted.

"I wouldn't be so cocky if I were you," he said. "Tucker Whitney was a stupid bitch who got herself caught in the wrong place at the wrong time, same as you. Came snooping around here and the Rousseaus scared her off, so you know what she did? Actually called me up to report suspicious activity."

He gave a short, harsh laugh and stepped toward her. Lucy felt her courage disappear like dirty dishwater swirling down the drain. She was utterly defenseless, hands pinned behind her back. She wanted to run, but she couldn't make her legs work. Horrified, she watched as he took another step closer.

How many seconds did she have to live? Was he really going to put his hands around her neck and strangle her, like he did Tucker? She couldn't let that happen.

"I have to hand it to you," she said, struggling to make the words come out of her dry mouth. "You're pretty clever. You planted that gum wrapper, didn't you?"

"It was so easy," Scott said, unable to resist telling her how he'd outsmarted everybody. "I knew I had to get rid of Tucker—she was starting to make a real pest of herself, calling the station and asking what I was going to do about the lobster pound. She even threatened to call the drug task force. Then I ran into Cummings at the coffee shop. He'd just left Tucker and he was real broken up. He couldn't wait to tell me all about it. How he was going to give her up and go back to his wife, even if it was the hardest thing he'd ever done. She'd been understanding, he said, actually encouraged him to do the right thing."

"From what I heard she didn't really care for him," said Lucy, hoping to keep Scott's mind off the next item on his agenda. It was all she could think to do. Every second she could delay his assault was a small victory. Maybe the Rousseaus would come back. Maybe help would come.

"Yeah, I heard that, too. But to hear him it was the love affair of the century. He was practically crying into his coffee, and popping those sticks of gum ino his mouth one after the other. He finished the pack and left it on the counter. I figured it might come in handy and picked it up with a napkin." He grinned evilly. "I was right. I called her up from a pay phone and asked if I could come over to her house to get a statement from her before she went to work. She was only too happy to cooperate."

"You even won a commendation from the state police for preventing contamination of the crime scene. That must have been icing on the cake."

"It just goes to show that if you do a really good job, people notice," said Scott, practically patting himself on the back. "But you know what the best part was? It was the look in Tucker's eyes when she realized that Officer Scott wasn't her friend."

He was now standing above her, and Lucy felt his leather-gloved hands closing around her neck. She squirmed, trying to kick between his legs, but he just laughed and pressed her legs down with his. She tried to scream, but nothing was coming out, she couldn't make a sound, she couldn't catch her breath. Then it came, a popping sound, and everything went dark in the room.

"What the fuck," she heard him say, and he dropped

his hands from her neck. She assumed he was moving toward the window, so she ran in the opposite direction, knocking something over as she dashed across the room and crashed into the big wooden desk. She felt her way around it, putting it between herself and Scott.

She heard the door open and for a second saw Scott's figure silhouetted against the dim, dusky light outside, and then he disappeared.

Her heart was pounding. This was her chance to escape and she had to take it. She ran to the door and cautiously opened it, intending to take a cautious peek to see if the coast was clear. Instead, she was suddenly blinded by an extremely bright light that was flooding the yard. She heard popping gunshots and ducked back inside.

What with the spotlights and guns, it seemed to her that the entire compound was under attack. She got down as low as she could and scuttled awkwardly across the floor, diving under the desk. She landed hard on her shoulder; she couldn't use her handcuffed hands to break the fall.

There was the piercing squeal of an amplifier and then an authoritarian voice boomed out. "This is the state police. Drop your weapons. Put your hands on your heads. Walk to the lighted area."

Thank God, thought Lucy, who was only too happy to obey. She couldn't put her hands on her head, but she could walk. She crawled out from under the desk, blinking her eyes against the light that was pouring in through the windows, and started toward the doorway, only to be immediately knocked off her feet. Scott had come back.

"Get up," he said, yanking her to her feet and holding her in front of him like a shield. "You're my ticket out of here."

The pain in her shoulder was agonizing as she struggled against his grip.

"Let her go." Lucy recognized J.J.'s voice. She heard a thud and felt Scott's body crumple behind her. "I've wanted to do that for a long time," he said.

Lucy found herself in wholehearted agreement. "Me too," she heard herself say. "Get me out of these handcuffs?"

J.J. began going through Scott's pockets, feeling for his keys while Lucy kept an eye on the door. It was quiet outside; the gunshots had stopped.

"Got 'em!" exclaimed J.J. "Hold still," he said, grasping her arm.

She bit her lip, refusing to cry out with the pain. First one cuff and then the other loosened, and she moaned with relief. She cradled her arm against her chest, watching as J.J. clamped one cuff on Scott's wrist and then with a grunt dragged his inert body to the corner, where he looped the other cuff around the gas pipe that fed the overhead heater.

"That takes care of Dudley Do-Right," he said, with a satisfied smirk. "Now, the heroic Jean-Jacques, having saved the lady in distress, gives himself up to the authorities. Ready?"

"You bet," said Lucy.

J.J. took her hand and reached for the door, but before they could step out into the light they heard the staccato of machine-gun fire, and it suddenly went dark again.

"What's going on?" Lucy gripped his hand tighter as they ducked back into the shelter of the office.

"Fatman." J.J.'s voice was a moan. "He loves that Uzi. I never saw him without it."

"It couldn't be," whispered Lucy. "Nobody'd take on an entire SWAT team."

"Nobody but Fatman. They named him after the atom bomb. I heard nothing can stop him. He shot five or six cops last time they tried."

"What about Rusty and Claw? Where are they?"

"On the boat. They're gone."

Lucy was stunned. "You could've gone—why didn't you?"

She felt his breath on her cheek as he sighed.

"I had enough. You know how all this started? We took out the boat and picked up one little package and brought it in. Never saw nobody. Just left it on top of a trash can in a highway rest area. That was gonna be it. Pay the bills, get a fresh start. But it don't work that way. Scott shows up. Somehow he knows all about it. He wants a cut, or he'll turn us in. 'Ti-Russ gets ahold of some, he starts dealing, and then he starts using and he's high all the time. Pretty soon we've got more dope than lobsters goin' through here, and the weird thing is, we're not gettin' any richer. What's worse, we're scared all the time. Scared of the cops. Scared of Fatman and his friends." He inched up the wall and looked out the window. "I wish I knew what was going on out there."

"Me too." Lucy found herself giggling.

"What's so funny?"

"I was just thinking about my family. They're proba- bly wondering where I am and why there's no supper. They probably think I went Christmas shopping and for- got the time, or something like that. They'd never believe where I really am."

"I don't believe it, and I'm here." J.J. slumped against the wall beneath the window, next to her.

Across the room, she heard Scott stirring.

"He'll get us all killed," muttered J.J., standing up.

He hadn't taken a step when his body was thrown violently across the room, slamming onto the desk and then slipping to the floor. On her hands and knees Lucy crawled to him. Frantically, she felt for a pulse. Touching something warm and sticky she jerked her hand back, as if she'd touched fire. She clutched her hands together in front of her, they were icy. Her teeth were chattering, she realized. There was another burst of gunfire, and she crawled under the desk.

She pulled her knees up against her chest and wrapped her trembling arms tight around them, hugging herself. She heard small, whimpering noises, and for a moment she thought a kitten or puppy had somehow gotten trapped with her. She had actually started feeling around for the poor, frightened thing in order to comfort it when she realized she was making the noises herself. She pressed her lips tight together and concentrated on breathing, just breathing, one breath at a time.

A loud crash made her jump, she felt as if her heart would leap out of her body. Then machine-gun fire was raking the room. It was so loud she involuntarily covered her ears with her hands and she smelled something like Fourth of July fireworks. The machine-gun staccato ended with a loud crack, and Lucy felt the floor shake as something heavy fell. Suddenly, there was a bright, white light.

She could hear voices. They seemed to be coming from very far away.

"She's starting to come around."

"I want to interview her, before you take her away."

"I can't let you do that . . ."

Lucy stirred, rolling her head from side to side. She tried to raise herself up, but she couldn't. She was wrapped up in something. Finally, it occurred to her that she could open her eyes.

"Well, hello, sunshine."

She blinked, recognizing Lieutenant Horowitz. "Wha'?" she asked.

"You're going to be OK." Another person, this one in a blue uniform, came into view, leaning over her. "We're taking you to the hospital to check you out, but right now it looks like you'll be home for Christmas."

Lucy closed her eyes, only to hear Horowitz's voice.

"Mrs. Stone! I have some questions. . . ."

Chapter Twenty-Two

Special Edition
The Pennysaver

Tinker's Cove, Maine   **December 26th**

Two Killed in Drug Raid

By Edward J. Stillings

TINKER'S COVE—Two men were killed and a Tinker's Cove police officer was wounded in a dramatic Christmas Eve shootout at a Cove Road lobster pound owned by Claude Rousseau, 63. The two dead men were identified as Jean-Jacques Rousseau, 42, of Tinker's Cove and Raymond "Fatman" Norris, 23, of Boston, Mass. Tinker's Cove Police Lt. Thomas Scott, 34, was wounded and remains in stable condition at Memorial Hospital in Portland. Also injured in the raid was *Penny-*

saver reporter Lucy Stone, who was treated for a dislocated shoulder at Memorial Hospital and released.

"From the evidence we have so far, it looks as if Norris shot the other two men with an Uzi machine gun," said State Police Detective Lt. C.G. Horowitz. "Norris was killed by a SWAT team member."

A fourth man, Eduardo Reyes, 20, of Boston, Mass., was taken into custody and will most likely be arraigned on Monday. Charges against him have not yet been completely determined, but will include illegal possession of one or more firearms, said Horowitz.

Horowitz said charges are also pending against Scott, who had been under surveillance for several months by the state police special crimes unit. Unit investigators allege that Scott accepted bribes and engaged in drug trafficking while he was acting chief of the Tinker's Cove Police Department. Police are also investigating allegations that Scott murdered Tucker Whitney, 20, of Tinker's Cove earlier this month.

Horowitz said the drug task force was alerted when Norris and Reyes were spotted by a New Hampshire toll collector who noticed their unique automobile. "It was a Mercedes, top of the line, really loaded, and you don't see a lot of those, at least not this time of year," said Fred W. Smithers, a member of the Classic Car Club of Portsmouth, N.H.

Drug task force members monitored the pair's progress, notifying the special crimes unit when they appeared headed for Tinker's Cove.

"When Scott, Norris, and Reyes all gathered at Rousseau's Lobster Pound, we knew we had to act fast or lose them," said State Police Capt. Willard Penfield, commander of the drug task force. "It was getting late in the day, and we were losing daylight. We decided to call in the SWAT team."

Tinker's Cove residents watched in amazement as numerous state police vehicles sped through town, with sirens blaring, en route to the lobster pound. Crowd control became a problem for officials as curious onlookers, including a large group of teens who had been attending a pool party at the nearby home of TV star Norah Hemmings, gathered on Smith Heights Road. Hemmings was unavailable for comment.

Charles Canaday, 41, who lives at 151 Smith Heights Road, said he was astonished to see SWAT team members in his backyard.

"I was taking out the garbage and saw what I thought were soldiers, dressed in camouflage and carrying weapons, trotting down my driveway. For a minute I thought it was World War III," said Canaday.

The SWAT team cordoned off the lobster pound and set up spotlights, which were immediately shot out by machine-gun fire from Norris.

"We called for replacements, but we knew that was going to take a while, so we improvised with vehicle headlights and fired tear-gas canisters," said Penfield. "Norris ran for cover and one of our snipers had a clear shot and took it. Once Norris went down, Reyes immediately surrendered."

Team members entered the lobster-pound office, where they found the wounded Scott manacled to a pipe with his own handcuffs. Stone was found, unconscious but otherwise apparently unharmed, beneath a large desk. Rousseau's body was also found; both he and Scott appeared to have suffered wounds from machine-gun fire. Norris was killed by a single bullet to the head.

Officials said that more indictments are expected as the investigation is still in its preliminary stages and will continue.

"We're especially interested in determining what role the Rousseau family played," said Horowitz.

Interviewed at home on Christmas Day, Stone insisted she was an innocent bystander caught in events beyond her control. "I was just picking up some lobsters for Christmas dinner," she said.

Chapter Twenty-Three

New Year's Eve

A week later, Lucy's arm and shoulder were still strapped, so she was a passenger in the Subaru while Elizabeth drove.

Even though she had a learner's permit, Lucy hadn't had much time to take her daughter driving, so she figured this was a good opportunity for her to get some practice.

"You're doing really great," she said in an encouraging tone of voice as they crept along Main Street. "Now turn on your signal and turn here—I need to go to the post office."

Elizabeth signaled left and turned right, picking up speed and heading directly for the brick post-office building.

"Brake!" shrieked Lucy, and the car lurched to a sudden stop, straddling two parking spaces.

"Sorry about that," said Elizabeth, who was checking her teeth in the rearview mirror. "I get them confused. Which is the gas?"

"The one on the right," said Lucy, opening the door. She wasn't sure which was more dangerous: the shootout at the lobster pound or teaching her own daughter to drive.

She reached back in the car for her purse and when she straightened up, smiled to see Sue leading her little group of day-care kids. They looked like peas in a pod, each child holding tight to a chunky, knotted rope. Bringing up the rear was a young woman Lucy didn't recognize, pushing an oversize baby carriage stuffed with several snowsuited toddlers.

"Hi!" Sue greeted her. "How are you feeling?"

"Much better. I didn't need any pain pills today."

"Kids, you know Mrs. Stone. Sometimes she helps us at the center."

"Hi, Justin. Harry. Emily. Matthew. Did you all have a nice Christmas?"

The kids smiled and nodded, and Emily held out her hands to show off her new dragon mittens.

"Granny made them," she said, opening and closing the dragon's mouth and revealing his hot pink tongue.

"Very nice," said Lucy.

"And this is my new assistant, Casey Wilson," said Sue, indicating a petite young woman who was adjusting Harry's hat.

"Hiya," said Casey, giving Lucy a big smile.

"I don't see Will," said Lucy. "What's happening with him?"

"Steffie's gone home to her folks, in New Jersey." Sue lowered her voice, mindful of the children. "I think she's going to divorce Tom. They weren't that happy, anyway. And now with all that's happened, she's definitely not sticking by her man."

"I don't blame her," said Lucy. "He's bad news. She ought to make a clean break and start over."

"I think she will," said Sue. "She was pretty shook up. Not quite the same Steffie. Said she was shifting her priorities, and now Will's going to be number one."

"Well, maybe some good will come out of this thing. But if you ask me, I can't quite believe little Miss Goody Two-shoes didn't know what her husband was doing all along. I still haven't forgiven her for bringing those leaflets to the cookie exchange."

"He was pretty controlling," said Sue, with a shrug. "I suspected all along that he was abusive. She even had a restraining order out on him around Thanksgiving."

Lucy's chin dropped as she digested this information.

"You never told me."

"Oops!" Sue's hand flew to her mouth. "Time to go, kids. I hear the bells. That means it's time for lunch."

Lucy watched for a moment as the little procession made its way across the parking lot, recalling how sad the noontime bells had sounded on the day she'd learned of Tucker's death.

Today, she thought they sounded hopeful. Ringing out the old year and ringing in the new.

She turned and went inside the post offtce, pausing at the letter slot, to check that she had all of Toby's college applications. She had just shoved them through the slot when she noticed Marge, also holding a handful of envelopes.

"College applications?" asked Lucy, noticing that Marge looked better than she had in a long time. There was color in her cheeks, and she seemed to have her energy back.

Marge nodded. "He got them done in the nick of time."

"Same here," said Lucy. "Did you have a nice Christmas?"

"Sure did." Marge nodded. "Barney's a lot happier these days. He says getting rid of Tom Scott was the best Christmas present he got!"

"I guess Tom will be going to jail for a long while— Ted says the Rousseaus are only too happy to cooperate and will testify against him. They want to clear the family name."

Lucy pushed open the door and held it for Marge, who paused on the stoop to wave to a passing car.

It was the Cummings family: Steve, Lee, and the girls, driving by in their big sport utility. Lucy also raised her hand in a wave.

"Happy New Year!" shouted Lee, waving out the window.

Steve beeped the horn.

"Happy New Year!" called out Marge and Lucy.

"Do you have any special plans for tonight?" asked Marge.

"Actually, the kids are all sleeping over at friends' houses, so Bill and I are planning some cuddle-and-bubble time—he's got a bottle of champagne chilling in the fridge."

"Good for you!" laughed Marge, getting in her car. "Barney's got a six-pack and a video called *Rolling Thunder*."

"Happy New Year!" called Lucy, as she watched Marge back out.

When she pulled open the door to the Subaru, Elizabeth handed her another letter.

"I found it after you got out," she said.

"You couldn't have brought it in? You just sat here like a lump?"

"Oh." Elizabeth looked at her blankly. "I was listening to my new tape—the Diskettes."

Lucy sighed and took the envelope.

She had just bought a stamp when she noticed Franny Small standing in the corner clutching a letter to her chest, apparently in a state of shock.

"Franny, what's the matter?" she asked. "Did you get bad news?"

"No." Franny's eyes were huge. "It's good news. Really good news."

Franny held out the letter and Lucy took it.

"It's from Neiman Marcus!" she exclaimed, scanning the text. "They want ten thousand pieces of your jewelry!"

"Do you believe it?" Franny's face was glowing. "That's a hundred-thousand-dollar order."

"Wow."

"And the letter says they plan to put them in their catalog next year and anticipate placing further orders."

"That's great, but Franny, how are you going to do it? Can you make ten thousand pieces of jewelry all by yourself?"

"Don't be silly." Franny's curls shook as she nodded her head. "I'm going to go right over to that economic development agency that's opened in Gilead and get myself what they call a start-up loan. Then I'm going to hire some of those folks who lost their crafts businesses in the fire and put them to work. While they're making the jewelry, I'm going to go out and see who else wants to buy it."

She pointed to the letter.

"If you notice, Neiman Marcus didn't mention anything about exclusive rights. That means I can sell to other customers."

She narrowed her eyes.

"This could be the start of something big."

She looked up.

"Listen, Lucy, I'm sorry, but I don't have time to talk right now. I've got to make some phone calls."

Openmouthed, Lucy watched as Franny bustled off. Then, remembering her errand, she looked down at the letter in her hand. It was the application to Toby's first choice college, Coburn University. She attached a stamp and, crossing her fingers, slipped it through the slot. Then she returned to the car and, saying a little prayer, took her place in the passenger seat.

"Okay, Elizabeth. Look over your shoulder and make sure it's clear. Then, put the shift in reverse, take your foot off the brake. . . ."

"Mom, my foot's not on the brake."

Lucy pressed her hands together to stop the trembling and took a deep breath.

"We'll start over. First, make sure your foot is on the brake. Then, look over your shoulder . . ."

RECIPES

Santa's Thumbprints

Lucy always brings these cookies to the cookie exchange.

1 cup shortening
½ cup granulated sugar
½ cup brown sugar
1 egg
½ teaspoon vanilla
½ teaspoon almond extract
½ teaspoon each baking soda, salt
1½ cups uncooked oatmeal
2 cups flour
6 ounces semisweet chocolate chips

Beat shortening, add sugars, beat till fluffy. Add egg and extracts; mix well. Stir in flour, baking soda, salt, and oatmeal. Shape dough into small balls about the size of a walnut, place on baking sheet, and press hollow in top of each cookie.

Bake at 375 degrees for 10–12 minutes. Melt chocolate and spoon into center of each cookie. Chill until firm.

Makes about 3 dozen.

Sand Tarts

My Aunt Helen, who was a lot like Miss Tilley,
used to bake these cookies every Christmas.
I always think of her when I make them.

Cream ½ cup butter.

Add:

1 cup sugar
2 egg yolks (beaten)
1 tablespoon milk
½ teaspoon vanilla

Beat mixture until light.

Sift together:

1½ cups flour
1 teaspoon baking powder
½ teaspoon salt

Add to first mixture and blend well. Chill for several hours. Roll dough very thin and cut with star cookie cutter. Place on buttered baking sheets and put a split, blanched almond in the center of each cookie. Brush with unbeaten egg white and sprinkle with mixture of 1 tablespoon sugar and ¼ teaspoon cinnamon. Bake at 375 degrees for 10 minutes.

Please turn the page for an exciting sneak peek of

Leslie Meier's newest Lucy Stone mystery

IRISH PARADE MURDER

coming soon wherever print and e-books are sold!

Chapter One

"I just want to say that this was absolutely the loveliest, most beautiful funeral I've ever attended," said the woman, grasping Lucy Stone's hand and leaning in a bit too close for Lucy's comfort. Some people were like that, and Lucy resisted the urge to draw away, and smiled instead at the woman, who was middle-aged and dressed appropriately for such a somber occasion in a simple navy-blue dress and pearls. Her hair was a warm brown, probably colored, and she had applied her makeup with a light hand: a touch of foundation, mascara, and soft pink lipstick. Lucy didn't know the woman, but she didn't know most of the people she was greeting in the reception line at her father-in-law's funeral, and she assumed she was a friend or neighbor.

"You know, it made me feel as if I actually knew Mr.

Stone," continued the woman, exploding that theory. "And what a wonderful family you have."

A bit weird, thought Lucy, wondering if the woman made a hobby of attending total strangers' funeral services. They were listed in the newspaper, after all, and anyone who had a passing interest could come. It was because of those listings that the funeral director had advised them to make sure someone stayed at the house, since burglars were known to take advantage of those listings, too.

"What a nice thing to say, and thank you for coming," said Lucy, passing the woman along to her husband, Bill, who was next in the reception line, and greeting Maria Dolan, who was Edna's best friend and one of the few people at the reception that she actually knew.

"Edna seems to be holding up," observed Maria, glancing at Lucy's newly widowed mother-in-law, "but I'll be keeping an eye on her and making sure she doesn't get lonely. I know you Maine folks can't be popping down to Florida every time she feels a bit blue."

"Thank you so much. I really appreciate that," said Lucy, who was finding her present situation somewhat surreal. It was only two weeks ago, when Lucy was still clearing away the Christmas decorations, that Edna had called, saying Bill Senior had suffered a heart attack but was going to be just fine. She had insisted on downplaying the situation, but Bill, an only child, had immediately booked a seat on the next flight to Tampa.

When he called Lucy from the hospital, he reported that Edna was either in denial or hadn't understood the seriousness of the situation, as his father was in the ICU in critical condition and wasn't expected to survive. He asked Lucy to inform the kids and prepare them for their grandfather's death. He also urged her to book a flight as soon as possible, as they would have to plan a funeral and support his mother. But even as her husband lay dying, Edna refused to believe there was any cause for concern and insisted that her son was making too much of a fuss. And when her husband finally did slip away in the final days of January, she opted for a quick cremation, to be followed by a simple memorial service. "No need for the kids to come all this way. My Bill wouldn't want a big fuss. He always said he hated funerals and didn't even want to attend his own," she said. "Elizabeth's in Paris, Toby's in Alaska, and Sara is just starting her new job in Boston, and their granddad would want them to look to the future. Young people don't want to waste time at some dreary memorial service, and why should they?"

But much to Edna's surprise, the kids immediately made plans to come to Florida. Elizabeth insisted she had to say a final *adieu* to her *grand-père*, Toby and his wife, Molly, brought Patrick to remember his Poppop, and Sara, who was waiting until June to start her new job at the Museum of Science in Boston, offered to stay with her grandma for a week or two to help out. Zoe, the youngest, who was still in college, wasn't sure she'd be able to make it, but in the end was able to postpone some exams and joined the grieving family that had gathered in Edna's spacious ranch house.

Lucy wasn't sure what to expect, but it turned out that people in Florida weren't much different from folks in Tinker's Cove, Maine. There was a steady stream of visitors offering sympathy, and many brought casseroles and desserts for the mourning family. And when they all finally gathered in the modern church, all angles and abstract stained glass, which was so different from the centuries-old church in Maine, with its clear glass windows and tall white steeple, the memorial service wasn't dreary at all, but was instead a true celebration of Bill Sr.'s life.

The service began with one of his favorite hymns, "For the Beauty of the Earth," and was followed by a favorite Irish prayer that he often repeated: "May you be in heaven before the devil knows you're dead." The kids all spoke of favorite memories they cherished of their grandfather. Elizabeth remembered the rainbow-colored Life Savers he always carried and shared with her, Patrick remembered catching his first fish with Poppop's help, Sara recalled the loud rock and roll he favored, which grew even louder as his hearing began to fail, and Zoe remembered countless games of checkers that Poppop somehow never won. Toby recalled that, as a child, he loved helping Poppop wash his car, but admitted that the time he tried to do it himself, as a surprise, didn't go well because the car was a convertible and the top was down, but Poppop had just laughed and said it was about time the inside got washed, too.

Lucy knew all these stories, of course, except for Toby's misadventure, which was a surprise to her. It was the minister's eulogy, however, that revealed her father-in-law's deep spirituality and faith, which she hadn't appreciated. "Bill Stone was a man who practiced his faith through action," said Rev. Florence Robb, "and he spent countless hours delivering Meals on Wheels, giving rides to the homebound, and working at the local food pantry. He helped at worship services, sometimes as an usher, sometimes reading the lessons and prayers. If something was needed, he provided it, often before it was missed. He replaced light bulbs, tightened screws, and polished the brass, and those were only the things he did inside the church. Outside, he mowed the grass, weeded the flower beds, pruned the bushes, and repaired the church sign when it was torn down in a storm. In his quiet way, he made a huge difference in many people's lives, and he will be missed." She paused, and her voice breaking, added, "Greatly missed."

All this was running through Lucy's mind as she smiled and accepted the condolences offered by the people who had attended the funeral—dear friends, neighbors, and people whose lives had been touched by Bill Stone Sr. And also, as the reception line finally petered out, at least one total stranger who admitted she hadn't known Bill Stone Sr. at all.

Finally released from her duties on the reception line, Lucy glanced around the room, making sure everyone was all right. Bill had taken charge of his mother and had led her to the buffet table, where he was filling a plate for her. The kids were gathered in a corner, taking advantage of this rare opportunity to hang together and catch up with each other. There was plenty of food and drink, and there was a steady buzz of conversation punctuated with laughter, as was usual after the solemnities had been dispensed with and people took the time to reminisce, renew acquaintances, and enjoy each other's company. As she scanned the crowd, Lucy looked for the woman in the blue dress and pearls, but didn't see her. She did see Bill, however, trying to catch her eye, and she quickly joined him and Edna.

"Quite a nice turnout," she said, taking Edna's arm and leading her to one of the chairs that were lined up against the wall. "It's good to know that Pop was appreciated by so many people."

"I suppose so," said Edna, pushing her potato salad around with a plastic fork. She sighed. "I don't know what I'm going to do with myself, now that he's gone."

"He was a force to be reckoned with, that's for sure," said Lucy, squeezing Edna's hand. "But you're not alone. We're here for a few more days, Sara plans to stay for a week or more, and I hope you'll come visit us in Maine very soon. There's always a place for you at our house, you know."

"I know," said Edna, but she didn't sound as if she really believed it.

A week later, the Florida sun was only a memory as Lucy was back at her job in late-winter Maine, working as a part-time reporter and feature writer for the *Penny-saver*, the weekly newspaper in the quaint coastal town of Tinker's Cove, but she was having a hard time concentrating on the intricacies of the rather complicated changes being proposed to the town's zoning laws. "What exactly is an overlay district?" she asked Phyllis, the paper's receptionist, who was seated at her desk across the room, tucked behind the counter where members of the public filled out orders for classified ads, renewed subscriptions, dropped off letters to the editor, and occasionally complained.

"Beats me," said Phyllis, with a shrug of her shoulders. She was occupied with entering the week's new batch of classified ads and was peering through the heart-shaped reading glasses that were perched on her nose and that matched her colorful sweatshirt, which was bedecked with hearts and flowers, in contrast to the dreary reality of lingering dirty snow outside. "I don't know where to put this thank-you to Sheriff Murphy," she groaned. "Is it an announcement?"

Lucy perked up, her curiosity piqued. "What thank-you?"

"All about his help for some fund drive."

"Who submitted it?"

"Uh, it's right here." Phyllis studied the slip. "Someone named Margaret Mary Houlihan, corresponding secretary of the Hibernian Knights Society. Do you know her?"

"No, can't say I do. The Hibernian Knights present the big St. Patrick's Day parade over in Gilead, but the thank-you is a new one on me."

"Where do you think I should put it?"

"That I don't know. Better ask Ted." Ted Stillings was the publisher, editor, and chief reporter for the paper, which he'd inherited from his grandfather, a noted regional journalist. Times had changed since his day, however, and Lucy knew that Ted was hard-pressed to keep the little weekly paper afloat. Like newspapers throughout the country, the *Pennysaver* was faced with a diminishing list of advertisers and subscribers, and constantly increasing production costs.

"Well, I would if he was here, but he hardly ever is these days," complained Phyllis. After a pause she added, "Is it me, or do things seem a bit weird around here?"

"Weirder than usual?" asked Lucy, who hadn't really been paying much attention since she'd returned from Florida. She'd been focused on staying in touch with Edna and keeping Bill's spirits up.

"Yeah. While you were gone Ted's had a lot of meetings with, well, folks who aren't from around here. Fancy types, in city-slicker clothes."

"Really?" Lucy's interest was piqued. "Like who?"

"Well, there was a middle-aged man, with quite a big belly, dressed in a suit and tie. He was nice enough, made a lot of jokes, and laughed a lot, but didn't give his name or business. Then Ted arrived and whisked him off—took him out to lunch, I think."

"And when Ted got back from lunch, did he offer any explanation?"

"Nope. I asked if he was buying life insurance. It kind of just popped out. I guess the guy seemed kind of like a salesman, but Ted just chuckled and gave me a big pile of listings for the Events column." Phyllis paused to polish her glasses. "I definitely got the feeling he didn't want to continue the discussion."

"He is always complaining about the rising cost of newsprint . . ." said Lucy.

"And the declining number of subscribers," added Phyllis. "And that's another thing. He had me research all sorts of facts and figures, like ad revenue, classified ad revenue, production costs . . ." She let out a big sigh. "Not exactly my cup of tea, if you know what I mean."

"How did the figures look?" asked Lucy, beginning to feel rather uneasy. Was it possible that Ted wasn't just worrying out loud but that the *Pennysaver* was really in dire financial straits? Was he thinking of selling the paper, or even shutting it down permanently?

"Not good," admitted Phyllis, "but I'm no accountant. I can't even balance my checkbook."

"Neither can I," admitted Lucy. "I just cross my fingers, and if the bank says I have more money than I think I have, then it's a good month."

"Wilf manages our money," confessed Phyllis, sounding a bit smug as she referred to her husband. They had married late in life, and she was clearly enjoying married life. "And then there was that woman, done up to the nines, with high-heeled boots and that bleached-blond hair that looks natural so you know it must cost a fortune."

Lucy noticed that Phyllis's tone had changed; she sounded worried when she spoke about the woman. "I'm confused," admitted Lucy. "Does Wilf know this woman?"

"No way." Phyllis dismissed that idea with a flap of her hand. "She came here to the office and, again, no introduction. Ted just dragged her off. He was gone for a couple of hours, and when he got back, not a word. He just sat down and started pounding out his weekly editorial."

"You have no idea who she was?" Lucy considered possible identities for a woman with a city hairdo and high heels. "Maybe she was some sort of sales rep? A high-flying real estate agent?"

"Your guess is as good as mine," said Phyllis, "but she looked like trouble to me."

Lucy was inclined to agree. She tended to be suspicious of women in high heels, who clearly did not have to negotiate the icy sidewalks and muddy driveways that were an annual feature in Maine as winter began to loosen its grip and temperatures began to rise above freezing in the day, only to refreeze at night. Everyone she knew, male and female, wore duck boots beginning with the first February thaw and right on through June.

"Any other suspicious characters?" asked Lucy, thinking this was beginning to sound like a Sherlock Holmes story. Of course, Sherlock would immediately identify the jovial man as having come from Portland, where he'd recently stopped for gas and a stale tuna sandwich. The woman, he would assert, undoubtedly came from Chestnut Hill, where she raised Dobermans and ran a sado-masochistic dungeon patronized by wealthy men with guilty consciences.

"A tall, skinny man in a plaid shirt and jeans, with a big Adam's apple," offered Phyllis, interrupting Lucy's thoughts. "He had a deep voice. He greeted me politely, 'Good morning, ma'am,' he said. That's how I know about his voice."

Ah, thought Lucy, a radio announcer for the country-western channel. "No introduction?"

"Nothing. He asked for Ted, called him 'Mr. Stillings.' Ted happened to be in the morgue, but he popped out like a jack-in-a-box when he heard the man's voice. Then they were gone, and again, no explanation when he returned."

"I dunno," said Lucy, shaking her head in puzzlement. "Either he's working on a feature story of some sort about little-known celebrities, or it's got something to do with the business. Maybe he's once again on the brink of bankruptcy and is trying to refinance, or . . ." Here she stopped, unwilling to continue and voice the notion that Ted might be selling the *Pennysaver*.

The bell on the door jangled, and they both turned to see who their next visitor might be. This time the stranger was tall, dark, and undeniably handsome. He was also young, and dressed in brand-new country duds: ironed jeans with a crease down the leg, a plaid shirt topped with a barn jacket, and fresh-from-the-box duck shoes that hadn't yet ventured into muddy territory.

"What can I do for you?" asked Phyllis, in her polite receptionist voice.

"I have an appointment with Ted Stillings. Will you let him know I'm here?"

Phyllis and Lucy both perked up, presented with an opportunity to ascertain the fellow's name. "Gladly," said Phyllis, with a big smile. "Who shall I say is here?"

"Rrr," he began, then caught himself. "Just say his eleven o'clock is here."

Phyllis's ample bosom seemed to deflate a trifle. "Actually, you'd better take a seat. Ted's not here, but I expect him shortly, Mr. Rrr . . ."

"Thanks," he said, smiling and revealing a dazzling white perfect bite. He sat down on one of the chairs next to the door, opposite the reception counter; even bent at the knee, his long legs pretty much filled the intervening space. He picked up the latest copy of the *Pennysaver* from the table between the chairs and began reading it.

Lucy took this opportunity to study him, taking in his thick, Kennedy-esque hair, his sweeping black brows, hawkish nose, square jaw, broad shoulders, and large hands. Dudley Do-Right, she considered, recalling the cartoon character. Clearly, she was no Sherlock Holmes.

"Did you travel far?" she asked.

"Not too far," he said, with a shrug.

"So you're familiar with Maine?" she continued.

"Sure," he said. "Lobsters, blueberries, and moose."

"Would you like some coffee while you wait?" asked Phyllis.

"No, thanks." He nodded. "I'm good."

"We also have tea," offered Lucy. "If you're a tea drinker."

"Thanks, but I'm all set," he answered, turning the page of the paper and burying his nose in it. Lucy doubted he was really all that interested in the Tinker's Cove High School's basketball team's recent defeat at the hands of the Dover Devils, and figured he was trying to avoid conversation. But why? Why were all these recent visitors so secretive, and what was Ted trying to hide?

She glanced at the antique Regulator clock that hung on the wall above the stranger's head, just as the big hand clicked into place at twelve, indicating it was exactly eleven o'clock. Like clockwork, the bell jangled as the door opened and Ted arrived, bristling with energy and rubbing his hands together. "Ah, you're already here," he said, extending his hand.

The stranger stood up and took Ted's hand, giving it a manly shake. "Good to meet you," he said.

"Same here," said Ted. "Did you have a good drive?"

"Not bad," said the stranger. "Bit of traffic in Portland, but otherwise clear sailing."

Lucy and Phyllis picked up on that last, and their eyes met. Was this a clue to his identity? Was he a fisherman? A yachtsman?

"That's great," said Ted. "Well, I don't know about you, but I'm usually ready for a coffee around now. We don't have Starbucks, but we've got our own Jake's. How about it?"

"Sounds great," said the stranger.

Ted opened the door, holding it for the visitor, who stepped outside. Ted followed, and the two walked past the plate-glass window with the old-fashioned wooden blinds, their progress followed by the two women inside the office. Then they were out of view, leaving nothing behind except questions.

"Who is he?" asked Phyllis.

"Why is here?" asked Lucy.

"What's Ted up to?" asked Phyllis.

"I wish we had some answers," said Lucy.

Connect with U s

Visit us online at
KensingtonBooks.com
to read more from your favorite authors, see books
by series, view reading group guides, and more.